Limbus, Inc.
Book II

A Shared World Experience

Harry Shannon
Gary A. Braunbeck
Joe R. Lansdale
Jonathan Maberry
Joe McKinney

Edited by Brett J. Talley

JournalStone
San Francisco

JOURNALSTONE
YOUR LINK TO ARTISTIC TALENT

JournalStone books may be ordered through booksellers or by contacting:

JournalStone
www.journalstone.com

ISBN: 978-1-940161-33-4   (sc)
ISBN: 978-1-940161-34-1   (e-book)
ISBN: 978-1-940161-35-8   (hc)
ISBN: 978-1-940161-36-5   (hc—limited edition—Fine binding)

JournalStone rev. date: October 24, 2014

Printed in the United States of America

Cover Design: Rob Grom
Cover Photograph © Shutterstock.com

Edited by: Brett J. Talley

This book is dedicated to Anne C. Petty, a woman whose kindness and generosity were matched only by her talent and wicked sense of humor. That talent gave *Limbus* to the world, and it will continue on even though Anne has left us. She is dearly and truly missed.

What is Limbus?

Limbus is Latin for "edge" or "boundary,"
but that's not the whole story.

Welcome to the world of Limbus, Inc., a shadow organization at the edge of reality whose recruitment methods are low-rent, sketchy, even haphazard to the ordinary eye: a tattered flyer taped to a bus-stop shed or tacked to the bulletin board of a neighborhood Laundromat, a dropped business card, a popup ad on the Internet. Limbus's employees are as suspicious and ephemeral as the company, if indeed it could be called a company in the normal sense of the word.

Recruiters offer contracts for employment tailored exactly to the job seeker in question. But a word to the wise… it's always a good idea to read the fine print.

Table of Contents

Limbus, Inc.
Book II

A Shared World Experience

Prologue: Český Krumlov

The tourists had not come to Český Krumlov that winter, for the heavy snows had dissuaded even the most adventurous travelers. That made it perfect for Conrad. He had needed somewhere to disappear after Prague had become too hot, even if no one yet knew his face or his name. After the Silk Road fell, anything was possible. Every day he expected Interpol to show up at his door, even in this sleepy and forgotten town, nestled deep within the Czech Alps.

But they had not come, not yet, and he hoped no one had or would connect Conrad McKay with the hacker known as Jack Rabbit, the same Jack Rabbit who had sold his skills on the dark net, sometimes to the highest bidder, sometimes to the one with the most interesting offer of employment. The same Jack Rabbit who had hacked the NASDAQ and the NSA. The first for fortune, the second for glory.

In Český Krumlov, he was only a college kid taking a year off from school to travel Europe, even if he never left the ancient city center of the medieval town. The locals didn't ask questions. The tourists had not come. It was cold and the snow piled high and they needed the cash.

He lived in a boarding house that doubled as a hotel and tripled as the home of the family who owned it. He spent his days and his nights and his *koruna* in the corner of a cellar bar called Van Gogh's that was not nearly as chintzy as the name suggested. He played chess with the bartender until the early watches of the morning. Then he spent hours reading message boards and TORchan, following the demise of the Silk Road and trying his best to ferret out any rumors of the infamous Jack Rabbit's hiding spot. They knew he was in Europe. That was it. But even that was too close.

Otherwise, he stayed off the net. He resisted the urge to play. To break through walls, just to see whether he could. They were watching. He had to lay low. And it was driving him insane.

There were worse ways to live. Conrad ate steak every meal in nearly empty restaurants and pubs, and every meal he washed it down with Budweiser—the original kind. And all for the price of a burger back home. Not that he worried about the money. The Bitcoins he still held were worth a fortune, and he could live for a month or more converting a single one to *koruna*. Not a bad life at all, and he guessed he should be happy here, a place lost to time where he could live like one of the city's ancient rulers. But the mountains and the medieval citadel ramparts built to hold back the Turks centuries before felt like prison walls. And as the snow piled higher and higher and the temperature plunged further and further, even his thoughts seemed to freeze.

He needed a release. One night, he found it.

It began in the midst of a particularly strong snowstorm when the heavy fall of powder-white flakes had dissuaded Conrad from venturing out into the darkened streets. He sat at a wooden table, rough-hewn and no doubt carved by hand some decades before. A fire roared in the hearth, and the barmaid— the youngest daughter of the owners of the place—dropped a flagon of beer and a large stein in front of him. He thanked her and smiled sheepishly. She stared back with lust in her eyes as she had since the first day he had arrived. Conrad wasn't much to look at, but he was new and different and exotic, and she wanted him. If he stuck around much longer, he might just let her have him.

Conrad opened his computer and signed on to Iram, a message board he had often visited when the Silk Road still ran strong and true. Iram of the Pillars they had called it. A pun, for

Iram was a lost city of the net, buried beneath the surface of the web in a place to those who knew it existed called the deep net.

Or, as Conrad preferred, the dark net.

There was freedom here. Or there had been before the FBI and ICE and NSA had found it. Now, he wasn't so sure, and in truth, it was foolish for him even to come, even to dip his toe into the black waters. Dangerous and deadly if they were watching. But it was exciting, too. To be back in the deep.

Most people don't know it, but the Internet is like an iceberg. The vast majority of people only ever see what is above the surface. But what lies beneath is so much bigger, and so much wilder. There is no law on the dark net. No rules. No limitations. Just vast possibility.

On that day, Conrad found one of those possibilities.

Among threads about 9/11 conspiracies, hacking conquests, and questionable porn, there was one that caught his eye. The title read simply,

"How Lucky Do You Feel?"

Conrad was intrigued. He felt quite lucky to be free at all. And it wasn't just that fact that piqued his interest. The thread had no responses logged. In fact, it had no views. Unusual in a world where most threads were posted, buried in crass profanity, and relegated to the trash heap, all in mere minutes. And yet this one remained pristine, as pure as the snow that still fell outside. Conrad couldn't help himself. He clicked the link. The thread opened, and a single sentence appeared on the screen.

Gallia est omnis divisa in partes tres.

Conrad grinned. A riddle. A diversion. He opened his bag and removed a notebook, plopping it down on the table next to his laptop. He poured beer from the flagon into his stein and took a long draw. He knew the sentence. He had taken Latin before coding had become his second tongue, and it had been the first thing they translated in Mr. Wheelock's class.

"All Gaul is divided into three parts," the first line of one of Julius Caesar's most famous works. It was the only clue he needed.

Conrad wrote out the sentence carefully in his book, sure to leave enough space between each letter. The thread was a test, he figured. And thus this sentence was most likely a code. A Caesar cypher, to be exact. A simple puzzle, certainly, but a little bit of fun, nonetheless.

A Caesar cypher was easy enough to crack if you knew what you were looking for. Just move up or down the alphabet a set number of spaces for each letter and, voila, secret message uncovered. Caesar himself had used a down shift of three spaces, so that's what Conrad tried, too. He counted in his head, even though he knew there were programs that could do this for him in an instant. But that would be cheating and he wanted to work through this riddle himself.

He leaned back in his chair and looked down at what he had produced.

Doo Jdxo lv glylghg lqwr wkuhh sduwv.

It looked like gibberish, and it was. Normally, you started with the gibberish and went the other way. But Conrad had a feeling that this particular code wasn't for reading.

He typed the letters carefully into his browser—one specially designed for navigating the dark net—and hit enter. The machine worked for a moment. And then . . . nothing. Just an error message. Conrad frowned, drumming his fingers on the table. That should have worked, he thought. Perhaps it was alpha-numeric. He ran the phrase through a program that assigned a value, 1-26, to each letter. Not cheating, he thought. Just a shortcut.

He frowned again. It was a lot of digits.

4-15-15 10-4-24-15 12-22 7-12-25-12-7-8-7 12-17-23-18 23-11-21-8-8 19-4-21-23-22

He doubted anything this long would represent a web address. Still, he dutifully typed it in anyway and hit enter. But his fears were confirmed. They came to nothing. He rubbed his chin and stared at the screen. Maybe he had made a mistake, gone wrong from the beginning. Maybe he shouldn't have translated the phrase to begin with. He looked at the numbers again. Studied them. And then he noticed something he had not seen before; several of them were primes.

7,7,7,17,23,23,11,19,23

Somehow, he knew he had found it. He typed the numbers into his browser. The screen went black and he grinned. Words began to appear, one letter at a time, as if they were being seared into the screen while he was reading them.

Well done, but a child could have solved that riddle. The test is not of your mind, but of your soul. Not of your intellect, but of your spirit. Will you be the master of your fate? The truth is far down the rabbit hole. How deep are you willing to go?

Conrad shuddered. It was a common enough phrase, he told himself. Surely it had nothing to do with his past, with the name that had made him famous, even if anonymously so. And yet, as the cursor blinked at him, something told him it was no coincidence. That somehow, whoever this was, *they knew.* It wasn't the FBI, though. Somehow he knew that too. It was something much more interesting . . . and dangerous.

He typed the only thing that came to mind in response to the questions.

Down, down, down.

The screen flashed white and then back to black. A cascade of numbers, letters, and arcane symbols poured from the top of the screen, filling it quickly before rolling down in waves. For several minutes they continued to appear, the scroll bar on the side shrinking with startling speed. By the time they had finished, Conrad guessed the code that now seemed to go on forever numbered in the millions of characters. It was utterly unintelligible, except for a message written at the top of the screen.

There is music in the noise, beauty in the chaos, truth in the lies, light in the void. He who has eyes, let him see.

The curser flashed beneath. Conrad understood. Hidden in this mass of text, of gibberish, was a message. But he needed the right key to find it.

Conrad considered closing out and going to bed, maybe seeing if the cute barmaid was still up, leaving this behind before he did go too far down whatever rabbit hole he had stumbled upon. Considered it so strongly that he actually grasped the top of his laptop screen and began to pull it shut. But in the end, he couldn't. The need to know had always been what had driven him, both to great heights of ability and infinite depths of obsession.

And if he stopped, where would that leave him? Waiting here until someone found him? Until the authorities tracked him down? Who would be the master of his fate then? The captain of his soul?

A light clicked on in Conrad's brain. Without thinking, his hands went to the keyboard and he typed,

Invictus.

The data on the screen began to reform. Blocks of text moved around, swirling, reordering, recombining. Then it settled on an image—three women. Then, it reformed again, changing into line after line of text. But not random letters. Words. Sentences. Conrad started at the screen for a full five minutes before he realized it was a story. There was only one thing he could think to do.

He began to read.

Zero at the Bone

By

Harry Shannon

A NARROW FELLOW IN THE GRASS

A narrow Fellow in the Grass
Occasionally rides —
You may have met Him —
did you not
His notice sudden is —

The Grass divides as with a Comb —
A spotted shaft is seen —
And then it closes at your feet
And opens further on —

He likes a Boggy Acre
A Floor too cool for Corn —
Yet when a Boy, and Barefoot —
I more than once at Noon

Have passed, I thought, a Whip lash
Unbraiding in the Sun
When stooping to secure it
It wrinkled, and was gone —

Several of Nature's People
I know, and they know me —
I feel for them a transport
Of cordiality —

But never met this Fellow
Attended, or alone
Without a tighter breathing
And Zero at the Bone —

-Emily Dickinson

* * *

"My name is Mike and I'm an addict and an alcoholic."

The group of men said, "Hi, Mike."

"I want to forget." Dolan looked down. His burn-scarred hands lay still on the cheaply laminated brown podium. He felt calm. Not long ago he would have been shaking like a teenaged boy opening his first blouse. He closed his eyes for a long moment then opened them again. The small room was crowded and smelled like unwashed males who'd been chain smoking. It was raining outside and the heater was on. Someone flushed the toilet at the back of the room and pipes rattled behind the peeling brown wallpaper.

Dolan said, "I want to forget but I can't."

A man whispered, "Amen."

"I started going to meetings in rehab," Dolan continued. "I hated them at first. Hey, who'd want to hang out with a bunch of assholes like you?"

The men chuckled politely. A white-haired old guy in overalls came out of the bathroom, zipping his fly. His name was Adam Gordon and he was a retired electrician with seventeen years of sobriety. He scurried across the back row and parked himself in an empty chair.

"I was in a bad place for a long time," Dolan said. "They gave me some pretty intense therapy in rehab, along with some medications I didn't like at all. I guess I was pretty messed up. I got better after that. Even though I'd still rather forget, I've been putting my mind back together bit by bit for nearly a year now."

Someone in the second row cracked his knuckles. A skinny teen speed freak responded to the abrupt noise by twitching. His metal folding chair squeaked like a mouse caught in a trap. Someone else whispered for everyone to be quiet.

"I'm supposed to tell you what it was like, what happened, and what it's like now," Dolan said. "So I guess that's what I should do."

The men waited patiently.

"Here's what it was like before." Dolan cleared his throat. "My dad was in the navy. He drank himself to sleep every night but never told us why. A lot of you guys know the story. He also beat us pretty bad sometimes. My mother left finally, just when I started high school, and then it was just the two of us fighting, the old bull and the young bull. Except this time, the young bull was the more ruthless one. One Saturday night, he got me really good, blacked up my right eye and made me reset a broken nose. I waited until he was passed out and just flat kicked the shit out of him. He could hardly move when he woke up. I told him I'd do it again every time he went to sleep unless he left me alone. He stayed off my case after that. It focused his mind pretty good. He happily signed for me when I went into the navy at seventeen. I never spoke to him again. He shot himself a few years back and nobody buried him because nobody gave a shit. I didn't cry. I haven't cried since I was little kid."

Dolan cleared his throat. The men listened intently.

"Okay. Here is what happened. I became a drunk too. I went for Special Ops early on. I made it, so there's a bunch of shit I can't talk to any of you men about. I'm not trying to hide anything, but I ended up in a branch of the service where most of the stuff we did was off the record. A lot of people died and sometimes it was the wrong people, not that a government ever wants to admit that. That shit really changed me. I'm not the first swinging dick who ever felt that way, and I won't be the last. I know that. I heard lots of stories like mine at the VA and again in rehab."

Dolan shut his eyes again and the world went black, but only for a second or two before it blew up in rage. He saw the multi-colored smear of tracer fire and heard screams of agony and felt the crunching thump of mortar rounds striking the earth. That last mission had been a horror show and the experience had stayed fresh in his brain along with every mistake he'd ever made and every life he'd taken. The past was out to get him. It was always happening in real time, like a video buried deep in the marrow of his bones.

"Excuse me." Dolan opened his eyes and the room returned and the men snapped back into focus. A bead of sweat rolled down his face, seeking a path through the stubble on his chin.

"I was drinking a lot, of course. I thought it helped me cope. I crawled through the grass and hid in the trees and I killed people with knives and guns and wires. I went to the desert more than a few times. I was good at my job, getting in and out of scary places to get heavy shit done. I became a pretty sneaky guy. In fact, the guys I worked with called me Snake. Look, I saw some things and I did some things. We were fighting in dirty little wars you didn't know about back home, but to be honest, the combat wasn't the real problem. The real problem was that I always dealt with it by drinking and doing drugs. In the end, you see, I wasn't any better than my old man—not really, except that I didn't beat up my own kid. Of course, I haven't had that opportunity."

The clock ticked. Someone coughed and another man blew his nose as if in counterpoint. Dolan tapped his burned fingers on the podium. He continued. "What I did was I beat up other men. Every chance I got, even back home. I fought hard and partied hard when the mission was over. I never questioned anything. I never cried. Never. Not in all those years, from my childhood on. Now I know that was a weakness in me and not a strength."

The electrician muttered, "Amen to that, too."

Dolan said, "So, what happened was the dude they called Snake was in his fair share of fire fights. He got real sick of it and drank a swimming pool worth of booze. Still, he did three tours straight up without complaining. So, eventually, when it was my turn to get my own shit blown up, bad leg and all, they shook my hand and told me thanks a lot for everything, here's some money, but now it's time to go home. I didn't want to, but I had to come back to the world. So I did. I came here. Back here to the States."

Thunder rumbled in the distance and Dolan heard the first rain drops ticking gently on the window pane. He felt his mouth going dry. The hard part was coming. The clock on the wall ticked forward remorselessly, steadily marking time as if alerting him to the approach of his own death. He wanted to forget, but the meetings kept forcing him to remember.

"I was home. But now I had no idea what to do or how to live. I wasn't Snake anymore. I was just another vet. It was... difficult."

The men listened and waited. Some of them already knew what was coming.

"The thing is, I understand the truth now," Dolan said. "The problem wasn't that I went to war. The problem was that I never came back."

And now a few of the men nodded together, like a bunch of puppets, and that simple gesture of solidarity communicated a level of understanding many of the other guys could not share. The support from the vets was palpable and it touched Dolan and enabled him to continue.

"A few years ago, I got married to a girl I'd known in high school," Dolan said. "Her name was Phyllis. She made me promise to stop drinking so I white knuckled it. I stopped. We got pregnant pretty quickly. I was working nights back then. See, the sunlight hurt my eyes and made me jumpy. Loud noises threw me off. I felt a lot safer at night. Some of you understand that."

More nods from the vets.

"Guys, I need to get the rest of this out quickly. The thing is, I started boozing again, and then one night, I was pretty bombed by the time I got home. There was somebody in the house, somebody who broke in while Phyllis was there alone. The cops said he was likely about to rape her just when I got there, but apparently, that hadn't happened yet. She was probably knocked out cold by then and her nightgown had been torn off. I was hammered and I came in loud and stupid and too damn drunk to know what was going on. I caught a glimpse of a big man wearing a stocking mask. The guy sucker punched me. He clubbed me and dumped my ass on the living room floor. He had a gas can with him and for some fucking insane reason started a fire just as he left."

Some of the men in the room who already knew this story started to wipe their eyes. Dolan's face remained expressionless, though his voice got a lot huskier. He did not cry. He rubbed his temples.

"I tried to make it to the bedroom," Dolan said. "God knows I did. I tried my best to get her out. It was too hot and they told me she was already gone by then anyway, probably from the smoke inhalation and the blow to the head. Not from the flames, thankfully. Me, I got these burns on my hands and lower arms, but that was it because drunks are lucky that way for some reason. The fire department showed up just in time and dragged me out of there and an EMT treated the burns or it might have been too late to keep my fingers."

He was on the verge of babbling now, so Dolan slowed down to take a breath. "What it's like now? Well, now is that I am sober almost nine months. I've worked my steps. I don't want to drink or get high again though I know this is a one-day-at-a-time proposition. I've made friends and want to go on. I can't say I've accepted everything exactly, but at least I've stopped hating myself every day for what happened. I would give anything to bring my wife back and make up for my mistakes but that's not the way life is. That's not the way things work. So I want to forget, but I can't."

More thunder, much closer than before. The rain was pouring down now, drops tapping on the roof like a line of Irish dancers. Lightning flashed outside, and a fork of shadows ran down the meeting room wall. Dolan decided he had nothing more to say, so he brought his share to a close.

"The shrinks tell me it wasn't my fault. Not her death or the war, any of it. They say that it makes no sense for me to brood any longer. They say that sometimes shit just… happens. You know something? They're right. In the end, it was just like all those times in action when my friends got hit or died instead of me. In the end, the sad truth about life is that it often comes down to simple random chance. It did that time. So I lived and Phyllis died."

Dolan closed his eyes. "And so did our unborn child."

Dolan left to sit down. The men applauded him but a fresh rumble of thunder drowned them out.

* * *

Big storms came and went for most of the week. Dolan found a room at a sober living house but only stayed there for two nights. The other guys in the room farted a lot and talked about sex and wanting to get high again. Dolan was fed up with that mindset. He wanted space of his own and longed for genuine solitude. He found a cheap apartment on the edge of the barrio and slept there instead. It smelled like dog shit and damp wood, but it was near the back stairs so he could come and go without having to talk to anyone. He ran a lot and found some ways to work out without equipment, but mostly at night.

During the day, Dolan went through the newspapers and down to the unemployment office looking for work. Nothing good came up. He figured the circles under his eyes and his burned hands and the long stint in rehab had something to do with not getting hired, but by this time, Dolan didn't really give a damn. He could just get by on his small check from the government, so being out of work wasn't the end of the world. Eventually, he'd need to find a job, but there was no rush.

The solitude helped. Dolan felt better away from other men, and though he bought a porn magazine for his room, in reality he'd pretty much lost the taste for sex, much less a girlfriend. His dark superstitions told him he was nothing but bad luck for women, just like his old man. It wouldn't be fair to get involved, and it just wasn't his way to go and hire someone.

He still hadn't cried, but Dolan survived. In time, he tapered off going to AA meetings. The constant stream of sad stories began to wear him out. He couldn't produce enough empathy to sustain them. He was also getting sick of the sound of his own voice. In truth, Dolan didn't care to feel anything anymore. He wanted to stay under the radar, maybe make some extra money and figure out some way to move on with his life. Most of all, he just wanted to forget.

The big storms stopped eventually but rain visited on and off, and the air stayed crisp and cold as if snow was coming soon. That sounded nice, the idea of having a white Christmas. The snow made everything seem clean and quiet. It wasn't long before Dolan went back to staying up all night and sleeping during the day. That was better than trying to fit in and talk to people. He got books from the library and read until his eyes burned. He slept at dawn. Ear plugs blocked the traffic noise and sheets of tinfoil taped to the window kept the sun out.

Dolan walked a lot, especially late at night when the dimly lit streets were empty. The city smelled nice right after the rain. Most of the time staying sober wasn't that difficult. Sometimes the liquor store on the corner winked at him with neon eyes as he walked down the sidewalk. Snake Dolan thought of it as a painted whore riddled with disease and he gave it a wide berth. Eventually, he walked in there to buy a candy bar or some beef jerky and prove to himself that he didn't have to buy any booze. The cold bottles of beer still twinkled in the harsh light and whispered obscene things Dolan couldn't quite make out. One night, he came close to getting a six-pack but he bought a newspaper instead. He stopped going inside unless it was absolutely necessary.

Dolan knew he had to get busy and find work soon or he'd end up taking another trip down nightmare alley. He took the newspaper for a stroll down to the all-night coffee shop to look at the want ads. He always skipped the front page and the stories about the sagging economy and the dysfunctional government he'd once been willing to die for because the whole politics thing threatened his serenity. He just folded the paper to the ads and stuck it under his arm. He walked on.

The sidewalk was damp with rain and a bum in the shadows near the glass entrance asked him for money for food. Dolan searched his pockets and found a few bills and some coins; he handed the change over, but it was only fifty cents or so. The man muttered something obscene and decidedly ungrateful under his breath.

The old restaurant was almost empty. A pair of stoners sat in the back, pigging out on apple pie and ice cream, and a wino wandered in to steal some crackers and take a piss in the men's room. Dolan sat down at the counter. The waitress was old enough to be his grandmother. She wore thick glasses and had white, pimpled skin like a plucked chicken. She looked ridiculous in her little skirt and white apron. Her name tag read AMY. Dolan called her by her name, borrowed a pen, and asked for a cup of black coffee. He had a twenty, a five, and a one in his pocket. He broke the five paying for the coffee.

The place was old with red plastic booths patched in spots by electrical tape. Fake plants managed to droop as if dying of thirst. The windows were dirty. Insipid music flowed from hidden speakers— some old songs he remembered from high school re-played by a mediocre, slightly out of tune orchestra.

Amy brought Dolan his cup. It tasted like thirty-weight motor oil. Dolan poured in sugar, stirred, and sipped anyway. He scanned the newspaper ads and circled the ones that looked promising. Some construction stuff that didn't require a particular set of skills, a phone sales job you could supposedly do from home, and a few other things that seemed legit. One ad was circled in black and popped off the page because it had a tiny globe covered with small dots. The miniature logo reminded Dolan of the waitress and her weird skin.

LIMBUS, INC.

The word Limbus seemed vaguely familiar to Dolan, but he couldn't have said why. Maybe he'd seen the logo somewhere over the last few days and just hadn't noticed? Had he seen it on a billboard or stapled to a wooden pole or something? Studying the ad gave Dolan an odd, slightly queasy feeling of disorientation.

Amy returned to re-fill his cup and her approach startled him. Dolan thanked her and asked for some water and went back to reading the ad.

LIMBUS, Inc.
Are you laid off, downsized, undersized?

Call us. We employ.
1-800-555-0606.
How lucky do you feel?

"Not very," Dolan said aloud.

"What, hon?" Amy asked. "Did you want to order? Maybe a piece of pie?" As if on cue, the two young stoners got up and headed for the door. They were giggling about something. In the neon glare, their eyes looked like sunburned flakes of skin. Like something he'd seen accidentally back in the burn ward. Dolan shivered.

He shook his head. "I'm fine with the coffee, thanks."

Amy went back into the kitchen to chat in Spanish with the fry cook. Dolan sat alone, just the way he liked it. He looked at the ad again and shrugged. It didn't say anything about the job. He assumed it was a company that would require an advanced degree or something. He did not circle it and folded the newspaper back up. He was down to his last twenty odd bucks. His next check wasn't due for a couple of weeks and rent was coming up. He'd have to get busy in the morning.

Dolan left the coffee shop and went back out into the night air. His breath looked like puffs of smoke. He hunched his shoulders against the cold and went for a long walk. The next block over had a couple of Indian restaurants and a trendy bar or two. He cut through the parking lot behind the bar, intending to come around to the back side of his place. The gangs owned the streets at this hour, no sense in cruising for a bruising. The sky above was speckled with bright stars. One street lamp and a sliver of moon lit the sidewalk ahead.

He spotted the two gang bangers immediately. They were holding up the wall of the trendy bar, hands in their jacket pockets, drooping baggy pants and fake gold chains. One was black and had his head shaved, the other Hispanic with a buzz cut. They had set up shop and it was going down. They were waiting for somebody. Dolan gave them a wide berth and acted like he hadn't seen a thing. It was none of his business, after all.

The door to the bar opened and a well-dressed man stepped out gingerly, like he was more than a tad drunk. Dolan saw him clearly in the street light. He was pretty good sized with a haggard face and a sharp nose and dark eyes. He wore a black suit and had his hair all slicked back like some villain in an old-time movie. He straightened his suit and sleeves, clumsily flashing what looked to be a platinum Rolex.

Dolan saw the two bangers shift position. One of them had a little piece of pipe in his grip.

Ah, shit...

Dolan was on the move before his conscious mind made the decision. He turned sharply and headed toward the drunk. He kept his hands in his pockets and the newspaper under his arm, like an ordinary man who'd just decided at the last second to get a night cap before last call. The bald banger seemed to sense something. He grabbed at his friend's sleeve but just missed it. The pipe was already up and the drunk turned just in time to block the blow and cry out from the pain as the weapon came down on his forearm.

Dolan feinted at the kid with the pipe but took on the one with the shaved head instead, slamming a shoulder into him, driving him back into the wall. The kid's breath whooshed out and Dolan kneed him hard, just to make sure he'd stay down. As Dolan spun around, the pipe caught him with a glancing blow on the lower back. It hurt his kidney. Pissed off now, Dolan leg-swept the other banger and the pipe clattered to the sidewalk. Dolan stayed in a crouch. He kicked the bald kid in the side of the head and took him off the board. He stepped back. It was over.

Dolan felt high on the adrenaline. He wasn't sure why he'd bothered to get involved, but had to admit the action sure felt good. He stood up slowly, rubbing his lower back. The drunk was still holding his forearm. He looked stunned by what had gone down and how fast it had all happened.

"Thank you," the strange man said. "Looks like I owe you one."

"I'm good." Dolan shrugged. "Just be more careful next time."

The dark man stuck his hand out. "I'm Mr. Cranston." He gave no first name.

"Mike Dolan."

Cranston took his burn-scarred hand without flinching. Music thumped from inside the bar. The two gang bangers sat up moaning and edged away along the cement while still on their asses. Dolan stared them down but ultimately let them stumble away. When he turned back to face Mr. Cranston, the older man was holding out a hundred dollar bill in one hand. His craggy face was half in shadow, and under the neon light of the bar sign, he suddenly looked a tad demonic. Dolan blinked away one harrowing PTSD flashback. He focused on the money.

"You don't have to do that," Dolan said without conviction. The cash sure looked good. The big bill waved in the breeze like a woman's skirt.

"Don't be foolish," Mr. Cranston said, reading his expression. "I'm very grateful for your kind intervention."

Pride warred with need. Snake Dolan still thought of himself as a soldier and the hundred bucks felt like chump change from a rich man's couch. He didn't have much left to cling to but right then, for some odd reason, integrity felt more important. Even than paying the rent.

"Like I said, I'm good. You can put that away."

Mr. Cranston took the bill back and Dolan felt a small burst of confidence return. Cranston returned the money to his thick wallet. He produced a business card instead. Dolan told himself to turn and walk away. He pretended not to see the card. Mr. Cranston did not lower his hand. His gaze was intense and his eyes somehow hypnotic enough to hold Dolan in his tracks. Dolan did not care for the feeling. He blinked first because a rain drop landed on his nose and rolled down his cheek like a long-forgotten tear.

"Perhaps you're looking for work," Mr. Cranston said. "A lot of men are these days. If so, here's the number of an associate of mine, a Mr. Goodfellow. Call him tomorrow and say I referred you. Believe me, I'm certain we can find something for a man like you."

Reluctantly, Dolan reached out across what felt like nine feet of open space and took the business card. He held it at the very end of his burn-scarred fingers. It seemed to vibrate. Words wouldn't come, so Dolan just nodded.

"That was a wise decision, young man." Mr. Cranston turned. He walked away without waiting for a response. Dolan watched him go, his right hand still holding the business card, which he lowered to his side and finally tucked into his right pocket. Strangely enough, Mr. Cranston no longer seemed inebriated. He walked briskly and efficiently down the long line of cars. He paused, took out his keys, and a burgundy BMW that was lightly beaded with rain drops chirped happily and unlocked itself. Mr. Cranston got in and drove off.

Suddenly Dolan felt sleepy and cranky, and it almost seemed like the whole thing had been some kind of a weird dream.

He walked down the main drag, heading home. The sleepiness persisted, unusual for him this far from sunrise. A police car passed by slowly, the cops inside taking his measure, but before they could stop to roust him, someone else sped through the stop light in a truck weaving back and forth. Their siren whooped once, kind of a solo war cry that reminded Dolan of a Confederate soldier, and then the cops hit the siren full on and took off in an explosion of color and sound.

Snake Dolan walked home and immediately went to bed.

He slept poorly.

* * *

The twenty bucks didn't last long. In fact, the cash ran out faster than a political promise. Dolan had to go to the Salvation Army and endure some preaching to get a bit of food the day before his next check was finally due. Then the slimy, fat landlord gave him some bullshit about needing the space and having to raise the rent if Dolan didn't want to move out. He claimed some company had come by and was going to buy the building. Dolan told him he was flat broke right now, which was true, but would make good soon. He got up that Friday and went straight to the mail box to collect his money.

But the check wasn't there.

Dolan went back to the mail box three times that day just to be sure. The money had always showed up on time before, but not this time. When he called the VA, he got the runaround. They told him it had been sent out and that maybe someone had stolen it from the mailbox, and if so, he'd have to fill out some forms and wait until his claim was processed. Their estimate was a few more weeks to cancel the first one and issue another. When he told them he'd be out on the street, they recommended he just go to a homeless shelter and wait.

Frustrated, Dolan finally remembered the earlier event by the coffee shop. He searched his pockets for the business card, but it wasn't there. He'd misplaced it somehow. He was now completely broke and without a single job lead to follow. He went for his usual walk that night, a sick feeling of dread growing inside.

When he returned to his room, the fat landlord had changed the locks. That motherfucker…

Dolan banged on the landlord's triple-locked door, though he knew the man wouldn't open it. He'd just call the police and have Dolan taken away. Stuck with the clothes on his back and no money, Dolan went back out into the cold, struggling to remember the ad he'd seen in the paper, the name of the company looking to hire. He couldn't quite remember it. He'd felt odd and groggy for days now, though he couldn't seem to fall asleep. Dolan was even more out of tune with the world than before.

Hopelessness nearly overtook him. The night tried to swallow him up. And that brightly lit liquor store seemed especially appealing.

Dolan stood outside in the night, unable to bring himself to ask the sparse collection of patrons for their spare change. His stomach rumbled with hunger. His throat felt parched. He watched the store with an idea growing in the back of his tired mind. The bored, stoned store clerk took frequent bathroom breaks and left the front of the place unprotected. He read porn magazines and rarely looked up.

Snake Dolan stood in the dark outside, planning his move. He'd grab one tall bottle of Wild Turkey and some beef jerky and cookies. He'd get in and out in a heartbeat. The bell would sound and the clerk would return but only to find the place empty. Meanwhile, Dolan would race down the side alley with the bottle and make for the safety of the park. A lot of homeless folks camped out there at night, sometimes huddled together for warmth, setting trash fires they had to run from if the police decided to roust their camp.

I'm down to this, Dolan thought. I can't believe I'm down to this. I just want to forget. I have to forget.

He stood in the dark, his cold breath billowing like dragon smoke in the air. The clerk flipped through a porn magazine, absently picking at his dried zits. He found something to study intensely. It was a fold-out photograph. He took the magazine with him and headed for the john behind the counter. Dolan walked briskly inside, grabbed some junk food and a bottle of whiskey and was out the door just after the bell sounded. He'd pulled it off without a hitch. He marched down the alley, forcing himself not to run and attract attention. Guilt chewed like a rat at the corner of his mind. It felt like his newly won integrity had just been run through a shredder.

The park was at the end of 5th, near Huston Street. Some of the homeless men had set fire to a trash barrel and they were all warming their hands and sharing bottles of cheap rotgut wine. Dolan stood for a time on the sidewalk perhaps twenty yards away. He opened the bottle of whiskey and sniffed. The pungent odor was at once disgusting and erotically tempting. Dolan remembered the old AA saying: "One's too many and a thousand's not enough…"

He walked over to a cold park bench and sat down with the bottle on his left and the junk food on his right. His ass nearly froze. Dolan ate some beef jerky and a couple of cookies and felt a little bit better. He'd find something. There was always something. Maybe he could do some manual labor or gardening. He could stand with the undocumented workers who hung out on the corner by the hardware store and ask for a day job of some kind. He'd get out of this. There had to be a way.

Dolan stood up. He examined the burn scars on his hands. They stung a bit in the chill. He took the whiskey bottle over to the group of ruddy-faced old men who were warming themselves by the trash barrel and he gave it to them without a word. A toothless fellow with a boxer's ear smiled and nodded and offered him a drink. Dolan shook his head. He turned and walked back into the darkness with absolutely no idea where to go next. The moon was nearly full and the streets were damp but brightly lit. He'd made his choice and now he'd just have to live with it.

Snake Dolan walked down the sidewalk, angling in the general direction of the Salvation Army, thinking maybe he could at least score a bed. Once he had some cash in hand, he'd have to go back to the liquor store to make amends and pay for what he'd stolen. That's what he'd learned would keep him sober. And he had to stay sober to have any chance at redemption.

Dolan turned down 4th street. The shops and fast food restaurants were closed. The neighborhood was beginning to slide into true poverty, so a number of buildings were boarded up. One had red tags all over it and had been marked for removal. Dolan stopped by an antique pay phone on a pole. He leaned on the cold metal to catch his breath. The battered phone and the metal support were both covered with graffiti and gang signs. The coin-gobbling gadget was easily as old as the building. The moon hung above the condemned structure like a giant unblinking eye. Dolan looked up at the wrecked edifice, the broken windows and splintering boards. This world was dying. He wondered if he had a red tag on his soul.

He tucked his hands into his pockets to keep them warm and felt something rubbing the burn scar on his right hand.

The business card.

It hadn't been there the night before, Dolan was certain of that, but suddenly he could feel it with his fingertips. It was vibrating in some strange way, just as it had the first time. The card was still there. He took it out and studied it in the moonlight.

LIMBUS, Inc.
Are you laid off, downsized, undersized?
Call us. We employ. 1-800-555-0606.
How lucky do you feel?

Dolan threw his head back and laughed out loud. He was standing in the damp darkness on a trash-strewn and condemned city street, out of work, hungry, and struggling to stay alive, without even the spare change to use an out of commission old pay phone that wouldn't have worked anyway, yet at least he'd been able to stay sober tonight. Hell, maybe that was as lucky as he was ever going to get.

Lucky enough, I guess.

An odd sound caught his ear. Dolan wasn't sure he'd actually heard it at first because the ring tone was so out of date, and the ancient pay phone was clearly out of order. It had to be out of order. The thing was dented and cracked and the land line would have been disconnected decades ago.

And yet it was ringing, a strange, brittle sound sent here from another century. Slowly, carefully, his flesh rippling with unease, Dolan lifted the phone to his ear. He swallowed dryly.

"Hello?"

"You've reached Limbus, Inc.," a mellow baritone voice said. "This is Recruiter Goodfellow speaking."

"Odd." Dolan's breath caught in his throat. "I didn't actually call you. Not yet, anyway."

"Well you've got me on the line now," Recruiter Goodfellow said. "Are you the gentleman Mr. Cranston referred to us, the fellow with a good deal of military experience?"

Dolan surrendered his skepticism. He had nothing left to lose. There was no other play to try but this one. "Yes, I met your Mr. Cranston and he gave me his card."

"Ah, I see," Recruiter Goodfellow said. "Then the card called us for you. It does that sometimes. Would you like to come in for an interview, Mr. Dolan?"

Dolan exhaled a white cloud of frosty air. It was starting to rain again and he shivered from the cold. "How the hell did you know my name?"

"We are very good at what we do, Snake. Would you be willing to work for us?"

"In what capacity?"

"Perhaps as something of a mercenary? We could use a man like you."

Dolan closed his eyes and shivered again. He just wanted a warm bed and some money in his pocket. He just wanted to forget. He kept his lids down and saw bright tracer rounds and dirt-encrusted entrails and heard someone screaming in pain, but his body did not go tense.

Not this time. Maybe the war was finally over, the one inside his head. Maybe he'd just needed to accept his fate and to be willing to die to finally feel better. Strangely, in a way, Dolan didn't much care, not any more.

"How much does the work pay?"

"Enough."

"That's pretty vague, Mr. Goodfellow."

"We promise it will be worth your while," Goodfellow said. "You will be well compensated."

That sounded pretty damn good right about now.

"Where do I sign up?"

"Come on in."

"What?"

The front of the condemned building trembled and gave off a strange creaking sound. Dolan dropped the phone, which had abruptly gone dead, and studied the front of the abandoned property. The front door was opening. Ice and dust flew up like talcum powder as an uncluttered entrance appeared. A bright light flowed out and Dolan felt the rush of warm air as it flowed out into the night. He walked up the steps. He could smell food and fresh coffee and even the long-forgotten fragrance of a woman's perfume.

That was nice.

* * *

When Snake Dolan stepped inside of Limbus, Inc., he half expected to hear someone playing jingle bells, because Recruiter Goodfellow was a Santa type, rotund and white bearded and ruddy cheeked. He wore a black suit Dolan figured to be worth the price of the average man's car, and on his wrist was a Rolex identical to the one worn by the mysterious Mr. Cranston just a few nights before. These guys did all right at this firm, whatever the hell it was. They were fat cats for sure.

Goodfellow closed the door behind him. The inside of the building was warm, brightly lit, completely modern and spotlessly clean. Strange fantasy art adorned the walls, imagined planets and what appeared to be alien life forms. For some reason, the odd change in environment did not seem unnatural. Not at this point, not after all that had already happened. In fact, Dolan had a very strange sense of déjà vu, as if he'd done all this before, or perhaps it was just that this was an event destined to happen.

Goodfellow was accompanied by a Viking-sized blond nurse in hospital greens. Two heavily muscled men in suits stood back against the wall with their arms crossed. Dolan immediately recognized them as ex-military by their physical bearing and short haircuts and that thousand-yard stare in their eyes. He nodded respectfully and they nodded back. They were professionals for sure.

"Perhaps you'd like to have something to drink and to get cleaned up a bit before we have our little talk?"

Dolan felt foolish and intimidated. He wanted to gain some respect. He wanted to have something to say in all of this. "I sure could use some coffee, sir. As for the rest, I can freshen up later."

Goodfellow nodded. "As you wish, Mr. Dolan. Follow me, please."

He turned and walked to a large, ornate wooden set of doors. He opened them and ushered Dolan into a plush, wood-paneled office. Recruiter Goodfellow left the nurse and the guards outside. He ordered them to stay with a dismissive wave of his plump fingers. Dolan stood blinking in the bright lights, abruptly aware of his body odor and filthy clothing. He instantly regretted his stiff-necked decision to negotiate first. He was in no position to strike a good bargain.

"Have a seat," Goodfellow said.

"I'll stand, sir. I wouldn't want to mess up your furniture."

"Again, as you wish."

Recruiter Goodfellow went around the huge desk. He plopped down heavily in the plush executive chair. He leaned forward with his elbows on the polished glass and moved some papers to one side. "I suppose you are wondering about this company and how we found you. You must have questions by now."

Dolan stood at ease. "Yes, sir."

"Unfortunately, I cannot answer them."

"I see."

"You have done covert ops before, Mr. Dolan, so you likely know that you will have to take all this at face value. We are a top-secret operation, much larger and more powerful than any you may have encountered before. Limbus is a Latin word, Mr. Dolan. It means an edge or boundary. We push things as far as they can go. We make and change history, figuratively and sometimes literally. We go to unusual places to accomplish great things. You will be doing very important work. You will be treated with the respect your services deserve."

"Go on."

"Only two conditions apply before we go any further. You are to follow orders without debate, and you will never be able to tell anyone you worked for us. Do you understand and agree to those parameters?"

"Certainly, sir. I know the drill. Now, what is the assignment?"

"I can't tell you yet," Goodfellow said. "Nor can I even be specific about what you will be paid for carrying out the assignment, should you choose to accept the job. I can only promise that, should you succeed at your mission and survive, you will not need to spend another night on the street."

"No offense, but that's pretty damn vague."

Goodfellow shrugged. "Beggars can't be choosers."

Dolan eyed a plush, needle-point chair. *Fuck them. They deserve my dusty ass print on their furniture.*

"Okay if I sit?" Dolan asked, seconds after having sat down.

"Certainly," Goodfellow said dryly, almost as if he'd read Dolan's mind. He looked through some of the papers on his desk. Dolan wondered why he'd still use paper instead of computers and tablets, but knew that wasn't his business. None of this made logical sense. Not the trashed building, the funky neighborhood, or the chance encounter with Mr. Cranston. But it all seemed appropriate and natural. Still, all Dolan knew so far was that these people had money, and that some other ex-military types worked for Limbus, Inc. He'd seen the two outside. There would likely be more. Men who were well-dressed and healthy and very well paid. So at least the job offer, whatever it was, was for real. And that meant a chance to forget and start over. He wondered why he'd been chosen if they had so many trained operators already, but that would have to wait. Just get hired. Right now, nothing else mattered.

"You are extraordinarily proficient in hand-to-hand combat, yes?"

"I can look after myself."

"And you have handled dozens of deadly weapons over the years. It says here you were even a member of an antique gun club at one point, and before your home burned down, you were quite the collector. You owned a small but enviable collection of antique firearms from the Civil War, the Revolutionary War, and the two great wars of the 20th Century. They were all destroyed in the fire. Is all of that accurate, Snake?"

Dolan did not respond. The question was rhetorical and they both knew it. Recruiter Goodfellow and his operation knew everything there was to know about him. They held all the cards. Dolan figured it was better just to wait, watch, and listen. He did not miss that Recruiter Goodfellow had called him by his nickname—for a second time, now.

"You have had your eye on me for some time, haven't you?"

Goodfellow nodded. "We've been nudging you our direction and waiting for you to see the light."

These people are something else...

Recruiter Goodfellow set the papers down. He leaned back in his chair with his hands over his ample belly. He looked even more like a plump department store Santa than he had just moments ago. "Incidentally, why did your team members call you 'Snake,' Mr. Dolan?"

"I had a way of sneaking up on people. One time I hid in the grass without moving for two days waiting for the target to show."

"So you were a sniper?"

"Not that time. I did it with a knife. Come on, Mr. Goodfellow, you already seem to know my back story. Why don't you get to the point?"

"Do you accept the job?"

Dolan sighed. "Maybe. Probably. But perhaps you could give me just the rough parameters of the job you are offering?"

"That's not how it works around this office," Goodfellow said. "Limbus has a formula. We offer you a job that will resolve your difficulties once and for all. A job perfectly suited to your unique abilities. You accept that job unconditionally. Then we decide what responsibility to give you and prepare you for the assignment. You promise your services and we promise compensation. These terms are simple and non-negotiable."

"You control everything, start to finish."

"Not quite accurate. We decide everything. When you are ready, we send you where and when we please and compensate you after. If you fail to execute the job properly, the deal is off. If you refuse to go on the mission right now or later, the deal is off. If you try to run away..."

"You'll terminate me," Dolan said, face still devoid of emotion.

"Well, not exactly," Goodfellow said. "We will just see to it that your mind is wiped clean. You will still be alive, Snake, but you won't remember anything about Limbus or what happened when you met with us, or even who you were before. We'll give you a brand new identity, all new thoughts and memories. You won't be a danger to us then, but you won't be you any more either."

Dolan's mouth dropped open. "You can do that?"

"Yes. Sometimes it works quite well."

"Sometimes?"

"Well, unfortunately, a few dishonorably discharged individuals have a breakdown of sorts waiting for them. Months or years later, he or she might suddenly begin to remember bits and pieces of a deeply buried former identity. The process usually starts with very, very bad dreams that gradually seep into the waking hours. They get worse. If it gets out of control, the subject might hear voices, see things, and then eventually go completely psychotic. You see some of those unfortunates on the streets sometimes, always talking to their inner demons."

"In short," Dolan said, "if I try to fuck with Limbus, I'll end up on the street corner wearing a tinfoil hat."

"As I said, we have created our share of those over the years, though rarely on purpose. But you will not be dead. Not just for refusing or failing to complete a mission successfully. We are efficient enough to find a way to avoid executing our own people over something as trivial as human error."

"And what do I get for all this exposure?" Dolan asked. "Never mind, I suppose you can't tell me that."

"No," Goodfellow said.

"Can I ask for something as part of my compensation?"

"You can ask."

"When this is all over, even with all the risks you just described, I want Limbus to make me forget."

Goodfellow pursed his lips. He nodded. "That can be arranged."

"I want your word on it."

"Do what we ask you to do without question and to the best of your ability. When it's all said and done, you will be discharged from the organization and I promise that you will be comfortable and happy and that you will forget about the mission and everything that happened in this life. You have my word."

"Sounds good," Dolan said, though now he wasn't so sure. His mouth went dry. He felt like a man signing a deal with the devil. "But first there's just a wee bit of danger?"

"Oh, yes. Quite a bit, but then, you already have had ample experience with putting your life on the line. You also have a special motivation that should prove useful, at least according to our intelligence. Those are the main reasons we have asked for your help."

Dolan stretched and yawned. "I'm pretty out of shape. There is some sense of urgency here?"

Goodfellow said, "Well, time isn't as much of a constraint on Limbus as it is on other organizations, but in this instance it is, shall we say, of the essence. Our reasons for taking on this project, and for the current need for speed, are complex and, unfortunately, well above both of our pay grades. Again, you must trust us. We start tomorrow. We need you to get in tip-top condition and back into the fray soonest."

"I endanger my life in unknown ways without an explanation as to why, for which I receive a promissory note?"

"Precisely."

Dolan smiled in a minor key. "Hell, I'm down with that. You have a deal."

"I want you to know that I heard what you said, Mr. Dolan. Once we clean your mind, it will be changed forever."

Then what have I got to lose? Dolan thought. Just pain.

"Why nothing at all," Recruiter Goodfellow said, once again as if reading his mind, and perhaps for real this time. Dolan wouldn't have put anything past Limbus at this point. "Nothing at all, except perhaps your life."

* * *

Dolan got a good meal, a long, hot shower, and one good night's sleep. After that, they flat out ran his sorry ass into the dirt.

The building may have been dilapidated on the outside, but as he'd suspected, Limbus was a very well-funded outfit. They had a large gym below ground. It was sterile white and packed with state-of-the-art equipment. Dolan worked out twice daily, roughly two hours a shot, lifted weights and did lots of cardio. He had the place to himself most of the time, although he did spot some of the stoic ex-military types leaving just when he arrived, or showing up as he headed for the shower. They were respectful but never said a word to him and their facial expressions did not invite conversation.

Limbus fed him well, generally sending meals directly to his room. They went heavy on the protein and vegetables to get him lean and strong again, and in between workouts provided him with a firing range and mixed martial arts training. The firing range was indoors near the gym, extremely large, with obstacles and rooms and windows that made it feel similar to those used by SWAT teams everywhere for urban training. Dolan worked alone with a variety of guns. The course changed daily, so he had to stay sharp to keep from being marked down. Overhead cameras watched his every move and doubtless reported back to Recruiter Goodfellow, Mr. Cranston, and whoever it was who gave those men their marching orders.

The mixed martial arts training hurt. Limbus had anticipated everything. They sent different instructors from several schools of fighting to each of the sessions so Dolan never got comfortable with an opponent or any individual style. The variety made him sharper and more confident. The routine was exhausting, and Limbus a hard taskmaster, but Dolan grudgingly came to admire its efficiency. He felt like a man with a purpose, even if that purpose was to disappear forever.

The powerful female nurse came to get him one morning. Dolan tried to engage the blond woman in conversation, but she was either mute or didn't speak English. Perhaps she really was a Viking. She walked ahead of him, her sneakers squeaking on the linoleum. The floor was cold on his bare feet. He was still in his shorts. The nurse did not look back to see if Dolan was following her; she just assumed it. He stopped trying to converse and hugged himself against the chill. She walked him into the infirmary and then into one small room. There were no furnishings and the walls were the usual bone white.

The nurse turned around. She motioned for him to lie down on a padded gurney. Nervously, Dolan sat on the edge of the gurney, looked in her empty eyes, gave up, and went flat. The nurse cleaned the inside of his arm with rubbing alcohol. She was good with the needle; it barely hurt. Then she hooked Dolan up to an IV bag full of something clear. He immediately fell asleep again. He slept deeply and did not remember any dreams.

Dolan woke up feeling great, better than he had in years. He got dressed and hit the gym and lifted nearly ten percent more on his bench press. Had they given him a brew of vitamins and anti-toxins, perhaps mixed with other kinds of performance enhancing drugs? Dolan didn't much care after one treatment. Whatever it was, it worked. He felt stronger and more confident. When the nurse came for him again a day or two later, he went along willingly. They were whipping him into tip-top condition.

It was hard to keep track of time, but Dolan figured by charting his sleep hours and workouts that he'd been training for about ten days when it happened. He'd eaten dinner alone in his room, set the tray outside on the floor, and already done his stretches. Someone knocked and the sound startled Dolan. He knew the outer door would lock itself soon, keeping him trapped in his quarters for the night. Dolan didn't mind that. He had a tablet in the room with seemingly unlimited movies and a substantial library of electronic books. He was exhausted from the training. It wasn't that boring. He noticed faint music started playing, coming from somewhere behind the wall. That was unusual. He hadn't asked for it.

Dolan padded to the door in his shorts and opened it a crack. "Yes?"

The girl had flaming red hair and large blue eyes. Her cheeks were dusted with freckles. She wore a low-cut black evening gown with one strand of pearls and black high heels, and she carried a velvet purse just big enough for feminine essentials. She smiled and his pulse kicked into high gear.

"My name is Colleen. May I come in?"

Dolan felt his mouth go dry. "Excuse me?"

"May I join you?"

Confused, Dolan stepped back from the door before remembering he was in just his shorts. Colleen swept past him without a second thought. Her perfume was intoxicating, the scent completely out of place in this harsh new world. Colleen was too beautiful and exotic to be found standing in the hallway in such a sterile, white, fabricated corporate environment. Where the hell had she come from? Was she one of them or just another recruit?

Colleen set her purse down on his desk. She hummed along with the faint music. She slipped out of her high heels and turned her back. She cocked her hip to one side. The girl had an amazing figure. She motioned to the light hair at the nape of her neck and the fastening gadget seated there. She wiggled her fingers.

"Please unzip me."

"What are you doing here?" Dolan asked finally. It was a rude question, pretty pointless in the end, and they both knew it. His erection was instant, visible and weirdly embarrassing. Dolan also became acutely aware of the security cameras mounted everywhere. When he did not move closer, Colleen managed to undo her own zipper. She slithered out of the little black dress. She turned to face him. Now she wore only a tight smile, a pair of tiny lace panties, and the one strand of pearls. Her breasts were perfect. She reached over to flip off one of the light switches so that the room was mostly dark. She stopped humming but the soft music continued. Colleen stepped closer and put her hands on his bare shoulders.

"Who sent you?" Dolan asked, his own voice seeming to come from somewhere else. He licked his lips. Again, too obvious a question.

Colleen kissed him. The effect was electric. Dolan sat down heavily on the bed and she immediately slid over to sit next to him. Her hand drifted down to his manhood and she kissed him again. Dolan fought against his own drugged-up physicality and long-dormant sexual desire. He took her hand by the wrist. She turned her head and he thought of his wife and the war and the fire and all the other things he badly needed to forget. His erection flagged.

"Wait a second, okay?"

Colleen stopped obediently. "Okay. Did you want anything special first?"

"I don't know you," Dolan said. "You don't know me. Someone paid you to come here. Or made you come. That's strange. Maybe I'm old-fashioned, but that just doesn't feel right."

He could see most of her pretty face in the light of the desk lamp. The rest was in shadow. Dolan read what was behind the sparkle in her eyes. She was actually relieved that he'd stopped her, not frustrated or annoyed. His erection went away. He held on to her hands. He ignored the prying cameras and thought about what he needed, really needed. And that was the death of his past.

"What can I do for you?" Colleen said.

"Lie down," Dolan said at long last. "Let's just talk until we fall asleep."

* * *

The next morning, Snake Dolan woke up alone again, though a female scent on the other pillow and a small, false eyelash proved she'd been there. He took a long, ice-cold shower. The animal part of him felt deprived and angry for having missed out on getting laid, but mostly he was glad to have done something thoughtful for someone else. He was turning back into a killing machine, so it felt good to remember he was also just a human being. This assignment wouldn't last forever. They never did. A man had to go back to the world and still be a man somehow, even if he didn't remember why. That part had never changed and never would. He'd blown it badly last time and didn't want to make the same mistake.

He left the room.

The building seemed virtually empty, unusual for this hour of the morning. Assuming it was indeed morning. There was no way to be sure without going outside. Dolan went to the cafeteria and made himself a protein shake with fresh fruit and oatmeal. He hit the gym, stretched, did five miles on the treadmill and then some light weights for toning. He didn't want to bulk up any more; it was better to be light on his feet when the time came.

And then it came.

"Mr. Dolan?"

Dolan turned from his position on the slanted bench and lowered the two thirty-five-pound free weights to the floor. The two burly mercenary types were standing in the doorway waiting for him. The big blond nurse appeared between them. Dolan felt an electric charge run through his body. Something was up. He could tell. He got up, toweled the sweat off his upper body and walked their way.

"Should I shower and change?"

The nurse spoke her first words. It turned out she had a bit of an accent; Dolan thought it might have been Swiss. "There is no time. You must come with us."

Dolan complied. His heart sped up with excitement. He was about to find out what this had all been about, what his assignment was, what was expected of him. He would face the actual mission at long last. Dolan followed the three employees into the hall. He wore only gym shorts and tennis shoes and socks. He assumed they would have his gear ready and waiting. Limbus was damned impressive that way.

"We are a go?"

One of the two mercenaries offered Dolan a quick nod.

It's on.

The nurse walked faster than the three men and so she led the way. With every step, Dolan felt more and more excited. It was finally about to happen. Everything he saw became sharp and crisp, the molding around the white doors and windows, the grout in the tiles running down the seemingly endless hallways, the vague scent of the nurse's antiseptic and some kind of old lady perfume she wore, the sour sweat drying on his own body. For a time, there was only his own slow breathing, heartbeats, and the sound of shoes and suit fabric to his left and right. These were perhaps his last few moments as Snake Dolan.

Fine by me...

They turned right, went through an entrance he had never seen before and gradually approached a large set of double-wide steel doors. The two mercenaries stayed a few feet behind, as if allowed no farther, but the nurse marched ahead. She punched a code into a small box near the center of the doors. The mercenaries exchanged nervous looks. Dolan studied them, wondering what would happen next.

The monstrous doors grumbled, squealed, and slowly parted. They boomed against the far walls and stopped.

The room beyond was even more pristine than the other parts of the Limbus branch. It was a laboratory, but like nothing Dolan had previously seen. The space was huge and full of odd-looking electronic equipment and long tubes filled with a powder-blue fluid of some kind. In the center of the room was a big table with a thin pad on top. It was covered with cups and bracelets and wires that gave Dolan a deep shiver. It looked like a torture chamber out of an old horror movie. Beside it were long needles and scalpels galore, all shining like holiday tinsel on their rolling metal trays.

No one was on the large, man-sized table.

Dolan became curious. As the nurse went to a control panel to confer with two strangers in white lab coats, Dolan approached the table, idly wondering who would ever willingly lie down on it and why. Bad joke. Another part of his mind recognized his fate and shivered, but Dolan buried the fear along with his questions. He'd come too far to back out now. He wanted to get this thing done and over with.

Above the table and yards away sat a gigantic, flat screen television, much like the ones in giant football stadiums. It was designed to hold one huge image made up of several smaller parts. It seemed to be a holograph of sorts.

"Snake?"

Dolan didn't catch his nickname at first. Then he turned and realized one of the new men in white coats had addressed him. The man was bald with a bulbous nose and thick eyebrows that gave him a clownish look. His name tag said DR. BARTLETT. Dolan faced the man.

Dr. Bartlett said, "We cannot delay this mission for long for very complex reasons, but I want to give you just a sense of what is about to happen so you will be better prepared."

"I'm listening."

"Do you know anything about time, Snake? What it is or is not?"

"Not really," Dolan said. His heart was thudding now. His bare body broke out in goose bumps. "I never gave that kind of thing much thought."

"Let's start with this. Everything changes constantly, because what we are and what we experience is made up of star dust—these tiny particles which are slowly separating and disintegrating in a pretty orderly fashion. We cannot comprehend the enormity of that universe, so we manage things by counting seconds and hours and years and decades and centuries. We use time. But we just made all that stuff up. Time is an invention of the human mind. Therefore it is always relative to how it is perceived. It exists in its own continuum and is in one sense as stagnant as visualized, although it also ebbs and flows in both directions."

Dolan took a deep breath, then another. "You're kind of losing me."

"Let's look at it this way then," Dr. Bartlett said. "Time is a lot like space. If we were floating around in a space suit, there would be no up or down or left or right. We all just measure time as we experience that for our own convenience. In reality, what we think of as time does not really exist. The past was just more organized, and the present and future are accelerated products of ever increasing entropy. Things fall apart, the center cannot hold, the poet wrote. As I said, time is a purely human construct, a way our level of consciousness manages the information it receives and the events that appear to take place around us. Viewed from a wholly different reality, those same events could be read in reverse, broken down into perpetual sections, or perhaps be thought of as happening at exactly the same millisecond. Are you following me now, Snake?"

He wasn't, but Dolan was clinging to that droning voice for comfort, so he nodded. Just then, the no-nonsense nurse took Dolan by the arm and led him toward the table.

She said, "Remove all of your clothing, please."

Dolan complied, but then when standing in the cold room naked but for battle scars, he felt an even colder ball of anxiety growing in the pit of his stomach. This felt more like facing a major surgery than preparing for a typical combat mission with a team of friends. He felt goose bumps ripple up his arms and the small hairs rise along the back of his neck. This whole op was getting spookier by the minute.

"Go on, Doc," Dolan lied. "I get it."

Bartlett waved his arms in the air. He was clearly excited by the topic. At least someone was having fun. "A fellow named Robert Lanza argues that the theory of biocentrism proves that even death is just an illusion. Biocentrism says life creates the universe—that it is not the other way round. And what this means for this particular operation is that since space and time do not occur in any linear fashion, nothing is really the way we experience it as individuals. Our perception is actually irrelevant."

The nurse stood waiting, her features deadpan. Dr. Bartlett smiled and shrugged. "I won't bore you going on about the famous 'double slit' experiment, Snake, because I think you get the general idea."

Dolan just stood there naked. "I'm going to travel through time?"

"Indeed you are. Suffice it to say, we at Limbus have spent many years and hundreds of billions of dollars and we finally have proven Lanza right."

Dr. Bartlett grinned and clapped his hands. The nurse motioned for Dolan to get up on the device. He pushed the terror down and fully committed himself to the choice.

I've got nothing to lose, nothing but this fucked life and a bunch of bad memories. I want to forget.

"Let's do this."

Dolan hopped on the edge of the table. The nurse touched his chest with one palm and pushed it away from her own body. She stepped to the side and put her other arm under his back. Dolan let her guide him until he was stretched out and flat on the medical table. She placed electrodes and attached wires to his flesh like someone who'd done this before. He thought he caught a trace of sadness in her eyes but wasn't sure.

"In essence, we are now going to drop you into the flow of time in one universe in order to change its course," Dr. Bartlett said. "You will be rather like a small rock thrown into a big stream. What I can tell you is that in one multi-verse, and at different places, unfortunate deaths have just occurred. That's where you come in. We want you to change the course of one particular stream so the future that results from those changes is one we deem optimal. We are not absolutely certain how many missions will be necessary. We will find that out soon by studying what happens after the first event is altered."

None of it made real sense to Dolan. All he could think about was his steadily rising adrenaline and the thought of the one final payoff, freedom from his mental agony. He closed his eyes, controlling his tense breathing. The nurse worked busily now, efficiently securing his head, torso, arms and legs into the various straps and cups. Below him, under the table, something began to vibrate and produce a low, whirring noise. The table grew warmer, then warmer still. Soon, Dolan felt hundreds of tiny needles as they rose up, pricking his exposed skin. How far would they go? He panicked and twitched and his mouth tasted sour. He panted for air.

"What is going to happen to me, Doc?" He hated the fear in his voice.

"You will be going into combat," Dr. Bartlett said in a whisper, now with the air of a man imparting precious secrets. "So be prepared for anything. Do your job. When you're finished, we'll wipe your mind clean and take away your pain, just as Recruiter Goodfellow promised."

Dolan wondered if he could finally get some real answers, since it was all actually going down. He figured that at this point anything was worth a try. Why not come right out and ask?

"Tell me, Doc, why did they choose me?"

The machine began to click and bang and hum. The nurse stood back.

"For a variety of reasons," Dr. Bartlett said, "including, of course, your expertise with antique weaponry and your combat experience. You are a man who has fought his way back from the abyss. That is a psychological skill we expect will come in very handy during this particular mission. Perhaps most importantly, Snake, you have one absolutely indispensable personal motivation that should see you through and bring us the result we require."

"This hurts," Dolan said. He grimaced.

The machine was loud and shaking around and something smelled like burning hair. The needles were moving, turning in his flesh and digging even deeper into his body. Dolan felt nauseous and woozy and had trouble concentrating on the conversation. Part of him was glad it had begun. Whatever this was, it would soon be over. The idea of having his mind swept clean was still oddly appealing, despite all the risks he'd been warned about. He liked the thought of being here but also gone forever. No more grief. No more shame...

Dr. Bartlett looked at something on the control panel. "Here we go!"

"What am I supposed to do when I get there?" Dolan asked.

Dr. Bartlett said, "Fight. Trust your instincts. Keep moving forward."

Someone else, not the nurse, called out, "Any moment now, sir."

"But what's my actual assignment?" Dolan whispered.

"Save the girl."

Dolan winced at the words. He felt as if they were mocking him at the very last second. A sickening flash of guilt ran through him. "What girl?"

Dolan tried to open his eyes again, only to find the nurse had secured something over them, some kind of metallic blindfold. He was completely blind. The countless little pinpricks steadily heated up until they fully scorched his skin. Dolan groaned. A strange new charge of energy rushed into and through his muscles and bones, flowing back and forth, like hot ocean waves were carrying him somewhere. He could no longer move his limbs. His body was twitching and jerking within the restraints. He shook like a child and pissed himself. He'd lost control of his body.

"What girl?" Dolan said again. Or thought he'd said, but now there was no sound but his breathing. No one answered him because no one was there. The world was total darkness and he sensed the enormous push and pull of unknown forces. He was drifting in the middle of nowhere, out between the stars. He'd never felt so damned alone.

Just as Dolan began to completely freak out, his vision returned. He registered not what had been there in the laboratory, but a reality existing somewhere else entirely. He was seeing from down deep in his soul, looking through a window into an unfamiliar countryside dotted with farms and cows and trees and long, winding dirt roads. The spot was verdant and the sun was just coming up in the distance. It was some other place and time, strange and yet oddly familiar. It was becoming real and rushing closer. Dolan knew it was his destination. He could smell the trees.

"What girl, damn it?" His last words to Limbus emerged in a voice that was someone else's. It came from way down a long, empty hall and echoed from off in the distance as if filtered through electronics to sound low and robotic. Again, no one answered.

And then Dolan saw a woman in an old, sepia-tinged photograph. She seemed familiar, yet he knew he'd never seen her before. Abruptly, her features morphed into the face of different female, a much younger one. Then she became someone else entirely, but by then, his vision was too blurred to take it in. Dolan felt completely baffled and curious but the physical and psychic pain dominated everything. His conscious mind was gone. His brain spun in circles and his flesh twitched. His body felt like it was literally melting away.

Dolan screamed. His pulse raced and the fear at last completely consumed him. The last thing he heard was more like a whisper than a human voice and it seemed to come from deep within his own psyche. He could not make out the words.

Everything went dark.

* * *

Something bit him on the neck.

Dolan swatted at it. He felt incredibly tired. He was naked and ached all over. His body was sprawled in the dirt and grass somewhere and his face was wedged into the trunk of a tree. The earth smelled rich and dark and damp. He turned over and stared to his right. A huge metal cylinder sat nearby that contained what appeared to be the table he'd been strapped to and some mysterious electronic equipment with blue and red wires, but even as Dolan watched, the strange device became transparent and faded away. It was gone in three seconds. He was completely alone.

"Shit."

Dolan sighed. He groaned and sat up. The morning sun spread orange fire on the eastern hills, which were dotted with what looked like white tents. Dolan brushed dirt off his body. He smelled something rank. He could hear something buzzing in his brain. He rolled over.

A corpse stared back at him.

Dolan recoiled in shock. It was just a boy barely in his teens dressed in faded and torn rags dyed a butternut color. One of his eyes and part of his face had been blown away. The buzzing sound came from the flies swarming in his skull. Maggots were already squirming in the exposed brain. Dolan tried to vomit but nothing came up. He stared. The dead body still clutched an antique .58 Springfield musket that appeared to be in near-mint condition. A long, blood-encrusted bayonet was fastened to the end of the barrel.

Stunned, Dolan shook his head to clear it and rubbed his eyes. The uniformed corpse and the old weapon were still there. So was the strange landscape. The delivery vehicle was gone. And Dolan was naked and unarmed.

Where the fuck is this?

Above him, from higher ground deeper into the squat copse of trees, came the awesome, thunderous racket of an army wakening. Dolan heard horses neighing, heavy cannon rolling along cleared dirt tracks, and men shouting and laughing and swearing and forming up into ranks. He crawled up the slope on elbows and knees, ass naked to the morning air, and peered up at the far hills. The sun broke the horizon and lit a wide battlefield already littered with rotting human and horse bodies and shattered wagons. The white tents on the slope were military. He saw huge cannons, also forming up in rows. The artillery was surrounded by men, an army in mostly blue uniforms.

The fucking Civil War?

Dolan mentally ran through the books he'd read, trying to guess where and when Limbus had dropped him. He had no time to wonder exactly how they had done it. He already knew why. They wanted him to find and protect some woman or women. And now he'd have to find a way to get the job done.

He stared upward.

The group on the ridge was definitely Union, and from the sheer size, probably one of the largest forces they'd assembled. So he was definitely somewhere in the early 1860s. Dolan thought fast. He had no sense of the size of the Confederate ranks because he was too close to take all that in. He knew nothing except that he was stuck among them. Perhaps the individual battle didn't matter. He'd just have to perform the task and somehow escape with his life.

He slid back down into the space by the tree trunk. He reluctantly stripped the boy of his uniform. It reeked of sweat and piss and blood and gore, but it would have to do. He rubbed dirt in his hair and took the small paper cartridges of gun powder and ammo along with the tall Springfield. Dolan had once owned one. He knew he'd have to load and fire one mini-ball at a time, but at least it was rifled.

He had one move. Dolan had to become one of them or die. If he was found naked and alone by either side on the eve of battle, he'd almost certainly be hung as a deserter or a spy.

"Hell you doin' there, son?"

Dolan spun around with the rifle up. He did not aim it. An older man wearing a sergeant's stripes and a battered old cap stood on a mound of dirt and dead brush. He spat tobacco juice into the dirt. The sergeant squinted into the sunrise, shading his eyes with one hand, leaning on the trunk of a tree.

Dolan waited and watched. The sergeant was a sour man. He had a feral look in his squinty eyes. Someone whooped and fired a weapon and the sergeant shouted for him to shush up and wait for orders. There was nothing in his tone but a studied indifference.

"Well?"

The sergeant was staring at him now, so Dolan kept his own voice hoarse and did his level best to imitate the thick Southern accent he'd just heard. He did a pretty fair job. "I jes' had to piss."

"Come on, then," the sergeant said. "Less'n you're gonna shit too, best git goin'."

"Comin'."

"Wass yer name, boy?"

"They call me Snake," Dolan said.

"Try not to get kilt, Snake." The older man laughed and farted large.

Dolan trudged up the slope. If the sergeant had noticed the naked body below, he said nothing about it.

When they cleared the top of the mound, Dolan saw an astonishing sight, thousands of men and horses and weapons in one vast formation. His mind worked furiously. He knew the Springfield had a default sight setting of one hundred yards, but that it could be set for three or even five hundred. He'd read that the hollow-based round could cause frightful damage to the foe because it tended to tumble as it hit. If he worked hard, aiming and firing and re-loading, he might get off as many as three shots per minute. Dolan prepared for combat. He fumbled at first, but managed to remember how to load the weapon. Meanwhile, the army rose to the ready. An average-sized man on a white horse rode behind them waving his hat. He gave the order.

It was time.

The men were packed incredibly close together, and Dolan knew this charge would be virtual suicide for perhaps one in four. Others would lose arms and legs due to amputation directly after the battle. These men had no medical assistance to speak of and most would get only alcohol for anesthetic, or perhaps nothing at all. Combat was a proud test of nerves to these people, and they were accustomed to suffering horrendous casualties, making charge after charge for a cause they barely understood.

Dolan studied their situation. The Union troops had the higher ground and at least as many cannons. He remembered what Limbus had ordered. He needed to find and save a girl. But there were no women here, just thousands of frightened boys and weathered, bitter old men. Dolan thought about trying to run away, but where could he go? Wouldn't Limbus just pluck him out of the grass and send him back again? Still, perhaps they'd wipe his mind clean then, just as promised, though it would be for failing at his mission. Did it matter why, if he'd never even remember it? Wouldn't the result be the same? No, it would matter, Dolan thought. You gave your word. And there's a girl.

There was no more time to think about Limbus. The officers waved the troops forward. Dolan found himself surrounded by rows of scared boys and sweaty, scowling older men much like the evil sergeant, most seemingly indifferent fellows who just urged callow boys into the fray.

As the men advanced, gear and sabers and bayonets and canteens rattling, bodies all packed together and oozing primal fear, Dolan studied the landscape ahead. He knew from reading that the boys in blue would fire cannon soon, and that the effect on his brethren would be nothing less than catastrophic. He shaded his eyes as he stumbled forward. One of the boys in front of him tripped and fell and was almost trampled. Dolan spotted something through a narrow break in the ranks. He saw a small brown farmhouse perhaps fifty yards ahead. A wooden picket fence surrounded the weathered property.

There was laundry hung on a rope line out back.

Women did laundry.

The sergeant shouted something Dolan didn't catch, and in response, the men let loose a series of terrifying, high-pitched rebel yells. They all began to jog forward. The sergeant stayed a bit behind, gleefully kicking reluctant men in the ass, always yelling and waving his arms while staying to the rear. Dolan ran forward with the house in mind. The cannon above them on the slope began to belch fire and an obscene screech filled the air above. Their advance was courageous but completely insane and ultimately doomed to fail. The huge balls and links of chain began to fall like mortar rounds.

The explosions were deafening. Guts and body parts flew.

Blood and gore splattered Dolan's face. The battlefield was now covered with smoke and there was chaos all around. The Springfields and pistols rattled and barked like small dogs. Terrified men paused to fire up at the ridge. They reloaded at once then ran a few dozen yards before kneeling in the stained dirt and green grass to fire uphill again. The Yankees had the high ground. It was suicide all right, and Dolan knew that better than most.

Dolan whooped and waved his rifle without firing it. He broke into a dead run, heading for the small farm with the white picket fence out back. A boy to his left followed him as if hoping to take cover there, but as Dolan watched, the top of his thin body vanished into a cloud of red mist. He'd been struck by a low-flying round from the Yankee cannon. His lower torso and legs collapsed, arteries pulsing blood into torn clods of earth.

The cannon screeched and the men screamed and the rifles belched flame.

Their ranks had already thinned when Dolan jumped the picket fence and rolled into the yard. He got up and ran for it. He passed some kind of wooden door set into a pile of dirt and rocks, hit the clothes line, shoved a white sheet out of the way, and made for the front door of the little home. He struck it with his left shoulder. When he did, the door flew off its hinges and collapsed into the small living room.

He looked up. Outside the window, Confederate soldiers raced by, firing and screaming in the thick white smoke.

Dolan rolled over to protect his sore shoulder. He was under the haze and could see another room to the back of the little house. He crawled that way. The building rattled and shook. As the troops closed in on the Union-held ridge to begin their ascent, the cannon fire finally ceased. It was amazing the house had not been hit. It was most likely just under the range of the guns. The fighting was beyond and above them now, fierce as ever, but of considerably less volume due to the distance.

Dolan reached up and opened the door. It exploded in his hand, and left him holding a wooden latch. A woman was inside the room, a small child at her side. She was young and dark-haired and her eyes were wide with horror. She held a one-shot handgun in her two hands. She'd just missed him. Dolan zeroed in on her face. He recognized her as one of the women he'd seen while lying on the table, the one from the sepia photograph in his mind. He surveyed the room. He crawled closer. The woman screamed and held the child to her side.

"I won't hurt you," Dolan said. "Do you have any place below ground you can hide until this is over?"

The woman was trembling and pale with terror. Dolan shook her gently. She snapped out of it, nodded her head, and pointed toward the west side of the property, back near the clothes line.

"I tried to get under," she said in a whisper. Her accent was unfamiliar. "But when I did so, someone shot at me."

The root cellar with the wooden door. Dolan realized he'd gone right by it on the way into the house. That would have to do.

"Bring the child," Dolan said. "Follow me and stay close."

He duck walked through the low smoke with the woman and child behind him. The kid was crying. Dolan didn't think anyone would hear that, or much give a damn under the circumstances. Most of the rebels had long left the farmhouse behind. He eased the front door open and looked out. In the distance, when the wind shifted, Dolan could see officers on horseback watching the assault through spyglasses and with shaded eyes. The smoke pretty much covered everything else.

The area seemed clear.

"Now," Dolan said. "Run for it."

"Much obliged, reb." The woman and child ran across the yard, heading for the wooden door to the root cellar. Dolan followed them a few yards behind, already wondering what to do next, if the mission was already over, or if he was actually just going to die here. The woman reached the root cellar. She looked up and to one side and screamed.

The scowling sergeant appeared in the smoke. He'd stayed behind, perhaps pretending to be wounded, and now saw a pretty woman out in the open. Dolan closed the distance. The sergeant looked his way. He grinned at Dolan as if they were both in on something good. He spat tobacco and stepped closer to the woman and shoved her down on the ground. Dolan raised the rifle but knew he could not fire the long Springfield from this far off without risking the lives of the innocents. He jogged a bit closer. Meanwhile, the sergeant set his own weapon down. He began to undo his breeches, clearly intent on raping the girl. He'd have killed her afterward just to shut her up; that much also seemed clear.

Dolan closed the gap. He fired. The Sergeant was hit in the leg and dropped to his knees. He glared at Dolan and fumbled for his own rifle to shoot back. Dolan lowered the barrel of the old Springfield and ran the man through with his bayonet. The sergeant screamed and shat himself.

The women threw open the wooden door and took the child down into the root cellar. She looked back once with wide and grateful eyes but then slammed the door behind her. Dolan immediately ran over to kick some rocks and dirt on top of the entrance to camouflage her hiding place. Dolan heard the sergeant dying noisily behind him. He felt an odd mixture of remorse and primal satisfaction.

The charge became a rout. Trumpets sounded.

The men on the ridge began to retreat and come back his way. Dolan got up and a round narrowly missed him to strike a white nightgown hanging on the clothes line. He spun around to see who had fired at him.

They'd seen him running away. Now the enemy lay on both sides. He was in a sandwich.

The officers and a few enlisted men raced toward Dolan. They appeared to be summarily executing stragglers and deserters. In truth, Dolan hadn't given much thought about what to do next. There hadn't been time. He ran for the house again to hopefully lead the soldiers away from the woman and her child. He made it up to the porch just in time. A round struck the door as he rolled through it.

Dolan loaded the rifle as quickly as he could, then turned facedown and brought the Springfield up. He sighted on one of the officers on horseback and fired. The man fell backward. Dolan struggled to reload the cumbersome weapon. It seemed to vibrate in his hands. Why was it doing that?

Just like the Limbus business card.

Dolan was shifting now, leaving the past, and he knew it. His sense of smell vanished, and then his hearing. The world blurred and then slipped the rest of the way out of focus. He shook on the floor, frothing at the mouth. He could no longer control his limbs. The painful feeling of a thousand pinpricks returned. His skin felt hot and dry and every muscle hurt.

Dolan wondered if they were bringing him back to Limbus and if the mission was already over. He prayed it was. And if not, that he would die. But a small voice within him disagreed. He'd proven useful again. He was proud of that. He'd won. He was alive and energized and felt good about himself for the first time in ages, even if just for surviving the first test. Did he really want all of that erased forever? Everything he was? Just...gone?

When the Confederate soldiers burst into the house, they found only an abandoned uniform and an empty .58 Springfield musket, its long bayonet covered with fresh blood. The man had vanished.

* * *

Snake Dolan did not wake up back on the table as he'd hoped. They had not wiped his mind clean. Not yet, anyway. He was not that lucky. He hadn't died, either. He woke up groggy and shivering and opened his eyes to complete darkness. It was also cold as a cast iron toilet seat. Dolan felt around with his fingertips. He felt damp, sticky earth and chilly water. Back on earth, but somewhere else, and in some other when. He took stock of the situation.

He was once again naked and on the ground, this time in what felt like a steadily widening pool of mud. Drops of cold moisture fell on his bare skin. It was raining hard. His entire body ached.

"Shit."

White lightning split the sky. Dolan gathered that he was outside in the woods. Maybe ten seconds later, he heard a long, deep, repetitive rumble. He felt relieved to note it was not cannon fire this time, merely thunder. Then the lighting came again, and he counted to six before he heard the booming noise. The worst of the storm lay in the distance.

Dolan sat up in the mud. His head throbbed. He rubbed his arms against the cold and watched the sky. Lightning again, thunder after, speeding up a bit. The storm front was moving closer.

Dolan sat up. He felt around in the dark. Another lightning flash, almost directly overhead and very bright, finally illuminated his immediate surroundings. He was next to a dirt road in the middle of what seemed to be absolutely nowhere. He had no idea where he was or what time zone they had dropped him into. But the dirt road had tire tracks on it. Not wheel tracks, tire tracks. So, automobiles.

Headlights appeared in the distance. Yes, a car. Okay, Dolan thought, at least we know this isn't the 1800s. That's a start.

Dolan realized he'd be in an exposed position. He forced himself to stand and jogged naked to some waist-high brush. He squatted down to watch the approaching vehicle. He could see it in the moonlight and with the help of the occasional forks of lightning. It was a medium-sized truck. The engine sounded odd, smaller than he would have expected for modern times. The truck slowed down as it bounced through a deep mud puddle.

Dolan noticed a large tree had fallen across the road. He decided he'd jump the driver when they stopped to move the tree and at least score some warm clothes. But something moved just below Dolan and to his right. He gently nudged some brush out of the way. He peered through the shrubbery.

Two men lay there in the darkness and the mud. They both wore rain slickers and held firearms of some kind.

It was an ambush.

Dolan squinted in the gloom, though now his eyes were beginning to adjust. The guns had round cylinders and looked to be from the early 20th century. They'd called them Tommy guns back then. He'd fired one once before, though he'd never owned the weapon. They were deadly and fairly efficient. These two men had carefully laid a trap for the driver and probably planned to steal the truck.

But what am I supposed to do about that? Why am I here?

The truck came to a halt but no one got out. The two men who lay in wait stiffened. One of them whistled a poor imitation of a bird. Someone across the road answered in the same manner.

The bad guys were on both sides of the road; all of them were guaranteed to be heavily armed. Dolan had no idea who was in the waiting truck, but if there was a girl around, she wasn't likely to be lying around here in the wet mud, clutching a gun, and planning to hijack or murder the driver. She had to be in the vehicle.

Before Dolan could move, he heard another sound to his left. He went flat in the brush and dirt, naked and wet and acutely aware of his helplessness. He saw another man who was smaller than the others, wearing a floppy hat and a black slicker. The new man crawled to the edge of the road. He carried a revolver in each hand and had a wicked Bowie knife stuck in the pocket of his raincoat. He was fixated on the truck.

The headlights lit up the area. The passenger door of the stuck vehicle opened. The men around Dolan stiffened and took aim. Whatever was happening, time was running out. Dolan eyed the Bowie knife. A burst of lighting snapped overhead.

One...two...three...

Dolan gathered himself and waited for the thunder to arrive. When it did, he rolled down the short slope and pounced on the back of the prone gunman. He grabbed the knife. The man tried to roll over to protect himself but Dolan was too fast. He slit the man's throat. The gun in his left hand discharged once into the road. The man getting out of the truck promptly shot back. Then someone else began firing. Men shouted and screamed. The entire area was immediately bright with muzzle flashes and the air dense with flying lead. The plants and trees around Dolan were being cut to pieces. It was all-out war.

Staying low, Dolan stripped the man of his raincoat and buckled it on. He returned the knife to its sheath. He stole the floppy hat as well, and the two hand guns. He crawled back to the side of the road.

The men in the truck were trying to back it up, but someone behind them had just dropped another tree in their way. It was a perfect trap. The attackers now seemed to be firing down at the tires, perhaps because they did not want to destroy the contents of the truck. One thing was for sure, once they forced the passengers to step outside, this was going to become a slaughter.

Dolan heard Bartlett in his mind, clear as a bell, saying "Protect the girl." But she had to be in the truck, not out in the woods. Dolan scowled and wiped the wet mud from his face. Frustrated, he came to a decision. He crawled back to his right. He did his best imitation of that crappy bird sound and cried out hoarsely, "Don't shoot, boys. It's me!"

The two men down below looked up. With all the noise and confusion, they bought it. One went back to firing.

"Get down here," the other man said. He lowered his Tommy gun. He looked up again to see Dolan in the raincoat and hat coming down from the brush. The other man stopped shooting but continued to aim at the road.

Someone far away shouted, "Get out of the truck! All we want is the fuckin' whiskey!"

Some other men laughed.

Above the two thieves now, Dolan raised the pistols, one in each hand. The lightning flashed overhead.

"The hell?" the man below said. His voice went thick with fear. He could see Dolan's size and bare legs now. He knew it wasn't his friend. He frantically tried to bring up his machine gun but lost his balance. He slipped in the mud and fell flat on his back with a splash.

Dolan shot him and then shot the other gunner in the back of the head. He tucked the two pistols into the pockets of the rain coat. He ran for the machine guns and picked one up in each hand. They weighed a ton, but he was in good shape. His hands shook from adrenaline. He stood up and waved one in the air. The wind and rain whipped his bare legs. Across the road, two other men stood up as well, thinking the battle was over. They seemed to be waiting for orders.

Dolan shot them, too. That deep rattling noise was all but drowned out by a painfully loud burst of thunder.

"Get out of the truck!"

The last man, one apparently stationed in front of the vehicle, appeared as a black outline just outside the glare of the headlights. He had a shotgun aimed at the front windshield. He repeated his demand. "The both of you get out and hightail it back to Canada if you want. We just came for the fuckin' whiskey."

You're lying to them, Dolan thought. You're going to kill them or I wouldn't even be here.

The man waited.

Dolan trotted along the mud bank just above the road, one gun in each hand. "We're comin' out."

The side door opened again and a woman's legs appeared.

There she is!

Dolan could just see the top of her head in the window. She stepped out into the open with her hands up. The woman wore a ridiculously incongruous evening outfit, a beaded white dress with some kind of funny little hat that had feathers in it. Her dress shoes sank ankle deep into the mud. She was crying and waving her arms. She was the younger girl he'd seen in his mind back at Limbus.

Dolan watched as the man in the headlights waited for the driver to emerge. He kept the man in his sights. He already knew how this would have to end.

The driver door opened. Someone tossed a rifle out into the mud. A man appeared. He was round and bald and had his hands up. He was nobody's fool. He went for a pistol at his belt and right then the girl took off running into the darkness. Dolan watched her go, his attention distracted.

The man in the headlights shot the driver dead.

Dolan dropped the large guns and charged after the woman. He could not stand his ground and shoot the other man dead and still keep track of where she was headed. It was too damned dark. His instincts told him to flank her in the woods and keep her from getting injured or killed some other way. He figured the last man might be true to his word, though that didn't seem likely. But if he was there for the hijacked whiskey, it was now his to keep. If he wasn't, they'd know in a matter of seconds.

Nope. Either he had orders to kill them all or the man feared leaving a witness. He came after the girl.

Dolan ran through the mud and twigs and roots. He knew his bare feet were bleeding. He paused by a pine tree and studied the ground ahead. Nothing was moving. And then he saw a flash of the white beaded dress. It made the woman an easy target. He could see in the moonlight whenever she darted into the open or whenever there was a flash of lightning. He heard the man from the road following her from above. They were in a triangle of sorts, with Dolan closing faster.

Dolan crouched. He saw her go by like a deer in flight and managed to wrestle her to the ground. She fought him like a panicked cat. He covered her mouth and whispered in her ear.

"Stay down," Dolan said. "I'm not with them. I won't hurt you. Let's just let him run on by."

She stopped struggling. Dolan scooped up handfuls of mud in one hand and covered her white dress with it and held her tightly against his raincoat and bare legs. He covered her up as best he could with the dark rain slicker and his muddy body. Her heart pounded against his chest like a small musical instrument. He could smell her cheap perfume.

The man crashing through the woods slowed down. Then the noise stopped entirely as if he'd sensed something.

Dolan waited. He thought he'd spotted the man, but wasn't certain. He had one of the pistols in his right hand now but didn't want a muzzle flash to give their location away. He stayed quiet. The girl breathed warm air between his muddy fingers, offering up a small puff of white to the frigid air. Dolan raised the pistol just a few inches. Some liquid, probably just sweat, slipped into his right eye and stung. They both held perfectly still.

The other man stepped out into the moonlight with the shotgun in his hands. His eyes roamed the woods, searching for the girl. Dolan sat up and took the shot. The girl screamed when the pistol went off and she tried to writhe away from him. He did not let her go.

"Please, mister."

"Wait."

The other man did not get up again. Dolan loosened his grip.

"Go back toward the road, turn right and keep on going," he whispered in her ear. "Go where you were both heading before the ambush. Get to the next town and just keep your mouth shut and don't tell anyone that you were ever here."

He released her. She seemed confused at first, but then sat up and stumbled away sideways, as if expecting to be shot in the back. He watched her go with a warm feeling in his chest. He'd done well. Then the girl picked up speed and confidence. She headed for the trees, going back the way they'd come and to the right, just as Dolan had suggested. She'd be safe.

Dolan rolled over on his back. He pictured the Limbus laboratory in his mind. He opened his mouth and drank some rain water. He waited to be picked up. He wondered if he could negotiate a little, now that he'd proven his worth. He wanted a conclusion that didn't involve any more death. He spoke aloud. "Was that it, Doc? Am I done?"

The mud became warm and then hot and Dolan felt his exposed skin begin to sizzle like bacon in a pan. His stomach flipped over and tied itself in a knot. His nerves caught up with him. He sat up quickly, which started his head spinning.

Mistake...

Dolan vomited the rainwater into the mud. Dizzy, he lay flat again. It had to be over now. He was tired.

Please.

He curled up into a ball just as he blacked out.

* * *

Dolan gagged. The overhead light was far too bright. It hurt his sore eyes. His throat felt dry and thick. He squinted. It burned through his lids even when they were tightly closed.

Snake Dolan licked his lips and said, "Can you please turn that off?"

It dimmed a bit but did not go out.

Dolan gathered himself and looked around. He could not move his body, only his eyes. He was back on the laboratory table at Limbus, but he was still fastened down. It was as if no time had passed. The room had not changed. Perhaps he'd never left? Had his physical body been here the entire time?

The nurse was taking his blood pressure with some concern on her face. Dr. Bartlett appeared in Dolan's vision, also looking down at Dolan. His features seemed strangely elongated. The whole world appeared distorted. Dolan figured that was likely just some side effect of the drugs they had given him. Had he experienced the whole mission in his mind? Was this some strange experiment with hallucinogenic medications? His body felt like he'd been through every inch of those missions; his muscles ached, his skin was cold, even his bare feet felt bruised and cut, but on another level, it didn't seem like he'd gone anywhere but deeper into his own unconscious. Maybe he was imaging those other times and places.

Hell, maybe Limbus wasn't real. Perhaps he was just going insane.

"Can you hear me, Snake?"

Dolan tried to nod. His head was still firmly gripped by the machine.

"I'm happy to tell you that you did brilliantly in both instances," Dr. Bartlett said. "I just chatted with Recruiter Goodfellow and Mr. Cranston and they are both very pleased. Thanks to you, the two women survived and will have the necessary offspring, and thus will continue their line as required. This is what Limbus, Inc. needed to insure that certain events in the future will also take place. A job well done, son. You are a fine soldier."

Dolan stared at him. Was it really over? Thank God.

"We're about to finish up now," Dr. Bartlett said. "Are you ready to…rest?"

Dolan tried to speak. He wanted to discuss his bonus for a minute or two. He wanted to say that he'd changed his mind about having his mind wiped completely clean. Couldn't they just give him some money and maybe a modest home in Montana, instead? Hell, he could still work as a mercenary if he needed to, so maybe not even a lot of money. He just wanted to remain…Snake Dolan. Or maybe they could just take the more painful memories and leave the rest. He wanted to be able to remember these two successful missions and the way he'd finally regained some self-esteem. He wanted to at least remember falling in love with Phyllis. He wanted to hold on to the faces of the good friends he'd known, living and dead.

In the end, Snake Dolan didn't want to lose his life after all. He tried to say so. He tried to tell them. He just couldn't. His mouth wouldn't work.

The nurse put something in an IV that was hooked to his arm.

Dr. Bartlett murmured some orders.

Dolan did not want to die. He tried to scream. Nothing happened.

They were going to do it. His memory, all that he was, would end now, even if his body survived. Dolan tried to beg for more time, a chance to barter, but his lips barely moved.

Dr. Bartlett smiled down at him. "Snake, be proud. You can now sleep forever, resting assured that you have not let anyone down."

Dolan tried to whisper but only produced a hissing sound.

The nurse took her eyes off of the IV rig. She shot Dr. Bartlett an odd look. Dolan felt queasy again and more than a bit high. Her face worried him. The woman was clearly emotional about doing this, which probably was not such a good sign. In fact, she seemed quite upset. Was that sadness or sympathy in her deep brown eyes? Both?

Dolan swallowed dryly. He found a word. "Don't."

Dr. Bartlett stood up and his face changed shape again. The world tilted and rolled like an old television set. "Your assignments are finished, son. Now, as we promised, it is time to erase you."

"Wait please." A faint whisper at best.

The nurse turned away. Her eyes were damp with tears. Her sympathetic reaction terrified Dolan because he was totally helpless now and unable to form a rational protest. His mouth was frozen shut. The world throbbed. The damned machine was kicking back into gear. They were going to do it, clean the slate and punch his ticket. Soon the nurse was openly crying.

They were about to kill him.

Dolan freaked out inside, but he could not move. He'd made such a terrible mistake. He'd been saddled with pain and sadness for so long that all he'd been able to dream about was being free of it. But now, faced the prospect of losing everything he'd ever been or would ever be, Dolan completely panicked. His life was not just about loss. It would be gone, all of it. The good would leave with the bad. The beautiful would end with the ugly. There would be no more childhood wounds, happy memories, no first love, no good experiences, no buddies from the war, no civilian life, no mission for Limbus, no Phyllis, no...anything. They were going to erase him and that would be the same as performing an execution. Everything he had been or would have ever become would be…nothing. He'd just be star dust again.

It would be as if Mike Dolan he had never lived at all.

No!

Dolan wanted the pain back. His pain.

The nurse wiped her eyes and sobbed. She turned a plastic knob on the IV. The blue fluid flowed into his veins as the machine roared to life.

Dr. Bartlett said, "Good-bye."

Dolan fought against the restraints but his body barely moved at all. He was still screaming in his mind but the hot feeling started all over again, as all those fiery needles punctured his skin. They had begun the final process. It was almost over. Dolan tried his best to scream in protest, to fight for who he was. He failed.

Don't!

The laboratory began to fade. Dolan realized that even now, at the prospect of existential nothingness, he was still unable to cry. He was a coward. He just wanted to stay alive, to stay Mike Dolan, to keep the small shreds of dignity he'd managed to recover through the last mission. But now it was too late to change his mind. He'd made his choice.

The awful mechanical sounds returned and so did the relentless physical pain.

The machine was merciless as it took him away.

* * *

Horror and confusion and more silent shrieks of panic. The now familiar shift in time and space. An eternal sense of falling that finally stopped.

The man woke up on someone's front lawn just when the sprinklers came on. He rolled over onto his back and looked up at the stars. The pocked moon was full and devoid of pity or remorse. He felt incredibly drunk, and when he looked down at his body, he was stunned to see that he was also stark naked. He sat up and held his aching head. He could not remember where he'd been, or who he'd been with, or what he'd been drinking. Hell, the man did not remember his own name.

The sprinkler water felt good on his aching body. He got soaked. The man got to his feet and shook off the inebriated feeling. No. He was not drunk at all. In fact, he was stone cold sober. He was just loopy from all the drugs they'd given him. He did not know who "they" were. He knew that someone had given him drugs, he was sure of that; people in white coats in some strange place with weird paintings on the walls.

Had he been in a mental institution? Why couldn't he remember anything? Who was he, and how had he ended up here?

He stumbled down the sidewalk, shivering from the cold, embarrassed by his condition but determined to get off the street.

He came to a corner and found a small strip mall flanked by huge metal trash bins. Some old clothing had been discarded by the homeless. It was wet from the recent rain. He slipped into oversized trousers and a torn jacket. The damp clothing reeked but it covered his nakedness. There was a half-empty bottle of wine sitting there. It looked inviting. He felt thirsty and he stared at it, but he did not touch a drop. He just stumbled down the alley and out onto the next block.

The man stopped in his tracks.

He knew this corner. It was near his house.

My name is Mike Dolan.

Dolan felt something very much like the wind pushing from behind. He had a job to do, even if he wasn't quite sure what that was. He stumbled forward. He jogged for half a block. His head cleared and he began to run. He passed by the next door neighbors' home. All the lights were off and the half-tilled garden was marked off by wooden posts and thick twine.

He'd need a weapon.

Dolan saw a shovel poking up from a pile of manure. He grabbed it as he raced by. It trailed along the sidewalk with a thin scream, leaving sparks. His heart slammed in his chest and he felt a terrible sense of urgency but couldn't have said why. He knew his name and the place to go but nothing else except that it was a matter of life and death.

Mike Dolan ran for his life. He crossed the alley and broke through the rose bushes and into his own front yard.

And that's when he heard the woman call for help.

Dolan burst up the steps with the shovel and somehow was not at all surprised when a big man in a stocking mask came out of the bedroom with a knife and an open can of gasoline. The intruder sliced at Dolan, but cut only thin air. Dolan was too fast for him. He swung the shovel. The tool whacked the man on the knee and then the left shoulder. Dolan swung again. The man dropped the knife and stumbled forward.

As the intruder turned away, Dolan noticed an odd logo on the back of his jacket, a globe with little dots of light. The man dropped the open gas can. Gas spilled out on the floor. The pool spread rapidly. The stench filled the air.

Dolan struck again, aiming for the back of the intruder's head, but the man managed to roll out of the way just in time. He got up slowly. Dolan got to his feet. He could see the intruder's eyes through the mask. They seemed oddly calm. They did not look angry or afraid. In fact they seemed vaguely...amused. The big man reached into the pocket of his jacket.

Dolan said, "Don't!"

The masked man held up a cheap, plastic cigarette lighter, an old-fashioned one. He flicked it twice and dropped the flame into the pool of gas between them, which exploded instantly. Dolan dropped the shovel and stepped away from the fire. The stranger raced for the front door and escaped into the night. Gone as if he'd never been there. And Dolan let him go without a second thought.

The woman...

Dolan instinctively turned and ran for the back bedroom. He saw her lying there in her torn nightgown. He did not recognize her at first, but he gathered her in his arms. She was unconscious but still breathing. He looked back at the front door. The flames were in the way. Dolan could hear sirens coming. He wrapped the poor woman in the old, damp clothing and carried her naked through the flames, but he was healthy and strong and sober and running so fast, with his skin and clothes still soaking wet, that he did not get burned or experience any pain. They got outside.

His house went up in flames behind them, but he had somehow managed to save the woman. He'd done it. He'd done it.

Outside, on the damp lawn, Dolan rolled her around just to be sure the fire was out. The old pants he'd picked up were smoldering a bit, but so what. He checked her out. She seemed okay. In fact, neither one of them had been hurt.

The woman's eyes fluttered. They opened.

And that's when Dolan recognized her.

Everything froze in time and space and the present vanished. Dolan felt his mind blink and somehow change channels. He had one disturbing vision of an unfamiliar white room that was packed with electronic equipment. Some people in white coats were looking down at him. A nurse was crying, but it was not because she was sad; it was because she was touched. The image went in and out of focus. It shifted until it became just a fleeting idea; just something disturbing and surreal, a half-remembered moment from a scary film, or perhaps just the vestige of a very bad dream. A faint voice in his head said, "Good-bye, Snake," and then even the odd trace of a dream was gone.

The house was a total loss, and so was his collection of antique weapons, but it didn't matter. Mike Dolan remembered exactly what he'd wanted all along. He was done drinking. He was going to change as of right now, once and for all. His wife was lying there on the grass, thankfully okay, and it was all because he was sober. Phyllis was alive, and she was his entire world. Her perfume smelled wonderful.

The fire trucks arrived, and the yard was soon filled with shouting men and flashing red and white lights. Puzzled neighbors in pajamas and robes stood in the street and stared at the two of them.

Phyllis opened her eyes and smiled up at him. She coughed up smoke. She put his unburned bare hand on her swollen belly.

She whispered, "You came home."

And Mike Dolan finally cried.

First Interlude: Whispers in Shadow

As Conrad read the last words on the screen, the text began to dissolve, to reform, and then Conrad was again staring at a mass of numbers, symbols, and unintelligible digital scrawl. The fire popped and crackled in the hearth, while the snow swirled outside the windows, backlit by the pale light of a gas lamp.

He turned the story he had just read over in his mind. True, it was a wild, insane, inventive piece of fiction. But that was all it was. And yet, something deep down, back in the reptilian part of his brain, screamed out at him. In warning, perhaps. But certainly in recognition. There was something familiar that tugged at him. Then there was Limbus itself, hinted at so darkly, yet never unveiled. Whether an entity of good or evil, he could not say. And why should it matter? It was, after all, a creation of the mind. A fiction. No more real than any other.

And yet...

Conrad felt the way he did when he needed a drink, which was ironic given that he had already had several. Instead, he decided he needed a walk, blizzard or not. He grabbed up his coat, leaving his laptop behind on the table—no one would take it—and headed out into the night.

As he opened the door, he braced himself for the cold wind. But it did not buffet him as he expected. Yes, the snow came down in handfuls, but the wind was stilled. As he stepped out into a fall of soft velvet, he felt a warmth inside that could not be attributed to the alcohol. At least not entirely.

He walked through the streets of that ancient city, sure to step carefully along the cobblestones. He jammed his hands into his pockets, strolling past shuttered stores and closed pubs. Always, the citadel towered over him, looming black and foreboding above.

The night, however, was not as dark as he would have expected. The accumulated snow seemed to gather the frail light from the flickering gas lamps that lined the corridor-like streets—collecting it and reflecting it back into the night. It was unnaturally quiet though, so quiet that when he stopped walking and let the seemingly thunderous pounding of his bootfalls die away, he could almost imagine he was the only man alive, such was the titanic totality of that silence.

Yet he was not alone. That much he suddenly knew. He could feel a pair of eyes on him, feel it as much as he would if a hand clapped down on his shoulder. He turned in place, slowly. Carefully. But as nonchalantly as he could manage. He didn't want to appear startled or afraid. Just a student, out for a stroll.

He saw him almost immediately. He was standing in the shadows—and in Český Krumlov, the shadows were somehow thicker than in other places. But while the man's face was shrouded, his eyes shone in the night. Then his face was illuminated too, lit in the glow of the cigarette he was smoking. Conrad shivered, and it wasn't from the cold.

He jumped when he heard the footsteps, sure that in that moment of shattered silence he was undone. He had been caught. This was the end. He turned in the direction of the sound, expecting to see a SWAT team or a squadron of police with guns drawn. That, however, was not what he found. Instead, it was a single man, turning the corner of the street, a load of what looked to be firewood in a sturdy leather sack slung over his shoulder. The bag was packed full to bursting, and as he drew close, Conrad wondered how he could possibly manage. He seemed not to notice Conrad, but as he was about to pass, he looked up, and Conrad stumbled back in shock.

At first, he told himself it was an illusion. Then, that the man was merely deformed. But both were lies, and he knew it.

He was from a different age altogether, and not an age of men. Conrad had seen a face like that before, but only in museums.

The man—if man he was—passed on, and a cackle split the night. The figure in the doorway roared with laughter. His unnaturally bright eyes mocked Conrad, as much as his voice ever could. His laughter had not ended when he turned and opened the door behind him, light flooding into the streets. He tossed the cigarette back into the snow, and the hiss of extinguished embers seemed to echo through the narrow alleys of the city. He looked at Conrad one more time and coughed out another laugh before turning and disappearing inside.

Conrad thought of Van Gogh's, probably the only place in the old city that was still open. It had been, he supposed, his destination from the beginning. But suddenly he didn't want to keep walking. Suddenly he felt like he should be back at his computer. That he had more, much more, to discover. He turned back, the snow still falling around him. He sincerely hoped he did not see the man again.

In this, his hopes held true. He returned to the Wolf's Head Inn without incident. His computer still sat on the table, as did his stein of beer. But when he opened the laptop, he noticed something he hadn't before. Another riddle.

Priceless work of art, made without hands—
An unparalleled treasure, as rare as the sands.

A shiver ran down his back, and his skin became gooseflesh. He turned and looked out the narrow window. In the glow of the lamplight, specks of white swirled.

"Just a coincidence," Conrad whispered, even as didn't believe it.

His hands found the keyboard again.

Snowflake.

The image swirled wildly, a chaos of mad electrons flashed across the screen. A new image formed, one that looked to Conrad like some great, prehistoric beast. A dinosaur maybe, but one that swam in the sea. Then that too dissolved, and Conrad watched as the unintelligible became sentences once again. It was another story.

He took a drink—deeper and more desperate this time—and then he began again to read.

Fishing for Dinosaurs

By

Joe R. Lansdale

When I climbed out from under the bridge that morning, it was raining hard and a cold wind was blowing and I guess that's what turned me, that and the fact my coat was as thin as cheese cloth and I was so hungry I felt like my backbone was trying to gnaw its way to my navel. Being wet, cold, and hungry, as well as homeless, can affect a man's judgment in all manner of ways. It damn sure affected mine.

I thought about waiting for the rain to stop, but then decided the rain was what I needed. It was a Sunday morning, and if I was going to break into a house or building to find warmth, and mercy help me, something to steal and sell at a pawn shop, it was as good a time and as good a cover as any.

The rain beat me like chains, it was coming down that hard, and by the time I walked along the highway, which was empty of cars, I had a throbbing headache from the constant pounding of the rain. Finally, I came to a row of buildings just outside of town, and I decided they were my best bet. I felt drawn to them, in fact.

Most of the buildings were part of a series of warehouses, and that made it all the better. At the worst it would be warmer and drier inside, and maybe there would be that little something I was talking about. Something to steal.

It was like the place was made for me to break in. Underneath one of the windows someone had laid a barrel on its side, and I managed to get up on that without it rolling out from under me, and by using my elbow, I broke the window out. I spent some time picking the glass free because it was a good position, out back of the warehouse, away from the road, and with the rain and lack of traffic, I could take my time.

When I crawled inside, I moved away from the window and through a row of barrels that contained who knows what. Through cracks in the stacks I saw bits of this and that, but the truth was I wasn't interested. I felt bedraggled and just needed a warm place to rest, and as I said, I was looking for something easy to steal. But it occurred to me that I might could hole up in the warehouse until morning, maybe even beyond. It didn't seem like a place people were coming to often. If I could find a way to get food, this might be my home away from home for a while. I tried to think about my own home, but my mind didn't co-operate; I had a hard time visualizing it.

Winding my way through the rows of barrels, knocking aside a cobweb or two, I came to a door and gently pushed it open. It was nicer in there, and I could see it was a factory floor. It looked old and unused for quite some time, a deduction I made from the fact that it, like what must have been the store room, was gently covered in dust. There were all manner of machines, and I walked between those and found an office, which I peeked into. There was a desk in there and a chair, and on the desk I could see a little plaque with a rotating world symbol with certain spots on the continents dotted in red. I had no idea what that meant, or if it really meant anything. There was an old-fashioned rotary phone on the desk. I hadn't seen one of those since I was a kid. My grandparents owned one forever ago. I thought of them for a moment, but couldn't seem to hold their faces in my thoughts, and I let it go. There was also a coat rack, and on the rack was a nice wool coat and a pork pie hat on one of the spokes.

I walked away from there and found the break room. There was a candy machine and soft drink machine in there, but I had no money, so outside of turning one over and beating it until it gave up the goods, it didn't look likely that they'd do me any good. I didn't think I was strong enough to break it open. Not the way I felt right then anyway.

Back in the office, I sat in the chair and opened the desk drawer. I found a tin of paper clips, a box of old-fashioned kitchen matches, a few sheets of paper, the nub of a pencil, a plastic container of business cards, and about four dollars in quarters. I took the coins and went back to the machines and bought myself a bag of animal crackers and a soft drink with someone else's money, then went back to the desk to enjoy it. While I ate I fiddled with the box of cards. They all had the same emblem that was on the plaque on the desk. A globe spread out and broken open to show all the views. I studied that world, determined it wasn't the earth as I knew it. It was similar, but there was a slight rearrangement of continents and the continents were marginally out of form. It didn't fit my geography lessons, but there was something about it that seemed right and sane to me, as if I had seen such a map somewhere, once upon a time.

Texas, the state I was in, was on the map, but the panhandle bent and went higher and twisted up through Colorado. At one time what became part of Colorado had been Texas. I remember my dad used to say, "Why Texas gave that part up, I can't say. There's good skiing up there."

There were a number of other things, including a large continent in the center of the Atlantic. I didn't know what that meant.

I studied the card for a while and read the words at the top. LIMBUS, Inc. Below it was a phone number. I fanned the cards out, saw they were all the same, but noted something odd. The phone number on each of them was different. That made little sense. I turned one of the cards over. It read:

LIMBUS, Inc.
Are you laid off, downsized, undersized?
Call us. We employ.
1-800-555-0606.
How lucky do you feel?

I studied the number. I looked at the phone on the desk. I thought, don't be a dumb ass. They won't give you a job. They've probably been out of business for years, and besides that, they don't even know how to make a proper map of the world. It was my hunger and desperation that was thinking about calling, not my common sense. It may have been one of those scam jobs where you worked for them and turned out in the end you owed them money. Forget it, I told myself.

I ate my animal crackers and drank my drink, and when I finished I was still hungry. I scrambled around in the drawer and found some more quarters, a few dimes, got myself another drink from the machine and this time went for a bag of peanuts. When I finished eating I got the coat and tossed it on the floor and lay down on it, using the hat to cover my face. Lying there with a full stomach, I went straight to sleep. I slept warm, and for some time.

It was dark when I awoke. I fumbled about and got the drawer open and found the matches. I struck one and looked about for a light switch, found one. I flipped it, and a light so dim that to see well by it you would have to set it on fire glowed on the ceiling.

I shook out the match. I picked up the phone. It had a dial tone.

All right. This place was not out of business, just not used frequently. Or maybe it was just this section. It was a large complex. Very large and this was just one end of it. Maybe there was more going on here than I thought.

I picked up the coat and put it on and sat back down in the chair and looked at the business cards that I had fanned out on the desk. I picked up one and studied it for a long time. I thought, well, what the hell?

I dialed the number on the card.

A man's voice answered on the first ring.

* * *

At first I was a little startled and said nothing. Then the voice said, "If you are looking for a job, it is highly possible you've called the right place. My name is Cranston. How did you get our card?"

I told him.

"Ah, our storage facilities in Owen Town."

"This is a town?"

"Once it was. It's just warehouses now and one long street, but it's still referred to by that name. The railroad went a different way some fifty years ago. The town went away with it. Actually, those are very old cards for a very different time."

"I'm confused, Mr. Cranston. You offer jobs to anybody?"

"No," he said. "We use Limbus to get our workers. You've called one of the numbers on the card, our number, which they have provided, and I should say all the numbers on those cards are our numbers. We offer jobs to those who have our number, or whoever we seek out or Limbus provides through its many methods. It's really not worth considering. It'll just cause your head to fill with cobwebs. Just talking about it makes my head a little musty and webbed. Here's the thing, Mr...."

I really was tired. I had to give that some thought. My name finally arrived, as if by a late plane. But instead I made up one. "Ray Slater."

"Mr. Slater, you have two choices. You can hang up the phone right now and leave our warehouse because obviously you're not supposed to be there. And I might add, don't be looking into any of the storage. You might find some of it...shall we say, uncomfortable."

"I was cold and hungry," I said. "I thought about stealing things, but didn't. Well, some quarters out of the desk drawer. I used them for the vending machine."

"That's all right. We only use that area for storage, as I said. But you will need to leave, unless you would like to accept our job offer. We can be very intolerant about someone probing about in our materials. The job is the second choice."

"What kind of job?"

"The way we work is simple. You accept the job, and then we find where we want to put you, what you'll be doing. Now and then, we come to you, but in this case, you have come to us. We can employ you or have you arrested."

"Or I can be out the window and gone in five minutes. Ray Slater is not my real name."

"But if you have left a fingerprint, any manner by which you might be identified, we will seek you out. The results may not be pleasant."

"Is that a threat?"

"Yes sir," said the voice. "It is. Our resources are unlimited. I might also add that we pay very, very well."

I let all of this move about in my thoughts like a drunk trying to find his apartment keys, then settled on the fact that I had nothing. My life had turned wrong since my father died. There wasn't a thing I had done that had worked out. Maybe this was all bogus. Maybe Limbus was a day job supplier. Raking leaves, hauling trash, cutting grass around curbing. It didn't matter. I needed work. I needed money. I was so low down I could look up and see bottom.

"All right," I said.

"We'll send someone for you."

* * *

I stayed in the office, waiting, expecting it to actually be the police that showed up. I thought that might be all right. A warm cell, a hot meal and a bed. Perhaps even someone named Bruno who I could snuggle with. Maybe they'd keep me a few days, or even send me to jail for breaking and entering. It had to be a better life than the one I was living.

I sat in the chair and sipped what was left of my soft drink. After a short while I heard the sound of footsteps, and then I saw them. Two very big men coming toward me. They wore black suits that no doubt had been specially designed for them; you didn't get those kind of suits off the rack for those kind of men. One of the men was about six-seven, broad shoulders, with very close-cropped reddish-blond hair and bronze skin. I had never seen skin quite that color before. Later, I saw his eyes were odd in that they were gray with flecks of what looked like bronze fragments in them. Strangest eyes I had ever seen. The other man wasn't quite so tall, but like his counterpart he was broad shouldered and muscular, a more lithe muscularity than his partner. His hair was jet black and his eyes were as gray as gun metal. His tanned, handsome face was marked with numerous small white scars.

They came in and stood looking at me, said not a word. I got up and went with them, walked down the long hall between them, feeling like an antelope between two lions. We turned a way I hadn't been, and I saw there were clear, glass vats visible between the barrels, and there were odd, fleshy things floating in the vats, but I didn't get too good a look because the men on either side of me took up my view.

We came to a big door. The dark man slid it aside, and we went out of it. Outside a long black car was waiting. There was a man behind the wheel, short and squat, wearing a black chauffeur's cap. He looked like one of those middle-list drawings from a chart of the evolution of man. Appeared as if he ought to be squatting in a cave chipping out flint arrow heads. He rolled down the window, looked at me, said, "I'm Bill Oldman. I will be your driver."

"All right," I said. "Don't they talk?"

"When they take the urge," he said.

One of the men, the dark-haired one, got in the front passenger seat. He said something to the driver in an odd language that contained clicks, exhalation of breath, and a few words that sounded like a monkey hooting. The driver nodded.

The bronze man sat in the back with me. He said in a voice as melodious as bird-song, "You will need to take a sedative."

"Now wait a minute—" I said. But I was too tired and too weak, and the man was incredibly strong. He stuck a hypodermic needle in my neck, and as the plunger went down, I was certain I was going to die, that I had been taken for body parts, or was being put to death by the vengeful owner of the warehouse, or at least by one of his henchmen. I don't even think I had time to raise my hands. I know I couldn't speak. My eyes began to close. The last thing I remember was the squat man driving us away into hot sunshine. The rain had passed but there were still clouds over my head.

* * *

The world crawled with fuzzy light. The light went from top to bottom in waves, and then from bottom to top. There was movement in the room, and there was sound. Footsteps. I felt like a wounded porpoise floating to the top of the sea. I had the sensation of tiny particles moving throughout my body, looking for a place to lie down.

A blond nurse wearing blue and white smiled at me. She was pretty. I tried to smile back, but moving the corners of my mouth away from my teeth was just too large a job. She moved out of my view and then a man came into my sight. He had arrived without the sound of footsteps. He was either a very light stepper or my mind was only picking up a bit of this and a bit of that. He bent over me. He wasn't as pretty as the nurse. He was what you would call roughly handsome with an emphasis on the rough. He wore a suit so dark it was the color of the end of time. He was lean and bony, had a long, long, crooked nose and hard gray eyes. His black hair was slicked back from his high forehead. Something about his face didn't lend itself to smiling. In fact, there was a cruelness to it.

"I'm the man you spoke to," he said.

I tried to call him a son-of-a-bitch, but I hadn't the strength for it.

"My name is Cranston," he said. "You can call me Mr. Cranston."

I managed to make my top lip quiver, but that was it.

"You called about a job. We have a job. It's an unusual job, but then again, all our jobs are unusual. We like to choose people who don't really have a lot of options. Desperate people. Sometimes the people we choose, or the ones who choose us, don't live through the job. No one will know what happened to you. Someone might care, but no one will know. It will be as if you have fallen off the face of the earth. If you succeed, it could still be the same. You may never go back to the life you lived, not in any manner, shape, or form. It isn't always that way, but frequently it is."

I didn't have a life to go back to, so that part didn't concern me, though the part about not surviving almost allowed me to speak. But not quite. Phlegm rose up in my throat, but no words. I was too weak to spit it out, so I had to swallow it. It was like trying to swallow a grapefruit.

"If you don't want the job, well, I have to say this. We have a man, the big bronze man who helped bring you here. He's a doctor, and he can wipe your mind clean and set you down wherever we like. We can give you new memories. It might even be a good life. But you won't be you, and you won't remember any of this. I realize right now it's a bit difficult to speak, so I'm going to leave you and let you think. There's an IV in your arm, and there's a drip feeding through it. It will put you asleep again. When you awake the next time, we will feed you, and it will begin. Or, we can make the other arrangements I mentioned."

My eye lids felt like falling boulders.

He moved away.

I tried to keep my eyes open.

I couldn't.

A mouth was close to mine. I could smell sweet perfume. The nurse. "I suggest you take whatever they offer," she said. "By the way. My name is Jane."

Someone turned out the light. It might even have been the one in the room.

* * *

When I awoke the second time I felt less weak. I couldn't get out of bed though. I had a leather band across my waist and my ankles were bound. I was propped up in bed and my hands were free and there was a tray in front of me. At first I thought I might make a show of things and toss it across the room, but the smell coming from it was divine. It was a big juicy steak with grilled vegetables and wonderful, aromatic seasoning. The pretty nurse, Jane, was sitting in a chair across the way. Sitting there in her white and blue dress and her white nurse cap, her long legs crossed. She was reading a magazine. She looked at me and smiled. I couldn't help myself. I had the urge to smile back, and this time I was strong enough to do it. It was a thin smile, but it was friendly. It was hard to look at her and not be friendly.

I ate my steak.

No sooner had I finished up my meal than Cranston came in.

The nurse came and took the tray away. Cranston pushed a chair on rollers next to the bed and sat down.

"Feeling better?"

"Enough to cuss you now," I said. "All you had to do was ask me to come."

"We didn't really want you to see the route. Did you know you slept in the car for two full days? Well, part of it was in an arranged house, but you slept the entire time. It took that long, with a stopover, to get here."

"How long have I been here?"

"This makes four days. We wanted you to get a deep rest. You needed it, and you will need it for what is in store, provided you choose to accept our employment."

"And if I don't, then I get my brain sand papered?"

"That's true. I can't say it's something I disapprove of, not when it's someone like you. I found out a lot about you."

"How do you even know who I am?"

"We have our ways here. I know you are adding nothing to society, and I think if you do not add, you should be taken away."

"You do, do you?"

"I do," Cranston said.

"Where is here? Is this a Limbus headquarters?"

"Limbus finds us employees. We have what might be called a complex and sometimes complicated relationship with them. We are independent of them, and dependent on them. But this is OUR headquarters. One of them."

"What do you do here?"

"Lots of things. Let me tell you something, Richard Jordan—"

"How do you know my real name?"

"That part was easy," he said. "Don't let it worry you. You have a chance at a better life. Here's what I know. You started out good, smart with possibilities, that kind of kid, but your father committed suicide. Or tried to, failed, and then was killed accidentally. Comical, actually."

"Not to me."

"Tried to hang himself from a light fixture. The fixture broke. He fell, banged his chin on the desk, broke his jaw, received a concussion, died in the hospital a week later having never regained consciousness. You went to the university. Two years if memory serves me, and it most likely does. You went through one job after another. Failed relationships—"

"How can you know all this?'

"Not your concern. But there's no use in me continuing. Pretty much your life is a wreck, and you were just on the verge of that shipwreck washing up on a rocky shore. All that's left was for the seagulls to peck out your eyes and devour your body."

"Enough with the metaphorical bullshit," I said.

"We can offer you a job. We can give you a new back story. A new life. We can also wipe your brain, give you new memories and send you out in the cold, cold world to survive. To be honest, over time, the ones we send back with that alteration, they tend to lose the back story. The depth of it anyway. They cease to believe it, but they know nothing else. Psychosis often results. And frequently they go back to their old ways. Now and again we have someone who succeeds as a new individual, but it's not really all that successful in the long run."

"So you're trying to convince me to take the job."

"Just stating the facts. You get to choose."

"I get to choose between two choices you've given me. One sounds bad, and the other one might be. I don't even know what the job is."

"True. But I can promise you this. It is unique. There is nothing like it. You will be part of a small crew. It is adventurous. We will prepare you for it, as much as someone can be prepared, and we pay extraordinarily well."

"How well?"

"One job and you're fixed for life."

"Are you with the government?"

"No. Unlike the government, we are efficient. We are not with or associated with any known government. You might say we are mostly unknown and a government unto itself."

"That doesn't sound like a good thing."

"Crime bears bitter fruit, Richard, but unlike the government, at least it bears fruit."

"So it's a criminal enterprise?"

"Only in the sense that it's off the books, not answerable to any government, so yes, it's a criminal activity with all manner of jobs, some of them sketchy by the standards of many citizens. That is neither here nor there. Here's how it will be. You agree to go to work for us, we get you in shape for it first. Some solid meals, exercise, a bit of preparation. You were once a top javelin thrower."

"You do your homework. I was being groomed for the Olympics. Things went wrong."

"That no longer matters. Do you accept the job?"

"May I ask why it's important to know I was once training for the Olympics with the javelin?"

"I didn't say it was."

"But it might be?" I said.

"It might be, but probably isn't. Still, the muscles for the javelin may indeed need to be aroused and rejuvenated to help with what we may consider you to do."

"You have something in mind already?"

"Yes, but it all depends. Mr. Jordan, are you in or out?"

I thought for a moment. What did I have to go back to? A bridge over my head. Cold winters, hot summers, stealing to survive. That was the world I knew, and I didn't find any of that enticing. Here I was warm and fed and being offered payment for a job. If I didn't like the job I figured I could find a way out later. They might not think I could, but I felt like it was a better shot than having my brain wiped—if they could actually do that—and being sent back out into the world.

"You're thinking you can say yes and maybe escape later, aren't you?" Cranston said.

"It crossed my mind."

"You can't. You're in, you're in. Let me put this simply. There are nine, sometimes twelve members of our board, and frankly, they run a lot of the world's affairs. Any one of them is smarter than you, and together they are considerably smarter."

"Perhaps they could do a better job running the world," I said. "Case you haven't noticed, it sucks like a vacuum cleaner out there."

"They fail from time to time. They are unique and wise, but they are also human. There are other factors, of course. Fate, humans, climate. Our group control more of that than what might be expected, but they can't control it all."

"The climate?"

"Yes," he said. "They work on a theory of balance. Sometimes bad things aren't all that bad, good things sometimes aren't all that good. They have to be balanced."

"You lost me at bad things aren't always that bad."

"You needn't know any more. Are you in?"

I thought it over again. I still believed I had a chance to get out if it came to it. And then again, I might just like the work. Whatever it was.

"I'm in," I said.

* * *

I guess I was there about a month. I didn't keep up with the time. Couldn't even tell you what day of the week it was. I saw the bronze-skinned man and the dark-haired man from time to time. I saw them in the gym, wrestling, nude, like in the old Greek contests. Neither seemed to be trying to win out over the other. It was almost as if they were afraid of discovering who was the best. Instead they practiced moves and throws and did so with an eerie kind of grace. I even saw them walking alone through the halls, gently touching hands, entwining fingers. It was obvious they were lovers.

I saw the nurse from time to time, but she never smiled at me again. She didn't smile at that pair either, but she watched the dark-haired man in a way that made me think of a chained dog smelling meat from a butcher shop.

My assignment of the moment was to eat right and exercise. My teacher was a long, lean black woman who looked like an African goddess. She put me through my tasks as if she were a drill sergeant. She sprang about with cat-like grace, taught me a few martial arts moves for muscle tone, had me kicking a heavy bag and running along the track outside. Where the outside was I couldn't tell you, and to be literal, it really wasn't outside. Just seemed to be. There was a huge dome over the track, and though it was transparent in spots, it was mostly covered in camouflage. A birds-eye view from above, and it would look like forest, or jungle. The flooring of the track was the color of swamp water, so even views through the gaps would make it appear wet and uninviting. I wondered if it were possible to see us from above on the track, running. I found the idea of that amusing, an aerial view of us running on what appeared to be the surface of water.

Again, I had no idea where I had been transported to, and still had no idea for what reason. But I decided in for a penny, in for a pound, and maybe a ton. I felt it was best to dedicate myself to the preparation of the task ahead of me, whatever it might be. I never lost the idea that I still could escape if I found my job odious. It was hard to imagine it being a positive assignment, what with all the secrecy. I felt like a character in a comic book.

I began to throw the javelin again in time. The goddess brought it to me and I was rusty at first, but I found my stride after a while. It didn't feel all that familiar though, in spite of remembering how good I had been at it in the past. It built my arms up, throwing it again.

I was also fed a very foul-tasting milkshake every day. I drank it without hesitation after the first week. I realized it was doing something to my body. I felt stronger, quicker. More than felt—I *was* stronger and quicker. Partly that was due to the training, the diet, but that milk shake had something in it besides the usual ingredients. I could feel it seep into my bones and innards. I didn't measure myself, but I was reasonably certain that not only was I leaner and more muscular, but that I had grown an inch or more in height, which I would have thought impossible.

They increased the size of the javelin over time, but I continued to be able to throw it with ease. In time the drinks were stopped, and when I inquired of the goddess as to why, she informed me it was no longer needed. Its effects by this time were permanent.

It had other aspects that were beneficial as well. I was not tired at the end of a day, and on a fine dark night, after a workout, the goddess became quite human, and the two of us shared my bed. It was as if we were competing in a sexual Olympics. By morning, she was out on the track. I showered and ate lightly and met her there. It was as if nothing had happened between us. She looked at me with all the warmth of a cobra.

One day the African goddess came to me and said, "Today, we take a day off from training."

Actually, I didn't want a day off. I had begun to truly love the workouts. They made me feel good and powerful.

"You have a meeting with Mr. Cranston," she said.

I went to meet Cranston with the goddess leading.

It was a large office with a desk about the size of a landing field. There was a computer on the desk, a chair behind it, and a row of chairs in front of it, eight to be exact. It occurred to me that with eight in front and one behind the desk that could be the nine who ruled the world. It was a crazy thought, but there it was. Cranston had said as much, and though I hadn't yet decided if he was crazy or not, no doubt the resources available to him seemed unlimited.

The rest of the room was lined with shelves of books. The books climbed three stories, and there were stairs that led upwards to the other levels, and there were long rows with railed pathways where you could walk along and look at the books.

The black goddess left me there and went away. I stood waiting. A short older man was on the far side of the room sweeping with a large push broom. He swept and then used a whisk broom to push the small, almost invisible dust pile into a hand-held whisk pan, and then dumped it into a trash can on wheels. He put the broom in the can so that the broom itself stuck up in the air. He pushed it past me, said, "Good luck to you," and was gone.

After a while I walked about, looking at the books on the floor where I had been left. There were what you might call classic literary titles. The entire collection of Twain, Kipling, Dickens, and so on. I pulled a few out for examination, saw they were first editions. I was even more impressed to find that many of them had been signed by their authors.

I strolled along and found a section of books with titles I didn't recognize. Like *The Book of Doches*, something called the *Necronomicon*, *Those Who Rule the Earth*, and *Outsiders and Insiders*. Volumes that were sometimes attributed to certain authors, others without author recognition.

I had just pulled one of these books from the shelf, *The Hounds of Tindalas*, when Cranston, standing at my shoulder, said, "That one I wouldn't look at. It will make you nauseous, not just due to content, but due to how words and images and numbers are placed on the page, the shapes of the letters are quite baffling."

That didn't make a lick of sense to me, but I returned the book to its position on the shelf. I was shocked to discover Cranston had been able to sneak up on me so easily, so silent.

I turned and watched him glide toward the desk and seat himself in the chair behind it. He motioned to me and I picked a chair directly in front of him and sat down.

"I hope everything has been comfortable," he said, "and to your satisfaction."

"It has, though I do feel a little kidnapped, baffled, and abused."

"Do you now?"

"Just said so, didn't I?"

He almost smiled. The corners of his mouth rose up as if they were hats being tipped, then settled back down.

"Do you believe that beneath our world there is a hollow that contains another world?"

"What?"

"Do you believe in global warming?"

"Yes," I said. "And as for the earth being hollow, no."

"Okay, you believe in global warming, but you don't believe the world is hollow."

"I know it isn't," I said. "I didn't sleep through all of science class. I even found out about things like gravity and evolution, and believe them. I also believe the core of the world is molten. "

He nodded. "All right then. What if I told you that inside our world is another?"

"I'd say you are nuttier than I first suspected."

"Fair enough," he said. "Let me lay it out to you in a different way. The center of the earth is not hollow."

"Now you're making me dizzy. Didn't you just say—"

"I said beneath our world—to be more specific, inside the earth—there is another world. But not at the core. There is a hollow band beneath our earth and it can be best entered through a gap at the South Pole, though there is, in fact, a North Pole entrance."

"The place where Santa lives," I said.

He ignored me. "I might also say that the hollow is not strictly hollow. There is a world within the hollow."

"Well, sounds like to me you may have had a bit too much coffee, so I'll just go back to the track and you can call me when you're ready for me to start to work."

"What I'm ready for you to do involves both global warming and the world within our world."

I could see that he was absolutely serious.

"All right," I said. "Tell me."

* * *

Cranston leaned back in his chair, placed his hands together and steepled his fingers beneath his chin. He said, "At both poles there are entries into the earth. They are subtle openings. It's like sliding down gently into a bowl. You don't realize the depth of the bowl because its sides slope gradually. The bowl has large openings in the walls of what appears to be a cavern of ice. Through those gaps are more direct entrances, many of them large enough for an aircraft to enter, or even for a boat to sail through. We'll come to that consideration shortly."

"Sailing to the center of the earth?"

"No, it's not the center of the earth, but those entries are how the stories were started. People who went there and came back claimed to have gone to the center of the earth, but they were within a rim world that circles the world completely around."

"It would be a dark world," I said.

"It is not completely explored, but has its own sun, or a substitute for it. The high roof of their world blazes with volcanic fire. This is something the writer Edgar Rice Burroughs knew, though he called it a sun. No one knows how he came by those stories, who told him about the inner light, but he knew. A large number of the things he wrote about were accurate, the bulk of it fabrication."

"If this is true, what has it to do with me? And I don't know who Edgar Rice Burroughs is."

"Doesn't matter. Let me backtrack. The job we had for you was uncertain. It might have been menial. Someone, for example, has to clean this library."

"You were considering me for a custodial job? You went through all of this to possibly have me sweep up? You have someone for that. I saw him."

"It was truly a consideration, having you replace the old man. He's been of service to us in so many ways, but right now, we feel he best serves us here, doing a menial, but important job. You could take his place."

"Again, I have a hard time believing you brought me here the way you did because you wanted me to sweep up and swab toilets."

"True, but the custodial job here comes with added chores you would never encounter elsewhere. It doesn't matter, however. That's not the job. You have been researched thoroughly. Your mother leaving you and your father, taking off for parts unknown. Your father's death. But I've told you I know about all that."

"That has nothing to do with anything," I said. "He was an unhappy man."

"Obviously," Cranston said. "But genetics has a lot to do with inclination, and so do events in your life. The two make you a great candidate for us. As to why, it's a long story and a study of psychiatry and genetics would be necessary to understand it."

"I'm not a total idiot," I said. "How do you know all about me?"

"For us, information comes easy. So does certain kinds of manipulation."

Cranston paused for dramatic effect. I said nothing. I waited him out.

"You are of a good type, blood and bone and flesh and genetic makeup. We ran tests while you were, shall we say, asleep."

"As in drugged?"

"More accurate, yes. I think the best way to short-story this is to say certain flaws in your DNA have been corrected, and strengths have been enhanced through the drinks and the diet we have been feeding you. We like a long employment, so all of these alterations will allow you to live a long, long time. You won't be immortal, and you will still be subject to accident or attack, some rare diseases, but otherwise quite hale and hearty for years to come. As long as we attend to you. As for your employment, your job, sir, is to fish for and catch a plesiosaur, or at least a beast similar to it. An unknown cousin, to be accurate. Well, unknown to the rest of the world, but not to us."

"A dinosaur?"

"A very large one," he said. "Technically it's a sauropterygian. Unlike the plesiosaur it greatly resembles, it has serviceable legs for taking to the shore, though not well. To simplify what we have in mind for you, I'll just repeat what I said before. You'll be fishing for a dinosaur."

* * *

The wind was cold enough to make a polar bear scream, sharp enough to shave with; the water was high and vigorous, and the icebergs were cracking and moaning as they melted all around me. The contrasting warmth of the water rose up and heated the great tuna boat we were in, giving me warm feet and legs; the howling wind in contrast gave me a cold head and body, in spite of my layered clothes, my fur-lined hood and heavy coat.

For all his abilities and knowledge, I could have told Cranston that while fishing for a dinosaur (and this conclusion I drew without any experience in the matter whatsoever), it is best to have a very large boat, and better yet, best not to do it, and if it has to be done, it should be done from shore with a very long line, not caught on the water and dragged to shore, which was their plan. They wanted it alive.

Also, I preferred a different sort of bait. Sticking the remains of dead bodies on a hook the size of a Town Car was not my idea of a good time, even if the corpses belonged to what might have been the last surviving Neanderthals.

But I am ahead of myself.

So it turns out I'm fishing for a dinosaur because it has come up from a world beneath our world. Not a Center of The Earth world, but a world that lies below the crust, a Rim World, Cranston called it. Still, it is deep down and may not be everywhere beneath the earth, but it is certainly beneath the poles, including the South Pole where I was at the moment.

Down deep in this world is a roof of burning fire that serves as a sun, and there are clouds and there is an atmosphere, and all manner of people live there in a primitive state, and oh yes, there are dinosaurs and mammoths and mastodons and ape-people and even pirates. I have not seen these things, but Cranston has told me. I thought he was out of his mind, but if you see one dinosaur it's easy to believe that there are others, and that all the wild and wooly things Cranston told me are true. That the ice caps are melting from Global Climate Change is obvious, but the worry for Cranston and his Secret Rulers is that the world beneath our world will be revealed. Why this is their worry, I can't say. But, you see, the water-going dinosaur likes to eat people. It's envisioned that it might swim through the newly acquired waterways, due to the ice melting and find its way to warmer waters and make its way to our civilization. Then, much like an old Japanese monster movie, start tearing down cities and eating fleeing citizens, stomping pedestrians, and receiving an air strike.

When that was said and done, the next step would be for our current civilization to find and invade the world below, destroying it in all its primitive glory, just because we can. This is Cranston's and the Secret Rulers of the World's concern. I guess that's a good thing, but with Cranston it's hard to tell. As for the remainder of the Secret Rulers, I assumed the two men who had brought me to the compound were part of that group, and after that, I'm not sure. Maybe they don't all live there, or stay there, and the others are spaced here and there about the world.

Not only had the climate changed, but when the ice melted it affected deep pockets of water below the surface. With it came hundreds of dead bodies, drowned out victims. Among them animals and dinosaurs and what I call Neanderthals, because I can't think of anything else close enough to how they look; large brows, short legs, stocky bodies, all of them drowned and bloated and convenient fishing bait. They are cousins to the man who drove the car that brought me to the compound. Oh yeah, he's one. He came up from the earth through a passage of some kind many years back, or so I've heard. He ended up with the Secret Rulers, went to work for them. They call him Bill Oldman. I think there's a weak joke in there somewhere. Me and him got along, were friends actually. That said, when it came to the Secret Rulers he didn't answer many questions. And contrary to what I thought about Neanderthals, he has the power of speech and is an A-1 thinker. You should play him in a game of chess.

The thing though is the water. A dormant volcano became less dormant. It heated up, and with the air temperature increase from global warming, this part of the world started to melt like a block of ice on a hot stove. The water that filled the dormant volcanoes rose to the surface of our world, brought with it the drowned from down below. And if that wasn't enough, the rising water contained one angry dinosaur. It survived by eating all manner of swimming creatures, not to mention at least one climate investigation team.

So there I was, with Bill Oldman and Cranston and sometimes, the two giants, and a crew of men and women who wore blue and white parkas and carried guns, all of them studying me with jaundice eyes.

Oh yeah, the goddess is with me too. She's my fishing companion. Ayesha by name, that tall African-looking woman with legs that seem to begin somewhere near that mythical world below, a head with a halo of black hair like a threatening storm cloud framing her face, drawing attention to her strong features and eyes so dark and deep they seem like tunnels leading you straight to hell. But oh that mouth, and how it tastes, and those legs, how they wrap, and that face shiny with beauty. Finally we had become lovers. Not just sex partners. During our long and fruitless fishing trips for the dinosaur, we had become not only sticky close, but soul-close.

I had never known a woman like her. Enigmatic, strong, purposeful, and someone with a bit of dinosaur fishing experience. And with something in her background I didn't know about, but something that lay coiled there like a snake about to strike. I could sense it. She was unique and wonderful, but inside her head not all was right with the world.

* * *

I climbed up the railing that led to the chairs in the conning tower. The tower was open to the sky, though the chairs we sat in for fishing could, with a touch of a button, cover our heads with a shield against sun and rain, sleet and snow.

Ayesha sat in one of the chairs with the great rod settled into a steel boot on squeaking swivels. The rod was a hundred feet high and made of steel and fiberglass and things I had no idea of. It rose up tall in the sky like a fat finger pointing to the clouds, then it bent at the tip, way up there, and a cable about the size of my thigh spun out of that and went off in the water with its great cork (aka bobber or float) the size of a kayak, and beneath that was more cable, dipping down deep in the water with that mighty, sharp hook with its meaty portion of a drowned Neanderthal.

"They're already dead," Cranston had said. "I see no sense in wasting the opportunities their corpses provide."

Bill Oldman had quivered slightly at that comment. But he said nothing.

That was then, this was now, and it was me and Ayesha on the tower in our fighting chairs with our rods, Bill Oldman down below, manning a cannon-sized harpoon launcher if things went wrong and we couldn't bring the beast in alive. Killing it was supposed to be the absolute worst-case scenario.

I fastened my shoulder straps and waist band, glanced at Ayesha in her heavy clothes and close-fitting hood, her hands on the gears that worked the rod and the great spinning reel that was six feet above us on our rods. It was the size of a large industrial drum with coils of cable squeezed around it like a hungry anaconda preparing for a meal.

Our chairs were about a foot apart. She with her line in the water, and me sitting with enough cable reeled out so that it and its huge hook were resting on the floor of the ship below. A stout, tall woman wearing a blue and white jumpsuit, an electronic cigarette hanging from her mouth, was struggling to stick a corpse on my hook. Thing I had noticed about the blue and white uniformed folks was they were not as strong as me, or Bill, Ayesha, Cranston, and the others. Oh, they were all solid and in shape, but they had not been given the tonic that had been given to me. I didn't know why. I didn't know a lot of things about my employment. What I did know was the world was far stranger than I had imagined. Dinosaurs and Neanderthals were in it, and down below it, living in a land with air and water and fiery skies.

As for our quarry, we had seen the beast a few times, even got hits on our lines, but the meat had been taken and the hooks had been straightened. New, bigger, better-made hooks had been brought in, but we got the same results. What I remembered most was seeing the beast rise up out of the water, massive as a whale, long as a train, flexible as a rubber hose, pulsing with color, blue and red and aqua green, grays and browns mottled about its head, an elongated mouth so full of teeth that when the sun hit them they threw off a glow that nearly blinded me. I thought then that we needed stronger hooks and a better place to be, but here we were, fishing for a dinosaur, re-equipped, courtesy of the Secret Rulers. More importantly, they had brought in with the new hooks and stronger cables peanut butter and wheat bread at my request; that was for me to eat, not for the dinosaur, though the idea of the big beast going smacky-mouth over a huge peanut butter sandwich had its appeal.

In the chairs the wind was cold and the heat from the water did little to warm my feet. The heat rose up through the metal but became cooler with height; those icy winds negated it in the end, up there in the chairs where we perched like birds. I pulled my scarf over my mouth and reached out and touched Ayesha's hand. She rolled her knuckles in my palm, then removed her hand.

She looked at me, said, "I have to concentrate."

"On what?"

"Fishing."

"Yeah. Well, when it hits, then you can fish, until then we can hold hands."

At that moment there was a call from below. My baiter had the corpse on the hook. Romance was over. I hit a lever and the cable began to roll up and curl beneath the tip of the rod, dangling the hook and the bait. I hit more levers. The rod flexed back and flung out, tossing the cable and the bait (the arms were still on the torso and they flapped in the wind as if trying to fly) into the water with a significant splash. I took hold of the toggle and worked it. My chair spun then, and the cable and its bait swung around our ship, and within instants, my chair's back was against the back of Ayesha's chair.

"I think tonight," I heard Ayesha say, "you get to be on top."

"That would be nice," I said, "but just so you know, positioning doesn't matter much to me. Just as long as you are connected, so to speak."

"Everything in life is about position. Everything."

We waited and waited, touched the mechanisms and swung our chairs to different positions, but never got so much as a nibble. The daylight was constant; we were in that part of the world where night could go on for months, and then it was daylight's turn, which was how it was now.

I could hardly believe it, but even fishing for a dinosaur, with my intent to save the world beneath us from discovery and exploitation, I was bored. The clock moved, the daylight didn't. My inner workings didn't respond properly. I looked at my watch, the fine one they had given me. We had been at our chore for four hours. Lunch time. I went below. I had peanut butter on bread, went up and Ayesha went down, came back with a kiss for me and caviar on her breath.

Time crawled on as if its legs were broken. Finally, twelve hours from the time I began my fishing shift, it was over. We hit the switches and rolled our lines, and the rotten corpses that remained were deposited in the freezers on the boat, ready for tomorrow's baiting.

The boat toiled its way through the boiling waves toward shore. It docked and we disembarked into a great fortress made of ice. It was beginning to melt around the edges, but was mostly firm still. Oddly, it was heated, and the heat held and the ice held. It was the changing of the climate and the boiling from below that was gradually eroding it.

Fishing for Dinosaurs

In our massive igloo rooms were large, inviting beds. Ayesha invited me into hers.

"You will think of me tonight as She Who Must Be Obeyed," she said, and showed me a grin that made me tingle from ears to toes. Later that night, I can assure you, I would have called her anything she wanted to have been called, and I would have called myself by any name.

In the morning we went out again on the ship. The light was still the same and the waters were still the same, and the job was just as it was before, except for one thing. An hour into our shift, Ayesha got a bite.

* * *

Plesiosaurs bite big.

Okay, not technically a plesiosaur, but the thing in the water bit big.

The beast was strong, even when it nibbled. A nibble and slight pull could make the boat quake and feel as if it were about to be yanked below the waters like a cheap, plastic float. Today we learned there were two of the monsters. They swam as a pair; we just hadn't realized it before.

We had our chairs back to back, were talking about this and that, sort of flirting, building up for another night in the sack that would involve wet gymnastics and happy determination. Then my reel screamed like an injured panther. Screamed so loud my ears felt as if they would bleed. The cable darted across the water, way out wide, and then it dipped.

I yelled out, "I got it."

This wasn't entirely true. It had me.

As my cable sliced across the water, Ayesha's reel whined and her line hummed, and she had a hit as well.

Since her line was on the opposite side of the boat, her chair having been swiveled back to back to me, it was clear that we both had a bite. And our bites were heading in opposite directions.

"Oh, hell," Ayesha said.

"Took the words right out of my mouth."

Now her line turned and went beneath the boat.

That wasn't good.

Oldman was at the wheel, and he saw the situation immediately. He turned the boat wide, letting the line glide out, and by this time Ayesha had turned in her chair so that we were side by side.

My catch rose up out of the water, showing us all its magnificent beauty and horror simultaneously. Drops big as my head flared off of its shiny teeth. It let out with a howl, if you can call it that. Frankly, the sound was indescribable. It reached down in my gut, deep in my soul, and ripped at me. I could see one great dark eye, big as a subway tunnel, and then it dipped down and the water exploded and the boat washed heavy.

"By the gods, it is so beautiful," Ayesha said.

Now the cables were swinging in close to one another, and there was no doubt that within instants they would cross. And they did. They came together with a whine of metal cable and a screech of our reels being strained so hard the oil on the reel and on the cables smoked with friction. Then the boat, I kid you not, spun like a top. I felt the hilt of the rod vibrate in my hands like a washing machine coming apart. I let go of that and went at the gears, trying to disengage, but no dice. It was hooked up tight as a banker's vault.

That's when one of the cables snapped. Ayesha's cable. The cable popped, whipped and flew back. It came with an explosion of glistening drops and what I think must have been blood from the mouth of the beast, and along with that came the hook, minus its bait, and minus its dinosaur.

It came back at Ayesha like a missile. Struck with an explosion of red and grey, black skin pieces and fragments of bone. Ayesha's decapitated body sagged in the chair. The side of my face, shoulder, and chair were soaked with her blood and brains.

My cable locked tight, pig-squealed, and then it too snapped. I yelled as if I had been struck. But I was unharmed. My cable swung loose in the water, minus bait and hook, and the reel's kick-switch went to work on its own and recoiled my cable.

I unfastened my belt, moved to Ayesha's chair. Her hands were still on the levers. Her right leg, which I knew when unclothed would show a fine little scar in the dent of her knee, was pushed out as she were trying to stomp a brake pedal. I watched as her leg went limp and her body sagged.

I sagged myself, right to my knees.

* * *

When the ship was brought in that night, Bill Oldman came to where I lay on the upper deck in a pool of Ayesha's blood at the foot of her chair. He tried to lift me to my feet, but it was as if I didn't have any feet. I couldn't get my mind to do what my body needed to do. Finally Bill picked me up like a rag doll and carried me down the stairs effortlessly, off the ship, and onto the shore. I think he may have carried me as far as my room. I don't remember anything after that. Not until I came out of a deep pool of shock, floated to the surface and screamed; that's when the fine-looking nurse I had seen before, when I had first been taken in by Limbus, appeared with a sedative, which I fought against. But Bill and two other men, thin men with gray faces as slack as paper sacks, helped hold me down as she gave me the shot.

The nurse said, "Let yourself go," and I went, racing along a string of smoke, or was it blood, or was it sweat, or was it a string of thought? I can't tell you because I don't know, but that's how it seemed, as if I were crawling like a spider along a string of matter that was sometimes soft and sometimes hard, sometimes the color of smoke, sometimes the color of blood, and in my mind's nose were scents that couldn't be, the cinnamon smell of Ayesha's skin, the stench of blood and brain matter, of feces and urine that she soiled herself with when she died, of the wet air and the strange odor of those huge beasts as they leaped out of the water and their stench was mopped up and absorbed by the air.

My sweat and fear were part of the stink. Along that line I crawled, and then I swung under the line, clung for dear life, scuttling with six legs and then no legs and there was no line anymore. There was just a wisp of smoke and the smoke had all those aromas and stinks in it, and then I was falling into a deep black pit that popped with electricity and contained the warm water of the ocean, but when I awoke, the pit was my bed. I lay there strapped down and weak in a pond of my sweat. It was the position I had first found myself when I had been brought to the Secret Rulers by connection to Limbus. It seemed a popular method of sedation and control. A theme was at work.

Cranston came in and sat in a chair by my bed. As he sat he carefully adjusted his trousers so that they maintained their crease, looked at me, said, "Sometimes it happens. An agent dies in the field."

"I'm going to kill that dinosaur and its mate, or cousin, or butthole buddy. Whatever it is," I said, "I'm going to kill it."

"Catch, not kill, that is our desire."

"But it's not mine. I'm going to kill it."

"As I explained—"

"Sometimes an agent in the field is killed. I know. But that doesn't change that sometimes a dinosaur in a vast expanse of water is sometimes killed, and his pal as well, and that's what I'm trying to explain to you, the sanctimonious ass-wipe."

"We can't allow that."

"You certainly aren't one for feelings, are you, Cranston?"

"Not particularly, no. But I will tell you this. Ayesha has been with us for some time, except for occasional trips back to Africa. She has been a good employee. She may have just naturally weaned herself out of her position."

I wasn't entirely sure what he meant by that, but I didn't care. Nature may have been involved in her death, but there was nothing natural about how it happened. All I wanted right then was for those dinosaurs to die, and if I could make them suffer, all the better. I suppose I could look at it as our fault. We were fishing for them. They were dumb beasts. They had no particular intent but to survive. Cranston was right, why kill them? But I wanted to anyway.

And then it hit me. Why did they want to capture them? What was the point? If they were trying to keep the lost world below the crust from being discovered, what purpose did they have in capturing a dinosaur, or dinosaurs?

I asked him what I was thinking.

Cranston nodded at the question, as if it were the first time he had ever considered such a thing, which, of course, it was not. "Very well," he said, "but it's not that mysterious. I've told you our main purpose, which is to protect the world down under, but there's also the scientific research we'd like to conduct. There is much to be learned from captured aquatic dinosaurs, and nothing to be learned from vengeance against a dumb creature."

"They are not that dumb, trust me."

"They are merely trying to survive. We have large places where they can live, where they can be contained."

"Why don't they just go home?" I said.

"Because they are trapped in a volcano of boiling water. They are comfortable this high up. We find the water uncomfortably warm, but they do not. Down deep, however, it's another matter. We've dropped devices into the depths to measure the heat, and for them to go to those depths, it would be like dropping a lobster into a pan of boiling water."

"After today," I said, "I love that idea."

"Ayesha understood the risk. We have global warming to contend with, which has made larger holes in the ice, larger gaps to the world below, and that in turn has been filled with volcanic activity, and dinosaurs. Now, I'm leaving. You will continue to be held. That will give us time to decide if you are in fact going to be useful, or if your employment for this job was a mistake."

"I'll kill those big bastards."

"That's what we don't want," Cranston said. "That is not your job. That is not what you were hired on to do."

"It's all I want to do," I said.

"I know, and that gives me pause for consideration. I think your wiring may not be just right."

"That's one way to put it," I said.

* * *

In the middle of the night I heard a noise and came awake, but the thick straps around my shoulders, middle and legs, the leather clamps on my wrist and ankles, didn't allow me to rise and investigate. I had gone down so deep into sleep again—perhaps a secondary rush of the drug—that I awoke as refreshed as I had felt in years; I felt brand new. No less sad, but brand new. It was like electric-hot spiders were crawling about in my brain, giving me juice.

It was dark in the room. Then there was a light. A single light. The light moved across the floor and came to rest by my bed. The carrier of the light sat in the chair by the bed and turned out the light. But as he lifted it to push a sliding button on the instrument, I saw standing behind the chair Bill Oldman. I got a glimpse of the man in the chair as well. Short, middle-aged, ruggedly attractive in a ravaged sort of way. He looked as if he had seen all there was to see and hadn't liked much of it, and what he had liked he was suspect of. It was the man I had seen cleaning the library.

"I know you," I said.

"My name is Quatermain," he said. "Alan Quatermain."

"What do you want?"

"I am thinking I might want you. Bill and I, that is."

"Bill, you're with him?"

"Yep," Bill said.

"He is a man of true source," Quatermain said, "as am I, though for a while I was tainted with a uniqueness of a sort that has worn me thin in spirit, something that was in me, eating away at my character like carnivorous worms."

"I'm not up for riddles," I said.

"Nor do I mean to bring you a riddle without a solution, though the solution may be hard to understand, as your brain is little more than a bundle of frayed impulses and a mess of contradictions. Let me begin this way. You, according to Bill, want to kill the dinosaurs."

I gave an honest answer. "I've thought it over, or rather I did so in my sleep. I don't want that anymore. My mind wasn't working right. They're just beasts, as Cranston said."

"You could just be saying that," Quatermain said.

"I know. But I mean it. Killing them makes no sense."

"It makes all the sense. That's why you must kill them," Quatermain said.

I didn't know how to answer that. Quatermain sighed and stretched his legs and then tucked them under the chair and leaned forward. He turned the flashlight on and flashed it on my face. The light was a pool of yellow against my eyes. I turned my head.

He said, "You didn't turn your head right away. Something in your skull made you think about it. Something short of common reaction. Something that has to do with quicker adjustment to light. You didn't like it, but you could take it."

I didn't know why this mattered, but I said, "I've been drugged. I've been under a bit of stress, as Bill might have explained to you… Bill, what are you doing with this guy? What is this about?"

Bill didn't answer.

"Let me say this first," Quatermain said. "They want the dinosaurs to examine. Bill, would you come around in front of the chair, please?"

Bill came.

"Show him," Quatermain said.

Bill took off his shirt, pulled his pants over his shoes and stood before me naked, except for his socks and shoes which he had not removed. Quatermain flashed the light over him. He was covered in huge scars, some of them puckered from stitches, others mounded up like some kind of huge animals had burrowed beneath the skin. Some of the scars were light-colored, nearly healed, others were angry and red. Even his penis was scarred.

I said, "Why are you showing me this? Put on your clothes, Bill."

"This is what happened in captivity," Quatermain said. "He would be there still, except on a whim, the Professor, the Doctor, the fellow with the bronze skin, decided he needed someone as an aide. And finally Bill, fortunately, at least at the time, began to work for The Fucked Up Rulers of the World. Goddamn shit-eating bastards."

Bill was putting his clothes back on.

"I'm growing old and weak," Bill said. "Not by common human standards, but by their standards, and I am denied the fuel."

"The fuel?" I asked. "What in hell are you talking about?"

"You drank it," Quatermain said. "Ayesha fed it to you. It was to be absorbed by your body. I used to have the drink too. They say it is permanent, but it isn't. It lasts for several years, and then it begins to fade, and so do you, faster than you would have from old age if you don't get it. But once they give that drink to you, and you learn how good it feels, and they finally let you know you really do have to keep drinking it, and they are the providers, well, then you owe them. You will want that drink. The things you'll do for that kind of strength, that near immortality."

"He said it was in my DNA—"

"You don't have your own DNA, friend."

"Of course I do… Come on, man. What is this?"

"I am your salvation if you choose it."

"Oh hell," I said. "And now you're going to tell me I'm going to be sucked up to heaven in some kind of rapturous blast. You may have converted Bill here, but I'm not interested. I went to church when I was young. I had enough of it then."

Quatermain leaned back against the chair and stuck out his legs again. He turned off the flashlight. "Church," he said. "Tell me about it."

"What?"

"Where did you go to church?" he asked. "Where was it? Tell me about it."

"Mud Creek Methodist, Mud Creek Texas. Minister was Reverend Crutcher."

"Tell me about Crutcher."

"Tall, dark-haired."

"No. Tell me about him, the man."

"I didn't know him that well."

"Tell me about your father. What happened to him?"

I hesitated, but finally went on with it. It was the same story Cranston had known.

"That is such an odd and unique story it would be hard to believe it isn't true."

"Of course it's true."

"And your mother running off, leaving you, that's good too. That way you couldn't have known her past a certain age. You've got a back history, but nothing else you have to remember about them. They are gone."

"I don't understand you at all."

"You are made of flesh and bone, but it's not yours."

"Bill, please take this man with you, and leave."

Bill had returned to his position behind the chair. I could see his shadowy shape more clearly now, quite clearly actually. My eyes had adjusted well. I saw him gently shake his head.

"You have microcosmic creatures running through your veins, pumping in your blood, the blood from transfusions. Bill here was one of the transfusions. Right, Bill?"

"Right," Bill said.

"You are not truly human," Quatermain said. "You are not born of man and woman. You are cells and borrowed blood and bone and skin. Your brain tissues, so wormed with microscopic wires, were essentially grown in a jar and fed little wires so small they are smaller than capillaries."

"Wires? A jar?"

"Well, a beaker and such. Large vats and electrodes and crawling flesh that attached itself to bone with the aid of microcosmic assistance. Nano stuff."

"Yeah," Bill said. "It's little. I mean small. You can't see it with the eye. It's like if a gnat were compared to them it would be, relatively speaking, to them, the size of an elephant."

"You're crazy. Both of you."

"I am crazy," Quatermain said, "but not as much as you might think. What you have in your head is information, stuffed there like cotton in a teddy bear. You have experiences you never experienced. Knowledge you never learned. A childhood that never happened. No parents. No dogs or dates to the prom; no connection between the two meant there.

"None of what happened to you happened. Ayesha, hell, boy, she was a fine looking woman, smart, but she was playing you like a cat plays with a mouse. They all are. You aren't but a few months old. You haven't even had your first birthday. You think you've had ass before, but I got to tell you, Ayesha, she was your first. You didn't screw that cheerleader from Mud Creek I read about in your computer file. An advantage of having been more important to the Rulers in the past and knowing what kind of codes they used in their computers, and being the fucking janitor and go-to-guy for all manner of shit. Beside the point. Thing is, none of the girls they gave you memories about ever happened. Now, close your eyes, think on things. See what you really know. Compare your long past to your recent past. The recent stuff, that's the real deal. You can feel that like a thorn in the side, the rest, it's not even as substantial as a cloud, now is it? You got loose from where you were born, broke free, picked up some old clothes that were meant for the trash, put them on, made a loop like a homing pigeon, and then didn't quite understand why you escaped. You had a moment of clarity, my man-made boy. You are a type of Pinocchio, but made from a chemistry set, not wood."

"You're reaching now, Alan," Bill said.

"Yeah, that was a metaphor too far, like trying to cross a bridge with bad support posts. Listen here, boy. You had a moment when you knew you were being bamboozled and buffaloed and filled with their shit, and then it was gone. In that moment you proved, man-made or not, you have free will. Then the coding kicked in. You circled back, came home. Your real home. That was no storage building, was it, Bill?"

"Nope," Bill said. "Least not all of it was storage."

"And that little trip you took from the warehouse to the infirmary, the library. Same building, son. They knocked your ass out and drove you around the block and turned that car into the glitzier side of their operation. The ones with the elevators that went down under, the compartments where they did their Doctor Frankenstein business on you in the first place.

"That building was your true-ass home, and your natural desire was to return to it, though your false memories were starting to kick in at the same time to confuse you. Those memories were made of little nano-bots, racing about, running up your cortex and flowing through your blood, tossing mini-miniature wires and doo-dads all about. And when they were finished, you knew what you were meant to know, nothing more. You're a human-made machine without the machine oil and the squeaky wheels. By the way, that DNA they made you with? Part of it's mine. You are my son in a sense, or at least part of you is. There's some of Bill in there too, the big guys, the hot blonde, Jane. You are the son of many fathers and mothers, a mass of meshed DNA. If you have a big pecker, that part is me. Ha!"

"He gets silly when it gets late," Bill said.

"Ah, hell," I said, because right in that moment I knew they were telling me the truth. And not just about the pecker.

* * *

I have memories, experiences, a childhood fall when I was ten that left me in the hospital for a week, lots of cuts and scratches. The fall broke my leg and left me in a cast and crutches for three months. But there are no scars. I attended school, college, but never really did much with my life, went homeless. All because my father killed himself accidentally while trying to kill himself on purpose. My mother ran off and left me.

Except none of it was true. I am the product of large machinery and small machines not visible to the eye. I am made of bone, flesh, and blood transfusions, none of it mine. I have knowledge, except I didn't actually learn anything for myself. I had never thrown a javelin in my life until Ayesha put one in my hand. I had been geared for the knowledge to see how it translated from brain to muscle and bone, but until then, I had never touched a javelin. I realized that now.

Bill Oldman is a Neanderthal from the Rim World. He was brought to the upper crust against his will because he and his kind reach the age of about forty in appearance and stay there. They do not continue to age. They live for over a thousand years and then die suddenly, their clock runs down, their light goes out. That was where Cranston and his people who rule the earth got their juice—blood and bone transfusions from Bill and others like him, others from way down under. And then, when they didn't have enough of it, they began to artificially create it. The only problem is, made from Bill or his kind, or synthetically made, they have to be injected over and over. And the originals, those like Bill, they begin to fade after a hundred years above ground. So it may be their DNA is activated by the strange fires of the Rim World, flaming warmth and light from miles up, fastened to the roof of their world.

Same with the dinosaurs. They had the natural juice, same as the primitives down below. They needed to be caught to be experimented on. Sliced and poked and cut and pulled and clipped and burned and twisted some. It was a way the Secret Rulers might discover a better formula to make them live longer, maybe with only one injection.

But those experiments, as Bill's body revealed, were ugly stuff for men and creatures. Terrible slicing and dicing, harsh chemistry and surgical operations so a bunch of men and women, Ayesha included, wouldn't get any older and wouldn't need injections to stay young. Ah, the vanity of it. The conceit. And me. I had been handmade as an experiment. That's all I was, something else for them to study tissue and wiring and new ways to live forever. They had already decided I was a failure. It was the damn free will.

"Bill," Quatermain said, interrupting my thoughts, "is fading, and he knows it, and they know it, of course. When they decide they have learned all they can from him, or can no longer use him for anything, he will cease to be of importance to them. Just like me, who no longer will accept an injection or drink their smoothies, and therefore has been demoted from a position of prominence to a position over a mop. Like me, who has killed everything in this world that flies or crawls or walks or swims. Like me, who has helped capture one beast after another, bring it into their realm, where they can torture it with their experiments in search of the secret of longevity. I am their awful puppet. Or have been. The water beasts should die rather than be subjected to such, don't you think?

"I am here to take you with me, if you wish to go. They have tired of you quickly. You have changed and matured rapidly. You see them for the shit stacks they are. Like me, they were once heroes. People to look up to, but then they got the immortality shots, and with that, they got power. Then the shots backfired, didn't do what they thought they would, and that realization gave them fear. The fear of losing youth and power. It soured them, made them bitter as unripe persimmons. Have you had one of those, it'll make your lips suck in behind your teeth. Wait a minute, of course you haven't had them, and I bet that isn't something they put in your brain. That's too unlikely. Too rare."

"Nobody gives a shit, Alan," Bill said.

"Sure, of course. Forget the goddamn persimmons. Richard, as they call you, don't you want to live your own life? Find your own rareness? Use your pecker more? Damn it. I got to go pee."

* * *

Quatermain peed in the corner of the room and made quite a moaning production of it.

"Kidney stones," Bill said.

They unstrapped me and gave me cold-weather clothes and put on their heavy stuff they had left by the door. They had a suit of it for me. They told me their plan as we went outside into the cold air and the constant sun-lit sky the color of wet pearl. It was a simple plan. Kill the dinosaurs to avoid them being experimented on for days, months, years.

Outside the air nipped at us like pinchers.

The blond nurse, Jane, lay dead by the doorway, her neck twisted around.

"Bill fixed her," Alan said.

"Snapped that bitch's neck like a chicken," Bill said.

"She was always nice to me," I said.

"Supposed to be," Alan said. "At some point they may have wanted you to reveal your true feelings. They were using her to gradually gain your trust. She would have cut your nuts off with rusty scissors if they asked her to."

I looked down at her, her mouth open, her tongue hanging out of it like a sock from an open drawer. There was a blood drip dangling off her tongue, frozen there like a dollop of strawberry jam.

One thing for sure, Quatermain and Bill weren't messing around, and now I was in the mix too. The thought crossed my mind that I had been bamboozled by bullshit and a fast shuffle, but it wasn't something that would stick. Deep down in my brain cells, I knew the truth, and it wasn't what Cranston had been feeding me. I was brand new with old knowledge of many things. I could tie a bowline. I could toss horse shoes and a javelin, recite poetry and quote from books. I knew special secrets of cunnilingus. It was odd to know I was so young and yet the size of a full-grown man, a young man with tremendous muscles and endurance. I was—

I busted my ass on the ice and it hurt, so that put some perspective on it. I was human enough. They helped me up and we hustled past more bodies in blue and white uniforms, scattered about like turds in a dog park, their weapons lying on the ice. And there were other bodies there, minus the blue and white. Men and women in white parkas, splotched with blood. I realized immediately that they had been on my new team, Quatermain and Bill's team.

As we passed, Quatermain said, "If we had time we'd bury them, but we don't. We have to kill those poor beasts before the word is out and we're dead as stones."

"Wouldn't it be better to make a run for it?" I said.

"Of course," said Quatermain, "but every creature I ever killed for sport and mounted, every possible redemption I might have is in those big ass swimming fish-lizards. I want to make amends."

"And if I don't want to help you make amends?"

"There's the ice," Quatermain said.

I looked about me. Yep. Ice. Melting. Out in the middle of nowhere. It wasn't like I truly had a lot of choices.

"You help me do this, and we kill the beasts, we'll sail away. Or motor away, and do our best to hide, because hide we must. They'll be coming. They don't even let small things go. With the drink comes not only muscle and speed, there's also intense focus. They'll lock onto us and won't unlock until they kill us."

"This is only starting to sound marginally better than the position I was in."

"That's exactly how it is," Bill said. "It's about doing the right thing because it's right and no other reason."

We had reached the edge of the ice now. Our dinosaur fishing boat bobbed in the water before us at the end of the dock.

"In or out?" Quatermain said.

"In," I said.

We hurried across the dock. I could feel it wiggle beneath our feet. The ice it was imbedded in was melting. We climbed on the fishing boat. It was crewed with other rebels. They were of various sizes, races and sexes. All four of them. Those four and us made seven. It was a small revolution.

One of the revolutionaries, a woman, was our captain. She was small and dark-skinned, but most of her face was hidden by her fur-lined parka hood. Nothing was said. Once we were on board, she disappeared into the wheel house. A moment later the boat was kicking about in the churning water. The three of us climbed to the upper deck. Steam rose up from the once cold sea.

"Stay to the middle," Quatermain called down to one of the men on deck, who rushed to convey the obvious to the captain. But that was all right with me. I surely wanted her to keep us in that middle, away from those crumbling towers of ice.

As we chugged out to the more central part of our icy "lake," the bergs continued to groan like old men on the john, sliding and scraping like shoes on tile. It was a horrible sound, and it was frightening too. Melted fragments larger than our boat dropped loose, sloshed and slid under water, bobbed up near us, or clanged against the side of our puny craft as if they were battering rams. But the boat held.

Into the fighting chairs went me and Quatermain, back to back. Ayesha's blood, brain, and bone matter had been wiped clean, and the rods were ready with new cable that smelled of fresh oil. Hooks dangled, and from the hooks there were no longer the bodies of Neanderthal, but instead they were baited with great chunks of what looked like beef to me. At least we had enough class not to use the bodies of the fallen, theirs or ours.

"We pull those dinos up, and then we shoot them," Quatermain said. "Right through their tiny brains."

He made it sound simple. He had two very large rifles up there, bagged. He opened the bags, gave me one, which I put in a kind of well at the side of my chair, as did he.

He said, "You've been taught to shoot, but you don't know it yet because you've never done it. But it's in your brain. I laid out all that information myself, they coded it, and in it went. Also, you have my DNA, so you may have the basic attributes that helped me have my skill. And let me tell you something, boy. I am the best shot that ever lived with any gun or tossing tool; the javelin, hell, you got that from me too. Let me add something I've already told you. Let me speak with perfect conviction once again. Hook them up and shoot them down. It's for their own good. In time the ice will melt, just as you were told, and out they go. Most likely, before that, they would have been caught by you and Ayesha, carried away and tortured for the sake of experimentation. Longevity drugs being the goal, maybe some toothpaste, or hair grower, or something that makes the dick hard would come out of it. But the bottom line is they will suffer, most likely without a drop of pain killer, because the experimenters want the full experience. It's horrible, and we humans, just as always, will be the cause. Screw up the water. Fuck up the air. Cut down the trees and shit on the world. We'll call it science. We'll call it sport. We'll…"

Bill yelled up from below where he was hustling out of the wheel house. "Alan, shut up and pay attention. He gets it."

"Yeah. Right. Sorry."

Bill came up to the chairs then. He was wearing thick goggles to protect his eyes from the glare of the ice, the shimmer of the water. He said, "I'll be your spotter."

"You have binoculars?" I said.

"Don't need them," Bill said.

"He doesn't," Quatermain said. "He can see a shit spot on a frog's ass from across these waters where we now float to the ice palace from which we came, can't you, Bill?"

"Probably. But it would have to be a large shit spot."

"Naturally," I said.

"Spot away," Quatermain said to Bill. Bill clambered up a long tower that rose out of the upper deck near us, nestled himself in a little crow's nest at the top. The thin tower shifted and rolled with the wind and the waves. There was a small harpoon gun with cables attached to a reel up there.

The tower hadn't been there before. It had been welded into place since yesterday. The boat chugged forward.

* * *

No sooner was Bill in his tower and us in our chairs, strapped and ready, our hooks in preparation for mechanical toss, when Bill said, "There be them two unfortunate sea-goers, Ar, Ar, shiver me goddamn timbers."

"He saw a pirate movie once," Quatermain said.

True to Bill's sight, along they came through the water, swiftly, partly out and partly in, the sun lighting up the ridges of their backs and making the water running down their exposed flesh shine like silver.

"I think they are mad from yesterday," Bill yelled down. "They hold grudges."

"He's not kidding," Quatermain said "Today, they are looking for us."

The beasts lifted their snakey heads and kept on coming. I touched my controls and my chair came alongside Quatermain's. Our mechanical devices tossed our lines with our baited hooks, and no sooner had they splashed the water than our angry dinosaurs hit them, thinking them maybe less as food, and more as an extension of us. Couldn't blame them.

Under our boat they went, dragging our lines. One line went left, one went right. Our chairs rotated about on squeaking bearings and kept turning, us to the back of one another, pivoting the circumference of our platform. Then they dove deep. The reels spun, the cables sang and split the water with a sound like someone tearing rotten sheets.

The boat went dragging across the water.

"They are way down under," Alan said, "and they are dragging us toward the ice."

"Reverse the engines," someone below yelled, and the engines were reversed. There was a straining sound like an apple being forced through a straw, followed by a grinding. The boat locked down and ceased to move quickly. The dinosaurs tugged. The boat's engines billowed with black smoke.

"Cut the engines," I heard another yell from below, and the engines were cut. Now the boat was going across the water like a wagon being hauled by two great horses.

"Harpoon them," I heard Quatermain yell out.

Chunk, came a sound from above. I looked up to see a cable unreeling from the harpoon gun, then glanced at the water as it hit one of the great shadows beneath the water, striking the beast square in the back. The harpoon went in smooth. A dark wetness trailed up and spread over the water. Another harpoon was fired, but now the hit beast was diving down, and the harpoon missed its mark. The other dinosaur followed its companion.

Down they went. The boat bobbed and tipped. For a long, agonizing moment it seemed as if we would be pulled under. Finally the boat rested firm, but you could hear all manner of squeaking and scraping as the cables tugged at us. A chunk came out of one side of the boat as a cable effortlessly cut through it like a hot knife through butter.

"They have gone down and intend to pull us with them," Quatermain said, "but the boat will hold."

"Are you sure?"

"Of course not," he said, "but would you have me say otherwise?"

The cable with the harpoon attached snapped loose with a *ka-ping,* ripped out of the water, whirled around our heads in a fan motion, wrapped around the tower like damp spaghetti.

"You dead up there?" Quatermain called out to Bill.

"Yeah," Bill said.

"Good," Alan said. "Don't get no deader."

Then to our surprise the fishing lines stretched out again and the boat began to move, and the beasts were pulling us in a new direction, but with the same intent. We were once again heading directly toward a great iceberg that rose from the water like the Empire State Building.

* * *

We were moving fast. We could ride it out and see what happened, or release our cables.

"We got time yet," Quatermain said.

I tried to believe he sounded sincere.

Trails of blood from the injured beast were causing the water before us to look like spills of ink. The iceberg loomed closer and closer, and we had no idea how much of it was underwater and in which ways it projected. We might feel what parts of it were below long before we reached the visible part above water.

If this wasn't enough of a consideration, there came a noise like someone beating a thick pillow with a belt. I looked up.

A black helicopter.

One at first, then two.

Bullets slammed into the boat and pinged all around us.

"Shit," Quatermain said. "Someone got word to Cranston and the Rulers. There's rat shit in the soup now."

Bullets pinged on the tower above as the copters flew past. Quatermain yelled out, "Bill, you dead again?"

"Yep," Bill said.

"Good," Quatermain said. "Hang in." Quatermain looked at me, said, "That's a joke, he isn't dead."

"Yeah," I said. "I got that."

* * *

So the monsters were pulling us fast as an arrow toward the icebergs, the boat was starting to come apart, black helicopters (five now) had appeared, and only luck had kept us from catching a bullet in the teeth.

Another pass from one of the copters. Bullets buzzed by my head like wasps. By this time we had thrown up our head shields, designed to keep the rain out, not bullets. The shots struck the head shields, and one came through and buried itself at my feet like a lawn dart. Before the shield had slipped into place, I looked up at the chopper. Saw Cranston. He was dressed in a sharp black suit, as if off to the opera and not an employee-killing spree. He had one leg hooked inside the copter and was hanging out of an open side with a .45 in each fist, spitting metal bees at us. I only glimpsed the pilot.

The copter dipped and rose and moved on.

Quatermain pulled a rifle from the well beside him, an old elephant gun. Another of the copters came near. He lifted the gun and fired. The glass eye of the copter exploded and there was a burst of red. The copter buzzed just over us, almost hitting the crow's nest, then hit the water and broke into pieces. I looked toward the water, saw the big, bronze man swimming with a speed a porpoise might have envied.

Quatermain fired again. His shot caught the bronze man in the back of the neck. I saw meat and water fly, and then the bronze man was gone beneath the waves under a wide swath of blood.

That's when my hooked creature worked the hook out of its mouth, leaped high in the air. For something that large it seemed like an impossible jump. Its jaws widened, then snapped around one of the low-flying copters, dragged it down. I saw the big, dark-haired man inside of it; it was just a glimpse, but it was him, and the inside of the copter was splattered with blood. The beast landed hard, swirling beneath the water with the machine in its teeth.

The wave caused a backwash. It hit the boat like a giant's fist.

The hook cut loose of the dinosaur's mouth. It whipped high on the cable, its tip catching sunlight.

I hit the levers, recoiled the cable so fast it was nearly subliminal, and saved us from that disaster.

Looking up, I saw Cranston's copter coming at us, the others behind it in formation. He was still hanging out of it, firing. I noticed now that on the front of his copter were the painted letter and number G-8. The pilot at the controls could be seen clearly through the great windshield. He looked as cool as the icebergs. They were so close I felt as if I were in the machine with them. Cranston swung out through the opening again, fired those .45's. A shot plucked at my shoulder and banged off the metal chair behind me, leaped up and kissed my ear lobe and whistled away. Neither wound was major.

I swung the rod, disengaged the cable, swirled the hook, splattered it against the front of the copter's windshield. The hook knocked through the windshield, hooked on something, and the copter spun. I wheeled my chair and flung the hooked machine way out over the water. But it wasn't enough. Something went haywire with the reel. The copter was jerked back toward us.

"Shit in a pan," Quatermain said.

For a moment, it looked as if the loose line would drop it short. But not quite. It caught the edge of the deck and there was a fiery explosion. The boat came apart like wet cardboard. We were dragged down by the warm waves. As I went under, I saw the shadow of one of the copters beating its blades above us.

Right before going under, I had instinctively gulped in a breath of air. The water was warm, but not boiling, as too much ice had melted into it. It wasn't pleasant though, and I was down deep.

I stayed down for as long as I could, and then I had to come up. When I did, there was Quatermain clinging to a large plank from our boat.

"Hi, kid."

I grabbed hold of the plank, feeling no more confident of it than if I had clutched a straw. There was an explosion in the distance that made the water rise high, and there was fire in the sky. The remaining helicopters, too low and too near the explosion, snapped and crackled in the flames like insects caught in bug zappers. Their great blades went sailing across the sky. Icebergs shot upward and came apart, and their fragments floated above us like clouds against a blazing sunset, began to fall down. The water heated up considerably.

"Balls," Quatermain said.

* * *

The volcano way down below had exploded, just to make sure we were awake.

A whirling blade from one of the helicopters whistled over our heads. Smoldering body parts splashed in the water. Ice chunks plunged down all around us.

The water began to move, fast, and then drop. It sizzled and smoked.

"Cheers, kid, nice knowing you."

The water plunged even more, and we went down with it. Then we were sailing along toward a great iceberg, and the water dropped away before it. We came to a massive gap in the ice. The water was flowing into it, and we went along with it.

I glanced back along the icy tunnel, could see the sky, the water. Fire was blowing out of the water, spewing high. Rolls of lava tumbled into the waves, turned them to steam. So steamy I could no longer see.

Down we washed, so far down that I accepted that I was doomed. Lava flowed in behind us, sizzling the water, creeping up on us like a cat on a crippled mouse. Then there was a strange rush of water as if we had been caught in a vacuum of some sort. We shot along as if taped to the head of a bullet. Went so fast I lost grip on the plank, lost awareness of Quatermain. I didn't know if I was up or down, dead or alive, still under that bridge, in the warehouse, on a gurney, or if anything I knew was true, or if it was all just a bubble somewhere in my brain.

Water gushed through my nose and mouth and flooded inside of me. The world went dark. I knew my short, real life had ended.

* * *

Okay. Sorry for the cliff-hanger. But that's how it was. I was doomed.

Except I wasn't.

I sat up. I don't know how long I had been out, but there was light and it was hot and sticky. Above me there were clouds, odd looking, bluish, sparked with pink. Through gaps in the clouds I could see a sky, rippled with fire.

There was a vast inland lake before me. I was on its shore, bedded down in deep mud. To my right I could see Quatermain. Down a piece from him I could see Bill. He was standing. The rushing water had torn all our clothes off. We were naked as the day we were born, or in my case, made in a vat.

I leaned to my side and coughed up water and tried to get to my feet. That was no harder than dragging a bus up a high hill with a rope, so I lay back down in the mud for a while. In time, Bill was looking down at me.

"Home," he said.

I sat up, not wishing to lie there with his penis swinging above me.

He grabbed me under the arms and backed up, pulling me out of the mud. Quatermain was already out. He was sitting with his back against a tree.

"This is my world," Bill said. "The volcano collapsed in on itself, opened a path, and we all came down it. Slanted easy and came down under, sliding down the sloping bowl that leads here. Had it been a straight drop we would have been drowned. Might have been drowned anyway. But we weren't. We're lucky to be alive."

"You can say that again," I said.

"We are lucky to be alive," Bill said.

"Not up for the humor," I said.

"By the way, there didn't use to be a lake here," Bill said. "Come walk with me, come see."

I was able to get my feet under me this time. Quatermain got up too. We went along after Bill. We came to a bend in the shoreline. To our left were great and primordial trees, and to our right, that vast lake, or perhaps a better name for it would be inland sea.

Scattered about it, close to shore, were fragments from the copters and our boat. There were bodies as well. I saw the great dark-haired man wrapped up in a propeller. His head dangled down and that was the only thing about him truly recognizable. His features were perfect, serene even, as if he always expected it to end this way. The rest of him looked like dirty taffy wrapped around those blades.

"Irony," Quatermain said. "They wanted to live forever. Now they're dead and we're alive."

"You haven't noticed," Bill said.

"Noticed what?" Quatermain said.

"Me," Bill said.

"So you've done something with your hair?" Quatermain said.

"Damn, you're dumb," Bill said, extended his arms and turned around and around a few times.

"Your scars," I said. "They're gone."

"The air," Bill said. "This place. My home. It's healed me. Well, there are some little white scars, but the serious stuff, it's healed up."

"So the question is solved. It's the DNA mixed with the air that keeps people here young," Quatermain said. "Look there."

It was the two plesiosaurs. They were swimming amongst the wreckage, around remaining fragments of melting ice bergs, pausing to eat an available snack of mutilated and burnt corpses. The one that had been harpooned looked healthy enough, as if it had received a nasty pin prick.

"We don't need to fish them now," I said.

"Or kill them," Quatermain said. "Of course, now we have a new problem. This world."

"My world," Bill said.

"No one owns a place like this," Quatermain said.

"We can live a life of our choosing," I said. "I'm only a few months old, and I'm ready to have some real experiences."

"I bet that will be possible," Quatermain said. "But as for the Secret Rulers, they aren't all gone. We may see them again."

"Then we will," I said. "But for now, we have this and we are free of obligation, our indentured servitude is over."

"I can show you how to survive, how to live here," Bill said. "I remember all that shit. Making fires, weapons, finding things to eat. It's right here in my head and in my heart. I have sort of lost the taste for grubs, though."

"That sounds all right," Quatermain said, "but what I wouldn't give for a pair of Bermuda shorts, some flip-flops, right now. This is no way to go about."

We stood there looking out at the wreckage in the water, at bodies both of our revolutionaries, and those from the choppers. That was done and couldn't be undone. We looked out at the beautiful and foreboding forest, touched by shadows, dappled by sunlight. It was full of fleeting figures, the sounds of birds and growling animals.

After a while Bill located a trail and we took fallen limbs to serve as clubs and went along together into the dark of the trees.

Second Interlude: No Good Deed...

The words fell away like rain on a window pane, dissolving again into the same jumble of text as before. Sometime during the story, the room had gone as silent as a placid sea at midnight. The wind had died away, and the fire was nothing but embers that glowed quietly in the hearth.

Conrad shivered. He could not say why, though he told himself that it was from the cold. He stood up and walked to the bin where the firewood sat in the open. He picked out two split logs, both dry and sinuous, and threw them into the fireplace. Smoke rose for only an instant before the wood sputtered and hissed into flame. He rubbed his hands together, suddenly painfully aware that he was not cold at all. He was, however, thirsty. The flagon of ale was long empty, and perhaps on any other night, he would have considered whether perhaps he had already consumed more than he should. But not tonight. Tonight he had too much on his mind.

He walked into the darkened kitchen of the inn and jerked open the refrigerator door. He'd been there so long that this sort of familiarity was fully condoned. He grabbed a *Budvar* and threw a dollar—more than enough—on the counter. He popped the top and took a deep, long pull. And his thoughts were deep and long as well.

He thought of the stories, of the impossibly long block of text on his computer screen. Of the riddles, the post that no one else seemed to have seen or opened, of the prehistoric men in the story he had just read, so eerily similar to the man he had seen in the snows earlier in the night.

It's all for me, he thought. He coughed out a laugh. "Absurd," he said to himself. It was just a game, a clever scam. Like so many others he had seen—and occasionally fostered—over the years. It was, after all, the way of the deep net. Layers of bullshit obscuring the truth.

And yet, it all seemed so familiar to him as well. Especially Limbus. He could have sworn he'd seen it before, or heard of it at least.

"Maybe I should Google it."

He walked back into the other room, intending to do just that. But then he saw her, and he forgot all about Limbus.

She was standing in front of the fire, shadows dancing across her face. Normally, when he saw her, she was dressed in the modesty her parents demanded. Not tonight.

Her dark hair hung long and loose, spilling over her breasts. And it was a good thing, too, as nothing much else did. Her blouse hung from her shoulders threatening to slip off at the slightest movement. The two cloth ties meant to keep it closed swung limply from the neckline, leaving her bare chest all but exposed. The simple skirt she wore was modest enough, but Conrad suspected there was nothing underneath.

"Hi, Veronica," he muttered, immediately feeling foolish.

She smiled sweetly. "Hi, Conrad."

There was probably a time in his life when he would have given into his basest desires in a situation like this, without a second thought. It was, in fact, the easy thing to do. Much easier than saying no. But he had matured. Or at least, that's what he told himself. In the moment, he wasn't so sure.

She stepped toward him, and as she did, Conrad was critically aware of just how young she was. A child who wanted to be a woman. And in that instant, the not insignificant temptation Conrad felt to take this girl and take her then and there melted away.

But she didn't know she'd already lost. Not yet. And as she took one graceless step after another toward him, as she tossed her hair in a comical imitation of a Hollywood starlet from twenty or thirty years before, Conrad realized how painful this was about to get.

"You have been with us for a long time," she said. "Will you stay much longer?" She rested one hand on the table, her other she placed, very deliberately, on her hip. Conrad stifled a laugh at this clumsy attempt at small talk, mixed with an even more clumsy attempt at sensuality.

"Veronica… darling…" He started to explain, but then he fell silent. He searched for the words to justify this rejection to her, to tell her that it was not her fault, that she would live a beautiful life without him.

But the words didn't come, and in the end, they didn't have to. She saw them in his eyes. Her own began to quiver. She reached up and pulled the top of her shirt closed. Shame and embarrassment spread from the top of her face, down her neck, and, Conrad was sure, all the way to her toes. She murmured something under her breath—not in English—spun on her heals, and veritably ran out of the room.

"Veronica, wait!" Conrad said, somewhat half-heartedly. But she did not wait. She disappeared into the back and into darkness.

Conrad felt like shit. That would pass, though. If he had given her what she had wanted? Now that was the kind of regret that didn't go away. He was painfully aware of that fact from past experience.

"Well," he mumbled, "I guess I'll be getting my own beer from now on." He chuckled joylessly to himself, and it echoed off the barren walls with such force that it scared him. The quiet of the place was immense.

Conrad took himself and his beer back to the table where sat his computer. He plunked down in front of it, having forgotten altogether what he had intended to do before. What he saw on the screen chilled him to his core.

He spun in his chair, expecting to see someone standing behind him. But there was no one, and so he leapt up, running to the window and peering out into the snowy night. The streets were empty. Chills coursed through his body so intense that his arms could have doubled for sandpaper. He turned and leaned his back against the wall, the cold from outside seeping into his bones. He stared at the electronic demon sitting on the wooden table across from him. The curser blinked furiously, demanding an answer. Even from here, he could still make out the words.

Every good deed deserves a reward. No riddle this time. Just hit enter.

His rational mind rebelled. How could they know? Were they watching him? Was this some kind of trick? He appealed to Ockham's Razor, but for once, conspiracy was the logical option.

Conrad shook his head. Really, he had no choice. Curiosity, after all, was his drug. And he needed a hit. He walked over to the table. He pressed "enter." Once again, the mass of symbols reformed, this time into the image of a grotesque figure—a man, but one with the face of a pig. Then it dissolved into words that Conrad could not help but read.

Lost and Found

By

Joe McKinney

I woke to a cop tapping his flashlight on my window. Red and blue lights filled the rearview mirror, so bright I had to shield my eyes. The traffic light in front of me turned from green to yellow.

Groaning, I sat up. I was nowhere near sober, and I felt like my head had been stuffed inside a bag. It took me a moment to get my bearings. The clock on my dashboard read 4:06 a.m. Great, I thought. I had to be back at work in less than three hours.

The cop tapped on the glass, a little harder this time.

"Yeah, yeah," I said, groping for the button that rolled down the window.

I didn't recognize the cop, which wasn't surprising. The young ones are all just faces to me these days. His nametag said ROBINSON, but that didn't ring any bells, either. He looked about six foot even, a hundred seventy pounds, probably ex-military. He had that look about him. Probably liked to fight too. His nose was crooked from an old break that hadn't set quite right.

"I'm Alan Becker," I said, trying to sound sober and not doing a very good job of it. "I work in Homicide." I gestured up at the traffic light and paused. It was still yellow. I stared at it for a long moment, but it held at yellow. I looked back at the cop and said, "Uh, I'm sorry about that, I…"

I trailed off. Drunk as I was, it was hard to concentrate. I kept looking back to the traffic light, frozen on yellow.

"How much have you had to drink tonight?" Robinson asked.

The light changed to red.

I grunted in surprise. I pointed at the light. "Did you...?"

"Sir, how much did you have to drink tonight?"

I thought about it, but I honestly couldn't remember. After work I'd hit a sports bar called Callaghan's, the closest bar to my house. I remember watching basketball and drinking vodka and Diet Cokes, but I couldn't remember much else. I didn't even remember leaving the bar.

"Put it in park."

"Huh?"

Robinson pointed to my gear shifter. "Put your car in park."

I looked down, surprised and a little scared that I'd passed out with my foot on the brake. I'd passed out like that once before, but it'd been in my driveway where there was no danger of me crashing into anything except my own house. I took a deep breath and tried to pull myself together. This was bad. I put the car in park and tried again.

"Look," I said, "I'm sorry about—"

"Step out of the car, please."

"Wait," I said. "It's cool. I'm a cop. I can call somebody. My phone's around here someplace."

He took a step away from the door and gave me a come on gesture with his left hand. "Out of the car, please."

I tried again to reach him. If a cop gets pulled over by another cop he doesn't know, he's supposed to show a little professional courtesy. Most of us are recorded by dash cam these days and you can't make it obvious you're about to get a pass. I put my hands where he could see them and gave him the usual line.

"No problem. I'm stepping out. But I just want you to know I've got my service weapon on my right hip. Next to my badge. My credentials are in my back left pocket."

"We'll get to that," he said. "Now step on out, please."

I did like he told me, but he kept having to point me in the right direction.

"Turn around," he said. "Stand there, with you back to your car. Face me."

He had my weapon out of the holster before I knew what he was doing.

"Hey!" I said.

"Just while we're talking," he said.

He stripped the magazine from the receiver, ejected the round from the chamber, and set the empty weapon on the hood of his car. The magazine and the round he slid into the cargo pocket of his pants.

Then he put me in position to start the standardized field sobriety tests.

I realized what he was doing when he took the stylus out of his shirt pocket.

"Hey, come on, man, what the hell?"

He assumed the officer's introductory stance for the SFSTs. "Stand with your feet together, hands down at your sides. Like this." He tapped the blue-lit tip of his stylus with his index finger. "Do you see the blue light here? I want you to follow it with your eyes; don't move your head. Do you understand the instructions?"

"I don't understand why you're doing this. Come on, let me just call somebody. I can get somebody to drive me home. There's a Park and Ride lot right over there. We can just park my car and I'll get it later."

"Sir," he said, "I need you to acknowledge the instructions I've given you. Follow the blue light with your eyes; don't move your head."

"Man, are you for real? You're really doing this?"

"Sir, are you refusing to comply with my instructions?"

"This isn't necessary," I said, though I'm sure I was slurring at that point and it probably came out as one long syllable. "Just let me call somebody."

"Sir, failure to comply with my instructions will be taken as a refusal on your part."

"I'm not refusing anything." I was yelling at him now, talking with my hands like a man whose head is swarming with bees. "All I want to do—"

He grabbed for my wrist.

I yanked it away and backed up. "What the hell, man?"

He tried to grab my wrist a second time and I shoved him back. "Back off," I yelled. "I'm a fucking cop! What's wrong with you?"

It was a mistake to push him. He was younger than me, stronger than me, faster than me. He knocked my hands aside, spun me around, swept my feet out from under me, and slammed me face down into the trunk of my Honda Accord so fast my vision was still a smeared swirl by the time the handcuffs bit into my wrists.

He was good, I had to give him that, even as I cussed him.

After he finished frisking me, he pulled me back up to my feet and led me, wobbly and off-balanced, toward the backseat of his patrol car. On the way there, still stunned by having my face slammed into my trunk, I glanced at the lightbar on top of his car. You can set a police car's lightbar to about twenty different configurations. There are flashers and alley lights and rear-only flashers and a whole host of other patters. Robinson had turned on his flashers and his takedown lights. The takedowns are a pair of intensely bright white lights designed to turn the area directly in front of a police car into broad daylight. Cops who work at night use them as much for the light they provide as for their power to blind a potentially belligerent subject. His takedowns were on, but that was the weird part, because they weren't all that bright. They should have hurt my eyes. Instead, they were at a dull glow, like a light bulb on its last leg. And inside the lightbar, where the bulbs should have been, was what looked like a slowly rotating globe. There was a belt of stars surrounding the globe, and little pinpricks of light on the globe itself, like you sometimes see on those company logos when they want to impress you with all their worldwide locations.

I tried to stop for a better look. "Wait!" I said. "What was—"

But he put his hand on the top of my head and pushed me into the backseat. Unable to use my arms, I had to roll over to get seated the right way. I must have looked like a whale on the beach. It took me forever to get my feet into the foot well. It was a pathetic display.

"Watch your head," he said, and slammed the door on me.

* * *

I got feeling pretty sorry for myself on the way down to the jail. Staring at the end of things will do that to you, and I was about to kiss my seventeen years as a cop good-bye. I was so wrapped up in my own misery I didn't even notice that we'd pulled into the prisoner off-loading dock behind the City Magistrate's Office. One minute I was swaying along with the motion of the car ride, the next I was looking up at Officer Robinson's broken nose.

"Step out," he said. "Watch your head."

I did like he ordered. Everything hurt. Having your hands cuffed behind your back is murder on your shoulders, and my feet felt like they had weights tied to them.

I looked around.

A prisoner under arrest for nothing but warrants goes directly to the county jail, but those with fresh charges, like driving drunk, have to stop first at the City Magistrate's Office. That's where you see the judge and get told the formal charges against you. In the San Antonio Police Department, we call that first stop "the Mag's Office." Though we claim it as ours, and City employees work as detention guards inside, the Mag's Office actually services all thirty-eight law enforcement agencies in Bexar County, not just the SAPD, so on the weekends it's crazy busy. The parking lot is so packed with police cars that sometimes officers are forced to park outside the security fence that surrounds the lot. But this was a Tuesday night, or rather very early on Wednesday morning, and the parking lot was nearly empty. The few police cars present were parked up near the metal doors that led into the holding cells.

We were parked way off to the right of the entrance.

I'd investigated a few cases that used evidence gathered here in this parking lot, and I knew from reviewing the video on those cases that the security cameras above the entrance covered most of the parking lot, but not all of it. Where we were parked the cameras didn't reach.

"What gives?" I asked, gesturing with a nod toward the doors.

He didn't answer. Once again he flipped me around like a rag doll and searched me, and this time he emptied my pockets and put the contents on the hood of his car. When he got to my wallet he opened it and turned to my agency credentials, where my badge and peace officer license were kept.

Like most cops with kids, I'd put pictures of my two children over my license. The trick is to position it just so, to hide the personal information. The public has a right to see my credentials, but they don't have a right to know my home address. I've seen beauticians do the same thing at the barber shop.

He turned my wallet so that I could see Nicole and Andrew's school pictures. "Your kids?" he asked. Seeing them smiling at me was like a knife in my heart. I missed them so much my legs nearly folded beneath me. I barely heard what he said next. "You know," he went on, "the rules say you're not supposed to cover up your credentials like this."

It took a moment to register. My thoughts, and my heart, and my soul, were still hanging on those pictures.

"Hello?" he said. "Detective Becker?"

I snapped back to the moment. I stared at him, suddenly so angry I wanted to kick his teeth down his throat. "You don't know me," I said, and I did not slur my words. Not one bit. "Don't ever think you have the right to talk about my family."

He studied me for a moment, frowning, then let the matter go with a shrug.

He put the rest of my things down on the hood. "You won't be allowed to keep this Swiss Army knife. It'll have to go in the Property Room along with your handgun."

I didn't respond. At the time it didn't occur to me that the Rules and Regulations required him to call a uniformed sergeant to the scene to seize an arrested officer's weapon, but I wasn't thinking straight. I just looked away, my anger still at a boil.

"Of course, there is another option."

That got my attention.

"You've had a rough time of it lately, haven't you? What's it been, a year since the crash?"

Exactly a year, actually. Two days from now, Friday, marked the one-year anniversary of the death of my wife and two children. One year, I thought. It sounded like a long time, but it still hurt like it was yesterday.

No, scratch that. It hurt even worse.

Every day was a fucking hellhole without them. And lately, with the one-year anniversary looming, it'd been absolute murder.

I couldn't drink enough vodka to make the loneliness go away.

I didn't tell him that, though. It's a common police interview tactic to suggest that you know more than you're supposed to know. A lot of times, at least with the inexperienced offenders, dropping a few informed guesses and passing them off as concrete evidence is enough to get them to take the bait. But I wasn't buying it. Drunk as I was, I'd been doing the suspect interview thing for a long time. Maybe even longer than this boot had been on the job. News of what happened to my family was more or less common knowledge around the Department. A cop loses his wife and kids in a hit-and-run accident, word gets around. I didn't begrudge him knowing my business, but I wanted to strangle him for trying to use it as leverage against me.

He organized my belongings on the hood of his car. He was meticulous the way he laid everything out, all my credit cards in one column, my pictures in another, my money in still a third. He counted my cash twice, out loud both times.

"Sixty-three dollars," he said. "Do you agree?"

"Who are you?" I asked. "Why are you doing this?"

He ignored my question. "I'll take your silence as an agreement to my count. Your cash will be in the Property Room once you bond out. Do you understand?"

"Guy, the only thing I understand right now is how much I want to kick your ass."

The smile never left his face.

"Okay then, sixty-three dollars it is."

I watched him make notes to himself in his pocket notebook. "Who are you?" I asked.

"I'm Officer Robinson, badge number three eighty-three."

"I can see that, asshole. I mean who are you? Why are you doing this to a fellow cop? Do you have any idea the kind of retribution that's gonna come down on you? No one is going to cover you on your calls. You get into trouble, nobody is going to put down their hamburger and run Code Three to bail you out. No one will sit next to you at roll call. You'll become a pariah. You arrest me, you end both our careers."

"Does any of that change the fact that you have sixty-three dollars in cash in your property?"

I stared at him, utterly dumbfounded. "No," I said.

"Okay then, do you want to know to how to make all this disappear?"

My eyes narrowed. "What are you talking about?"

Robinson reached into his shirt pocket and took out an expensive-looking cream-colored business card. He put it on the fender.

LIMBUS, Inc.
Are you laid off, downsized, undersized?
Call us. We employ.
1-800-555-0606
How lucky do you feel?

"What's that?" I said.

"Exactly what it looks like. An opportunity."

I looked at the card again. How lucky do you feel? I didn't like the sound of that. "If you have a point, you should make it."

"Okay. In addition to the San Antonio Police Department, I represent Limbus, Inc. Sort of my off-duty job, you know? Limbus is an employment agency. People come to us with jobs that need doing and we find the right person to do that job. And we've got a job for you."

"I already have a job."

He gestured toward the door that led into the Mag's Office. "Not after I take you in there you don't."

Somewhere along the way a shred of sobriety came back to me. Maybe it was the car ride. Maybe it was this new twist he was giving me. I wasn't sure either way, but I did know the hairs on the back of my neck were standing on end.

About four or five months into my first year as a patrolman, a group of eight San Antonio police officers got caught up in an FBI sting operation. They were paid a pittance, a few thousand dollars each, to escort what they thought were drug shipments through the city. Turns out it was sheetrock ground up to look like cocaine. The eight were arrested and dragged through the mud on the news, but it was a huge disgrace for everybody wearing the uniform. I was working the day the news broke, and I happened to be going to lunch at a Taco Bell when I heard some sixteen-year-old peckerwood in line behind me tell his girlfriend, in the loudest stage whisper he could muster, "Did you hear about those eight San Antonio cops who got busted dealing drugs? Didn't I tell you all those guys are corrupt?"

It put my blood to boil hearing that. I wanted to pop that kid across the mouth. Instead, I forced myself to stay calm. To think about the integrity and honor I'd learned at the Academy.

I did the same thing then, while staring at Officer Robinson.

"If you're about to ask me to do something illegal then just lead me inside. I won't ever soil my badge by doing something illegal."

"You mean except for driving drunk?" he said. His smile grew wider. "I mean, you know, except for that."

I looked down at the hood of his car, at the Limbus, Inc. business card and the rest of my belongings spread out on display. My mouth was set in a frown. I wanted to lash out at him; I wanted to lash out at the whole world, but instead, I focused on controlling my breathing. A slow pull in, a slow exhalation out.

After a long moment I said, "Just take me inside and be done with it."

His smile faded. I thought I saw pity on his face, and that pissed me off. I looked down at my feet and tried to breathe.

"You deserve better," Robinson said. "You deserve better than to drown yourself in vodka. You were a good cop once, and you can be again. I know how bizarre this must sound to you, believe me I do, but what we're offering you is a good thing. And I can assure you there's nothing illegal about this deal. In fact, if, in the course of doing this job, you come across anything illegal or even unethical, you should consider yourself free from your relationship with Limbus, Inc. and encouraged to make whatever arrests you see fit."

I didn't say a word, just went on staring at my feet.

"Really," he said, and leaned against the fender of his patrol car. The scar across the bridge of his broken nose looked pale under the sodium vapor lights. "You'll find nothing illegal in what we're asking you to do," he said again. "I promise you that. In fact, you might just save a life."

I didn't trust him. I've been a cop for seventeen years. I've learned to trust my gut when it tells me something is not right, and my senses were telling me that something was very wrong here. My mind kept turning back to that image I'd seen in his takedown lights, that slowly rotating globe with the belt of stars around its waist, and I couldn't help the feeling that it was familiar somehow, like I was supposed to know what it was. It was that vague sense of familiarity that kept me from telling him I wasn't interested.

He caught me looking at his lightbar and said, "Something on your mind?"

"Why me?" I asked.

His eyebrows went up and his smile grew even wider. "You're interesting," he said. "That's not why Limbus picked you. That's just a personal observation. Here I've been talking all around this job we're offering you, and you haven't once asked what it is. Rather, you go to the more important question of why you. I find that interesting."

"That doesn't answer my question."

"True. And you won't get an answer. Not from me, anyway. But I can tell you that Limbus, Inc. has a special knack for pairing up available talent to do the job at hand. Nothing Limbus does is random. You were picked because you're the right man for this job. That's really all you need to know. And, really, it's all you'll be told."

"So what's the job?"

"You'll find that on the back of that business card. There's a name written there. We need you to find that man."

"And do what?"

"Nothing. We just need you to find the man whose name is written there. Do that, and the job is finished."

"What's going to happen to the man once I find him?"

"I've already told you, nothing illegal. I will tell you this, though. There is some sense of urgency to this job. There are others looking for this man, and when they find him, they won't bother with questions of legality. They have their own brand of justice."

"People are trying to kill this guy?"

"I told you, doing this just might save a life."

"So…what happens next?"

"I let you go."

"No DWI?"

"And you get to keep your job. Consider it half your payment. An advance, if you will."

"Half my payment?"

"Limbus pays very well. Not always in cash, but always very well."

"Am I supposed to know what that means?"

He shrugged.

"How do you know I just won't walk away from here?"

Robinson nodded like he'd guessed I was going to ask that. The scar across the bridge of his broken nose seemed to shine. "It's like I told you," he said. "Limbus, Inc. has a knack for finding the right person to do the job at hand. You won't walk away. You'll want to finish this job once you get started."

And with that, he turned me around and undid the cuffs.

Still facing away from him, I rubbed my aching wrists and thought of laying him out with a punch. I had forty pounds and about three inches on him. Wouldn't be that hard.

"I wouldn't if I were you," Robinson said, and I could just picture the chuckle that went along with his smile. "I was a Golden Gloves champ for the San Antonio Area Conference from the time I was sixteen till I was nineteen. Chances are I'd knock you on your ass before you landed a single punch."

Fuck it, I thought, and spun around on him with a half-cocked roundhouse ready to fly.

A moment later, with two hard left jabs to my ribs and a right-handed uppercut to my chin, he made good on his promise.

Stunned to find myself on the ground, and unable to work my legs, I watched as he swept my belongings from the hood of his car, got behind the wheel, and drove off. When at last I could move again, I crawled on my hands and knees toward the business card and read the name written there in red ink.

I shook my head in disbelief.

For all the buildup, I'd expected some big name, somebody famous, somebody I'd recognize.

Instead I found the name Gary Harper printed there in a firm, masculine script.

I spit blood on the ground and rubbed my aching jaw. It felt like I'd taken a bite out of my tongue. But the name had me in a state of disconnect. How many Gary Harpers were there in the world? Probably a hundred or more in the San Antonio area alone. And with no identifiers, no race or date of birth or last known address, what he was asking of me sounded even more absurd than when he'd first described it to me.

Yeah, I thought, fuck this. Robinson and his Limbus crew could kiss my ass.

* * *

The downtown substation is right next door to the Mag's Office. I went there and used their locker room to shower and try to look presentable again.

I halfway managed it.

On the way out, I found a patrolman I knew and he gave me a ride over to Headquarters. I sat through roll call in a haze, turned down offers to join the guys for breakfast, and went back to my desk with a case of acid indigestion that made me feel like somebody had tried to scrape the inside of my throat with a metal barbeque grill brush.

At my desk I fired up my computer and ran the Active Duty Officer Database to see what I could learn about Officer Robinson. He'd said Limbus, Inc. wasn't into anything illegal, but I didn't buy that for a second, and the fact that I couldn't find any Officer Robinson working for the Department only confirmed my suspicions. He'd no doubt used an alias, which wouldn't be all that hard to do. Go to any cop shop and you can buy the needed indicia of authority to pretend you're a cop.

But it did make me wonder how he had managed to target me the way he did.

Surely he hadn't just happened upon me.

I'd been asleep at that light for probably an hour, maybe longer. Had he been watching me, waiting for the right moment to approach me?

That bothered me a lot.

I went to Google and tried to find information on Limbus, Inc., but that was a dead end, too. I tried the FBI's Online Law Enforcement Database and the SEC's Law Enforcement Online Directory for strikes two and three. The company didn't seem to exist, at least under that name.

I took out the business card and looked it over. At first I thought Limbus spelled backwards was SUBLIM, which might be short for subliminal. It was weak, but maybe. I tried that and was asked if I meant SUBLIME instead. I didn't. Then I realized I'd transposed a letter. SUBMIL seemed less intriguing.

The other references for Limbus were to a hotel and a CGI studio, both out of France.

Neither seemed likely.

I did find that the word "limbus" meant something in Latin. In anatomy it meant the border between one part of the body and another, like in your eye where the cornea changes to the white part.

But that didn't make much sense either.

Frustrated, I tossed the card back on the desk.

I was tired and my head ached. Exhausted, I decided to head across the hall to the Night Detectives' Office. They had all gone home as I was coming in to work, and their office was dark and deserted.

I found an empty desk in the back and put my head down and tried to sleep.

I woke two hours later to my boss calling my name.

I sat up, groggy and still feeling like warmed over dog shit, but trying hard not to show it.

"Hey, Steve," I said and wiped the drool from the corner of my mouth.

Sergeant Steve Hernandez was a big, heavyset man with a black mustache and a graying crew cut. Though he was the supervisor of an investigative unit, and therefore authorized to wear a suit if he wanted, he usually opted for the uniform instead. He rested his arms on his gun belt as he stared at me. "What are you doing, Alan?"

"Working my way through a migraine," I lied. "The lights were hurting my eyes."

Steve Hernandez had been an SAPD sergeant for twenty-two years. He'd been my sergeant in Homicide for ten of those years. He'd seen his fair share of broken policemen.

But he was good enough not to call me on the lie. "I'm worried about you, Alan."

"I'll be okay," I said.

"I don't know," he said. "Alan, you've had a rough time of it since the crash. I can't even imagine what it must be like losing your family like you did, but I'm worried about you. You know that, right? I think about you and what you're going through. I sit at my desk and I watch you come in. You share an office with the guys who are supposed to be investigating your family's death, and everyday they've got nothing new to tell you. I see that. I may not get what you're feeling, but I worry about how you're doing just the same. You can see that I'm worried, right?"

"Don't be," I said. "I'm fine."

He looked down at his feet and fidgeted some more. "Look, Alan...I'm sorry, this is hard for me to say. I know it must be hard for you to hear, but I really think you're in trouble. You just haven't admitted it to yourself."

"Steve, I don't want to talk about this. I feel better now. I'll get back to work."

"No, you won't." The iron in his words made me sit up and pay attention. Steve Hernandez was the pushover supervisor, the one you told to just go away, and he usually did, but this time he wasn't giving in. "You're not going back to work," he said, and the note of finality in his voice sobered me up fast.

"But, I'm fine—"

"No, you're not fine, Alan. Look, a man loses his wife and two kids in a car crash, it's heartbreaking. I watch you every day when you come into work. You're dragging all the time. Your eyes are always bloodshot and you slip off here nearly every day to sleep. I don't know if you're not sleeping at home or if you're drinking heavily or what, but you're going downhill fast. I'm about one step away from recommending you to the Officer Concern Program. You don't want that, do you?"

"I'm keeping up on my cases, Steve."

"Yeah, because I'm spoon-feeding you the easy ones."

I started to object, but didn't. What he was saying was actually the truth. In the year since Sheryl and the kids died, I'd handled the follow-up investigation on twenty-four suicides. I'd also handled three murders, but one of those was a murder-suicide and the other two came with on-sight apprehensions. From an investigative standpoint, I hadn't done much. Just a lot of paper pushing.

"Go home, Alan," he said. "Please. You didn't take any time off after the crash. At the time, I thought it was just your way of dealing with it. Throw yourself into your work and all that. But whatever this is, it's not working. And I think it's killing you. You need some time off. You need to regroup."

I didn't like the tone of that. "Are you putting me on Admin leave?"

"No," he said. "Nothing like that. You don't deserve to get suspended. You haven't done anything wrong. What you deserve is a few weeks off. Take the time, Alan. I checked the books. You've got nearly three hundred hours of vacation time due to you. You can afford it. And it wouldn't hurt you to talk to somebody about what you're feeling. There's no shame in that."

"I don't need a shrink, Steve."

"Fine. Then a minister or something. Somebody. Alan, you need help in pulling back from this. What you're going through, it's bigger than you are."

Of that, he had no idea. I couldn't help but agree to that. Since Sheryl and the kids died, I'd been going through the motions, but I was dead inside. I could barely sleep, except here at work, and even then I slept in fits. I felt weak and heavy, violent and confused. Sometimes I was so miserable I couldn't get out of bed. In the car sometimes I'd just start balling my eyes out. Sometimes I'd wake up in the middle of the night, the sheets soaking wet, thinking I'd heard Nicole or Andrew crying in their rooms upstairs. Sometimes hearing them scared me. Other times, it just made me numb inside.

Finally, I nodded and got up. "Okay," I said. "I'll go home."

"Good man. I'll tell you what, I'll drive you myself. You look like you shouldn't be behind the wheel."

I nodded again. No need to tell him my car was at a Park and Ride twenty miles away. "Let me go to the bathroom first," I said.

"Okay, I'm parked out front. I'll meet you in the lobby."

After using the men's room, I walked out to the lobby that Homicide shared with Sex Crimes, Financial Crimes, Traffic Investigations and the Records Division. During business hours, the lobby was usually packed, and today was no exception. There were at least eighty people standing around, waiting to speak with a detective. I went over to the Memorial Wall to wait for Steve Hernandez.

I'd passed that wall a million times over the years, but I'd never really looked at it. Set into the wall was a large shadowbox that contained row upon row of plaques, each one commemorating the death of a San Antonio Police Officer killed in the line of duty. All but the earliest plaques had pictures of the officers they celebrated. As I stood there my gaze slid over the pictures, just like a million times before, but then suddenly locked on one of them.

It was Officer Robinson, right down to the broken nose and the wide grin.

Glenn Patrick Robinson.

Entered service October 16, 1994.

Killed by a hit and run driver while on a traffic stop on August 17, 1997.

My legs turned to water beneath me, and I staggered away from the case, bumping into the woman standing behind me. She said something mean to me, but I didn't hear her. The room swirled around my head and I couldn't catch my breath. I couldn't focus. The floor seemed to rock like the ocean. People were staring at me, but they were just a sea of faces, some of them watercolor smears, others twisted and grotesque with laughter. My heart felt like it was beating so fast it might explode, and the last thing I remember going through my head before Steve Hernandez caught me and guided me toward a wooden bench in the middle of the lobby was that Glenn Patrick Robinson was killed sixteen years to the day of the crash that took my wife and children.

* * *

I could have asked Steve to drop me off at the Park and Ride so I could drive myself home, but that would have brought up more questions than I was ready to answer. He was already looking at me like he wasn't quite sure what to do with me, like he was seriously thinking of driving me to a hospital rather than leaving me alone at home.

He pulled into my driveway and said, "You sure you're going to be okay? You still look a little pale."

"I'll be fine," I said. "Thanks for the ride."

He nodded. "Yeah, well, at least you're not shaking anymore. You really had me worried, Alan."

"You keep saying that."

"And you keep telling me you'll be fine. I don't know if I believe you."

I climbed out before he had a chance to say anything else. I waved once in thanks and then went inside.

I headed straight for the pantry and took down a bottle of vodka from the shelf, noting with an air of self-defeat that I'd need to buy more by tomorrow or face a dry spell, and I wasn't ready for that. Not yet.

With vodka and Diet Coke in hand, I sat down at my computer and signed on to the City's Citrix account, so I could access personnel records. I was still trying to get my head around what I'd seen, and now that I'd had some time away from that initial shock, I thought maybe I had just been seeing things. I accessed the SAPD's Memorial Wall webpage and scrolled through the entries there until I came to Glenn Patrick Robinson.

I clenched up inside.

It was Robinson all right, and there wasn't enough booze in all the world to change that.

"But how?" I said. "I don't..."

I ran his name through the city's archived personnel database and found him right away. Glenn Patrick Robinson, born in San Antonio, Texas, March 6, 1971. Date of employment, October 16, 1994. Date of separation from the Department, August 17, 1997.

All the dates matched.

I am not a superstitious man. I'm not a religious one, either. I am a man of facts. Being a detective, I've built my life and my reputation on the reliability of the facts I uncover. But the facts were right there in front of me, and I didn't know how to process them. For the first time in my life, I felt like the facts were lying to me, and that was like being lost on the ocean. I refused to believe I had encountered some kind of ghost. I couldn't make myself accept that. And yet I had seen his face, both in person and in that picture from nearly two decades before. They were the same. That I couldn't deny.

I went to the master bedroom to get undressed. Sheryl had left me with the habit of putting my laundry into hampers in my closet, and after nearly fourteen years of marriage, it had become second nature. I stripped down to my undershorts and tried to sort the clothes into the right hampers. But being a serial drunk requires a little effort. Though a measure of sobriety had returned during my car ride home with Steve Hernandez, the first few sips of my vodka and Diet Coke had brought back that numbing warmth with a vengeance.

It had brought back the stagger as well.

I reached for the top shelf of my closet by habit, meaning to put my gun up there, where it'd be safe from little curious hands as Sheryl used to say, but only managed to sway wildly off balance and go staggering into a stack of boxes I'd put there to get them out of the way.

The contents spilled all over the floor.

I was about to cuss the work I'd made for myself when I noticed one of Nicole's drawings on top of the pile of spilled papers and toys.

It was a globe. A globe drawn by a ten-year-old, the continents not quite right.

And a belt of stars surrounded it.

My mouth fell open and my legs couldn't hold me. I dropped to the floor, fell back against the wall, still clutching Nicole's drawing. I stared at it, simultaneously stricken by the horror that this was the same image I'd seen in Officer Robinson's lightbar and cut down by the love that had been ripped from my chest.

It was too much.

I tried to fathom what it could mean, but only managed to break into sobs.

Nicole, I thought. My beautiful, sweet, innocent Nicole.

* * *

Nothing hits harder, or with less warning, than grief. I was wrecked by it. Sheryl and the kids, I missed them so much. Their passing had left a hole in me so deep there was no way it would ever be filled again. Without them, I had absolutely nothing. I looked at my future and saw a place I did not want to live in, a place I couldn't live in. As a homicide detective, over the years, I'd handled hundreds of suicides. It was almost an everyday thing. But no matter how deep into somebody's personal history I got, no matter how much I came to know him or her after their death, I'd never been able to truly understand why they'd want to kill themselves. I got the reasons. Fatal, painful illnesses. Deep depression. The collapse of a marriage. I got all that, I understood it in an academic sense, a clinical sense; yet even with that understanding, the idea of ending it all was so alien, so not right, that I couldn't wrap my head around it. I was raised to fight to the end. You never give up, no matter how much it hurts, no matter what stands in your way. But in that moment, seated on my closet floor, my service weapon just inches from my hand, I nearly gave in to the dark.

I wanted to.

Only one thought held me back.

The star-belted globe in Nicole's drawing was identical to the glowing image I'd seen in Officer Robinson's lightbar.

Was it a coincidence?

I thought there was little chance of that.

She'd seen this image at some point before her death, and it had struck her with enough importance for her to reproduce it.

What did that mean?

Limbus had selected me to find this Gary Harper guy, which meant the DWI arrest with Officer Robinson had to have been a setup. And to do that, they would have needed to keep me under observation. I'd done undercover work before, and I knew from that experience that you could learn a lot of information about people real fast. It wasn't hard, even if the person was paranoid. Cops are trained to spot someone watching them, and I knew what to look for better than most, but of course I hadn't been on my game for a long while. If I was being watched by pros, they could have learned everything about my family and me in a matter of days. And all of that led me into some unpleasant conclusions.

I'd always thought my family was killed in a random hit-and-run accident. Sheryl had been driving them to school one morning. It happened at the entrance to our subdivision. A red Ford pickup had lost control on the curve on the main road and spun into the driver's side of Sheryl's Camry, killing her and the kids instantly. But what if the crash wasn't random? What if somebody had targeted them? Or even Limbus? Could Limbus be behind the murder of my family?

Maybe this Gary Harper fellow was connected to their deaths.

Somehow that felt like a stretch, but nothing about what I'd experienced so far made sense. I didn't know what to believe. All I had were a bunch of questions.

But I did know somebody who might have answers.

I called the number on the Limbus, Inc. business card Officer Robinson had given me. I knew he would answer even before it started ringing.

"What kind of game are you playing with me?" I demanded.

"This isn't a game."

"You're damn right it's not. I want to know what happened to my family."

"I know you do."

"Did you kill them?"

"No."

"Did this Limbus, whatever it is, did they kill them?"

"No."

"How can I believe that? Why all this secrecy? Why bother setting me up like you did?"

There was a long pause on his end. I was about to say his name when he finally spoke. "Which question would you like me to answer, Alan?"

"Why are you doing this to me? Why are you doing this to my family? Why did this happen?"

"There are no answers to those questions, Alan. At least, I can't answer them."

His tone was soft, almost apologetic, but I wasn't about to let him off the hook. "Why not? What's the truth here?"

"I'm sorry, Alan. You have to answer those questions yourself. I can't do it for you."

"Why not?" I was screaming into the phone now. "Why the hell not? You tell me, goddamn it! You tell me right fucking now!"

"Good-bye, Alan."

I heard a click.

"No!" I screamed. "Robinson, damn you. Don't you hang up on me. Don't you…"

But he was gone. I was talking to dead air.

I held the phone to my ear until it clicked again and the connection closed. Only then did I put the phone and the business card down on the dresser. I sat on the edge of the bed and stared at the wall, my whole body humming with rage. I felt like a live wire, like I was ready to rattle myself to pieces.

And then the grief hit me again and the tears came and I was lost to everything but the pain.

* * *

Later that night, I went to get my car from the Park and Ride. It was dark by then and the lot was six miles away. There was no way I was going to walk that far in the dark and along the highway, so I called a cab. Though I'd done absolutely nothing all day but sit and wallow in my grief, I was exhausted. Riding in the back of the cab, my second ride in the backseat of a Crown Victoria in as many days, I could barely keep my eyes open. I let my chin sink to my chest and I was almost asleep when the cabbie started speaking.

"Huh?" I said.

"Which car is yours?" He was an older Hispanic man, lean and slight of build, with a thin, black mustache and black hair that looked like he used some sort of Just for Men product to color the gray away. He smelled of cigarette smoke and hair oil. Ranchero music played softly on his radio.

I shifted in my seat. My back was hurting again, the lingering memory of a rear end collision I'd been on the receiving end of twelve years earlier, back in my days as a patrolman. I pointed across the lot toward the back row. "I'm in that maroon Honda Accord over there."

He pulled up next to my car and said, "Seventeen-sixty."

I fished my wallet out of my back pocket and looked at the few miserable bills I had there. I did some quick figuring. Twenty for the cab ride, and I'd need another thirty for a bottle, because I was almost out of vodka at home. That'd leave about ten dollars for gas. That wouldn't buy much, but seeing as I wasn't going to work for a while, I wouldn't be driving much. I saw myself sitting at home, watching TV, and trying my hardest to drown away any thought that dared to enter my head.

Does any of that change the fact that you've got sixty-three dollars in your property?

Hearing Officer Robinson's voice in my head was like a punch in the gut and I groaned in pain.

"Hey mister, you okay?" the cab driver asked.

It took me a moment to answer. "Yeah," I said. "Yeah, I'm fine."

I reached into my wallet and took out a twenty. He had his hand out to take it. As I put it in his hand I saw movement at his wrist. I glanced at the spot, not sure of what I'd seen.

A long, red, fleshy vine appeared.

It coiled around his wrist and then moved toward my hand, snakelike and dangerous.

I yanked my hand back, the twenty falling to the floor.

"Hey man, not cool!" the driver said.

But I wasn't listening. I groped for the door handle and tumbled out of the backseat, backing away from the cab in shock and horror.

The cab driver got out, gave me a long, disgusted glare, then got the twenty from the backseat and shut the door. "Asshole," he said. Then he got behind the wheel and took off, leaving me under the buttery yellow glow of a street lamp that hummed like a bug zapper.

I stood there, trembling, wondering if I was losing my mind.

It sure felt like it.

My chest felt tight and it was hard to breathe. I closed my eyes and willed myself to calm down. It hurt, but I drew in two deep breaths, and then two more. The tightness in my chest cleared a little, and so did my head.

You need a drink, I thought, and just as quickly blocked that thought from my head. That was the last thing I needed.

I didn't need a drink. I needed to think.

I reached into my shirt pocket and removed the Limbus, Inc. business card again. One of the edges had darkened and turned soft where I'd held it with tear-stained fingers.

The name Gary Harper was still clear as a bell.

I didn't believe Robinson for a second when he said Limbus was on the level, and while I couldn't see any reason why they would want my family dead, I knew that if I was going to get any answers and have any chance of putting my head back together, I was going to have to follow the only lead I had. Whoever this Gary Harper was, he was going to be my guide down the rabbit hole.

But first I had to find him.

And that meant becoming a policeman again.

* * *

Unless there's an officer-involved shooting or some other high-profile event going on, the Homicide Office is dead in the middle of the night. Once the daylight detectives end their shifts around 6 p.m., all the hustle and bustle moves across the hall to the Night Utility Detectives' Office. I glanced into their office on my way in and saw at once they were busy. They had officers and witnesses and suspects at practically every cubicle, which was good for me. There was nothing wrong with me coming in off hours to look into cases, but still, it would be a whole lot easier if I didn't have to explain myself to anybody.

I sat at my desk and fired up my computer. My first online stop was the San Antonio Police Department's Master Name File. Anybody who's had dealings with the SAPD in the last forty-five years, regardless of the reason, is in the Master Name File. So I typed in Gary Harper and got exactly what I expected, about thirty hits, the earliest of which dated from July, 1974. The software also gave names that were phonetically similar to the search parameters, so I got another one hundred sixteen Gerald Harpers, George Harpers, and Garner Harpers added on to the end of my list.

"This is stupid," I said, and pushed the keyboard away.

Without a date of birth or an address or a particular incident, how was I supposed to figure which of these guys was the right Gary Harper? With all Robinson's talk of Limbus, Inc. finding the right man to do the job, I'd just assumed the man they were looking for was located somewhere in the San Antonio area, but now I realized that might not be the case. Hell, he could be from anywhere.

Still, it seemed logical to start locally and exhaust those leads before going elsewhere, so I went to the kitchenette, made myself some coffee, and got busy going through names and their reason for contact, trying to see if something stood out.

Nothing really did.

Three of the men made it into the MNF as witnesses, and I thought maybe I'd find something there. After all, Robinson had confided in me that time was of the essence in finding this guy, and that others were looking for him who wouldn't worry themselves with obeying the law to do it. I thought witness tampering, maybe.

But that was a dead end. All three of the cases were for small-time misdemeanors that had already been adjudicated and the sentences long since served. Minor league dope and forgery cases that didn't merit a second look.

The search was going nowhere.

I sat back in my chair and thought about where to look next. All the logical openings seemed closed, and the information I did have was so vague as to be practically useless. What I needed was more information. I needed some context. Without it, I'd have better luck finding this Gary Harper guy by throwing a dart at the phone book.

But there was always a way to dig deeper. My years as a homicide detective have taught me that. In our investigations, when you don't have a suspect to research, you research the victim. The closest I had to a victim in this case was Officer Robinson, so I turned my attention on him.

The first time I looked Officer Robinson up, I was only interested in figuring out who he was, and if he was really a cop. As a result, I'd only searched the city's employee databases. Now that I was looking at him as part of my investigation, I turned to the case file for the crash that caused his death. I kept coming back to what Robinson said about Limbus, Inc. having a knack for finding the right man to do the job. Maybe that meant Robinson was also the right man for recruiting me. Maybe he was chosen for the same reason I was.

Whatever that was.

Homicide shares an office with the guys from the Traffic Investigations Detail and our open historical cases are kept in the same file room. Police car crashes and fatality accidents are kept separate from the other case files in the Traffic Section, and I had little trouble finding Robinson's file. It was about eight inches thick, which surprised me until I remembered that back in 1997 we were still working with print copies of nearly everything. These days so much information is stored digitally that an average physical case file consists of little more than a few handwritten evidence receipts. But Robinson's file had a print copy of everything the Traffic boys had generated during their investigation, and I took it all back to my desk and started wading through it.

The top page was a Pending Further Investigation report written by a detective named Randall Fehrenbach. I didn't know Fehrenbach personally, but I knew of him. In the seventeen years since writing this report, he'd promoted to the rank of lieutenant and was put in charge of the Research and Planning Division before retiring a few years back. He had a reputation for being smart and thorough, well suited for the number crunching that was the bread and butter of the Research and Planning Division, and the case file in front of me was proof that the reputation was well deserved. His narrative of the crash and the subsequent investigation was exhaustive in detail, and the hand-rendered scale diagram of the crash that took Officer Robinson's life looked like something an architect would have drafted.

From the narrative section of his report, I learned that Officer Robinson was passing through the intersection of Spencer and Grissom on his way to a burglars-in-action call, when he was T-boned by a green Dodge Diplomat. The Dodge hit the rear door on the driver's side of Officer Robinson's Crown Victoria, sending it into a spin that led to a series of barrel rolls. Fehrenbach's calculations put Officer Robinson's speed at about eighty miles per hour at the time of the crash, and the photos of his car wrapped around a telephone pole were about what I would expect from a crash at that speed.

But then I saw something that made me forget all about the photos and the diagrams and the speed calculations.

The Dodge that hit Officer Robinson's car was disabled during the crash.

The driver ran from the wreckage to a nearby subdivision, where he disappeared.

The Dodge had paper dealer plates on it, and Fehrenbach was able to trace the Dodge back to a used car lot several miles from the crash site.

And the name on the point of sale was Gary Harper.

* * *

During most investigations there comes a tipping point, a moment when you feel things starting to come together. The big picture suddenly makes sense. Your pulse quickens. Your skin is flush with heat. You can't stop smiling and licking your lips. You develop the focus of a hawk about ready to dive toward its prey.

I used to live for that moment.

I was feeling that tipping point now for the first time since Sheryl and the kids died, and it felt good. It felt really good.

Until I realized that it couldn't be that easy. After all, if Fehrenbach had located this Gary Harper guy, I would have found a record of him when I searched under that name in the Master Name File. He would have stood out from the others from the start.

I read deeper into the Robinson file and soon found out why he was missing from the Master Name File.

Apparently, Gary Harper didn't exist.

Witnesses reported seeing a white male, slender build, blond hair, about seventeen years of age, fleeing from the crash scene. The owner of the used car lot reported selling the green Dodge to a kid that matched that description. The kid said his name was Gary Harper, and he'd signed a bill of sale under that name.

But it was a fake name.

The case file included all of Fehrenbach's 2057s, the five-by-eight cards detectives in the SAPD used to use to record all phone calls, status updates, meetings, interviews and evidence processing they performed during the course of an investigation, and from those I could tell he'd exhausted every lead available to him. He'd even gone to several area high schools and looked through old yearbooks hoping to find his suspect. But in the end he'd come up empty-handed.

I glanced at my computer screen and coughed in surprise. It was nearly 6:30 in the morning. I'd been at this all night. Steve, my supervisor, usually arrived in the office about thirty minutes before roll call, which meant he would be walking in the door any moment.

I didn't need him to find me here.

That would not be good.

I hurriedly scooped up the case file, tucked it under my arm, and ran out the back door that led to the detectives' section of the parking lot. I managed to make it to my car without anybody seeing me and set the case file on the passenger seat.

I let out a long breath and looked at myself in the rearview mirror.

The bloodshot eyes of a lost and hollow man stared back at me.

I'd been up all night. I needed sleep. I was a mess. I should have been exhausted, but I wasn't. I felt jittery and tense, like I'd had too much coffee. For the first time in a long time, I was hungry. I had leads in hand and enough brick walls in my way to wake my need to break something. But I still needed more information.

What I needed was to talk with retired Lieutenant Fehrenbach.

Of course it was just now 6:30 a.m. I couldn't call him before sun up. That wouldn't be cool. So I leaned the driver's seat back, took out my iPhone, and asked Siri to wake me up at 8:15 a.m.

That done, I closed my eyes and tried to sleep.

* * *

One of the scariest statistics cops live with is the knowledge that over half of them will die within five years of retirement.

It's not hard to count the reasons why. Thirty-three years of working a cop's long hours, rarely getting enough sleep, will do a body in. So too will getting banged up in fights and torn up jumping fences. Spend hours out of every day sitting in a police car and the blood clots will form. Three decades of fast food eaten off the dashboard doesn't help either.

But the thing that does most cops in faster than all the rest of it is entirely mental. When you spend a lifetime wearing a badge, you learn to see yourself as synonymous with the mission behind that badge. You become the job. You live for the camaraderie, the friendships, and the sense of purpose that comes with wearing the uniform. Hobbies fall by the wayside. Wives get frustrated and lonely and walk out. Children become alienated and resentful. And for a long time you tell yourself that you're strong as an ox, and that you're feeding on the stress and the emotional isolation, rather than the other way around.

But then comes retirement, and you go from working nearly every damn day to waking up, showering, shaving, and getting dressed, only to face a day that is a desert of nothing to do.

Those who once loved you are gone, and those who once worked alongside you are still on the job, still slogging away. They have no time for an old man with nothing to do.

You're still part of the family, but the feeling of being kicked to the curb and passed by leads to a bitter and terrible loneliness.

Five years of feeling like that is a long time.

Randall Fehrenbach had retired three years earlier, and as bad as it sounds, I was hoping to use those feelings to my advantage. I was hoping he'd jump at the chance to get back into one of his old cases.

"Is this Lieutenant Fehrenbach?" I asked him over the phone.

He sighed. "This is Randall Fehrenbach. I haven't been Lieutenant Fehrenbach in a few years. Who is this?"

"Detective Alan Becker, with SAPD Homicide. Do you have a moment to talk with me, sir?"

"Well, I was gonna spend the day clipping my nails and waiting on a bowel movement, but I guess I can spare a few minutes. Whatcha got?"

I couldn't help but smile. "Sir, I'm looking into the hit-and-run case that took the life of Officer Robinson back in 1997. You were the lead detective on that one, weren't you?"

"That's right," he said. "Worked that case for nearly three years before I had to give it up. Why are you looking into it now?"

"Well, it's not the case itself, actually. It's the suspect you developed, Gary Harper. That name has come up in one of my other cases."

"Gary Harper is a made up name," he said.

"Yes sir, I know that. I read through your 2057s. You were thorough. I just can't figure out how anyone could buy a car without showing any ID or insurance or any of the rest of it. How did the owner of the dealership explain that?"

"He didn't have to," Fehrenbach said. "Things were different back then. Even if the dealership had been an upscale one, and believe me, this one wasn't, our suspect wouldn't have needed anything more than cash to buy that car. I was lucky to get what I did from the guy who owned the place."

"Was the place dirty?"

He laughed. "You mean were they crooked?"

"Yeah."

"No, not crooked. At least not in any sort of organized way. It was just a fly-by-night kind of place, you know? And my god, you should have seen the owner. He was so fat he looked like Jabba the Hutt. Every time I talked to him, he was wearing the same sweat-soaked clothes. And he had these two young guys who ran around the place and did everything for him. It was weird."

"Weird how?"

"Just, you know, creepy. They weren't related to him or anything, but they waited on him hand and foot. It was just creepy."

"I read that you went to some area high schools. Nothing came of that?"

"No," he said. "We even canvassed the neighborhood he disappeared into and came up with nothing. Of course, that area was out in the county back in those days, so for a lot of the searching we had to rely on County to do it."

"Do you think they might have missed something?"

"No," he said, but it came out slow. "I don't know. Maybe. There was a cop involved, so they were honor bound to be thorough."

"But you sound doubtful," I said.

"The County used to be the big deal around these parts. How long you been on?"

"Seventeen years, sir."

He grunted. "Well, you're probably too young to remember this, but when I first started, we didn't have any patrol sectors outside of Loop 410. The city was a lot smaller then, both geographically and in terms of resources. If we wanted anything, a helicopter, a dog team, we had to ask the County to let us use theirs. But by the time I'd promoted to detective, things had really started to change. The city was starting to grow, and annexing County land everywhere you looked. There was a lot of animosity on the County side, a lot of jealously. You know what I mean? For ten years we gobbled up everything they thought was theirs without so much as saying please, put a lot of their guys out of work. And then this mess happens and all of the sudden we come to them with our hats in our hands. You kind of see what the scene was like back then?"

"Yeah," I said.

"What it amounted to was that I didn't have full access to their records. They made me work for every piece of red tape I cut. Typical interagency crap."

"I can see that. You think there are any loose ends?"

He laughed again. "I'm sure of it."

That was what I wanted to hear. "Well, listen, would you like another crack at it? I've got the case file with me. Want to meet me for breakfast? Tommy's is still in business. We could meet there. Spread the case file out on the table. Get deep into it."

He didn't even hesitate. "Hell yeah, I'd love that. I can be there in about twenty minutes."

"Cool. See you there. You got my number from the caller ID, right?"

"Is this your cell?"

"Nobody uses a landline these days."

"Great," he said, with just the faintest note of sarcasm. "This ought to be fun."

"I hope so. Maybe the old dog can teach this new dog some tricks."

"Yeah, we'll see," he said.

* * *

Tommy's was a taco house about eight blocks south of the old Police Headquarters. Back when I first promoted to detective, it was one of the regular restaurants on our breakfast circuit. It serves good, old-fashioned Jalisco cuisine—menudo, picadillo, barbacoa, carne guisada—all the basics. There were times in my early days as a detective when you'd walk into the place and it'd be jam packed, but there'd only be a handful of people in the place who weren't cops. Auto Theft would take up one table, Arson another, the Bexar County Sheriff's Office Command Staff still another. Homicide, Narcotics, Financial Crimes, Robbery: you'd see them all there. We used to joke that if someone dropped a bomb on Tommy's during breakfast, they could wipe out nearly every detective in San Antonio.

But then, when Police Headquarters moved to the new building in 2012, a few of the old taco houses fell out of the rotation, Tommy's being one of them. I knew a detective from back in Fehrenbach's day would remember it well, though.

I also figured there was little chance of running into my fellow detectives from Homicide. Joining a retiree for breakfast was an easy explanation. Spreading a seventeen-year-old case file on the breakfast table was tougher to justify.

So I pulled into the parking lot next to Tommy's and waited for Fehrenbach to show up.

An hour went by, and he never showed.

Curious, I called his number.

He answered on the third ring.

"Lieutenant Fehrenbach?" I said. "Sir, this is Detective Becker. We spoke just a little bit ago."

"Oh," he said. He sounded distant and preoccupied, like he wasn't all there. "I'm sorry, I can't...I gotta go."

"Wait," I said. "Lieutenant, wait, sir. Please."

"No, I—" He broke off with a gasp of surprise.

"Sir, are you okay? Lieutenant Fehrenbach...sir?"

But he hung up on me.

The phone clicked to let me know the connection was lost, but I stayed there holding it to my ear for a long time, wondering what in the hell was going on.

I didn't like the way he'd gasped before he hung up.

Something was wrong. I knew it. I could sense it. I don't know how, but in that moment I knew it.

Fehrenbach didn't live far away. His house was a small blue and white one story off Martin Street, just west of downtown. There was a blue GMC pickup in the driveway that looked about two years old. The yard and garden were well tended, and the chain link fence that surrounded the front yard had a latched gate that was hanging open.

I scanned the front of the house. There were several windows and the blinds were drawn on most of them. I could see inside the house, but nothing seemed to move.

"Hello?" I called out.

Nothing.

Frowning, I went up to the house and climbed the steps to the porch. I peered into the windows and saw somebody moving in there in the shadows toward the back of the house. I knocked hard on the door.

"Lieutenant Fehrenbach," I yelled. "You in there?"

Again, no answer.

I looked at the window, and the shape I saw toward the back of the house suddenly became two.

Somebody was in there with him.

It was a man in a dark suit, and there was something weird about his head. It was too big, and strangely shaped. I saw Fehrenbach staggering away from the figure, his hands up in front of his face like he was ready to fight. Or perhaps fend off a blow.

"Hey!" I yelled.

The man looked up, and in that instant, I froze. He had huge, bat-like ears and an elongated face that tapered into a snout. It looked like he was wearing a pig mask or something.

"What the hell?" I said.

But he was already running out the back door. I heard a screen door screech open on rusted springs and then slam shut. I pulled my gun and ran around the back of the house. It only took me a few seconds to get to the back yard, but the man in the mask was already slipping over the six-foot wooden privacy fence that separated Fehrenbach's back yard from an overgrown service alley.

I tried to follow, but the alley was thick with a tangled screen of huisache and briars. The thorns cut up my hands after only a few steps. They didn't seem to bother the man in the pig mask though. He was already well ahead of me, and increasing the distance with every passing second.

I gave up and went back to Fehrenbach's house.

The back door was closed and locked.

I knocked on the doorframe. "Hey, Lieutenant Fehrenbach, it's me, Alan Becker. Are you alright, sir?"

No answer.

I beat on the door with my fists. "Lieutenant Fehrenbach? Sir, open the door. I'm gonna kick it down!"

"Don't," he said. It sounded like he was standing just on the other side of the door. His voice was faint, but I could hear the strain in it. He peeked through the curtains next to the door, met my gaze, and then let the curtains drop. "Go away," he said. "I can't help you."

"Who was that guy?"

"Just go away."

"Did he hurt you?"

"No, I'm fine. Go away, Detective. I told you, I won't help you."

"What are you talking about?" I said. "Less than two hours ago, you were excited to talk to me about the case. What's going on?"

"I can't talk to you."

"Can't or won't?"

"Go away," he said.

"Did they threaten you? That man, if he threatened you, I can put him away. Tell me what's going on. What did that man say to you?"

"This isn't a case anymore, Detective. There's nothing for you to investigate."

"Bullshit," I said. "Somebody got to you. Tell me who the hell that was."

No answer.

"Lieutenant Fehrenbach, I need you to help me. I can't do this without your help."

"There's nothing to do," he said. "There's no case. Gary Harper doesn't exist."

I hit the door again, but all my strength was gone. The best I could do was a dull slap against the wood.

I leaned my forehead against the door.

"Talk to me, Fehrenbach. Why won't you help me?"

"You don't have the first clue what this is really about," he said, and from the sound of his voice I guessed he was leaning against the other side of the door, head against the wood, same as me. "Maybe Hell is real. Did you ever think of that, Detective Becker?"

"What are you talking about? You're not making any sense."

When he didn't answer, I beat on the door again.

"Open up, Fehrenbach! You hear me? Somebody got to you. I want to know who. Open the door. Talk to me, dammit!"

I reared back to kick the door, but before I could, Fehrenbach threw it open and leveled a pistol at my face.

"Whoa!" I said. I backed up, my hands in the air.

His face was pale as ash. His eyes were wide and wild. I looked into the barrel of the gun. His hands were trembling and his finger pulsed against the trigger. Runners of sweat dripped from his brow.

I kept backing up until I was in the grass.

"What's going on, Fehrenbach? What happened? Who was that guy?"

He raised his chin and shook his head in warning. He was breathing hard through clenched teeth.

"You get out of here," he said. "Don't ever, ever, come back here. You leave me alone."

"I'm looking for answers," I said. "Why won't—"

He jabbed the air with his pistol and that shut me up straight away.

"Easy," I said. "Just talk—"

"I won't tell you again. You leave me alone. Get out of here!"

I didn't like the way his eyes were bulging from the sockets, or the way his finger kept tightening on the trigger. "Yeah, okay," I said. "I'm leaving."

He watched me as I rounded the side of his house and headed up his driveway, the pistol still leveled at my back.

I felt like a coward walking away.

Someone had gotten to him. Someone had scared him so badly he was willing to pull a gun on a brother officer.

I looked back. He was still standing next to his garage. He'd lowered the weapon to his thigh, though. His eyes had lost their wild stare, and the color was coming back to his face, but he still looked small, shrunken by fear. Fehrenbach shook his head and raised the gun a few inches.

"Just leave," he said. "And don't come back here."

* * *

As I pulled away from Fehrenbach's house, it occurred to me that I hadn't seen any other cars when I pulled up. The man in the pig mask had escaped into the alley, but where had he come from? Had there been a car waiting for him, and if so, where was it? It wasn't like he could have counted on me being there to drive him into the alley, not dressed in that black undertaker's suit of his, so it didn't make sense that his car would be parked anywhere but in front of his house.

It made me wonder if he was still around.

I rounded the corner at the end of Fehrenbach's street and parked near the entrance to the alleyway. I pulled up to the curb and watched it for a few minutes, trying to figure out the man's next move.

It was late April, but summer had already come in hard and mean. According to the thermometer on my dashboard, it was ninety-two degrees, and I was willing to bet my drinking money that the guy in the pig mask wasn't going to be running around in this heat in a suit. Or a mask for that matter. And besides, this wasn't exactly a suit kind of neighborhood. He'd stand out for sure, and a pro would be smart enough not to draw attention to himself.

So he was in a car by now. That much I could be sure of.

It also seemed logical that he'd still be in the area. After all, I'd interrupted whatever it was he was doing to Fehrenbach.

It made sense that he'd come back if he could.

I circled the block around Fehrenbach's house, then went one street west and circled that one. My plan was to make a series of widening circles around Fehrenbach's house and look for a car that didn't belong.

Unfortunately, they found me first.

I had just made another right turn when I heard an engine roaring behind me. I glanced in the rearview mirror just as a big black Chrysler that looked like something straight out of 1966 smashed into the back of my Honda and pushed me toward a line of parked cars.

The wheel shook in my hands and I felt the back end of the car start to drift. My instinct was to mash down on the brakes, but I knew from my tactical driving training back in the Academy that hitting the brakes would allow the Chrysler's momentum to take over and put me into a spin. And if these guys were half the pros I thought them to be, they'd pin me against the parked cars, climb out, and shoot me like a fish in a barrel.

I wasn't about to let that happen.

I put my foot down on the gas. My Honda revved, shuttered, and broke free of the Chrysler. I yanked the wheel to the left and missed the line of parked cars by inches. I sped up, ran the stop sign at the next intersection, and kept going, bottoming out the car and kicking up a cloud of leaves and dust as I lengthened the distance between us. So long, Pig Face, I thought. And then I looked in the rearview mirror. They were gaining on me, the front of their car looking like a mouth full of teeth rising from the depths.

"Shit," I said. I hit the brakes and turned hard to the right, cutting down a side street.

The Chrysler skidded through the intersection, backed up, and came after me again. It wasn't going to work. I could see that. The Chrysler handled like a boat, but they wouldn't have any trouble catching me on the straightaways. My Honda just didn't have the legs their car did. I needed to get to a busy street where I could get lost in the crowd. And even if I couldn't lose them, I could at least attract the attention of a patrol car. The end result would be the same.

But I had to get there first, and that was going to be a problem. The nearest major street was Zarzamora, and that was a good ten blocks to the west. I'd have to risk a straight shot to get there.

I made a few quick turns, enough to put some distance between us, and then turned my car west and floored it.

My lead fell apart fast though.

A van crossed in front of me at an intersection and I had to lock up the brakes to avoid smashing into it.

The bug-eyed look on the driver's face would have been funny if the roar of the Chrysler's engine hadn't suddenly filled my world. I tried to speed up, but they were already coming up alongside me on the passenger side. The narrow suburban streets didn't leave much room to maneuver. Their car was twice the size of mine, and they used that advantage to force me to the left. There were parked cars up ahead, and I had to do something before they made me crash.

I rolled down the passenger window and pulled my pistol.

Their driver's window came down at the same time, and I got a good look at the driver with the pig's head and I thought, Oh dear god, that isn't a mask. I lost focus when I realized what I was looking at. I nearly dropped the gun. My Honda started to drift to the left. The man, pig, whatever it was, flared its nostrils, opened its mouth wide enough to reveal a pair of short tusks, and then rammed the Chrysler into mine.

That woke me up. I slammed on the brakes and slid into a trashcan, but managed to miss a parked car.

The Chrysler skidded to a stop in the middle of the road.

In that moment my training took over. I threw my car in park and jumped out. If I could get on them before they had a chance to exit the vehicle, I had a chance of beating them. I pulled my weapon, trained it on the driver's side window, and started firing as I advanced on the car. Shooting a pistol while running with any accuracy at all is next to impossible. They train us at the Academy to do it at a walk. Slow yourself down, focus on the target. Be relentless, but be accurate. Nobody ever won a gunfight by missing what they were aiming at. I landed five or six hits before I heard a shriek that didn't sound like any kind of noise a man would make, and the next instant the Chrysler peeled out and shot down the road, leaving me standing in the middle of the street.

I lowered my weapon.

Score one for the good guys, I thought.

Only then did I turn my attention to my surroundings. People were looking at me from their doors and windows. More than a few of them were on the phone, calling the cops no doubt.

I've been a member of the San Antonio Police Department's Officer-Involved Shooting Team for five years. From past experience I knew how this scene would play out if I stayed around for the cops to show up, and I wasn't about to allow myself to go through all that right now. There was no way I could explain it anyway.

So I got in my car and hauled ass out of there. As I drove away, I heard the wail of approaching sirens.

* * *

I drove until I couldn't hear the sirens anymore. I spotted a McDonald's and pulled into the parking lot, feeling like I was about to come unhinged. I think if I'd driven any longer I would have completely lost my mind and caused an accident. As it was I put the car in park and stared down at my lap, unable to catch my breath.

That wasn't a mask.

How was that even possible?

I looked at Fehrenbach's case file on the passenger seat and thought of what Robinson had said about others looking for Gary Harper, others who wouldn't concern themselves with issues of legality.

I'd thought he'd simply meant there were violent men on Harper's trail.

But they weren't men at all.

Oh dear god, that wasn't a mask.

I sank low into my seat and ran my hands through my hair.

What in the world had I gotten myself into?

* * *

Fehrenbach's file.

I'd been sitting behind the wheel, watching the traffic pass by on the street for I don't know how long when I realized I'd referred to the file as Fehrenbach's, not Robinson's.

It's funny how the mind works. I'd been so focused on getting Fehrenbach to tell me what he knew that I'd completely disregarded what he'd already said. When I asked him about loose ends, he'd said he was sure there were plenty. And he'd also mentioned that there'd been more than a little jurisdictional cock blocking going on. That was nothing new. I'd experienced it before, especially when dealing with the Texas Highway Patrol and the Texas Rangers. But the San Antonio Police Department and the Bexar County Sheriff's Office had long since gotten over their differences, and getting information from them was a piece of cake these days. In fact, I had direct links to their local databases saved in my favorites.

I went to the downtown branch of the public library, found a computer, and signed on to my Citrix account. Once I had that up, I had all the County's criminal records at my fingertips.

I searched for the license plate of the car that had killed Officer Robinson and hit pay dirt right away. On the same day the car was purchased from the fat man Fehrenbach told me about—and two days before it was involved in the crash that took Officer Robinson's life—a seventeen-year-old kid named Thomas Brandt was issued a ticket in it for Excessive Display of Acceleration.

Apparently the Precinct Two Justice of the Peace dismissed the ticket two months later, without explanation, but that was no matter.

I had a name now, a real name, something I could work with.

Thomas Brandt, white male, thirty-four years old, five-ten and a hundred eighty pounds, it turned out, was no stranger to the police. Aside from the dismissed ticket back when he was seventeen, he'd racked up four DWIs and eleven arrests for driving with a suspended license. He even had a warrant outstanding for his latest DWI, and as it was his fourth, and therefore a felony, I had legal authorization to kick in his door if need be.

And as I sincerely hoped there was going to be a need, I printed up the warrant and slipped it into the case file.

I was close. So close my palms were sweating.

Thomas Brandt was about to be mine.

* * *

He lived in a subdivision called The Hills at Sonora Parkway. I didn't see any hills. Just a bunch of low-budget homes that had seen better days.

Brandt's home was a squat one-story with blue paint and sagging gutters. The yard was cut and the hedges trimmed, but the house still had a look of quiet desperation about it, like it was two steps from falling in on itself.

I studied the house from my car, looking for signs of movement.

Nothing. It was quiet, no lights on in the windows.

I folded the warrant and put it in my shirt pocket. Then I went to the trunk and got my radio. Last thing I needed was for a neighbor to call me in as a burglar. At least this way I could answer up if the dispatcher put a call out at my location.

I drew my weapon and tried the front door. It was locked so I kicked it in.

"Police!" I yelled as I entered the home.

I went from room to room, clearing the house quickly and systematically, the way I'd been trained.

Brandt wasn't home.

Everything was neatly arranged, the beds made, the magazines stacked, fresh bars of soap by the sinks, and yet there was a worn-out dinginess to the place that was unmistakable. A subtle, baked in funk hung in the air. It wasn't a bad smell, not like a dead body or anything like that, just a lived-in and hadn't-been-cleaned-in-a-long-while funk. Brandt was keeping up appearances, but I could tell he wasn't far from falling down. I could tell because his house looked a lot like mine.

Once I cleared the house, I holstered my weapon and started looking around, trying to get a bead on what kind of man Brandt was. There were pictures on the wall that looked like they'd been there since he was in high school. I saw a few large framed photos of a nondescript, middle-aged couple, a few of Brandt as a younger man, but nothing recent. Brandt had probably been raised in this home, I figured, and probably inherited it from his parents. But he'd done nothing to make it his own. The little porcelain figurines in the curio cabinets looked like the treasures of a housewife. So too did the Bible verses framed on the walls and the quilted blanket on the edge of the couch. I got the feeling the house hadn't changed much since the late '90s.

I was walking through the master bedroom when I realized something was wrong. I couldn't tell what it was at first, but I had a feeling I was missing something important. I remember once, back in my street cop days, I pulled over this beat-to-hell pickup for rolling through a stop sign. I got up to the driver's side window and saw this skuzzy-looking white guy in his early forties behind the wheel, trash all over the floorboards, the ash tray overflowing with crushed cigarettes, and a cute-looking Hispanic girl just a hair passed eighteen sitting in the passenger seat beside him. The girl was nicely dressed in a tartan skirt and white blouse, expensive-looking jewelry around her neck and on her fingers, well-cared for by somebody. And she looked so scared. I swear to God I saw her shaking. The picture didn't add up.

I got the guy's driver's license, ran it, and he came back as a registered sex offender, out on parole for aggravated sexual assault of a minor. The girl was eighteen, but she didn't look it.

My first thought was *Oh crap, that girl's about to get raped and left for dead in a ditch someplace.*

I went up to the truck and told the guy to get out.

He said, "What for?"

I said, "Because I fuckin' told you to. Now get your butt out of the truck before I yank you out by your teeth."

I searched him, cuffed him, and stuffed him into the backseat of my patrol car. After that, I went up to the girl. I got her out and we stepped around to the front of the truck. I positioned her so the cab of the truck was blocking the guy's line of sight, and I asked her the guy's name. She didn't know it. I asked her how she knew him. She didn't answer. I asked her if she was okay. Is this guy taking you somewhere you don't want to go?

"If he's up to something, tell me. I will help you. I won't let him hurt you."

The girl didn't answer me. She was looking at the shine on the toes of my boots, at the dirt on the ground, everywhere but at my eyes.

"If you need help," I told her, "this is your chance. Tell me what's going on, and I'll help you. I can have another officer come by here. He can take you home, or to a friend's house. Anywhere you want to go."

When the girl answered, her voice was so quiet I had to lean in to hear.

"I just want to leave," she said. "Please don't bother us."

I said something else, but she turned away and climbed back into the truck. I couldn't believe it. I just stood there, staring at her profile through the passenger window, the girl wringing her hands in her lap, her black, shampoo commercial hair falling around her face.

But I had no choice in the matter. There was nothing I could use to justify arresting this guy beyond the voice inside my head that kept yelling she was a lamb headed for the slaughter. But she was eighteen, free to do as she liked, and I had no probable cause to make an arrest for anything. No leg to stand on.

To this day I think about that traffic stop and I have a sick feeling in my gut that I missed something important that day. I didn't do something that I might have done. I just know it.

And I had that same feeling standing in the bathroom of Brandt's master bedroom. Something was wrong, and I wasn't seeing what it was.

"Think," I told myself. "What are you missing?"

I couldn't figure it out until I got to the kitchen. The counters had been wiped clean and there were no dishes in the sink, a fresh garbage bag in the empty trash can. The whole place had the feel of finality about it, like it had been packed up and organized in preparation for something.

And then I saw the paperwork on his kitchen table. He'd laid out his driver's license, Social Security card, homeowner's insurance, his last two tax returns, and bank account statements in an orderly, fanned out pile. It reminded me of the way Officer Robinson had organized the contents of my wallet on the hood of his car. The whole thing was meticulously arranged.

Next to the paperwork was a plastic grocery bag full of prescription pill bottles. I took a few of them out. They were for high blood pressure and depression, plus a few pain pills. Nothing major though. No hepatitis or cancer drugs, nothing like that.

It's a myth that all suicides leave a note. Some do, but definitely not all of them. Quite a few, in fact, leave absolutely no clue as to why they've decided to end their lives.

But I'd seen this before. This was Brandt's version of a suicide note, laying out the details of his life and making it easier for whoever would come along to do the paperwork on his death.

I picked up his driver's license and studied his picture. He was thirty-four, skinny, almost no chin and a caterpillar-looking thing that was supposed to be a moustache on his upper lip. He had short, blond hair and his eyes were wide, making it look like he was frightened of something.

Thomas Brandt was going to kill himself, I thought.

The realization didn't rouse any pity in me though. More like irritation. How was I supposed to find this guy before he carried it out? Most suicides, and I mean the ones who actually intend to do it and aren't just making a lot of drama to get attention, find someplace where they can take their last breath without interruption. He lived alone. I would have thought he'd go into a back bedroom and hang himself or something. Maybe take a crap load of the painkillers he'd so carefully stocked in the bag and wash them down with a gallon of booze. Go out easy.

I frowned down at the pile, wondering what thread to pick up next. I tossed Brandt's license down on the stack and was about to go looking through the house for more clues when my eye caught a sales receipt next to his tax returns.

It was for the Bellum Salvage Company. Back when I first promoted into Homicide, I was put on the Gun Detail. My job was to go through the Property Room Gun Files once a month to see what guns needed to be pulled out of evidence and destroyed, which usually meant weapons used in a crime where the incident had been adjudicated. Obviously, we weren't going to give a weapon back to a convicted felon, and the Department didn't want to burden itself with becoming a gun dealer, so once a month I'd go to the Property Room and load up the bed of a pickup with guns and drive them over to the Bellum Salvage Company. From there we put the guns into the backseat of a junked car that was then fed into a compactor that smashed and formed the vehicle into something about the size and shape of a bale of hay.

But Bellum generally only worked with commercial clients.

What was Brandt doing with one of their receipts?

I fished it out of the pile, and what I saw there made the bile rise in my throat. Thomas Brandt had paid $800 to have a wrecked Ford pickup, red in color, crushed and disposed of almost exactly a year ago. My face grew hot. My breaths whistled in my nostrils. I balled my hands into fists so tightly they'd gone numb.

Witnesses to the crash that killed my wife and children managed to get a fairly decent vehicle description. A red Ford pickup, later model, with one of those cartoons of Calvin pissing on a Chevy emblem on the back windshield and a partial Texas plate that started with either BR or BK. The witnesses couldn't agree on the plate, and nobody got the full number.

Thomas Brandt had paid to have a red Ford pickup destroyed just two days after the crash that killed my family, and the license plate recorded on the sales slip was BR6D31.

I remembered what Officer Robinson had said about Limbus having a knack for picking the right person to do the job at hand, and the realization that the man I was hunting was the same man who had killed my family was like a red cloud settling over my mind, blocking out everything but hate and rage.

"You fucking bastard," I said. "You goddamn lowlife little fuck."

I let the receipt fall to the table.

"You killed my family."

I beat my fists on the table. I wanted to put my hands on Thomas Brandt's neck and strangle the life out of the little bastard.

I wanted him dead. By my bare hands.

In the silence of that house, my rage seething inside me, my police radio suddenly seemed very loud.

"Seventy-two Fifty and Seventy-two Sixty, and I need you guys to make Grissom and Spencer for an MV-Ped. I've got EMS already on scene and a possible ten-sixty."

An MV-Ped was a motor vehicle-pedestrian accident. A ten-sixty a dead on arrival. The kind of calls patrolman dread getting.

But then I thought of the location she'd put out. Grissom and Spencer. Grissom was the road that ran along the southern edge of Brandt's neighborhood, and Spencer the cross street where Brandt had crashed into and killed Officer Robinson. The bastard was going back to the scene of the first fatality crash he'd been in to commit suicide. I could just picture it, that bitter little drunk walking into traffic. He probably even thought he was offering his death up as some sort of penance, like maybe that crazed act would somehow wash away all his sins.

I shook my head, the rage pulsing through me harder than ever.

That was not going to happen.

Thomas Brandt was not going to die thinking he'd made it all better, because he hadn't.

He could never make it all better.

* * *

I got in my car and I drove to Grissom and Spencer as fast as my little Honda would carry me.

The intersection was a circus of red and blue lights. Cars were parked along the road and people were standing next to their vehicles, watching what was going on. Firefighters and paramedics were standing around a white Honda minivan that had crashed into a row of cars. The woman who had been driving it was holding a crying baby in her arms as she sat on the curb, rocking back and forth in shock.

"He came out of nowhere," she kept saying. "I couldn't stop."

The EMS guys were loading a gurney into the back of their wagon. I ran over to them and caught a glimpse of Thomas Brandt's bloody face as he disappeared into the ambulance.

"Whoa!" one of the paramedics said, putting his palm up to my chest. "Hold up there, buddy."

"It's alright," I said. "I'm SAPD. Is that Thomas Brandt you got there?"

"No clue. We didn't find any ID."

"That's him," I said. "We've been looking for him."

"Was he running? That woman over there said he just walked right into the middle of traffic."

"We weren't chasing him," I said. "Where are you taking him?"

"University, it looks like."

"Is this life-threatening?"

The EMT glanced back at Brandt. "Nah, he's gonna be fine. Just some cuts and bruises, maybe a broken wrist."

"Okay," I said, struggling desperately to keep myself from jumping into the ambulance and finishing what the minivan had started. "Thanks," I said. "I'll probably see you guys at the hospital."

The EMT shrugged and closed the door.

But as I made my way back to my car, I knew Thomas Brandt was not going to be all right. He had a reckoning ahead of him, and I was going to see to it that he faced it.

* * *

The ambulance ran lights and sirens down to University Hospital, but it wasn't hard to follow them. Firefighters and cops have different takes on what it means to run code. Firefighters stick to the ten miles an hour over the speed limit rule. Cops, not so much. Staying with them wasn't hard.

But once we got to the hospital I had to hang back.

I had a gun and badge on my hip, so nobody bothered to stop me. Cops are pretty common in emergency rooms. But I couldn't get in the way. I had to watch, my rage barely contained, as the nurses check him over and tended to his hurts.

But finally they left him alone.

The nurse stepped out and pulled the curtain closed behind him. The trauma room was crowded, with nurses and doctors running every which way, but nobody was paying me any mind. Hospitals are designed to deal with crises, matters of life and death hanging in the balance, and so minor injuries get a quick fix and little more. Some bandages, some pain killers, and out the door—and out of mind—you go. As a plain-clothes detective, I was just part of the woodwork. They walked right by me. Nobody even bothered to give me a double take as I slipped through the opaque plastic curtains to talk with a man with minor injuries.

He was bare chested, wearing only jeans and boots, a few bandages on his right arm. His shirt was in a pile on the chair next to his bed. His face was red and puffy, like he'd been crying, and his blond hair was damp with sweat and sticking up all over the place.

He grunted when he saw me. "Who are you?"

I grabbed his wrist and held it up so I could see the ID bracelet they'd put on him.

"This says John Doe," I said. "Your name is Thomas Brandt."

His eyes went wide with alarm, but he said nothing.

"On August 17, 1997, you T-boned a police car and killed a policeman."

Brandt swallowed hard. I saw his Adam's apple work up and down like he was trying to force himself to breathe.

He tried to pull his hand away from me, but I held him fast.

"Sixteen years later you crashed into an SUV and killed a woman and her two children."

I was seething inside, but my voice was flat. I squeezed his wrist tighter.

Horror spread across his face. "Who are you?"

"You know what you've done? Your entire life has been about causing hurt and misery. You miserable little sack of shit. You think you can kill yourself and make it all better? Because you can't. You have caused more pain than your life can ever make up for."

"Oh my God," he said and rolled off the bed. He yanked his arm out of my grasp and staggered backward. "You're one of those pig men."

He fell into the plastic curtain and pulled it to the floor.

Nurses and doctors stopped what they were doing and stared at us. But all my attention was on Thomas Brandt.

He climbed to his feet and backed away from me, his eyes wild with panic and fear. "You're one of those pig men." He looked wildly around the emergency room, pointing at me. "Pig man! He's a pig man!"

All around the room people were staring at him, and then at me. Brandt grabbed one of the nurses by her collar and pointed at me.

"Don't let him get me. You see what he is?"

The woman pushed him away, and he backed into the hall.

I followed after him.

Brandt ran down the hall, raving the entire way, and charged through the doors that led to the stairwell. I broke into a run and reached the doors just as he was rounding the landing below.

"Brandt, stop!"

He screamed and ran faster.

I charged down the stairs. I felt intensely focused. The rage that had burned so hotly within me as I went through Brandt's belongings back at his house had narrowed to a fine and deadly point. My whole body was humming with electricity and it seemed the rest of the world lensed out of focus. Brandt was the only thing that mattered. Putting my hands around his throat and choking his life away was the only thing that mattered.

I heard him skid to a stop two floors below me.

He let out a scream.

I was on him a moment later. But he wasn't looking at me. His eyes had gone wide again and he was backing away from a side corridor.

"Leave me alone," he pleaded. "Please."

I heard a hammering sound coming from the corridor to my right and I spun around toward it. Halfway down the hall, one of those pig men stood over a body on a slab, hacking away at it with a cleaver. He wore a black suit covered with a blood-spattered butcher's apron.

He locked eyes on me and slammed the cleaver into the slab, then started toward me, taking off his apron as he came.

Brandt was running downstairs again, screaming like a lunatic.

I drew my pistol and leveled it at the creature.

"He's mine," I said through clenched teeth. "You can't have him."

The creature stopped, its hands opening and closing in a gesture that might have been frustration.

"Stay back," I said.

Below me I could hear Brandt throwing open a set of doors. I turned and went after him. At the bottom of the stairs a doorway opened to the basement. Greenish overhead lights sparked and sizzled and mechanical generators and water pumps snapped and bumped with a deafening noise.

Brandt was standing in the middle of the room in a pool of green light with nowhere left to run.

He turned to face me, tears streaming down his face.

"Leave me alone!" he shouted. "Go away!"

Rage washed over me again and I charged him. I flew into him, driving my shoulder into his chest and sending him sprawling across the floor.

I didn't give him a chance to get up.

I got on top of him, my knees on his chest, and brought the butt of my gun down as hard as I could on the bridge of his nose. His screaming broke off clean. Blood erupted from the wound. The sight of all that blood silenced my rage for just a moment, long enough for me to holster my weapon. But when I looked Brandt in the eyes again, all I saw was a red haze covering the entire world. With every fiber of being I hated that man. I wanted him dead, and though he raised his hands to try to ward off the blows, he was powerless to stop me. Blood spattered across the floor, on the ceiling, on my clothes. Gouts of it splashed across my face, and still I couldn't stop. I hit him over and over again. Over and over.

But as I continued to rain punches down on his pulverized face, I heard somebody call my name.

Gradually, the red haze bled away and my vision cleared.

Only then did I see what I'd done.

Brandt was a ruined mess. Bubbles popped on the surface of the blood pooling in his mouth. It looked like he was still breathing, but he wasn't moving.

I turned his face to one side so the blood could drain out without choking him. I wanted him dead, but I wasn't ready to let him die.

"Alan."

I glanced over my shoulder. Officer Robinson was standing there, watching me.

"What are you doing here?"

"You found him. The job's finished."

"It's not finished." My chest was heaving. My knuckles were beginning to burn where I'd torn them up on his teeth. "He killed my family."

"That's right, he did. And me too."

I looked down at Brandt. His eyes were swollen shut and he was missing teeth.

I let him drop to the floor.

Seeing him now, a bloody wreck, my rage drained away. I didn't feel anger, or pity, or remorse. I felt nothing but disgust for him now. I got to my feet and turned on Robinson. "He said I was one of those pig men. I'm not...one of them...am I?"

"Always with the interesting questions."

"Tell me, dammit."

"Okay. To him, yeah, you are."

"But only to him?"

"Maybe to others."

I thought about Fehrenbach and how frightened he'd been. "You mean like Fehrenbach?"

Robinson nodded.

"Why?"

"Some people, when their minds are clouded by guilt, see only devils when they're standing on death's door. Others, those whose minds are at peace, see angels in the architecture."

"But I saw them too. Is that what they were, demons?"

He nodded again.

"And the fact that I saw them means what? That I had been at death's door?" I felt like I was going to be sick. "Oh God."

"Do you still see them?" he asked.

"Huh?" I looked around the basement. "No," I said.

"So, what's changed?"

I started to speak, but stopped short. There was no way I could answer his question. The feelings were too raw, the problem still too big to see.

I glanced back at Brandt. He was coughing blood on the floor.

"You said if I found anything illegal I could make whatever arrests I wanted."

"That's right," he said. "You can even use my cuffs."

"I have my own."

"Suit yourself."

Brandt groaned. I flipped him over and cuffed his hands behind his back. Then I helped him sit up against a metal shelf.

Then I turned my attention back to Robinson.

"So it was all for this? This was the job?"

"Yes."

"What good happened here?"

"You solved four murders."

"Bullshit," I said. "You did this. You set all this up. Why did you hire me? Why go to all this trouble?"

He laughed, but not to be mean. His expression was actually one of honest pity and sympathy, but this time, I didn't hate him for it. I just felt lost, sick and confused.

"You still don't understand," he said. "I didn't hire you. Limbus didn't hire you. We are an employment agency. We match the right job with the right person, but we don't come up with the job. The client does that."

I was even more confused now. "The client?"

He gestured with a nod at something behind me.

I turned, and felt a fist squeeze around my heart. I gasped and nearly fell to the floor.

Over by the stairs, halfway across the basement, holding my two children by the hand, was my wife. The air seemed to vibrate and hum like it was alive with electricity, and suddenly, I was drifting. I was moving through space. All around me were images of my life. They came in a flood, and not in any sort of order. Andrew on his bike as he took his first solo turn down the sidewalk. Me holding Sheryl's hand as Nicole came into the world. Sheryl screaming in delight on a roller coaster. Her screams turning to terror as a red pickup spun out of control and smashed into her car door. Andrew lowering his chin to the table to watch a goldfish swimming in a bowl of water. Nicole at four years old singing to herself as she cut snowmen out of construction paper. Sheryl in my arms as we slow danced in the living room, an empty bottle of wine on the coffee table. Her brown hair spreading over a white pillow as she settled into the softness of it with a sigh and said, "Are you happy?"

And then the images faded. The sense of flying was gone. I was left with my chest so full of love and joy and loneliness and pain that I thought for sure I'd burst open. I wanted to explode. I wanted to let it all go. But it was in me, and I couldn't get it out.

In answer to her question lingering behind the visions, I could only answer, "I was, then. Now it's all hurt."

Sheryl was still standing at the foot of the stairs. Nicole and Andrew were smiling at me. The hand that held my heart in its grip refused to let go. I could barely breathe, but even still, I moved toward them.

A gentle hand fell on my shoulder. "Alan, no."

I turned and saw Robinson looking at me sadly, shaking his head.

"But…"

"You can't," he said. "It's not possible."

"Bullshit. Let me go."

He held me with a grip I couldn't break.

"You can't go with them. It's not your time."

"But I want it to be. I can't go on like this. I'll put a bullet in my head right now if I can go with them."

"Do you really think she'd want that? Do you really believe she did this for that? You *can* go on, Alan. It'll be hard, but you can. She understood that. She did this—all of this—for you. So you would understand."

I nearly fell over. Robinson caught me and held me up until I could find my legs again. I looked from Sheryl back to Robinson. I thought about Nicole's picture, the one of the globe with the belt of stars, and it somehow seemed like a loophole to me, a fault in the logic that kept me from them.

"Where did the picture come from?" I asked.

"She did that," he said, nodding towards my wife. "Put it there when you needed something to keep you going."

"Has she been watching me?"

"We're never far from the ones we love, Alan."

Sheryl smiled at me. In that smile I saw our life together, and it was glorious. I had loved her so completely that her absence nearly killed me. It wasn't until that moment that I realized just how close to death I had come. Robinson had said I just might save a life. I had no idea he was talking about my own.

Behind Sheryl and the kids, the stairs filled with sunlight. The light pouring down was so bright I had to shield my eyes. For a moment, Sheryl and the kids were silhouettes against its brilliance, and then the light overwhelmed my vision and everything turned white.

When my eyes cleared, Sheryl and the kids were gone.

"No," I said. "Please, God, no."

I turned around, expecting to see at least Officer Robinson standing there, but he was gone too. Only Thomas Brandt remained.

He was the last piece of the puzzle in my hand, the last thing left for me to understand.

I went to him, and I lifted him to his feet. He was punch drunk, and a heavy weight to navigate, but he came along willingly enough. I led him toward the stairs, and toward justice, but in my mind I was thinking about what Robinson had said.

Limbus doesn't always pay in cash, but they always pay very well.

Third Interlude: Beyond the Veil

Conrad didn't wait for the story to melt into random symbols before he was on the net, looking for answers. He started by searching for Limbus, and he actually laughed out loud when the results came back to him. He had thought it was just a story, a work of fiction, and now he was sure.

Limbus had been familiar from the beginning. Looking at the cover of the book by the same name, he knew why. He'd actually bought it, sometime in the year prior, but he'd never had the opportunity to read it. Life had intervened.

So there it was. He had stumbled into some sort of viral marketing campaign. Nothing more than that.

He could have left it there. Ignored the gaping holes in that theory. Brushed away the logical inconsistencies. Finished his beer and gone to bed. He could have done that, and maybe he should have. But that wasn't the way he was wired.

He'd been the kind of person other people sometimes hated. He was the one who would explain—some would say ruin—all the magic tricks. He did not believe in suspension of disbelief. Plot holes were his bane. And when it came to Limbus, he couldn't just let it go. Whatever else could be said about it, hiding a viral campaign for a book this far down in the dark web where only he would find it made no sense. No sense at all.

He closed out his browser and once again launched TOR, the internet submersible that would take him down into the depths where he needed to go. Here the task became more difficult. There was no search engine in the deep, no cheerful cartoons to mark the occasion of the day and guide his way. None that worked, anyway. Just vast, unordered information to wade through.

He began trolling his ordinary haunts—TORchan, the Abyss, and of course, Iram. And in that mass of inane babbling and wild speculation, he was able to discern some truth. Most of the discussion was about the book. But there were the ones who said it was more than that.

"Flame me if you want," said one, "but Limbus is real. I've read the book, and it's not far from reality. A buddy of mine found one of their cards and went to see them. They told him they had the perfect job for him. He took it and I never saw him again."

The poster got his wish. He *was* flamed, mocked into silence. But he was not alone. There were others who claimed to have seen the mark of Limbus, heard its name echoing throughout the world's underground. Scrawled on bathroom walls, spray-painted across subway tunnel exits, written on paper that fluttered through bleak side-streets in the winter wind, printed on cheap business cards tacked to corkboard displays in darkened hallways. And always with the same question.

"How lucky do you feel?"

And it seemed those who answered that question weren't that lucky at all. Story after story spoke of disappearances, vanishings, of things unexplained and unnumbered. But of course, none were told first-hand. No one on the boards had actually seen these things or personally experienced them. None of them had dealt with Limbus. They had only heard the whispers, the warnings, and the twice-told tales.

The others cursed them. Called them fools and much worse, as the way of the dark net—and all the web it seemed—demanded. Some claimed they were liars. Others, agents of whatever publisher had decided to peddle these tales in the first place. Their protestations of truthfulness fell on deaf ears. The denizens of the dark web were willing to believe many things. But this particular conspiracy was not one of them.

But Conrad, he was beginning to believe. He was beginning to believe very much. And as the fire continued to crackle and pop, as the wind picked up outside and shook the panes of glass in their frames, he felt the ordered world he'd always known melt away.

He opened the impossible block of text again. He stared at it, wondered why it was there. He couldn't imagine why they had picked him, and he needed to know more. There was another question, one as simple as Conrad now felt it was pointless. Conrad knew the questions were only for him.

When it comes, no friend will take note of thy departure.
All that breathe will share thy destiny.
The gay will laugh,
When thou art gone,
the solemn brood of care plod on,
and each one as before will chase his favorite phantom.
While you descend…

The cursor blinked, the sentence waiting to be finished, to be completed. Conrad put his fingers to the keys and typed.

Into the grave.

The text flashed and reformed, and for an instant, Conrad saw the image of books piled one upon another. And then more words, more sentences, another story.

The Transmigration of Librarian Blaine Evans

By

Gary A. Braunbeck

... and now there were bodies scattered on the ground in front of him as a result of the panic firing but Evans kept up his pace across the compound's main yard, increased it even, because nothing slowed him, nothing tired him, nothing stopped him, not even the bullets strafing down at him from the security towers. There was less gunfire now than a minute ago, but that was only because they were getting ready to release the dogs. He'd expected that, and the gas too, only someone had gotten impatient and given the order to use the bombs too soon and the yard was now impenetrable with gas-clouds. Security guards were running this way and that, firing indiscriminately because they couldn't see a damned thing, and that was good, that was very good, because Evans always came prepared, he'd put on his CX-47 mask, and could breathe easily, and that was really, really good.

The sirens were getting louder, screaming like monsters, and that wasn't so good, not so good at all because it was giving him a headache, but then a guard came out of the smoke, plowing off shot after shot; a second guard fired off a round and accidentally caught the other right smack in the knee, pulping it, and the guard did a flip, landed hard, tried to crawl, and Evans smiled behind his gasmask because no one crawled too damned far with a kneecap gone, so he pulled the Colt Python from out of his shoulder holster and just to be a good sport about things blew the guard's head clean off his shoulders on the way past because, after all, what was the guy going to do with the rest of his life, having a knee all shot to hell like that?

He rounded the last corner of the main yard and headed toward the gate now visible through the haze of gas and smoke and gunfire, but now there was the outline of another guard, one stupid hero guard, armed, one stupid hero guard armed with one mother of a semiautomatic rifle, and Evans charged toward him with all he had and Mr. Hero got off a couple of shots, one pretty close, one grazing Evans's shoulder, but that didn't stop him. He kept charging forward until he was close enough to make a fist of his right hand, a club of his arm, and one swing later, the guard was out cold on the ground and Evans grabbed up the rifle and spun around, switching it from semi- to full-automatic, and with one squeeze of the trigger began to hose the yard behind him.

The scream of the sirens was nearly drowned out by those of the guards he was laying to their final rest on the hollow-points of bullets, and now things were good again, things were very good indeed, so Evans let fly with one last burst of gunfire and ran through the gate into the snow-covered street, running, running, running along the route he planned out months ago, running toward the frozen lake and the special box of supplies he'd planted there before breaking into the compound forty-seven minutes ago.

He could hear them spilling out of the gates behind him, firing their warning shots, the idiots, but underneath the crackle of gunfire was the snarl of the dogs, so Evans picked up his speed and flew around a corner of the lake road and lo and behold, thank'ya Jee-zus, here came a car straight toward him, and the driver saw what he was in for and hit the brakes and the car came to a shrieking, fishtailing halt in a cloud of snow and ice, but Evans didn't have time to be polite or even wait to see if the driver's side door was unlocked, so he just skidded up beside the car, blew out the window and most of the driver's skull with the last bullet from the Python, tossed the body out into the snow, slammed closed the door, ripped the car into drive, and took off in a straight line right through the middle of the guards, cutting through them like a machete through foliage, clipping a couple, fender slamming two of them, then he whipped the car around, skidding for all it was worth, but the driver had been a conscientious one, yessir, because the snow tires were good ones, giving Evans traction to spare, so it was easy for him to plow through the rest of this first wave of guards and dogs, flattening several of both like pancakes before flooring the accelerator and heading on down the lake road.

Six minutes later, he was deep in the woods surrounding the frozen lake, discarding his clothing and slipping into his specially modified wetsuit, inflating it, strapping on his air tank, checking the oxygen regulator, donning the underwater mask.

The boots Evans wore were specifically designed for ice divers who, rather than chance the force of changing currents, chose to walk upside-down below the ice. Five-inch spikes covered the soles of each boot. Nothing short of a bomb blast could loosen their hold once they were entrenched.

Evans activated the oxygen tank, put the regulator firmly into his mouth, swung the speargun strap around his chest, secured his quiver of spears to his person, and double-checked to make sure he had the disks he'd just stolen securely sealed in their protective case in his belt. His last pistol, a deadly Colt Anaconda .44 Magnum, was firmly held in a water-tight holster strapped to his thigh. There were those who would probably think Evans paranoid for taking a gun underwater with him, but years of experience and wounds had taught him to take nothing for granted.

He had a gallery of scars from the rare occasions he'd forgotten that rule.

Admittedly, he'd made a few slips the last couple of years, but nothing serious, nothing he'd told anyone about. Though he knew he might be getting too old for his particular line of work, he tried with all his still-considerable might to deny it.

Even to himself.

Especially to himself.

It was, perhaps, one of the few genuinely human foibles he possessed.

He checked his air-timer: Thirty minutes. More than enough time to get from here to the drying shed three-quarters of a mile down the lake.

He'd chosen this method for his getaway for several reasons, not the least of which was that he loved the peace that lay beneath the water. It would give him time to regroup after the violence at the compound—a form of psychological decompression that was necessary to keep himself in one solid mental piece.

Aside from the ethereal quiet he found beneath the ice, Evans had chosen this method of escape because many of the roads leading in and out of the area were too bombarded with snow and ice to be traveled by any vehicle besides a snowmobile, and a snowmobile would attract too much attention.

He lowered himself down into the hole in the ice he'd cut earlier, readied himself, then pushed back his legs as if readying for a somersault until he felt the spikes take hold.

A moment later, he was under the ice, walking across the lake upside-down.

Christ, he thought to himself. Five years ago, I was a goddamned librarian.

But that was before the Limbus Corporation had come into his life, albeit in a sideways manner....

* * *

It didn't occur to Blaine Evans that he might have a problem trusting happiness until his wife, Jennifer —a week before filing for a divorce—pointed out that his reactions to movies fell into one of two categories: unstoppably weepy or bitterly amused. "Haven't you ever noticed," she asked, "that movies with happy endings make you cry? *Field of Dreams, My Neighbor Totoro, The Sting, Pinocchio* for chrissakes, even *The Hills of Home*, that saccharine Lassie movie, all of them turn you to goddamn jelly! But then you watch something like *Midnight Cowboy, Seconds,* or *Taxi Driver* and you laugh—and don't get started on all those horror movies where everybody gets slaughtered by the last reel! I mean, it's not like you fall out of your seat guffawing or anything like that, usually it's just this series of short, scratchy chuckles that make me think you believe the characters got what they deserved, even if they didn't deserve it. Seriously, has that never crossed your mind?"

"Not really, no."

"Doesn't that worry you?"

A shrug. "I don't know why it should. They're just movies."

"It should bother you because I think it shows how you really feel about everything—me, the kids, your purpose and worth as a human being, the way you see the world, how you see life in general."

"Do go on."

A scowl. "I think happy endings make you cry because at heart you don't believe in them, but that doesn't stop you from wishing they were real so you could know what it's like to feel that kind of joy. And downbeat endings, well, they just reaffirm for you that every last one of us came out of the womb screwed to the wall and can't do a damn thing about it. Look at your movie collection! A full eighty-five percent of them are movies where everyone dies—or, if they don't die, they're fated to spend the rest of their miserable lives alone and lonely with zero hope of things ever going their way. How many times have you watched *Bring Me the Head of Alfredo*-fucking-*Garcia*? Don't answer that, it wasn't a real question—but do you understand why this bothers me?"

"Not really, no. You said you've enjoyed all the movies we've watched together."

"And I have...some more than others, obviously, but because they were important to you, I wanted to share in them. It's just, over the past year, I started noticing the pattern of your reactions getting worse."

A sigh. "Is this why you've been telling me that we've got quote-problems-unquote? Because I have a bias toward movies with unhappy endings?"

"We've got problems because you've never really been happy and refuse to do anything about it. I understand that you had a...less than spectacular life before we met because of what happened to your sister and then your folks, but there comes a point when you have to take responsibility for creating and owning your own peace of mind."

"You've been watching *Oprah* re-runs, haven't you?"

"Don't trivialize this! For I don't know how long, you haven't smiled or laughed at anything in your life. Blaine Evans's body performs all of its expected daily functions—it goes to work, it comes home, it eats dinner, it asks its family how their day went, sometimes it even fucks me when it remembers to, but mostly it plops down in front of the television and watches depressing movies that only underline how useless it thinks everything is, including itself and all the effort it puts into keeping a roof over its family's heads and clothes in their closets and food in the fridge and cupboards. But it's not you anymore. Your physical body is present but you're just not here. It's like you're breathing and taking up space and that's it."

"Have I been mean? Abusive? No. I've never cheated on you—I've never even thought about it. I don't drink, I don't yell, I don't smack anyone, I always do what I say I'm going to do and never expect to be thanked for it. I love you and I love the kids."

"You haven't shown it for a long while. The kids don't even know how to act around you anymore. You're not the dad they used to know; you're just someone who looks and sounds like the person they remember. You've removed yourself from your own family, and we'd kind of like you to come back over to our side."

He knew this much was true. He'd been feeling more distant from everyone and everything, and so he'd stopped making a concerted effort to remain a vital part of their lives, resigning himself instead to being simply peripheral. Sure, he asked the kids about school and listened to their chatter over dinner and half-smiled when they lined up to kiss him good night, but beyond that, he was just the guy they called "Dad," who handed them their weekly allowances and nodded in approval when they came home breathless and beaming, proudly displaying their report cards with all the As and Bs. Blaine could feel himself becoming more and more...diminished. Maybe that was what happened when a man reached a certain point in the arc of his life, realizing that more of it was behind him than ahead, and maybe a man's spirit was tied to his time remaining; the fewer days he had left to walk upon the Earth, the less excitement, gratitude, and hope he had for those days. Hell, maybe it was just good old-fashioned male menopause, the laughable "midlife crisis" that sent too many men into auto showrooms to purchase gleaming sports cars with sticker prices that were too high and engines that went too fast and parts that cost more than most people's weekly paychecks to replace. If you could add a much younger hot babe to this picture, then your crisis was guaranteed to be a fiery one and your inevitable downfall and disgrace historic.

"Earth to Captain Blaine," said Jennifer, "Earth to Captain Blaine, do you read?"

He almost laughed. Almost. "Sorry. I was just thinking how you still look thirty, if that. You look younger now than on the day we met."

She grinned, as if hoping that she was getting through to him. "And I've never had any work done."

He nodded.

Jennifer reached down and took one of his hands in hers. "Talk to me. Let me in again. I want you to tell me about all those things that happened that you never talk about."

Standing up. Time for a clean getaway. "I'm sorry, but...the length of this conversation has now far surpassed my interest in it."

A resigned nod. A coldness in her voice when next she spoke. "Fine, if that's the way it's going to be. I think it only fair to tell you that I decided to take the job offer from Limbus."

That stopped him mid-stride. "What?" He whirled back around. "The company on that card Matt found? I can't believe you contacted them." He recalled the day that Matt, the youngest of their three children, discovered the card on a cork bulletin board hanging next to a restroom in the mall. Matt had pulled the card off the board because he thought the logo was "...cool." It showed a globe of the Earth with needlepoint beams of light shooting out of it from all directions. It reminded Blaine of the logo used by the law group Engulf & Devour from Mel Brooks's *Silent Movie*. The card had only a phone number under the company's name and logo, and on the back were the words, "Your ideal job is waiting for you. Don't be indecisive. Dreams never wait. We employ." Blaine thought the whole thing smacked of a scam and said as much, but when Jen took the card and put it in her purse, he began to wonder if his wife wasn't thinking about greener pastures—but he believed that she wasn't so naïve as to call a number on a card found outside a public crapper. Evidently, he'd been wrong.

"I didn't just call," said Jennifer. "I've already interviewed. A lovely young recruiter named Tasha Willing talked to me for about forty minutes and then offered me a position with the company."

"Doing what? You're a former social worker who processed food stamp applications."

"I'll be doing something like social work for the company, except I'll be overseeing the development and implementation of … I guess you'd call them 'mental health' programs designed to reduce employee stress in and out of the workplace. It's something I've always wanted to do and Tasha just offered it to me"—she snapped her fingers—"like that! I've never had an interview go so well."

He could think of nothing else to say at that moment but this: "What's it pay?"

"Because I signed a non-disclosure agreement, I'm only allowed to say that the salary is excellent, more than either of us combined has ever made. They'll even pay for the family to relocate, including the cost of a new house."

Blaine shook his head. "You're being scammed."

"I thought you might say something like that." She walked into the other room and returned moments later with her open laptop. She typed in a few commands with her free hand while she held the computer in the crook of her arm like a newborn. Finding what she was looking for, she turned the screen in Blaine's direction. "Our joint account. I could have had it deposited to my own account—and believe me, I thought about it—but I didn't. Hopefully I get Brownie points for that."

Blaine took the laptop and looked at the screen. The balance in their joint checking account stunned him so much he nearly dropped the computer.

"Wh-what is…where did that kind of money come from?"

"It's my signing bonus."

"Signing bonus? That's more money than I've made in the last six months!"

Jen took the computer. "And my salary makes this look like … well, not quite chump change, but close enough to call it." She closed the laptop. "Still think it's a scam?"

"Okay, okay…maybe the company's on the level, I'll give you that. But what about this 'relocation' shit? We are not going anywhere."

"Thus Spake Zarathustra time, is it? You giving me some kind of ultimatum?"

"What if I am?"

"Christ, Blaine! Are you that attached to the library? You've been there for almost fifteen years."

"I like it there. There are never any surprises. The day porter rolls the carts of books and movies in, I scan them into the system as returned, re-enter them into circulation, and send everything out to be re-shelved. One-two-three, lather, rinse, repeat. I worked my way up to assistant day librarian without any kind of college education. Over half the people there have degrees in library science and they come to me when they need help."

"And what about the people you work with? Do they treat you as anything more than your function? I know all of you probably talk and joke and maybe share personal information of the most surface and non-intimate variety, but when all is said and done, are you seen as an individual or only your function?"

"That doesn't make any goddamned sense." But it did. For the last few years, Blaine had begun to feel as if his presence at the library was an afterthought to everyone around him. Sure, they might miss him the first couple of days after he left, but soon enough, he would be just another someone-who-used-to-work-here-once; a fading face, a forgotten voice, nothing of himself having made enough of an impression to linger in the mind or heart after the chair at his desk became an empty space soon to be filled by someone else.

Jennifer reached over and gently shook his arm. "Hey you."

He blinked, exhaled, and looked at her. "Sorry, I guess I ... went around the corner there for a moment."

"This could be a new start for all of us, a better life, one where you could drop your guard and allow yourself to feel happy, to feel needed, to feel useful. That's the biggest problem, honey. Somewhere along the line, because of all that violence that happened to you before we met, you started believing that you or anything you did or hoped for was meaningless. Come on! What say we blow this pop stand and make like the old-time settlers? Create a new life in a new location."

He stared at her for several seconds, trying to find the exact words—something he should be much better at since his livelihood revolved around books—but no matter how tried it out in his head, it came out sounding awful.

"Look at me, Jen. I'm fifty-three years old, I'm thirty pounds overweight, I wear a partial denture, and the most interesting thing about me is that I can reserve new books and movies for people months before they're released. I've got a bad leg, more gray hair in my beard than I wish I had, type II diabetes, high blood pressure, and, for the icing on the middle-aged cake, I take Prozac every morning—I'm a goddamn living wreck on my best days, let alone those where I feel every damn minute of my existence crawling along over broken glass. I'm...I'm done, Jennifer. Probably have been for a good long while now. Pulling up stakes and moving to a new place to start a new life, that's for younger people who still have something of value to offer the world." This said knowing that his wife was ten years younger, and suspecting what this younger woman would do once she heard those words.

"You're not a used-up wreck," said Jennifer, reaching toward him.

He stepped back, out of her reach. "You can't say that—you can't know that. I am sickeningly aware of what lies in here"—he touched the center of his chest—"and I'm telling you, whatever mechanism it is that allows people to acknowledge and embrace happiness, I don't have it. Okay, maybe I did once, when I still wore shoes the size of my hand and got up on Saturday mornings to make sure I didn't miss the new episode of *Scooby-Do* or *Aquaman*, but it's gone, poof! Without so much as a 'sayonara, sucker.'"

"Self-pity doesn't look good on you."

"It sounds better than saying I'm sad and tired all the time and feel comfortable with it."

She stared at him for several seconds before saying it. "It wasn't your fault. You were both just kids."

He pointed at her, angry that she'd brought up his sister again. "Don't. Just...don't. You know goddamned well I've played it over in my head a thousand times and there's...there's no excuse, okay? Sure, we were both just kids, but if I would have gone in first, then –"

" —then Carolyn would be the one still around and beating herself up every day because she'd think she should have gone in first!"

"Stop it, please."

Jennifer took a deep but unsteady breath. "This is killing you, honey. It has been for years. It's this place, this town. We have to get out of here, Blaine. We have to. Or we'll all suffocate."

"There are worse ways to go. And I'm done talking to you about all of this."

The next day Jennifer took the kids (who didn't say good-bye) and went to her parents' house.

* * *

For the first fifteen minutes, Evans's otherworldly underwater walk was bliss. He had cut out two exit holes, in case of any trouble with the oxygen tank, but he didn't think he'd need to use it.

Then he heard something like a drum. As he neared his exit, the sound became louder, and irregular—not like a drum at all.

The water, so much denser than air, conducted sound as air molecules never could. As a child, Evans had liked to lie in the bathtub, his ears in the water, and hear the enormous clanks and knocks his toy boats could make as they bumped against the porcelain. It made his boats real. Now Evans heard sounds that seemed like footsteps: far away, yet all around him, the water carrying vibrations too long for air to carry. As he approached his entrance, they did not seem to grow louder from there—the water unlocalized sounds—rather, they grew louder from everywhere.

Evans stopped and stood still. Tried to listen. The sound was too confused.

Then, since he stood inverted, Evans looked "down," as it seemed, and saw very clearly, in front of him, one black, ripple-sole footprint of a man on the ice, directly over him.

Another joined it—perhaps the man had raised a knee to fix a boot.

Two black bootprints. Guard's boots.

A guard from the compound was standing on the opposite side of the ice from him: right side up on the other side of the ice which Evans stood on upside down, like figures on a playing card.

Evans tried to figure out how the guard had gotten here so quickly—probably used a hover-car—then decided it didn't matter.

The guy was here now, and that didn't figure into Evans's Scenario.

The ice was translucent, not transparent: only the black boot soles pressing flat against the ice could be seen. Evans's silver air bubbles began to congeal on the ice's surface, and he stiffened, deciding they were too light for the guard to see. Evans's boots, suspended from the ice by crampon spikes, should be similarly invisible.

The man's shadow fell across the ice.

Evans flinched and looked around, then realized he cast no shadow in his other-world.

The black soles turned, and Evans saw the unmistakable outline of a gun fall across the ice.

It looked thin, but that could be a trick of the light; thin and long like a rifle, not a gun you'd use to hunt anything out on this ice. In winter there were only ducks and geese out on the marsh. Any hunter worth the price of his ammo would use a shotgun to hunt.

The outline turned again. Evans saw, unmistakably, the shadow of a protrusion above the barrel, thicker than the barrel, that began above the pistol grip and ran no more than a quarter of the barrel's length, where it flared out in a bell. A scope.

Only rifles had scopes. Shotguns didn't even have ordinary sights.

The bootprints started walking in front of him. Evans followed them, walking upside down beneath the man, a pace behind him.

From the way the bootprints stopped, made half-turns to each side, and from the way the shadow of the rifle swept in an arc along Evans's glowing ice, back and forth, Evans knew for certain this was a guard.

The bootprints kept on—Evans stalking the stalker, walking upside down beneath him. He found them moving in a curve toward some point. Every five steps the prints would stop, the long compound shadow of the rifle and scope would sweep along the ice like a shadow searchlight across a glowing sky, then the bootprints would continue. Evans gradually became sure.

So he knows. And he's hunting me.

Evans followed the bootprints in their curve, certain they were heading for his second exit hole. They were waiting for him to come up.

Good God! And I think of myself as an intelligent person. He'd cut the hole in his idiosyncratic way. He had his own ways by now.

He had cut his exit hole near the ice-divers' drying shed a quarter-mile away. He hoped they hadn't found the shed, but they'd guess it wouldn't be far from the hole. They'd know he would need to get inside shelter quickly once he came up. The water was never colder than twenty-eight degrees, but the wind above on the lake gave a chill-factor of sixty below zero on this ice. At that rate he would turn into an ice statue unless he dried off within a very few minutes of surfacing. How in God's name could he get out of this? He had only the Anaconda .44 Magnum pistol and the speargun; they had a gun each, he presumed. He didn't doubt there was another one. They'd know it wasn't safe for only one of them to try to take him.

Evans trailed along beneath the guard's bootprints and the gun's searching shadow. This was what you wanted, wasn't it? You against them? But not here, Evans thought.

Dinoflagellates twinkled above him. He walked shod in silver on the glowing pearl of the ice.

And marring his pearl: black bootprints, and the shadow of a gun.

They were at the exit hole. Waiting for him. And they knew goddamned well there was no other way for him to get out. He was screwed if he didn't think of something soon. And if he did think of something, and if he did get out of this, the Limbus folks and he were going to have a little chat about pay grades....

* * *

Five days after Jennifer and the kids moved out, Blaine was served with divorce papers. It took exactly four months to completely dismantle the life and home they'd shared for twelve years, and Blaine Evans found himself, at age fifty-three, alone and living in a small apartment near the library, hoping the house would sell before the year was out. He could use the money. Jen wanted nothing from the sale of the house; thanks to her hefty salary from Limbus, she didn't need it. And as if to rub his face in how wonderful her life and those of the children were going to be, she'd left ten thousand dollars of her signing bonus in the joint account. Okay, okay, he told himself, maybe she wasn't trying to rub his face in it—she wasn't a vindictive person.

Maybe she just wanted to be civil, leave behind a peace offering to let him know it would be okay for them to stay in touch. He had no way of knowing. For months after the divorce he tried getting in touch with her but no one, including her parents, knew where she and the kids had moved to—or if they did, they weren't about to tell him. He hired a private detective to track them down, but she'd come up with very little. By the end of the year (with the house still not having sold, despite his dropping the price), Blaine was as lonely and uncertain as he'd ever been, even more than when he was a kid and teenager. At least he didn't have to fall asleep listening to his mother ramble on, stoned on sedatives, as Dad drank himself unconscious, both of them going on about their wonderful daughter who was no longer there and their disappointment of a son, the little shit who should have been looking out for his sister; at least he didn't have to worry that he'd be awakened in the night by the sound of gunfire, only to go downstairs and find both his parents dead after Dad finally lost it; at least he wouldn't find himself being continuously shuffled through the foster care system, going from family to family, some good, others too horrible for words who did even more horrible things to him; at least he'd managed to survive to see fifty-three, even if it was arguably a self-imposed isolated survival.

He began drinking in order to fight the insomnia that took hold of him since the divorce. It was nothing serious at first, just a couple Johnny Walker Blacks over ice, enough to make him groggy and ensure he wouldn't be in noticeably bad shape for work the next morning, but after a while, a couple turned into three as his system built up a tolerance, and then three turned into five, and five into six, and instead of feeling groggy, he began to simply pass out on the sofa in front of the television that was usually showing one of the downer movies he'd put into the Blu-ray player.

After his third reprimand for coming in late and obviously hung-over, the library board suggested he take an unpaid leave to get himself and his life straightened out. He didn't argue with them, only nodded his head and, without making eye contact, thanked them for not outright firing him. Maybe he was needed here after all.

The dreary routine of the following days were spent reading, taking walks to no place in particular, and finding new restaurants with food that did nothing to help reduce his waistline; nights were spent with Bailey's Irish Crème (Johnny Walker had worn out his welcome) and watching as many bummer movies as he could make himself sit through before crashing out hard. Every so often he'd break up the routine by staying sober for the night and watching something with a happy ending; if Jennifer had been around, she would have shaken her head at the way he always cried himself to sleep after these joyous films. He was turning into a pathetic caricature of the recently-divorced, middle-aged, unemployed loser. And he hated it.

Which is how and why he found himself one evening walking to a nearby church that had advertised an Alcoholics Anonymous meeting. He knew that his drinking was getting serious. Whether or not he was an outright, raging drunk like his dad had become was still in question, but he knew he had to do something. This was the first time in years he'd taken the initiative to shake up his life, and as anxious as he felt about it, he also felt a small sense of pride. Maybe he could get better. Maybe he could get past all the lousy stuff he carried inside that always reared its ugly head when he least expected it to. Maybe he could become the kind of man who'd be worthy of a woman like Jennifer. Maybe he could become the husband she deserved.

He was almost to the church when the car horn sounded behind him. He ignored it at first, figuring the person was honking at someone else, but when the car pulled up at the curb beside him and the door opened and someone called his name, Blaine turned around just in time to note three things: the Limbus, Inc. logo on the side of the car, the two men who were approaching him, and something small and sharp jabbing into the side of his neck. After that, it was dizziness, the sidewalk rushing up toward his face, and then darkness.

* * *

He'd sunk an Ikelight below the exit hole in the ice for safety. The clouds overhead were thick, perhaps they had noticed his light, even so deep? It was too strong, the Ikelight? No. They'd just been lucky. But if he survived this, he wouldn't use the Ikelight any more if an assignment involved ice-diving. There'd be more chance of becoming lost beneath the ice, but it would be better than this: one single-shot speargun against the rifle.

Ahead he saw more shadows by his entrance hole and another pair of black bootprints.

The prints Evans was following reached the other set and they faced each other, conferring. Shadows now of two guns, two scopes.

Two men with rifles waiting at his exit hole. Odds were they knew his single tank couldn't carry much more than forty minutes' worth of air.

I'm dead, Evans thought.

He could feel a tug when he tried to breathe and had a spasm of fear. Sucking at the air as the tank emptied was like trying to breathe through a pillow that was getting pressed tighter and tighter against his face.

That wasn't his only problem. He had lost great quantities of body heat the whole time he was underwater. Not just from the exhaustion but the water, with a specific heat exactly one thousand times greater than air, had been conducting warmth away from his body twenty-five times as rapidly as would air at this temperature, Fahrenheit twenty-eight. The lake had been leeching heat from him—heat of energy, of strength and redemption, of life itself—while he was under.

He had very small reserve.

The shivering and the coldness he felt in his hands were signs his extremities had already fallen below thirty-six Celsius. His body's thermoregulatory system had turned on its defense mechanisms and he'd begun to shiver.

Damn!

Heavy shivering increased the body's basal heat production five to seven times. The vasoconstriction called gooseflesh meant his skin had begun sealing itself tighter to keep body heat in, stop blood flow to his periphery, where heat evaporated faster, and preserve it around his core organs. These were signs his body was chilling toward death, had gone through its heat and fallen onto its last reserve.

It was getting damn cold under here.

His blood temperature was dropping too fast.

Time was running out on him.

They knew it.

He knew it.

All God's chillun knew it.

All they had to do was wait him out. Perhaps that was why they were both at the hole now, anticipating his return.

He couldn't think of alternatives. He could walk to some spot of shallow ice by a tide island and break his way out easily enough—and freeze to death. More than air, he needed to get into that drying shed, which his heater had been warming since he began this assignment, where hot liquid was waiting in a thermos, where his cache of Just-In-Case weapons was sitting, and—most importantly—where his two-way radio waited, powered by a portable generator that had maybe thirty minutes' worth of juice left.

If his core temperature—the deep tissue areas of his body, as opposed to his extremities—had fallen only two degrees Fahrenheit below normal, to ninety-seven degrees, or thirty-six Celsius, as he thought of it, then Evans had already begun to die of hypothermia; when his deep tissues reached thirty-four degrees Celsius, his brain would begin to go; and at thirty-two Celsius, his heart.

In the wind above, that could happen within minutes. Even if he could manage to kill them within two minutes of his exposure to the air, there was a chance there might be damage to his brain.

Evans stood upside down, opposite the guards standing above him. All they had to do was wound him badly and everything would go haywire—even if he killed them. In his current situation, even a mere scratch could prove instantaneously fatal.

He had to kill them; all they had to do was hit him. And he was wildly outgunned.

Evans, fumbling in the cold, removed his tri-cut point from his speargun and took a stempoint from his bandolier. He could take one shot, then had to reload. There were, after all, two of them.

He looked at his timer. Seven minutes of oxygen left. His cheeks inside the mask were collapsing as he sucked air like a baby straining at an empty bottle. It took precious effort not to panic.

A pair of bootprints stood near the hole. Evans's heart beat intensely: Near enough?

He walked underneath the man and knelt, inverted directly below him. He studied the boot soles. Rubber. Really meant for mud. Not bad for ice, but Evans's spikes would have the edge on traction.

Where there was an ice break like his exit hole, water usually bled around it for several feet. The weight of the ice pressing down on the entire lake kept forcing water slightly up, like a pressure valve giving. Helpers would spread sand by the hole if they were backing up an ice diver so that they wouldn't slide in. But Evans had no backup crew; he hadn't prepared the ice with the sand. Immediately next to the hole, then, he could hope for a slight slick on the surface, over and beyond the slipperiness of the ice.

Was the man close enough?

As Evans watched, the bootprints stepped closer, and the gun shadow swung in the arc he knew. The guard was scanning; his gaze was raised.

Evans dug his spikes into the ice, held his breath, remembered the pathetic creature that was the man he used to be, and reached out of the water.

* * *

Before he'd even fully opened his eyes, Blaine knew he was restrained; his shoulders were screaming from being pulled too tightly in toward his chest, he could barely feel his hands at all, and his chest...Christ, it felt like crisscrossing iron bands were cutting into him.

As his eyes adjusted—he had to look away from the large, round medical lights that seemed like they were only a few feet away from his face—he saw that he was lying on a hospital gurney, that his legs were restrained at the ankles by thick leather straps, and that he was in a straightjacket. Part of him—the part still recovering from whatever drug they'd shot into the side of his neck—almost laughed at the thought of being straightjacketed like this: how many time had he joked to Jennifer (who'd never found it funny) that he could well imagine himself spending his retirement years in just such a fashionable coat while relaxing in a room with rubber walls?

The amusement didn't last long. Several figures in surgical scrubs milled around the operating room, making preparations for God only knew what. All of them wore filter masks so that the lower portions of their faces were obscured. Blaine rolled his head from side to side, trying to crack his neck bones and ease some of the tension in his muscles.

"He's awake," someone said.

Like vultures clustering over fresh carrion, the gurney was immediately surrounded by a circle of masked faces staring down at him. He blinked at the medical team as they shone a penlight into his eyes, turned his head from side to side, and conversed with another in that maddening medical-speak that might as well have been in Croatian for all that Blaine understood.

After a few more moments, a female voice outside of the circle said, "Stop crowding the man already!" The medical team pulled back and away, one of them readjusting the overhead lights so that none were shining directly into his face. Blinking away the mini supernovas exploding across his field of vision, Blaine was soon able to focus on the face looking down at him; it belonged to a young black woman of perhaps twenty, maybe less. She stared into his eyes for a moment and then smiled as one of her hands took a cool cloth and daubed at the sweat forming on his face. It felt wonderful.

"Hello, Mr. Evans," said the young woman. "My name is Tasha Willing. I apologize for the somewhat...unconventional manner in which you were brought here, but you've been volunteered for a new program our company is the process of implementing—after, of course, we get a few bugs worked out."

At her saying "bugs," someone elsewhere in the room barked out a short but loud laugh.

Blaine had never seen this young woman before but recognized her name. It didn't take long for him to place it.

"...ennifer," he managed to croak. "...you hired Jennifer..."

Tasha nodded. "I did. And this program that she volunteered you for is her baby."

"I'll be doing something like social work for the company," Jennifer had said, "except I'll be overseeing the development and implementation of ... I guess you'd call them 'mental health' programs ..."

"Where am I?"

Tasha daubed at his face a little more. "You're in one of our volunteer medical facilities. Please don't worry. No one here intends to hurt you but—and I'm saying this so you'll know that I am not in the habit of lying or euphemizing things—there is a good chance that some of this process is going to be kind of unpleasant for you. We'll provide you with all the vitamins and nutrients your body will need, we'll provide all the pain medication necessary, and our physical therapy department is hands-down the best on this world or any other. In short, Mr. Evans, your ex-wife has made certain that you are in the best possible hands."

He glared at her. "So why am I in a fucking straightjacket?"

Tasha waved a finger in front of him like a scolding parent. "I don't insist on many things, Mr. Evans, but I do ask that you not curse in my presence. It only makes things more tense than they need to be."

He blinked. "Understood. Why am I in a straightjacket?"

Tasha smiled. "See? Was that so difficult? You're restrained in this manner because you've been injected with a certain substance that has, in the past, given us some trouble. Violent outbursts, people unable to control their limbs, people harming themselves and others."

Blaine was even more frightened than before. "What have you done to me?"

"I'm getting to that. Your medical history—including your ongoing trouble with alcohol—has resulted in your nervous system being in many ways severely compromised, but it's been compromised in a way that—ironically enough—may very well allow us to not only heal but enhance it. In short, if you weren't such a physical wreck, the injection would probably have destroyed you by now and we wouldn't be having this conversation."

"What did you put inside of me?"

Tasha stood, tossed aside the cool cloth, and turned toward someone unseen. "I think this where you come in, Ted." She turned back to Blaine and smiled. "I'll be seeing you again soon, Mr. Evans. In the meantime, you'll be working with Ted—Dr. Copeland. He can speak with much more insight than I. Try not to worry, Mr. Evans— and please don't bother trying to do something heroic like fight your way out of here. You'd never find the exit, believe me, and if through some series of skewed coincidence you did manage to find the exit, you'd never find a way off the island."

"Island?"

Tasha shrugged. "This is a very private facility." She patted his hand like a babysitter comforting a two-year-old at bedtime, reassuring the child that there were no monsters under the bed. "Don't worry yourself. You're going to be treated like a star." And with that, she did not so much walk out of the room as glide, as if the everyday weight of gravity had no effect on her physical grace.

"Yeah, she's got a nice ass," said a male voice that sounded as if its owner gargled with Wild Turkey five times a day, in between packs of filterless cigarettes.

Blaine looked up into the gaunt, weathered face of a man whose age could have been anywhere between a gee-you-don't-look-it fifty and a raggedy-ass thirty-five. His bright green eyes were sunk into their sockets so deeply Blaine wondered if they'd fall into the man's skull if he were punched hard enough.

"I'm Ted Copeland," said Sunken Green Eyes. "And unlike our Ms. Tasha, I don't give a flying fuck what kind of language you use, just so long as you do not interrupt me. Do you read my meaning?"

Blaine nodded. He really didn't like this guy. Kind of a lot.

Copeland nodded. "Good. Now, pay attention. Before I explain to you what we've done to you and why, you're going to get what I laughingly refer to as a mission statement. Limbus is big on the idea that its various departments and companies and organizations and what-nots all have individual mission statements. Me, I think it's all a bunch of horseshit, but as long as I go along with the program, I get to see my family twice a month. That makes me happy. You can probably already tell that I am simply filled to the fucking brim with a joy for life and an overwhelming love of my fellow man, so—my whimsical wit and sparkling conversational skills aside, pay attention.

"There's a tribe in Africa—well, what's left of the tribe, anyway—called the Masai, and every so often they chose one of their elders, or a cripple, or some other useless member of the village, and they give them a huge party, then take them out into the jungle and leave them there for the hyenas to eat alive. It's their way of not only controlling the population but of thinning out those elements that might taint the purity of their tribal genetics. This world, Blaine—may I call you Blaine? Doesn't matter, that's what I'm going to do. Now where was I? Ah, yes.

"This pitiful excuse for a world, Blaine, from pole to pole, is a jungle. Whether that jungle is composed of vines and swamps or boardrooms and contractual pen strokes, it's all the same, no different from the one where the Masai feed the hyenas. It's inhabited by various species of beasts, some which rut in caves and devour their young, others that wear tailored suits and dine on their business rivals' broken stock speculations. All of these beasts have only one honest-to-God function, and that is to survive. There is no morality, no law, no imposed man-made dogma that will stand in the path of that survival. That humankind survives is the only morality there is. And for us to survive as a race, we must be superior, we must dominate all lesser creatures. And in order to ensure that, it is not only vital but necessary to destroy, to eliminate, to thin out and expunge any undesirable element that threatens to stop the march of progress. Don't look at me like that, I'm not talking about genocide or anything that banal, no. I'm talking about expunging all the things that make us, on an individual basis, potential victims, be it to our surroundings, ourselves, our circumstances, or any of the myriad elements that we're trained from birth to believe will crush us the moment the opportunity arises. The things that hold us back from real achievement, things like fear, like doubt, jealousy, resentment, shit like the lack of knowledge that is both applicable and useful on a day-to-day basis. In short, I'm talking about expunging all those niggling little...stop-gaps that make it so easy to justify hesitation or non-action. Do you read my meaning?"

"If I could move my hands, I'd applaud."

Copeland glared at him. "I can't tell if you're being sarcastic or merely stupid."

"I get a lot of complaints about that."

Copeland nodded. "So your wife told us. She's really quite a brilliant woman, your ex-wife. If this program she's designed works out as we all hope it will, it may very well change the, you should pardon the expression, course of human events. But I'm getting ahead of myself." Copeland turned around, pulling something that looked like a small four-wheeled control panel toward him. Hitting a couple of buttons and typing in commands, he activated something beneath Blaine's gurney—which Blaine now realized was not a gurney at all but some sort of hospital bed or table—and Blaine felt himself being tilted upward as his feet lowered. Within a few moments, he was in an all-but upright position, facing a large, round dais rising silently from an opening in the floor about five feet away.

"See there?" said Copeland. "We give you a wardrobe, a comfy bed, wonderful drugs—and now, a floor show, all for you. Are you feeling special? You should be feeling special. We only do this for special guests. Are you reading my meaning?"

"I get it. I'm special."

Copeland glowered. "Sarcasm?"

"Just agreeing with you."

Copeland almost smiled as he entered more commands. "You were injected with a nannite, Blaine. A nannite, in case you aren't familiar with the term, is a microscopic-sized robot. The one in your system looks something like a mechanical spider. Nannites are programmed to build anything—organic or inorganic—from the base up. The one injected into your system can also self-replicate. If all my calculations are accurate—and there's no reason to think that they wouldn't be—within a few hours there will be thousands, millions, theoretically trillions, of them swimming inside you along with your cells. They're beginning the process of breaking down and rebuilding your molecular structure, but at a rate at which your system can safely adjust to the changes."

Blaine's only recourse to completely flipping out from panic was to focus on the situation from as detached a point of view as possible. Clearing his throat, he asked, "Rebuilding my molecular structure how? I mean, are you specifically targeting certain areas, certain organs, what?"

Copeland smiled. "Watch the dais. Nothing up my sleeve..." Activating a holographic imager constructed into the center of the dais, Copeland rolled himself and the control panel back a few feet, allowing Blaine an unobstructed view. The lower portion of the imager rose from its circular chamber while its sister component lowered from the ceiling, each stopping with four feet of space remaining between them. Adjusting a few controls, Copeland pressed a key, and a life-sized, three-dimensional image of a human brain appeared, hovering at a comfortable viewing level twenty-five inches above the surface of the table. The image was crowned with bright and vivid patterns of red, orange, and yellow; below them was a band of broken green; and scattered throughout the back-brain area were violet-and-blue streams.

"What you're looking at," said Copeland as the brain began slowly rotating, "are the positron emissions tomography readings of a normal-functioning brain. The brightly-colored areas—red, orange, yellow—indicate where maximum brain activity occurs. The green areas delineate mid-range activity, and the blue-and-violet areas signify minimum activity. Now remember—this is what a normal, everyday-functioning brain looks like."

He entered another series of commands, and the brain split horizontally, opening up like a book to its middle chapter; the frontal, temporal, and occipital lobes were also colored accordingly, as was the cerebellum. "I want you to look here"—he magnified the image—"at the mid-brain area. Can you make out the pituitary gland? Right there? Good." He magnified the area once again, this time focusing on a tiny cave just behind and above the pituitary gland, housing a cone-shaped organ that, minus the magnification, would have been roughly the size of a pea.

"What you're looking at now is the pineal gland. You'll note that its particular shade is a bit softer than the other green-colored areas. That's normal, trust me."

"What's its purpose?" asked Blaine.

Copeland smiled, but there was no humor in it. "Here is what, after centuries of study, testing, and theorizing, we know about the pineal gland: it is attached to the third ventricle of the brain, it processes light from the suprachiasmatic nucleus via the retinohypothalamic tract—in layman's terms, the passageway between the optic nerve and the hypothalamus—and it produces melatonin which is secreted throughout the night with the absence of light.

"And that's it. Believe it or not, that's all we know about its function—which is why, when this PET scan was taken, it was in a mid-range activity state. Mid-range is all the higher function the pineal gland achieves under everyday, known circumstances, even in the most healthy and active of brains. When light reaches the pineal gland during the day, it inhibits the production of melatonin, which is then produced and secreted as we sleep. Whenever in-depth study of human behavioral disorders is conducted, one of the standard results is almost always an unusually high level of melatonin in the system, such as those found in people who suffer from chronic insomnia or night workers who have to sleep during the day in places where light cannot be filtered out." He cropped the magnified portion of the brain and moved it away from the rest, then deleted the three-dimensional PET scan of this brain and replaced it with that of another.

"This is a PET scan I performed on you after you arrived at this facility. The nannite had been in your system for a little under thirty minutes. Notice anything about the color scheme?"

Blaine studied it for a moment as it rotated. He said nothing after the first rotation, but as the second one began, he spoke up. "The blue-and-violet streaks—those are...what'd you call them...the 'minimum-activity' areas, right?"

"Correct," said Copeland.

"They're hardly there."

"Right," said Copeland, splitting this brain and magnifying the lateral view. "Your brain was functioning almost solely at mid- and high-range levels, which is nearly unheard of. Now, take a look at the pineal." He magnified the area. "A Kewpie doll for the first correct answer."

Blaine felt as if ice had been injected into his veins. "It looks cracked."

"Close. Look again." Copeland doubled the magnification.

Blaine leaned forward. "What the—? It looks...deformed."

What he had described as looking like a crack was, as now clearly shown, a growth along the length of the pineal gland's surface; it look to Blaine like a raised vein—albeit one with no blood to give it color—or the outline of a too-smooth spinal column.

"What is that?" he asked.

"One more thing first. Hang on." Copeland cropped the pineal, moved it, then replaced the second PET scan with a third. "Just so you can put this in perspective, this was taken while you were still unconscious."

The 3-D PET scan rotating before them now would have been almost laughably psychedelic in its impossibility, but coupled with Copeland's grim expression, there was no denying its reality; its entire surface was covered in nothing but red, orange, and yellow, the colors so bright the brain appeared to be shimmering.

Copeland looked at Blaine. "The strength of the sedative in your system at the time should have lowered your brain's overall functionality into the green and violet-and-blue. Yet here it is, a virtual rainbow of activity." Once more he halved the brain and magnified the pineal gland until it alone was the size of a normal human brain.

Blaine shook his head, not looking away. "That's...just...not possible." He remembered the line from Sherlock Holmes that was among his favorites, "When you eliminate the impossible, whatever remains, however improbable, must be the truth."

And the truth, however improbable, was that he was looking at a pineal gland that branched into two separate cones while still connected at the tip.

"Is that...is that what my pineal gland looks like now?" said Blaine, almost numbed from the shock and near-terror. These people had gone inside his head and fucked around with his brain.

"Have you ever heard of Rene Descartes?" asked Copeland.

Blaine nodded. "The French scientist and philosopher—'I think, therefore I am'—yes, I've heard of him."

"Descartes has been rumored to have called the pineal gland 'The Third Eye' but it was, in actuality, Nils Holmgrenin, a Swedish anatomist, who gave it that name, in 1918. He called it 'The Third Eye' because medical dissection had shown that the front section of the gland is equipped with the complete structure of the human eye. Since it exists inside the skull, it was dubbed 'the vestigial eye' by the scientific community of the time, but Holmgrenin, like Descartes, was something of a classical Romantic, so 'The Third Eye' it became. 'In man,'" said Copeland, quoting, "'soul and body touch each other only at a single point, the pineal gland in the head.' That's what Descartes said about it. He believed that it was the nexus between the mind and the body, the...what did he call it?...the '...seat of the human soul.'"

"So you've done all of this to me to...what? Find physical proof of the existence of the soul? Goddammit, you messed with my brain!"

Copeland gave out a short, soft laugh. "Descartes was approaching it at that point in his life from a more philosophical vantage. He theorized that the pineal was the direct doorway to the subconscious mind—God knows that Wilhelm Wundt, Freud, Jung, Skinner, Weiner, and dozens of others referenced him enough in their studies. Descartes was also fond of pointing out that the ancient Egyptians believed the same thing—the headdress with the cobra protruding from the forehead exemplifying the symbology. It's been said that everything from the Eye of Horus to the Masonic Capstone on top of the pyramid on the Great Seal of the dollar bill represents this belief, as well.

"But Descartes also cited scientific evidence of the time to back up his belief that, when fully activated, the pineal gland opens not only the subconscious but enabled our dormant Psi abilities—what used to be called 'the sixth sense,' allowing us to perceive higher planes and alternate dimensions of existence—but not before both physically and physiologically altering our cells until we became what George Bernard Shaw referred to as the 'superman'—a being possessed of both immeasurable physical power and near godlike intellectual superiority.

"That's what we're going to do to you, Blaine. We're going to take this living wreck of a psyche and body you're walking around in and turn you into something just shy of a god." With the simple press of a button, the show was over. Copeland removed a hypodermic from his the pocket of his lab coat, rolled closer to Blaine, and uncapped the needle. "In ever-increasing gradations, naturally." And with that, he slipped the needle into Blaine's neck and sank the plunger.

* * *

The guard, from the corner of his eye, saw something black move out of the water and seize his ankle: Evans's suited arm and mitt. Before the guard could fire, Evans pulled him across the slick ice and into the hole.

To Evans, inverted, it was as if he had pulled the man, upside down into a cloud of air bubbles that lived in his world. The guard fought like a great fish hauled on a line from the depths but he weighed nothing. Evans held on to him and tottered away from the hole, carrying him at arm's length. Even under water the guard's gun fired twice, but he couldn't aim. The thousands of bubbles this manfish had brought with him moved upward to the ice and rolled about, trapped against the frozen surface of the lake. The guard gasped and struggled exactly like a fish in air, except that he kept seeming to want to fly upwards out of Evans's hands. His boot kicked Evans in the face, and Evans's mouthpiece wrenched out but Evans held his breath, keeping the guard above him like a weight lifter pressing a barbell over his head, going for a world record—until he saw the guard take heavy gasps of water and go inert. The gun finally slipped from the man's grip. Evans let him go and got his mouthpiece back in. He was so cold he was dizzy—his stomach and chest felt like frozen lead. The guard's body, like a slow balloon, floated up in space and hung among the starfish.

Beneath his feet Evans saw, in flashes, the bootprints of the other guard appearing and disappearing on the ice. Evans pulled desperately on the scraps of air in his regulator, but the pillow was pressing tighter and tighter across his face. He tried to prepare, but the cold was reaching his brain and slowing it down.

This guard must have seen the first go under, perhaps seen where all the bubbles the first one brought in coagulated, because suddenly there was a terrible noise inside Evans's head, inside it, all around it, and from the center of the bubble mass he saw a streak of bubbles fly through the ice fast as a tracer bullet in wartime night.

The guard, panicked, was shooting at the ice.

Evans moved away from the bubbles as shot after shot punched through, each bullet marked by a brilliant silver bubble trail that bent in the water after a few yards and arced in all directions.

Evans pushed himself away from the eruptions.

The bullets followed.

This guard had quickly learned to distinguish where Evans's bubbles were beneath the ice.

Evans held his breath and moved. The bubble he had breathed a second ago bounced down his side and reached the ice. A second later a bullet burst up through it, angled in the water, and almost caught him. He saw the trail of bubbles it made go past his eyes.

Evans made a sharp right. Inadvertently some air left the regulator and reached the ice. A bullet came up through it instantly.

Evans guessed, and made a quick dodge backward: he was right—four bullets pulled up through the ice in the direction he had been going. The guard had seen the track of the bubbles and was leading him. He was a better hunter than the one Evans had just killed. Evans's air was nearly gone and he was freezing. He couldn't keep this up much longer.

He held his breath and angled—no bullets. The guard must be changing clips. To fire so quickly the gun must be a semiautomatic.

Evans crouched, let out one breath, pushed the shaking bubble with his hands, and sprang away from it. The second it hit the ice a bullet lanced it, probing for him.

Evans moved in a circle, trying to get his little speargun into position to fire. Each time he breathed, he shoved the bubble from him and danced a different way to the side. The bullets came up through them, the water shook with the sound, but he was not hit. Evans fought to watch the bootprints with one eye and the bullets with the other. His mask limited his field of vision dangerously. Evans circled, working to get the open entrance hole between him and the bootprints.

A bullet, perhaps a hysterical shot, came up through the ice almost at Evans's feet.

The guard was close to the hole now, on the other side from Evans. The last few shots he had been pivoting—Evans would see the heels disappear as the man rose to his toes in the pivot. The ice, Evans imagined, must now be awash from the fountains of water that had sprung up whenever the bullets plunged through the ice. The man was not trying to move on the slick ice but was wisely holding still, turning, and then aiming his weapon. Evans doubted that, unless he was an ice diver, the guard knew his boots could be seen—and he could see nothing of Evans but the ghosts of bubbles.

Evans blew breath out, pushed the bubbles behind him and to the left, leaped with his ten-pound weight a long moon-leap sideways from the boots so that at last he had the open water of the exit hole between him and the guard. Thunder, water vibrations, bullets whizzed like bees through his bubbles as they touched ice. Evans landed kneeling. Through the shining surface he saw, as if beneath him, blue sky and the gray parka of the guard, aiming a long brown stick toward the water. The water magnified everything, so that Evans saw the guard, shimmery but large, saw the gun fire and kick, saw him as clearly as if he, Evans, knelt on a rock, and looked at a six-foot long fish just beneath him in the clearest water.

The guard would see him just as clearly too.

Before the guard could swing his gun and shoot through the hole, Evans fired. The speargun's stempoint, nine times larger than a .45 Magnum, hurled up out of the water into the guard's stomach, glanced off the inside of his ribs, and—with the one-ton stainless cable holding it to the stem—the five-inch blade swung like a clock hand inside the man's tissues, from eleven o'clock to five o'clock, slicing through half the organs in his body.

Evans saw the print of the guard suddenly on the ice. One cheek and the side of his nose were pressed against it, enlarged, like a child's against a store window, while his rifle was trapped beneath him.

Evans straightened and walked around the hole. The guard lay under his feet. The ice turned pink: the icy water on the surface had diluted the blood.

Evans looked up. The guard lay with his arms stretched above his head, like a ballet dancer.

Evans no longer felt anything when he killed. Gore no longer startled him.

God, it was so hard to breathe; he sensed his reason going. Get out. Evans stepped over the hole into the other world. The suit ascended.

Hooking his inflated legs over the edge, then drawing his floating body out with short pulls of the spikes, Evans lay, suited, in the water beside the hole, looking at sky. He ripped his mask aside and breathed.

Evans pressed his suit valve down, deflated it.

He stood up, slowly.

The enormous weight of his body returned as the Earth's pull reasserted itself. He had not weighed more than ten pounds during the last thirty minutes, and now he weighed one hundred and seventy. It was like being yoked with cannonballs. The extra fifty pounds of his tank was a crushing weight on his back.

Evans looked down at the water and felt dizzy; looked up at sky and felt confused, out of his element. The guard lay next to him in a red pool already partly frozen. Evans put down his pistol. He would hide the man in the water.

As soon as the Comanche left Evans's hands, he heard someone behind him say, "Hold it right there."

* * *

The process was a long one but not nearly as painful as Blaine had expected. There were the headaches, of course, as the nannites enhanced his pineal gland and, in concert, the rest of his body. Scars from childhood seemed to fade away in a matter of hours. His blood pressure stabilized. His eyesight improved. His physical dexterity increased, as did his overall strength. They fed him well, trained him well, treated him well, and within a few weeks, he even managed to make himself forget that he was, in essence, a prisoner, their guinea pig, a subject who'd been "volunteered" and taken by them at his ex-wife's request.

He often asked if he could see Jennifer and the children, but each request was met with either flat refusal or hasty excuses. Once he even refused to perform the tests Copeland had ordered until he was allowed to at least speak to Jennifer.

"You mustn't do that," said Tasha Willing during one of her rare visits. "The nannites have a secondary programming that can be activated by anyone at Limbus with the proper security clearance—admittedly, that's only five people, but any one of them can do it."

"What do you mean, 'secondary programming?'"

Her face was, for the first time, cold and expressionless. "The process is a bit complex, but what it comes down to is this: with the push of a button, the nannites in your body can send you into the most

Gary A. Braunbeck

painful convulsions you've ever experienced. Push another button, and the pain doubles."

He stared at her. "You wouldn't dare kill me, not after all the work that's been done and all the money that's been spent."

"True. But things could be made very unpleasant for you, and I've come to understand that you're feeling rather sprightly for a man of your age and previous health concerns."

"Just tell me—am I ever going to see my ex-wife and children?"

"Eventually, yes. But if you continue to cooperate, I think we can...how does the saying go? 'Sweeten the deal,' even more."

It was four days later, as Blaine lay on the examination table while a robotic X-ray camera traveled up, down, and around his body, that he found out what that meant.

"The Enticement," said Copeland when Blaine asked him about it. "That's what I call it. It's a fucking carrot they dangle in front of you. In my case, it's my family, too. Twice a month I get to see them for twenty-four hours off-site. The rest of the time, I'm here. Always read the fine print on employment contracts, especially with this bunch."

"So they're not lying to me? I mean you got to see your family eventually, right? So they'll let me, as well?"

"Remain still, please. Yes, they do keep their word, amazing as that might seem." Copeland looked around, noted the locations of the security cameras, and rolled closer to the examination table. "Don't react to this. I'm serious. In fact..." He removed a hypodermic and gave Blaine a shot. "That's a muscle relaxant to make certain you won't react. I'll just wait a moment. All relaxed? Good. You'll be asleep in a few moments, but I want you to know what it is they're going to use for your Enticement.

"Your sister Carolyn is alive and well. Whatta you think of them apples?"

* * *

From that moment on, Blaine Evans's soul was freed, and with that freedom came, as Copeland had promised, a kind-of godhood—if godhood is measured in lives that are spared and taken away, and Evans's almost was a certain day on the ice a few years and many assassinations down the line.

* * *

Idiot!

Why had he thought there'd be only two guards? Hover-cars moved fast and furiously, could cover half a mile in a few seconds. The sound of shooting must have been heard for miles along the ice! They probably fired up the first of the hover-cars before he'd even escaped the compound.

Oh, you moronic horse's ass!

The ice was forming white crystals around Evans's suit. The skin on his face tightened: ice crystals were covering it. He had to dry.

He was preparing himself to turn and face them down—he thought now only in terms of them because to think otherwise could be lethal at this point—and had just begun to pivot when he saw a thin leather strap come flying down across his field of vision. He managed to get his hand up in time to prevent the strip from constricting around his throat.

Evans spun around, his would-be strangler holding tight, and saw that there was, indeed, a fourth guard. This one had a pistol and was trying to aim at Evans's head but there was too much movement right now for the guy to get off a good shot. Any hit right now would just be lucky, even though the guy could take Evans with it if he were quick enough, which he wasn't, but that was all right with Evans because, right now, he was dominated by pain both from within and without, and pain changed his world, put a cloud around him he couldn't see through, preventing him from acting in accordance with logic and experience and training.

For a moment, as the thin leather strap cut into the flesh of his hand, Evans was feeble and clouded and clumsy and ripe for death.

Standing stock-still—a target on a shooting range.

But the other guard, the kid with the gun, was too slow and the moment went by.

Evans's brain began to clear. *You're the best there is!* he raged at himself. *Maybe you're getting too old for much more of this shit, but right now you are STILL THE BEST THERE IS and you have to do something NOW!*

He hit those words hard in his mind because the kid with the pistol was moving around, trying to get a decent aim again, and so what if his mind was clearing up? A bullet could crush clear tissue as well as cloudy, and the strangler-guard behind him was strong, almost as strong as Evans, and he had to use that to advantage somehow, had to do something extraordinary, something remarkable, something unique, jaw-dropping, and awe-inspiring, that was all, nothing to it, and he had to do it in the next five seconds.

Go.

And think about raising your rates next time.

The Strangler was strong but the Strangler was shorter than Evans—

—the kid with the gun was getting closer—

—the Strangler was quick but the Strangler was now stationary—

—the kid raised the gun into the firing position, supporting his firing arm with his free hand, a classic shooting-range stance —

—so if you can budge the Strangler, if you can unsettle his balance, if you can do that—

Evans faked going right—

—and went right.

The kid whirled left and fired into empty air and the surprise on his face was all that Evans needed; he powered everything he had into completing the next move, and behind him, he could feel the Strangler's strip loosen slightly as the man's balance momentarily deserted him.

And with all the power in his great body, Evans hunched forward, pulling the Strangler with him, and when he had his balance, Evans put all of his strength into a shoulder throw, sailing the Strangler helplessly over him and into the too-slow kid.

The two of them went down hard on the ice, and the kid was stunned as he hit, losing his grip on his weapon, and the gun skidded across the ice. Evans saw it but so did the Strangler, and the Strangler went for it, scrabbling and sliding along the ice like a desperate roach.

Evans let him.

His right hand was next to useless, bruised and bleeding from the leather strap, so he merely watched as the Strangler got closer to the gun—

—then Evans kicked the Strangler's head off—

—or tried to. The Strangler was ready and grabbed Evans's foot and snapped it around, tripping him—but not before Evans got off one good, spiked kick into the Strangler's shoulder, then followed it up with a blow from his left hand, but it only grazed the Strangler's head because even on his knees, even still dazed from the throw, even bleeding from the deep gashes left by Evans's spikes, the Strangler could still move, and Evans went for another left-hand blow, and again the Strangler spun free; another left-hand barely connected as the Strangler writhed and twisted, and he really was like a roach, a water bug that you could see and chase but somehow never catch, and both of them went for the gun then, but it was clumsy going for both of them, pained going, skidding-on-the-ice going, and when Evans saw that he might not get to the gun first, he kicked at it and sent it spinning toward the exit hole and smiled as it teetered on the edge then fell in with a soft *plop!* as the Strangler chopped him on the neck, but Evans faked sideways enough so that the Strangler missed a death-spot—but that didn't mean it didn't hurt like hell, didn't make his nerves shriek, didn't start his brain to clouding again which—coupled with his desperate need for heat, for warmth, for drying—served to slow him momentarily, but Evans would not allow that to happen, not for long, anyway. *If I cloud, I'm gone, it's that simple,* so he wriggled away from the Strangler's grip and connected with a spiked kick to the side of the Strangler's head, ground-zero on a death spot, and when his spiked boot hit, there was a double cry of pain, and who was to say whose was the greater agony, his or the Strangler's. All he could be sure of was that the Strangler's was over a lot sooner.

Gasping, cramping, bleeding, Evans managed to get to his feet, then moved past the dead Strangler and finished off the kid quietly before staggering into the drying shed. It was so blessedly warm, so heavenly toasty and welcoming, and he fell onto the pile of blankets he'd left there, wrapping himself in them like a child hesitant to leave its mother's womb, and then he reached for the thermos of hot tea and sipped it, then gulped it, not caring about the searing pain in his throat, and soon he was able to breathe easily and move freely with only a little agony. He managed to get out of his wetsuit and into some dry, warm clothes, taking care to check out the window for signs of other guards who might have heard the shooting earlier. As he looked, he saw maybe a dozen hover-cars rising out of the compound, swarming together, massing like dark, angry hornets, but before they could clear the distance, the air ignited in a thunderous flash and Evans grinned because the first of the six bombs he'd set in the compound were now detonating, seven seconds apart, and would level ninety-percent of the main building by the time they were finished, so that meant he was probably safe for a little while, thirty minutes tops—and that reminded him about the radio, so he staggered over and flicked it on, turned the transmission dial until he got the frequency he needed, instructed the person on the other end to patch him through.

When the person he wanted to speak to was on the other end, Evans said, "It's 'Come-And-Get-Me-Time.'"

"Did you get the disks?"

"You'll have to pick me up to find out, won't you?"

"I'm not in the mood for attitude, Blaine."

"Neither am I. I need medical attention, so have a doctor ready."

"You'll have everything you need. Give me your location and I'll have the chopper airborne in five minutes."

"You'd have a little trouble landing where I'm at." He gave them an alternate location, a field less than half a mile from his present location. "I'll be there in twenty minutes."

"The chopper will be waiting."

"It damned well better be," said Evans, "or your precious disks are going right into the lake."

"What a trusting soul you are."

"Just my warm and fuzzy nature. Don't be late. Oh, and this time, I want to see live footage of my sister, not just fucking photographs. And Copeland gets an extra day with his family."

"You're making demands?"

"Let's call it 'negotiating' and remain friends."

And with that, he killed the connection, gathered up his weapons, and set about preparing to blow up the shed and most of the ice supporting it.

As he made his way through the surrounding woods to the rendezvous area, Evans couldn't help but smile at the memory of the man he used to be, back in the life that now seemed like some pathetic dream. From librarian to guinea pig to assassin; the next step, according to Copeland, was just short of becoming a god.

And gods could make demands. Gods had bargaining power. Gods were not to be fucked with.

Especially the crazy ones.

And the librarian Blaine Evans, now having reached the end of his transmigration, knew damned well that he was crazy.

There was a certain comfort in that.

Fourth Interlude: A Pawn in their Game

The witching hour had long since come in that village ringed by unforgiving cliffs of basalt. And to Conrad, it seemed as though he had entered some strange world beyond our own, where nothing was as it appears, and anything could be possible. He looked down into his empty stein. He needed another drink, but more than that, he needed someone to talk to.

He pulled his coat tight around him once more and headed out into the night. He did not turn to or fro from his path this time. This time he headed straight to the Van Gogh. He ignored the eyes that peered out at him from beneath darkened eves. He did not stop to ponder what appeared to his passing glance to be the image of a globe, etched into the crumbling façade of an abandoned building. He continued on through the snow-filled streets, stopping only when he reached the door of the pub. He said a silent prayer it would still be open and pushed.

But of course it was open. Mikhail was a creature of the night, and as the bar's door swung wide, there was Mikhail, standing behind the bar, drying a glass.

"Ah, my American friend. I was beginning to wonder if you were going to come around tonight."

"Yeah," Conrad mumbled. "I'm sorry. I've been busy."

Mikhail squinted in the dim light. "Are you alright, my friend? You seem…distracted."

Conrad pulled himself up on a stool and collapsed on the bar. "I've just got some things going on. It's nothing." He looked down at the chess board. Mikhail had left the pieces where they had been the night before, as was their custom. He studied the position, but he could not concentrate. He picked up his knight, but then he put it back down again. Mikhail smiled. Conrad grabbed his bishop and moved it to attack the white queen.

Mikhail made a clicking sound with his tongue. "You *are* in bad shape." He picked up his queen and moved it to check the king. "I believe that is the game."

Conrad glanced at the board and let out a deep exhale. "I believe you are right."

"What is wrong, my friend? Tell me." Mikhail removed a stein from beneath the bar and pulled a draught from the keg that rested on the bar. He slid it across to Conrad who caught it and took a drink in one movement.

"Do you ever feel," Conrad said, staring down into the frothing liquid, "that everything you know is falling apart? That things will never be the same?"

Mikhail laughed deep and heartily. "Yes, my friend. During that period of my life when I decided to make a change of profession."

Conrad nodded knowingly, feeling somewhat embarrassed. Of course he had. They had grown close over the past few weeks, and Mikhail had told him much of his past. Including his time in Moscow, a member of the *komitet gosudarstvennoy bezopasnosti*—the KGB. He had spent years at the Lubyanka, and had even been close to a certain future Russian president.

"But I suppose I understand why you feel like you are in a particularly difficult transition."

Conrad saw the almost playful glimmer in his eyes.

"Oh, come now," Mikhail said, "did you really think a man of my particular talents could be kept in the dark about something as simple as who you are?"

Conrad started to object but Mikhail waved him off. "Please, my friend, your secret is safe with me. Besides, I am beginning to think that I am not the one you have to fear."

Conrad suddenly felt cold, and it wasn't from the draft whipping around the pub. "What do you mean?"

Time seemed to slow down. Mikhail stared him cold and hard in the eyes. Then he reached down behind the bar. When his hand came up, he was holding a business card.

"A man came into my bar today. He asked me if I had seen anyone fitting your description. I told him I had not, and that I had never heard of you. He told me I was lying, but that he understood, that I was only being a good friend. He told me that he wasn't looking for you. He said you were looking for him. He said that when you were ready, he would be waiting."

"Did he leave a name?"

"No," said Mikhail. "He left only this."

Mikhail dropped the card on the table and Conrad thought it landed with the sound of thunder.

"I know this group," Mikhail said, as Conrad's trembling fingers touched the corners of the thin piece of cardboard. The image of the globe seemed to glimmer in the candlelight.

"What do you mean you know them? They aren't real."

Mikhail's laughter rebounded off the walls and ceiling of the darkened pub. "Oh they are real, my friend. Very real—and very dangerous."

Conrad downed his drink and slid the tankard over to Mikhail, who filled it and slid it back without a word of question or answer.

"During my time at the *kontora*, I had a run-in with one of their, how do you say, representatives. A man came to see me. He said he had a business proposal. It was very unusual, of course. Such things did not happen in the old Soviet. He knew what I did for a living, knew my title and position. I threatened to have him arrested, but he just smiled. 'You must choose,' he told me. 'Only you can do this job, and this job is only for you.'"

"Did you take it?"

Mikhail nodded.

"And what happened?"

Mikhail gazed down at the bar top, wiping it with an old, dirty towel, seemingly lost in the swirl of stale beer and spilled whiskey.

"The job is your own, my friend. And as much as I like you and trust you, it is not something I can share with you. Maybe one day, but not tonight. I suppose that this is all to say—the world is a stage, life is a play, and we are the puppets. It's better not to ask who pulls the strings. Now you are on the line. You have been chosen for something, and it will no doubt change your life. Forever."

Conrad glanced down at the card in his hand. He slipped it into his pocket and drank down his beer. For a single moment, he considered that he'd drunk enough during this night to slay a small horse, and yet he felt fine.

"How much do I owe you?"

Mikhail shook his head. "Tonight, it's on the house. I have a feeling you are going to need all the good will you can get."

Conrad nodded. "Thanks for the beer and the game. I'll get you next time."

"Sure you will." Mikhail smiled and held up his massive hand in a gesture of farewell. Conrad wondered if it might be farewell forever.

"Until then," Conrad said, trying to fight off that feeling of finality, the feeling that he was walking into something so massive and so potentially dark that he might never escape its gravity. He left the bar behind and stepped into the cold night.

The walk back to the inn was uneventful, as he knew it would be. The city had gone to sleep, and he was perhaps the only person still awake now that Mikhail had closed up shop. Yet he knew that was likely not to be true. There were others as well. Watching.

The fire was burning low when he closed the door of the ancient building behind him. He sat down at his computer and was not surprised to see another riddle meet his eyes. But this one was different. There was no question, just a blinking cursor and a request for an answer. He might have been lost. But he wasn't. He wasn't at all.

He pulled out the card and flipped it over to its back. Written in black pen and looping script were the words,

"When life asks a question, three is always the perfect answer."

Conrad laughed out loud at the absurdity of it all. But he couldn't help himself. Instead he spread his fingers across his keyboard and pressed the number. The block of text swirled and spiraled, forming the image of what looked to be a full moon, partially obscured by a cloud. Then the words formed, and Conrad began to read again.

Three Guys Walk into a Bar

By

Jonathan Maberry

Chap. 1

The card was tucked into the cleft of a crack in the vinyl of my old Ford Escape's dashboard. The car was locked, the alarm functional but silent.

Card was still there.

I hovered there in the open doorway of the car and looked at it. Whoever had placed it there crinkled the end so the card folded back to make it easy for me to see what was printed on it.

LIMBUS, Inc.
Are you laid off, downsized, undersized?
Call us. We employ. 1-800-555-0606
How lucky do you feel?

"Balls," I said.

Chap. 2

I plucked the card out and threw it on the shotgun seat, got in, fired up the old beast, and headed out of the parking lot of the medical offices of Dr. Frieda Lipschitz.

She's a great doctor, but, seriously, no one should ever have a name like Lipschitz. I know it doesn't mean what it sounds like it means. Dr. Frieda—and I have to call her that or I can't keep a straight face—makes a point of telling everyone that it's a bastardization of Leobschütz, the German name for the Polish town of Głubczyce. Okay, sure, fine, nice history lesson. Change your name. Go with Lefkowitz or Lipstick or anything.

I mean, if you're a proctologist, you have a certain responsibility to your clients. It's a thing. Go with it.

So, there's me, driving away from Dr. Frieda's office after her telling me that I need a colonoscopy because I'm looking at fifty close enough to read the fine print and guys my age who eat like I do and drink like I do and generally act like overgrown frat boys like I do need to have someone stick a hose and a flashlight up their ass. Not how she put it, but words to that effect.

I told her I'd think about it.

She then browbeat me for twenty minutes and somehow I wound up agreeing. But...I really don't know if I could or should do it. There are complications with guys like me going under general anesthesia. Those complications could be life-changing for anyone in the E.R. if I have a bad dream.

Funny thing is, the thing she harped on the most was my cholesterol.

"You eat too much red meat," she said.

I tried to make a joke and tell her that it wasn't by choice. She didn't get it and, let's face it, it's not like I could explain.

So, she stuck her fingers in my butt, told me my prostate was okay, and cut me loose with a date for the procedure and a prescription for stuff that would "cleanse my bowels" the night before.

Given a choice between marathon pre-procedure bowel evacuation and, say, getting mugged by an entire hockey team, I'll take my chances with the hockey team. Sticks and all.

That was what I was thinking about as I drove.

The card was still on the seat next to me.

Still saying "Limbus" on it. Still reminding me of the last card with that name on it I'd had.

What was it now? Three years ago and change.

One of the nastiest cases I ever worked. Some psychopaths skinning young girls.

Yeah. Skinning.

Turns out, when I finally ran it down, the skinning wasn't actually the worst thing happening to those girls. I know, you're thinking how could it get worse than that?

There are more things in heaven and earth, Horatio.

Some of those things come into my life dragging a lot of very ugly baggage.

That case haunts me.

Absolutely fucking haunts me.

Sometimes, in the middle of the night, I wake up and see those dead girls standing around my bed. Naked of flesh, stripped of humanity, bloodless and lost.

I know I'm dreaming, but I think I'm awake. The things those girls say...

When I really wake up, I try to remember their words, but I can't. Not really. It's like the dead speak in a language that the living can't really understand. Can't, and shouldn't try.

What scares me the most is that the older I get, the more I think I'm starting to understand a few words of that language. It's becoming more familiar.

I leave night-lights on now.

Me. Sam Hunter. Ex-cop, occasional bodyguard, working private investigator. Whatever else I am. Tough and scary.

A night-light.

Shit.

The card refused to evaporate or fly out the window even though there was a breeze whipping through the car. As if it was anchored there. As if it didn't want to leave.

Limbus, Inc.
How lucky do you feel?

I stopped at a red light and watched a father cross the street while holding the hands of two little girls. Twins. Maybe four years old. Curly blond hair on one, curly red hair on the other. Otherwise identical.

The little girls looked at me. Both of them.

They smiled at me.

I smiled back.

Innocent little kids. Pretty, happy. Their whole lives ahead of them.

The group of assholes I hunted for Limbus flayed the skin from girls only a dozen years older than these two. Girls who also expected to have lives, a future. Happiness.

Dead. Destroyed.

Consumed.

The father shepherded his daughters to the other side. The little redhead kept looking back at me.

And, as the light turned green, she gave me a single, silent nod.

It was such a weird thing. Not a kid thing. It was an adult gesture, and for a flickering moment her blue eyes were filled with a much older light.

Then she turned away and the guy behind me beeped his horn.

I hit the gas too hard and jerked the Escape forward, cursed, adjusted the pressure on the pedal, and drove away from the moment.

The card was still right there.

When I pulled into the slot outside of the creaky old building where I have my office, I left the card where it was. I didn't want to bring it inside. It would mean that I was at least considering giving them a call. No way that was going to happen.

I locked my car, went up into my office.

Read the mail.

Most of it was bills. Some of it was junk.

Some of it was threatening letters.

Usual stuff.

I made some calls. Did some Net stuff for clients.

Didn't think much at all about the card.

Except that's a lie.

I couldn't *help* but think about the fucking card.

I was thinking about the card when Stevie Turks walked in with two of his goons. Card went right out of my head at that point.

Here's the thing about Stevie. His real last name is Turkleton, and he's a six-and-a-half-foot-tall lump of ugly white boy with more biceps than brains. I was warned about him when I took a missing persons case last year. Stevie likes young chicks. Ideally fifteen or so. He gets them high, gets them naked, and videotapes them having sex with Stevie and some of his crew. The video files are uploaded to a server in the Netherlands and sold to foreign buyers. I found this out while looking for a ninth-grade girl who was last seen in Stevie's storefront business—a video gamer shop on Broad Street near Girard. The girl's mother let me look around the kid's room, and that allowed me to pick up her scent. Everyone has a distinctive smell. Even kids with good hygiene. Most people can't tell.

I'm not most people.

It took me a week to find the kid. Unfortunately by then Stevie had spent way too much time with her. The kid was so far out on the edge of a heroin high that she didn't know what day it was. Barely knew her own name.

They'd been busy with her. Three video sessions a day. Different outfits. Schoolgirl clothes, cheerleader uniforms. Shit like that.

I'm no prude. But I have a very clear set of rules. Rape is, to me, no different than murder. It kills a part of the victim's soul. I've seen it way too many times. As a cop in the Cities and as a P.I. in Philly.

And when it comes to the rape of a child? When it comes to white slavery? Sex trafficking? Forced addiction?

Well...

Stevie was in the hospital for three months. Did that without changing, either. Just me, a blackjack, and a lot of moral indignation.

Would have been worse if I'd let him see the real me, but I actually wanted him to stand trial.

He lawyered up, of course, and they're taking their sweet time getting the trial started. Jury selection is next month.

Honestly, though, I didn't expect him to be stupid enough to come here, to my office. He thought he was being smart by bringing two guys who were as big as he was. The three of them looked like bridge supports. Muscles on top of muscles.

Stevie opened his jacket to show the gun tucked into his belt. One of the goons closed the door. It was after-hours; there was nobody else in the building. Again, they thought they were stacking things in their favor.

I stood up from behind my desk.

Stevie pulled his gun and pointed it at me. "You don't want to fucking move, dickbag."

Chap. 3

The killer moved through the shadows. Running low, running fast. The winding ribbon of the game trail twisted and turned, whipsawed and plunged down the backs of the hills. Night birds screamed and fled the trees, flinging their ragged bodies into the cold sky. The last of the season's crickets held their noise, their insect minds unable to process anything other than the concept of danger.

Of death.

A brown bear raised her head and sniffed the air. Then it pulled her cubs close and sheltered them with her bulk. The bear closed her eyes, not wanting to see what it was that passed so fast and so close.

The killer was aware of these things.

It drank in the intoxicating richness of sight and sound, of smell and taste. There was no drug that could match this rush. Not even the most powerful psychotropic pill or magic mushroom. Nothing came close.

It reveled in the thousand things that flooded in through its senses. The enormity of the information had been staggering at first.

At first.

Now…

Now it was greater than a sexual thrill. Greater than anything.

Almost anything.

There was one thing that sent an even more potent thrill through the killer's dark mind.

It raced toward that experience now.

With claws that tore the soft ground.

With teeth that gleamed as the killer smiled and smiled and smiled.

Chap. 4

I stayed where I was. "You really want to do this, Stevie?"

"No, I'm still fretting over whether it's a good idea."

We both grinned at that. It was a good comeback.

"They already have my deposition. On video. I signed the transcript in front of witnesses."

He shook his head. "Don't mean shit. It's your word against mine. And that little slut isn't going to be worth shit on the witness stand. My lawyers will rip her a new asshole. Not that her last asshole wasn't good. I tapped that shit. Damn if I didn't. Tight? Holy shit was she tight."

"Stevie," I said quietly, "you'd do yourself a big favor to shut the fuck up right about now."

He chuckled. "Why? Thinking about that tight little brown-eye giving you wood?"

"Stevie…," I said.

"Fuck this guy, Stevie," said one of the two goons. He had a big nose that looked like it wanted to be punched.

"Yeah, fuck him," agreed his colleague, who had no noticeable chin. "Let's do him and get the fuck out of here."

Stevie shook his head. "I'm not in a hurry. I spent three months thinking about this. This asshole suckered me and stomped me when I was down, and I need him to appreciate the consequences of his actions."

"Who writes your dialogue?" I asked. "I'm serious. Joe Pesci couldn't sell lines like that. You sound stupid, Stevie. No, let me correct that, you sound cheap. You're a third-string kiddie porn asshole and your father would have done the whole world a favor by jerking off instead of banging your mother. Now you come here and try to lay some tough guy Goodfellas rap on me like I'm supposed to go all knock-kneed. Are you kidding me?"

He brightened. "Wait, you think I'm putting this on? Really? 'Cause I think that you're going to realize just how wrong you are when I cut your dick off and stuff it in your—"

And that was as much of this bullshit as I could take. It wasn't a good day to begin with. Doctor sticking both hands and one foot up my ass. That damn card from Limbus. These assholes. The memories of the hurt in the girl's eyes when she was done with rehab and sitting with the cops to tell them what she remembered. A hurt I was sure would always be there, polluting her life, darkening her skies.

I know I said I wanted Stevie to go to trial.

I really did.

Past tense.

I jumped over the desk at him.

He wasn't expecting that.

Not a knock against him that he wasn't expecting it. The average person wouldn't be primed to make that kind of intuitive leap.

I was only a medium-sized, middle-aged man when I started the jump.

I was something else when I hit him.

I saw the way his eyes changed as he realized just how much trouble he was in. As he realized exactly what tough really was and how little judgment he possessed. As he realized that the world was so much different than what filled his limited understanding.

He'd come with superior numbers and overwhelming force to kill a man.

He did not bring enough of anything to kill the wolf.

Chap. 5

A solitary headlight cut through the forest and the killer stopped.

He froze into the moment, becoming absolutely still. The breeze blew past it, rifling hair, but the killer was now part of the vast and complex darkness of the woods. Beneath the canopy of oak and pine boughs, the floor of the forest was as impenetrable as the deepest part of the ocean. Not even a spark of moonlight fell through that ceiling.

But the headlights...

They moved along the serpentine fire access road, pushing the engine buzz in front of it.

The killer watched the light, amused by it like a traveler seeing a will-o'-the-wisp. The road the bike drove came from the southeast and curved around toward the northwest.

Toward where the killer waited.

The killer felt drool worm its way from between his lips, hang pendulously from his chin and then fall. He could hear the release of the ropey spittle. Could hear the splash as it struck the grass. He could hear everything.

The sound of the motorcycle and the glow of its light ignited a burning hunger deep in the killer's mind. His mind, first. Then in his chest, and then in his stomach.

Always in the mind.

That's where hunger began.

That's where lust lived.

The killer turned, peeling itself out of the featureless black of the forest as it stepped onto the winding road.

To wait.

Chap. 6

It takes a long, long time to bag three grown men.

Takes even longer to clean up the mess.

My office is prepped for it, though. Everything is waterproof. Everything is cleanable. I keep a bucket and mop, bleach, paper towels, rags, soap, sponges and brushes in the closet. A big box of heavy-duty contractor black plastic bags. And a wheeled mail cart.

Took me nearly five hours to clean everything up.

Played Tom Waits and Steely Dan really loud while I did it. Sometimes you got to play loud music to distract you from what you're doing. And, yes, I have playlists for this sort of thing.

My life is complicated.

I killed two more hours driving to a landfill I knew of and dumping the bags, then driving back. Tried not to look at the card while I was driving. Still hoping it would blow out the window. Still didn't. Came back to the office, drank some beer. Watched a DVR of the All-Star game and fell asleep on my couch.

I didn't start thinking about the card until I woke up. Took a poor-man's shower standing in front of the sink and washing myself with paper towels. Thought about coffee and decided to go find some.

The card was still in my car when I came outside at a quarter to seven in the morning.

Except it wasn't where I left it.

It should have been on the passenger seat. Instead it was tucked into the cracked vinyl where I'd found it the first time.

But this time it was turned backward so I could see what somebody'd written in blue ballpoint. One word.

"Now."

I looked at the card.

I got out of the car and looked around the area. The usual suspects were doing what they usually do. Cars passed on Street Road, heading everywhere but where I gave a shit. No one was looking at me. No one looked like the kind of person who'd leave this kind of card.

I didn't want to call the number. They might as well have printed *nothing but trouble* in red embossed typeface.

I said, "Fuck."

I went back into my office.

And called the goddamn number.

Chap. 7

The motorcycle rounded the curve in the road and the light splashed its whiteness ahead. The pale light painted the figure standing in the road.

The driver tried to stop in time.

He swerved.

He braked.

The bike turned and began to slew sideways toward an inevitable collision. One that would break bone and burst meat and splash the landscape with blood that would be black as oil in the night.

The killer did not move.

Not right away, at least.

As the bike and its driver skidded and spun toward him, the killer rose up from four legs to two. He bared his teeth and with red joy reached out to accept the gift that was being given.

It was not just meat and blood that fed him.

He feasted on the screams as well.

Oh, how delicious they were. And he made sure they lasted a long, long time.

Chap. 8

The voice that answered did not belong to the beautiful woman who'd hired me last time.

The voice was male.

Nasal, high-pitched, fussy. If a Chihuahua could talk, it would be like that.

Funny and cute if it was a cartoon. Less so on a business call.

Instead of saying "Hello" or any of that shit, he picked up halfway through the second ring and said, "Mr. Hunter."

My name, not his.

"Who's this?"

"We're delighted you called, Mr. Hunter."

"I'm not. Who is this?"

"Limbus," he said.

"No, your name."

A pause. "My name is Cricket."

"First or last?"

"Just Cricket."

"Jeez."

"And, as I said, we're delighted you called."

"Why?"

"My employers were very satisfied with the manner in which the last matter was, mmmm, handled."

The humming pause was for effect. He wanted me to know that *he* knew exactly how that case was handled. I had to use some irregular methods. Irregular for most P.I.s. Only semi-irregular for me.

"Can I speak with the lady who hired me before?"

"Mmmm, which lady would that be?"

"Don't jerk me off."

Another pause. "That person is no longer a part of this organization."

"What happened to her?"

"She is, mmmm, engaged in other work," said Mr. Cricket. "And before you ask, Mr. Hunter, I am not at liberty to discuss the matter."

"Balls."

To be fair, it was what I expected. I would have been genuinely surprised if I ever saw her again.

I sighed. "Okay, so what do you want?"

"Are you, mmm, familiar with the town of Pine Deep, Pennsylvania?"

"Sure. In Bucks County, on the river."

"Have you ever been there?"

"No. I heard it burned down."

"There was some trouble," Cricket said diffidently, "but that was a number of years ago. It has been, mmmm, substantially rebuilt."

"Big whoop. How's that matter to me?"

"We would like you to go there."

"Why?"

"To conduct an investigation."

"What would I be investigating?"

"There have been a series of, mmm, attacks."

"What kind of attacks?"

"Murders."

"Murders? Plural?"

"Five murders," he said. "And one person seriously injured."

"That's too bad. Correct me if I'm wrong, but don't even one-Starbucks towns in Bucks County have police departments?"

"They do."

"Maybe you haven't heard, but unless you're in a movie, it's pretty rare for anyone to hire a private investigator to go anywhere near a police matter. Cops, as a rule, take that sort of thing amiss."

"Amiss," he repeated, apparently enjoying the word.

I waited.

Cricket said, "You used to be a police officer."

"'Used to be' is a phrase you should look at more closely."

"You're *still* an investigator."

"Private. And let me reiterate that P.I.s do not—I repeat *do not*—interfere with active police cases. Cops tend to get cranky about that. Cranky cops can make life very difficult for working P.I.s, even small-town, cranky cops. If I interfered, I could get my ticket pulled."

"I do not believe that would happen in this case, Mr. Hunter."

"Why, are you cats going to pay for my lawyer?"

"Mmmmm, no."

"Are you going to run interference between me and local law?"

"No."

"Then have a swell day."

"Mr. Hunter, the reason you won't have those kinds of problems is that the Pine Deep Police have requested our assistance."

I said nothing.

"They have, in point of fact, requested *your* help."

"Me?"

"Well, perhaps I should clarify...your actual name was not included in the request."

"Then what—?"

"Well, mmmm, through various channels, the chief of police in Pine Deep has been searching for an expert in a certain kind of crime."

"I'm no expert. More of a general practitioner. Jack-of-all-trades, master of none," I said, trying and failing to make a small joke.

"Forgive me, Mr. Hunter, but we disagree with that assertion. You are exceptionally well qualified for this particular kind of crime."

"How so?"

"Because of the unique nature of the murders."

That's when I got the first real tingle of warning. Small, but serious. The smart thing to do would have been to simply end the call. No goodbyes, no polite refusals, just hit the button, put the cell phone in the bottom drawer of my file cabinet, and go to the multiplex to watch a movie about things blowing up. Maybe get some Ben and Jerry's afterward.

That's what I should have done. I knew it then, and I sure as shit know it now.

Instead, I felt my mouth speak, heard my voice say, "What do you mean?"

I swear to Christ that I could *hear* him smile. Like a fisherman who knew that his last tug had set the hook.

"The victims," he said after the slightest pause, "were torn apart and partially, mmmm, consumed."

"Oh," I said.

"And at the scene of each crime the forensics experts took castings of an unusual set of prints. Do you, mmmm, care to guess which kind of prints?"

I pinched the bridge of my nose. "Not really," I said.

"Just so," he said.

There was a very long silence on the line. Mr. Cricket did not seem interested in breaking it. He wanted me to jump out of the water into his little boat.

And, damn it, I did.

"Tell me the rest," I said.

Chap. 9

The killer sagged back from the orgy of its feast.

Sated.

Swollen.

His mouth tingled from the hundreds of tastes present in fresh meat and blood.

His cock was turgid from the frenzy of the kill.

His eyes were glazed from the intoxicating beauty of it all.

He rolled over and flopped onto his back, letting the night breeze cool the blood on skin and mouth and hands.

Hands now. Not paws.

He lay there and stared up through the trees. They were sparser here above the road and he could see a few stars.

He could see the moon.

It was a sickle-slash of white. So bright. So bright.

Chap. 10

After the call was over, I sat slumped in my chair, staring a hole through the middle of nowhere.

Cricket hadn't told me much more, saying the local law in Pine Deep would give me the whole story. He suggested I familiarize myself with that troubled little town. The story was readily available on the Net.

When we finally got to the question of my fee, Cricket made his mmmm-ing noise again and said, "Third drawer down."

After which the line went dead.

I pushed my wheeled chair back from my desk and looked at the bottom drawer. It was closed, the way I'd left it and I hadn't checked it since getting back. The wall clock ticked its way through a lot of cold seconds while I sat there. I hadn't told Cricket I was taking the job. We had no formal agreement. And whatever was in that drawer did not constitute acceptance on my part. Not unless I put it in the bank.

So, I could just leave it there.

Or I could mail it back to them.

Except that there was no address on the card. Just the number.

I drummed my fingers very, very slowly on the desktop.

The minute hand had time for two whole trips around before I opened the drawer.

The usual stuff was there. Yellow legal pads, box of disposable mechanical pencils, extra rolls of Scotch tape, plastic thing of staples, a dog-eared Jon McGoran thriller I was rereading.

And the envelope.

Placed very neatly and squarely in the exact center of the drawer's interior space. Fussy. Like I imagine everything was on Cricket's desk. I think he even straightened the stuff in my drawer.

"Mmmm," I said in acknowledgment.

The envelope was a standard number ten, off-white, with nothing written on the outside.

I could tell right away that it wasn't a check. Checks are flat. The contents of this envelope distorted its shape. Bulged it.

I sighed and reached for it. Hefted it, weighed it in my hand.

Heavy.

Heavy is nice. First nice thing about this matter.

I tried to judge how much would be in there. If it was fives, tens and twenties, it could be five hundred. Half a week's income for me, on a good week.

I tore open the top and let the bundle of bills slide down into my hand.

The top bill was not a five, a ten, or a twenty.

Mr. Benjamin Franklin smiled at me with a smug awareness as if to say, "Yes, son, we all have a price."

I took a breath and folded down the corner of the top bill.

The next one was a hundred, too.

So were the next thirty-nine.

My scalp began to sweat.

The stack didn't end there, though.

There were six bills with the face of someone I'd never seen on a piece of paper currency. Read about them, but never actually looked at one.

William McKinley.

The denomination insisted that this was a five hundred dollar bill.

There were six of these.

Six.

I turned on my computer and did a search to see if these were even in circulation anymore.

They weren't. The last five hundred dollar bills had been printed in 1945.

These were all from 1934. All crisp and clean as if they'd never been used.

I did a second search to see if they were still worth five hundred.

They were not.

Not even close.

I found auction sites that listed them, that sold them.

My scalp was sweating even more. So was every other part of me.

I called the number for one of the auction houses, a place in Doylestown. The receptionist transferred me to the rare coins guy. When I explained what I had, the man snorted and asked me if I was making a prank call. I assured him I was not.

"And you have *six* such bills?"

"Yes," I assured him.

"Would you mind reading the serial numbers to me?" The skepticism was thick in his tone.

I read the numbers. They were all in sequence.

He made a sound somewhere between a gasp and a growl.

"Please," he said, "assure me that this is not a joke."

"Not unless someone is playing one on me. But, look, just tell me...are these still good? I mean, could I deposit them in my bank?"

He made that sound again. Much louder this time.

"Please, sir, do not even *joke* about that. If these are legitimate bills, and if they are in the condition you describe, then they have considerable worth."

"Yeah...I saw something on your site that they might be worth fifteen hundred or—"

"No," he said abruptly.

"Oh," I said, deflated, "then—"

"If these bills are real then they are worth a great deal more than that."

"Like...how much more?"

"Do you have any understanding of rare currencies?"

"Not beyond that fact that it's rare for me to *have* currency."

He gave a polite little laugh. Enough to tell me that I wasn't as funny as I thought I was, or maybe that this was no time for jokes.

"Rarities of any kind are what drive the passion for collection. Art, coins, stamps...they have value based on a number of factors. Condition—even a scratch can take hundreds off of a rare penny, and—"

"Right, I understand that part."

"Condition is one factor in determining value. The actual degree of rarity is another. Take, for example, the 1933 Saint-Gaudens Double Eagle. When the Depression was in full swing, President Roosevelt took the country off the gold standard and recalled all gold coins for melting. About a dozen of that particular coin never made it back to the mint or were smuggled out again by enterprising government employees. One of those coins resurfaced in 1992 and was confiscated by the Secret Service but was not melted down. In 1933 it had a face value of $20; in 2002, it was sold at auction for over seven million dollars."

"Jesus Alexander Christ."

"Exactly."

"Now the third thing that can influence the value of an item is provenance. You know what that is?"

"Sure—who owned it, when they owned it, how it moved from owner to owner. Like that."

"Like that, yes. In the case of the 1934 Five Hundred Dollar Bills, there is a sequence of them that were part of a private collection of rarities. The entire collection, by the way, was appraised in 1973 and at that time valued at just under nine million dollars. It would be worth considerably more now."

"And these bills?"

"They are all from the missing sequence. There were ten bills in sequence. One turned up in Lambertville, New Jersey, in 2006. The rest have remained completely off the radar since the owner of that collection died."

"Who was he and when did he die?"

There was a pause. "Excuse me, Mr...?"

"Hunter," I said. "Sam Hunter."

"Excuse me, Mr. Hunter, but would you be willing to engage our firm to handle any auction for these bills? I can assure you that no one else would be able to get you a higher price for them, or a quicker sale."

"If I decide to sell them," I said, "we can talk. Right now I need to know more about the bills. That'll help me decide what to do."

"I understand."

"What's your name?" I asked.

"Milton Peabody," he said. It seemed about right. He had a Milton Peabody kind of voice.

"So who owned the bills?"

"They were part of the private collection of a foreign gentleman who moved to Eastern Pennsylvania in the late nineteen sixties. His name was Ubel Griswold."

That name rang a very faint bell. Not a nice bell, either, but no matter how hard I scrabbled for details there was nothing in my memory. I wrote it down so I could do a search later.

"And where did this Griswold guy live?"

Mr. Peabody said, "He lived in Pine Deep. And that is where he was murdered."

Chap. 11

The killer got slowly to his feet. He stumbled once in the dark. The man could see less than the beast. He longed to revert, to stay in the other shape. Always.

Always.

Always.

But that other mouth was not made for speech, and he needed to speak.

He was naked, but around his neck was a small metal disk on a sturdy chain. The chain was painted a flat black so that it caught no light. The disk had a single button.

He caught it between thumb and forefinger that were sticky with blood. He pressed the button.

"I...," he began, then coughed and spat out a wad of clotted blood. "I need a cleanup team."

He did not speak in English.

Chap. 12

So, yeah, I took the case.

Cricket told me that an email with some case details would be in my inbox. It was. Somehow, though, Cricket had blanked out his own return email address. Like most P.I.s, I know some tricks about tracing emails. I hit a dead end right away. Whoever these Limbus people were, they were very tech savvy. They left me nowhere to go.

So, I opened the email. There was no text, just an attachment with five photos. I opened them and sat for a long time looking at the pictures. Five people. Two men, two women, one child.

They were all dead. They had all been torn up.

These were morgue photos rather than the more useful crime scene photo. Two of the victims were in pretty good shape—relatively speaking. They had massive chest and throat wounds, but were otherwise intact. Whole.

The other three were not.

Whole, I mean.

Each of them had been torn to pieces. Actual pieces.

"This was no boat accident," I said in my best Richard Dreyfus, but there was no one around to get the joke.

I zoomed in on the photos and studied the wounds. I'm no forensic expert, but I know how to read wound patterns. To guys like me, they tell a very clear story. Flesh torn by bullets and flesh torn by knives tell one kind of story. Friction injuries of a certain pattern can indicate a motorcycle accident or a fall down a mountain. There are distinct differences in dog bites, rat bites, and snake bites. You simply have to understand human tissue and bone, something of physics, something of anatomy.

What I was seeing told a very specific story. Maybe a coroner might have some problems with it because of the angle of certain wounds, the depths of the bite marks, the apparent bite strength needed to crush bones like the humerus and femur. Me? I could read this like a book.

Personal experience is a great teacher.

I saved the images to my computer and thought about the money.

The money would go into my bank, but not riding a deposit slip. Before I did that, though, I ran a high-res scan of each side of each bill and sent the files to myself via DropBox.

I also sniffed each bill.

I do that. I'm not weird the way it sounds. I'm weird in a different way. My sense of smell is better than most. Better than most dogs, if you want to make a point of it. Sniffing the bills told me a lot.

First, I could tell that they'd been handled by someone, but not recently. It was an old scent, just a trace. And that's really interesting because it meant that no one had handled that money recently, and by recently I mean in years. The scent was really old, barely there. How had those bills then been placed in the envelope? The hundreds were mixed bills, most of them relatively recent. Late nineties into the early

2000s. Stuff that's still in circulation. The same human scent was on them, too.

That scent and no other.

"Curiouser and curiouser," I said to the empty room. I did not for a moment believe that the scent was that of the mysterious Mr. Cricket. There was also no residual smell of latex from gloves. What had they used to stuff the envelope? Plastic tweezers?

I spent some time going over the envelope, but if there was anything to find, not even my senses could pick it up. That was very disturbing.

And, also…intriguing.

Before I left for Pine Deep, I spent a few hours on the Net reading up about Ubel Griswold and the troubles in the town. A lot of it was new to me. I used to live in Minneapolis and Pine Deep is a rural suburb of Philadelphia. Griswold, according to the news reports, had been a foreign national who'd moved to America in the 1960s. His name was German but one reporter implied that the man was either Russian or Polish. Or, maybe from Belarus, from back when that little country was known as the Byelorussian Soviet Socialist Republic. Either way, Griswold moved to the States, bought some land, and set himself up as a small-time cattle farmer in a section of Pine Deep known as Dark Hollow. In 1976, the area was rocked by a series of particularly savage killings. There was a whole slew of them and it was believed they were the work of one man, whom the papers nicknamed "the Reaper." Reporters love titles like that.

The manhunt for the Reaper was intense and the leading suspect in those killings was an itinerant day laborer and blues musician named Oren Morse. Known locally as the Bone Man because he was as thin as a scarecrow.

Ubel Griswold vanished on a—you guessed it—dark and stormy night, and his body was never found. The locals apparently ran Morse to ground and lynched him. The killings stopped at that point, so it seemed pretty clear they'd killed the killer.

If the story ended there, it would be weird and sad enough, but there was a second part. Thirty years to the actual day of the Reaper killings, another psychopath came to town in the person of one Karl Ruger. He was a real piece of work. A former mob button man who'd gone way off the reservation into Hannibal Lecter territory. Apparently Ruger had ties to a local group of radical white supremacist militiamen and they put together a terrorist attack that still stands as the worst example of domestic terrorism on U.S. shores. You read about it in the papers, maybe saw the movie they did. Or read the books. The Trouble. That's what they call it.

Ruger and the other assholes spiked the town's water supply with hallucinogens during a big Halloween festival. Pine Deep was wall-to-wall with tourists. Everyone went apeshit nuts. Eleven thousand people died.

No matter how many times I read and reread that number, it still hits me in the gut.

Eleven thousand.

Three times that many were injured, and more than half the town burned down.

The Trouble.

According to the Net, the town was trying to come back. Some of it was already back, though it was no longer a Halloween tourist spot. It was settling back into being a blue-collar farming community with a scattering of craft shops and some galleries.

That's what I learned from web searches.

So, while I drove out there, I tried to make sense of those events—forty years ago and ten years ago—and how they might connect with recent murders. There was damn little about the new killings in the press, and every story I read suggested that each of the victims died in a violent car crash or farm-related accident. Not one word of anything criminal. The news stories didn't mention anything about animal attacks either, which means either that was squashed or the reporters out there are dumb as fuck. My guess was the former.

I hit Route 611 and turned north.

Chap. 13

The killer watched the big man in the woods.

The man was dressed in dark clothes. Battle dress uniform, boots, a shoulder rig with a holstered pistol. A Beretta. A knife clipped to the inside of the right front pants pocket.

The killer crouched on the thick oak limb and leaned down to watch.

The big man walked around the wreck of the motorcycle. He touched nothing. He stood for long moments studying it. He walked the perimeter of the crash scene, then out to the road, then back.

Occasionally the big man spoke out loud even though he was alone.

The killer strained to hear.

"Bug," the big man said, "looks like we got another one." He read the bike's license plate number. He gave a physical description of the driver. Or what was left of the driver. He stood as if listening. "No, tell Top and Bunny to check out that car crash in Lambertville. I'll call if I need them to come a'running."

He listened again.

"No. I think I'm going to have to talk to the locals on this. Yeah, I know the chief. Ornery little bastard. Okay. Cowboy out."

The big man suddenly straightened as if he'd heard something. His gun was suddenly in his hand. It was like a magic trick. The man was fast.

So fast.

He crouched and turned, bringing the gun up into a two-handed grip, eyes tracking at the same time as the gun barrel. The man was sharp.

Very sharp.

He even looked up at the surrounding trees.

For one fragment of a moment he looked directly at the killer.

But he did not see him.

The camouflage was too good, the intervening foliage too thick, the place of concealment too well chosen. So the narrowed eyes of the big man moved away. Reluctantly, though, as if the big man's instincts were not in harmony with his senses. As if his instincts were sharper, more primitive. Limited by the sensory awareness potentials of the modern human.

The killer smiled.

He could understand that.

He did not move at all.

But he watched every single thing this big man did. This was a dangerous, dangerous man. This was a killer in his own right. That much was obvious. His speed, the confidence he demonstrated as he turned to face the unknown. As if he'd faced — and fought — things that came at from unexpected directions. Many times.

He had that kind of aura.

The killer in the trees watched the killer with the gun.

He wanted so badly to fight this man.

To battle with him in the most primal of ways.

To revel in defeating him.

To taste the blood of another predator.

To eat a warrior's heart.

Chap. 14

Pine Deep is a triangular wedge of fertile farmland and mountains in Bucks County. It's bisected by Interstate Alternate Extension Route A-32, lying hard against the Delaware River that separated Pennsylvania from New Jersey and framed on all sides by streams and canals. A-32 wavers back and forth between the two states, across old iron bridges and up through farm country and then plows right through the town. To the southwest was the much smaller town of Black Marsh, and above Pine Deep was the even tinier Crestville. A-32 was the only road that cut all the way through those three towns. All other roads inside the triangle lead nowhere except someone's back forty or to the asymmetrical tangle of cobblestoned streets in Pine Deep's trendy shopping and dining district. Bigger and more prosperous towns like Doylestown, New Hope, and Lambertville were pretty close, but Pine Deep felt more remote than it was. Like a lot of farming towns in America, it covered an astounding amount of real estate for the number of people who lived there. Some of the farms had ten thousand acres of corn or pumpkins or garlic and maybe a dozen people living in the farmhouse and related buildings. Migrant workers did a lot of the labor.

I rattled across the bridge and drove into Pine Deep in the middle of an afternoon that was hotter than the weatherman said it would be. The trees were heavy with lush growth, and the brighter greens of spring had given way to the darkness of summer leaves. Towers of white cumulonimbus clouds rose like the pillars of heaven, but the distant western sky was softer, painted with cirrus clouds in brushstrokes of gray-white. There were birds up there, and at first I thought they were hawks, but they were too big. Probably turkey vultures.

I slowed to a stop on the shoulder of the road and leaned out to look up at them. Counted them.

Thirteen.

I tried not to make anything of that.

Spooky town, meaningless coincidence.

I kept driving.

A-32 rolls on for mile after mile and I didn't see a single living soul. The corn was half-grown and stiff and tall. The pumpkins were only pale knobs. Way off in the distance the farmhouses looked like toys from a Monopoly set. I drove past a tractor sitting at an angle in the middle of a fallow field, the engine rusted to a bright orange. A threadbare crow stood on the curve of the seat-back, his head turning slowly to follow the passage of my car. Flies swarmed in the air over a dead raccoon whose head had been squashed flat by a car tire.

I turned the radio on to find some music to lighten the load. Couldn't get reception worth a damn except for some religious blood and thunder stuff. I dug a CD at random from the center console and fed it into the slot. Tom Waits began growling at me. Song about a murder in a red barn.

"Balls," I said and almost turned it off.

Didn't though.

Drove on, listening to Tom's gravelly voice spin dark magic under the blue summer sky.

Chap. 15

The highway wandered around between some hefty mountains and then spilled out at the far end of a small town. Kind of a Twin Peaks vibe to it. One main street. Lots of crooked little side streets. Low buildings, lots of trees. From the crest of the hill, I could look down and count all five of the streetlights.

I took my foot off the brake and let the car find its own way down the hill, coasting, in no hurry to get there. As I reached the main drag, I switched the CD player off and drove in silence through the center of town. There were people here and there, but you couldn't call it "bustling" without lying. Most of the houses and stores had been rebuilt or repaired, but here and there I could see some blackened shells. Even after ten years the town still wore its scars.

Eleven thousand people.

Were there eleven thousand ghosts haunting these hills and this sad little town? I sure as shit wouldn't buy real estate here. Not at a penny an acre.

According to the Wikipedia page for the city of Pine Deep, there were currently two thousand, one hundred and nine people living here. In town and on the farms. It was hard to believe. I'd have guessed maybe five, six hundred.

I tried to imagine what it must be like to live in a place like this. It had been devastated by domestic terrorism. It had taken a worse hit than New York on 9/11 in terms of deaths. Maybe worse still when you considered that it hadn't been done by enemies of our country or religious fanatics. This terror was homegrown. It was brother attacking brother. That's some hard shit to accept, hard to get past.

As I drove down the main street, I saw the haunted looks on the faces of the people of Pine Deep. Some looked furtively away, unwilling or unable to meet the eyes of a stranger. Fear, paranoia, shame. Hang any label on it you think will fit.

Others stared at me, their eyes dark and intense, their attention focused and unwavering as I rolled past. I don't think I saw a single smile. I don't think I could blame anyone for being that grim, that detached. I sure as hell would be if this was my town.

I passed the Saul Weinstock Memorial Hospital, but the place was only half built. Creeper vines had crawled over the stacks of building materials and there were no lights in any of the windows.

Halfway through town, I saw the sign for the police department. It was a storefront place with big ceramic pots with dead evergreens beside the door. I nosed my car into an angled slot and killed the engine.

The sign on the glass door read:

PINE DEEP POLICE DEPT.
Chief Malcolm Crow

Turn around and go home, said a little voice inside my head.

"Too late for that," I murmured, and got out. As I did, a woman came out of the office. Tall, with short black hair and dark blue eyes. Slim and very pretty in a no-nonsense country way. Around fifty but fighting it and winning. A touch of makeup and a mouth that looked made for smiling, but which wore no smile. She stopped five feet in front of me and gave me an up and down appraisal. Impossible to tell what she read from my scuffle of brown hair, JC Penney sports coat over jeans, and Payless black sneakers. Probably not much.

But something flickered in her eyes and she half turned, opened the door to the police office and called inside. "He's here."

She left the door ajar.

I pasted on a friendly smile. "Are you with the police?" I asked.

A little smile flickered on her mouth. "I'm married to it."

"Oh. Then you're Mrs....um...Crow?" I ventured.

"Val Guthrie. I kept my maiden name." She offered her hand and we shook. Her hand was hard and dry and strong. She didn't go for a manly bullyboy handshake. She was strong the way women are strong. This one had zero interest in defining herself by comparison to a man. I liked that. I liked her.

"Sam Hunter," I said.

"You're the private investigator?"

"Yes, ma'am."

"Named 'Hunter?'"

"Yes."

"That a stage name or something?"

"No. It's a coincidence, but I've come to embrace the cliché."

That upped the wattage on her smile as she reappraised me. "You're a smartass."

"Says so on my business card. Sam Hunter, Professional Smartass."

She laughed. "You're going to get along fine."

She patted me on the shoulder and, still smiling, walked toward a parked Ford F-250 pickup whose bed was piled high with burlap sacks of seed. I watched her go, admiring both the straightness of her posture, and the curves that went with the whole package. Smart, sexy, and powerful. Nice.

I turned to the open office door and wondered what kind of a husband a woman like that would have. My guess would be someone who looked like Thor from the *Avengers* movies. Some big, tanned Nordic son of a bitch with muscles on his muscles and maybe a bit of aw-shucks in his voice. Or one of those redneck giants who bench press Hereford cows. Probably politically to the right of Sarah Palin. Rural Pennsylvania bears a lot of resemblance in attitude and culture to the less progressive back roads of Mississippi.

As I went in, the man I saw behind the desk was the precise diametric opposite of my guess.

He stood up to meet me, a wide grin on his elfin face. He was shorter than the woman who'd just left—call it five-seven and change. Slight build, curly black hair that had gone mostly gray, a sallow tan crisscrossed with white lines from old scars. His nametag said CROW.

"Mr. Hunter?" he asked, extending his hand.

Chap. 16

The killer followed the big man back to the road, then hid behind a rhododendron while the man got into a black SUV and drove away. The killer noted the license number, but if this man was what he thought, that plate number would likely be a dead end.

That was fine.

The big man was hunting now.

Hunting him.
The killer wanted to make very sure that the big man found his prey.

Chap. 17

"Sam Hunter, sir," I replied, taking the chief's hand. For a little guy, he had a good, strong hand. Shooter's callus on his index finger, and a ring of calluses all the way around to his thumb. Only other guy I know with those kinds of hands trained with those Japanese swords. *Katanas.*

"How can we help you?"

"I was asked to come here and—"

Still smiling, Crow interrupted, "Let's see your driver's license, P.I. ticket, and any other I.D. you'd like to show me. That's it, spread it all out on the counter."

I did as he asked, and he scooped it up and took it over to his desk. He didn't offer me a chair. Cops have a right to ask private dicks to jump and to ask how high on the way up; and if we don't jump the right way, they can get a judge to pull our license faster than you can say Sam Spade. At best, P.I.s are an irrelevant fact of life to cops; at worst, we are flies to be swatted. I did not feel like being swatted.

I stood like a schoolboy in the principal's office while he studied my cards and then typed my information into his computer. Crow made a few calls and I watched his face. He frowned, he grunted, his eyebrows arched. He'd be a lousy poker player. Finally he sat there, lips pursed, for maybe fifteen seconds. I wondered if he was jerking my chain and decided he probably was. A wiseass comment struggled to get past my lips, but I clenched my teeth and kept it trapped inside.

"Okay," Crow said, rising and crossing to the counter that served as the intake desk. He placed my stuff down and slid it across to me. "No wants, no warrants."

I nodded and put the cards back into my wallet.

"I called Minneapolis P.D. and some buddies in Philly. You don't have a lot of friends out there."

"Hoping to make some here," I said.

He grinned. "Let's see how that works out."

We stood there and smiled at each other for a moment. Then Crow waved me past the counter to his desk, nodded at the patched and creaking leather guest chair, and sank into a slightly bigger one on the other side.

"Chief," I said, "before we begin—"

"Crow," he corrected.

"Hm?"

"Everybody calls me Crow. I don't like 'Chief' 'cause it makes me feel like I should be wearing feathers, and I don't like 'Mister' 'cause my dad was Mr. Crow and he was kind of a dick. So, Crow."

"Fair enough. I'm Sam."

We nodded to seal that.

"Crow, before we begin, I'd like to understand why I'm here."

"Me, too," he said.

"Um...what now?"

He went to a Mr. Coffee and poured two cups, handed me one. "You go first. How'd you get here?"

I sucked my teeth for a moment, then decided to tell him the truth. Most of the truth. I left certain parts out, as I'm sure you'll understand.

"Limbus," he murmured, echoing the word.

"They said you reached out to them. That you were looking for some help on a case."

"Is that what they said?"

"More or less. They said the Pine Deep P.D. did. I guess that's you, right?"

"Mostly me. Couple officers hiding somewhere, sitting speed traps, generally fucking off. And my best guy's out at a crime scene."

"Related to this?"

"To be determined."

"Okay," I said, "but *did* you call Limbus or not? Didn't you ask them to bring in an expert?"

"Not exactly."

"Then what?"

He opened his desk drawer and removed a business card, looked at it for a moment, then handed it to me. I didn't need to read it. I already knew what it would say.

LIMBUS, Inc.
~~Are you laid off, downsized, undersized?~~
~~Call us. We employ.~~ 1-800-555-0606
How lucky do you feel?

However someone had drawn neat, straight lines through most of the text.

"Look on the back," he suggested, and I turned it over.

In very neat script someone had written a note:

We can provide a consultant
familiar with matters of this kind.

Before I could ask, he opened his desk and removed a second card. And a third. They were identical, front and back.

"I found one of these near each of the crime scenes."

"Near?"

Crow studied me for a moment. "Near. One was in my cruiser, apparently placed there *after* I arrived on the scene. My cruiser was locked."

"Ah," I said.

"Ah *what?*"

I explained where I'd found mine.

He gave a sour grunt. "The others showed up pretty much the same way. I even had an officer watch my car. He did and no one approached it that he could see."

"How sharp is your officer?"

"Sweeney?" Crow's smile was thin and wide and weird. "He's pretty sharp. Nothing gets past him."

"Except someone did."

Crow gave me a crooked smile. "That note on the back. Want to tell me what it means?"

I shrugged.

"Sorry, Sport," said Crow, "but I'm gonna need something more than a shrug. Explain to me how you are an expert."

"I never said I was an expert."

"You're here as a 'consultant,' though."

"Sure. Why not?"

"Exactly what do you consult *on?*"

That was the question I'd known was coming but didn't really know how to answer. I'd hoped that he would have been in some way clued in about me, but it was pretty clear he wasn't. Or maybe in place of a good poker face, he was a bluffer. If so, I couldn't read him.

So, I reached into my jacket and produced a set of color prints I'd made from the email attachments Cricket had sent me. I spread them out on Crow's desk, neatly, side by side.

"The news reports say these were accidents," I said.

"So do my official reports."

I shrugged. "But we both know different."

He looked at me instead of the pictures. "And you're certain these were murders?"

"I am."

"What makes you so sure?"

"Because," I said, "I've seen these kinds of murders before."

Crow nodded, gathered the photos up and handed them back to me. "So have I."

Chap. 18

The killer heard another car coming, and he faded deeper into the shadows as a police cruiser came bumping and thumping, trailing a plume of dust.

An hour ago, this same cruiser had been out here, but the officer had abruptly left minutes before the big man had arrived. The killer now understood. The big man had somehow lured the police officer away so he could have a few minutes alone at the crime scene. Now the officer was returning.

The killer shifted downwind so that he could not be detected and then climbed another tree. He settled in, drew his camouflage cape around him, and watched. The officer who got out of the car was not the same one who was here before. That first officer had been a redneck with a beer gut. This new arrival was lean and hard-muscled. Very tall. With red hair and sunglasses that he never took off, not even when he walked through shadows.

The breeze was blowing past the crime scene toward where the killer hid, and that allowed him to take the officer's scent.

Suddenly all of the alarms inside the killer's mind began to ring.

This officer was not at all what he seemed.

He was something much more.

Something powerful.

Something very like the killer.

Very much like him.

Chap. 19

Crow told me he wanted to take me to the most recent crime scene. We took his cruiser, which was a battered Ford Interceptor SUV that looked like it hadn't seen the inside of a car wash since Bush was president. As I got in, I peered at the side panel of the door.

"Is that a bullet hole?" I asked.

"Good chance," he said.

I got in. There was a hole on the inside too. A through-and-through. "You didn't get it fixed?"

He shrugged. "Air conditioner's busted. Gives a nice cross breeze."

"Uh-huh."

As we drove he talked about everything except the case. The Phillies and the Eagles—teams I didn't give a fuzzy rat's ass about since my heart belongs to the Twins and the Vikings. I said "Uh-huh" a lot. He talked about his wife's farm, which was now the fifth-largest independent garlic farm in Pennsylvania. I asked him if he had kids. He didn't answer and didn't say anything for a couple of miles. Then he started a new conversation about what he liked on TV. As if I hadn't asked the question.

So, fuck it, we talked about TV. *The Walking Dead. Game of Thrones. 24.* We both liked typical man stuff. Monsters, guns, and boobs. Big surprise. He was a closet fan of *So You Think You Can Dance.* My dirty secret was *Downton Abbey.* Total tough guys.

For most of the drive, we were backtracking the route I'd taken to get to town, but then he made a turn down a small side road. I caught the name on the sign.

Dark Hollow Road

It was a name I'd seen in the news stories. There had been murders here. And that murdered rich guy, Ubel Griswold, had lived in Dark Hollow.

I asked him about Griswold.

And Crow goddamn nearly drove us off the road and into a tree.

Chap. 20

The killer watched the big police officer.

The cop spent several minutes taking photographs and measurements.

Then the officer abruptly stopped, stiffened, and turned in a slow circle. It was very much like what the other man had done earlier.

Except the officer raised his head and sniffed the air.

Chap. 21

The Ford slewed around and kicked up gravel and leaves, barraging a weathered fence and nearly knocking the slats out. He threw it in park and wheeled on me, took a fistful of my tie, and jerked me forward so that we were inches apart.

"How the *hell* do you know about Ubel Griswold?" he snarled.

His face was insane. I mean it. Like bugfuck nuts. There was nothing in those eyes but a wild madness that scared the living shit out of me.

The moment stretched and I could feel the heat of each of his ragged breaths.

When I didn't answer, he leaned an inch closer. "Listen, dickhead, this is not a game you want to play. Not with me."

"What the fuck?" I said. And I said it slowly.

Crow shoved me back against the door. His hand rested on his holstered pistol. "I'm going to ask once more. Real nice. And believe me when I tell you that this is not an opportunity for wiseass comments or calling for a lawyer. This is you and me here in this truck and we are going to have an open and frank conversation, am I making myself crystal fucking clear?"

I held my breath.

I had an escape hatch for when things really hit the fan, but I didn't want to use it. Not on a stranger, not on a cop. And not on someone who might actually be an innocent. Not sane, by any stretch, but probably not a villain.

Besides, if the wolf came out to play there was no way to ever reclaim the moment.

So I had that ace but knew I couldn't play it. I'd be alive but in jail, or in the wind, and I didn't want to live the rest of my life that way. On the other hand, he was a cop, a stranger, and, clearly, a fucking lunatic. Or something close to it. He could mess up my entire life.

When I didn't answer, he snapped, "Do you understand me?"

I nodded. "Loud and clear. It's your game, man. Just calm down."

"I'll calm down when I have a reason to. And don't you tell me what to do. You're on the wrong side of the badge to do that. Now…let's try this one last time—how do you know Ubel Griswold?"

"I don't know him."

"How do you know *about* him?"

"From Google. I looked him up."

"Why? What's your connection to him?"

I said, "Limbus."

He frowned. "What?"

"Limbus. That's how I know about Griswold."

"No," he said, shaking his head. "Give me more than that."

You have to develop good instincts about people if you're going to shoot hoops in the kinds of playgrounds I frequent. My nerves were telling me this guy was half a keg short of a six-pack. My senses told me that he was scared out of his goddamn mind. And that he was primed to attack. I could smell the adrenaline. I could almost taste it.

My gut, though…

My gut told me he really was one of the good guys.

Call it instinct, call it whatever.

I held up my hands in a no-problem way.

"Okay," I said. "I'll tell you, but you're scaring the shit out me with that gun."

He looked down at his hand, at the fact that he'd unsnapped the holster. He made a little grunting sound. Surprise at what his hand was doing while he wasn't watching.

"Fuck," he said.

"Fuck," I agreed.

Didn't snap the holster though. Instead he laid his hand on his thigh. A token gesture that lowered my blood pressure by maybe half a point.

"Talk," he said.

I took a breath, and told him about Limbus, about Cricket, and about the envelope of money.

Crow didn't say a word the entire time. Didn't ask a question. Instead he sat there and chewed on his lower lip and looked strange. Older. Confused. Tired. He took his hand off his lap and rubbed his eyes, then spent almost a full minute looking out the window.

"Shit," he said.

I cleared my throat. "Don't suppose you want to tell me what the hell's going on? 'Cause, Chief, I'm pretty sure I've never been this confused before."

"Welcome to Pine Deep," he muttered.

"Huh?"

"Nothing."

We sat there for another minute. Doesn't sound like a lot of time until you're peeling the seconds off one at a time while seated next to an armed crazy person.

Out of the blue, Crow asked, "What do you know about the Trouble?"

I shrugged. "What everyone else knows. Maybe a little less. I mean, sure, it was big news for a while. Domestic terrorism, over ten thousand people dead. Worst day in U.S. history. Got that. I didn't hear Ubel Griswold's name in any of that, though, except in a footnote about a coincidence. Him getting killed thirty years to the day before the Trouble here."

He nodded. "Yeah. You ever see the movie they made? *Hell Night*? Or read the book?"

"No. I read a review when it came out. Saw it on Redbox but didn't get it. I heard they changed the story around. Made something supernatural out of it."

"Something like that."

"So? Why are we talking about it?" I asked.

He looked out the window at the cornfields to the right side of the road and the deep, dark forest on the other.

"If you weren't here because of that Limbus card, I wouldn't be saying what I'm about to say," said Crow.

"Um...okay."

"The story about the white supremacists spiking the town's water, driving everybody crazy?"

"Yeah?"

"Kind of true."

"*Kind* of?"

"Kind of. It was a cover story."

"Wait," I said, "are you saying there was a government cover up?"

Crow shook his head. "Not exactly. Not the way you're thinking. The Feds *did* cover some things up, but there was a group of white supremacist dickheads operating in town, and they did, in fact, dump a bunch of hallucinogens into the water. Fritzed everyone out. They also planted bombs to blow up the bridges, knock down the cell towers, take out all phone and cable service, and generally turn the main part of town into World War III."

"I don't—"

"That happened," he said. "But the tricky thing is that all of that was itself a cover for something else."

"Wait, the white trash dickheads were covering up for someone? Who? I don't understand. And, if that was a cover-up, why'd the Feds use that story, too?"

He smiled at the windshield. No visible humor in it, though.

"Because the cover story was something everyone could sell. Domestic terrorism. White power. Racism. Drugs in the water. That's doable. That makes sense. That's something, scary as it was, tragic as it was, people could live with. The rest of the country, I mean. Maybe the rest of the world. They could live with that story, especially since all of those militia assholes died that night."

"You lost me a couple of turns back, man."

"No," he said, "I just haven't gotten to the part where it makes sense. Or, maybe I should say I haven't gotten to the truth. 'Cause unless you're who or what I think you are, this isn't going to sound like the truth and it isn't going to make any fucking sense at all."

"You are scaring the living piss out of me here," I said.

He nodded. "Yeah, being scared is absolutely the appropriate response. I was scared then. More scared than I've ever been in my life. But I have to tell you, Mr. Hunter, that I am starting to get that scared again."

"Why?"

"Because I'm afraid that what was happening then is happening now. That it's happening again."

"Okay...but what did happen back then? If there was a cover story, then what was it covering up?"

That's when he finally turned to me and I saw all sorts of dark lights glimmering in his eyes. If he'd looked crazy before, then he looked absolutely lost now.

"The whole thing, the drugs, the violence, all of that was done to hide the fact that there were monsters in Pine Deep."

I had to take a moment on that. "When you say...'monsters'...?"

"I mean monsters. Vampires and..."

When he didn't finish, I pushed him.

"And what?"

He looked me right in the eye.

"And werewolves."

To which I said, "Oh shit."

To which he replied, "Yeah."

We sat there.

Talk about the elephant in the room.

I said, "You're looking at me funny."

He said, "I guess I am."

"Am I going to regret asking?"

"Depends on how this conversation goes," he said. "Could play out a bunch of different ways."

"You're making a lot of assumptions. You know how that usually turns out."

He shrugged. I noticed he'd placed his hand on his lap again. Very close to the gun.

Again.

Balls.

"I'm going to say a word," he said. "It's a word that the Limbus guy used. He didn't explain what it was. He figured I already knew. Which I do."

"Okay."

"I'm going to say it and then you're going to tell me the first thing that comes to mind. Fair enough?"

"I don't like games," I said.

"Not a game."

I said, "Shit."

Then I said, "What's the word?"

His hand moved an inch closer to his pistol.

Let's face it, I expected the word to start with a "W."

Instead, he used a different word. A lot more precise. A word that changed the entire dynamic between us.

He said, "Benandanti."

I looked at him, at his face, his eyes. At the expression he wore.

I took a breath and said, "Yes."

He closed his eyes.

And said, "Thank God."

Chap. 22

Without another word, he turned in his seat, restarted the car, put it in drive, and hit the gas. We drove for maybe a mile before he said anything. I sure as hell wasn't starting any conversations.

Crow said, "Tell me."

"I don't talk about this with anyone."

"Tough. Tell me."

"You used the word," I said. "You know what it means."

"Sure," he said, "I know what the word means. 'Goodwalker.' I want to know what it means to you."

"I think you already know."

"That's not what I mean. I want some background on you. Because if the stuff that's happening is what I think it is, then there's only two sides. Black and white. No gray area at all."

I nodded. He was being very cagey about it. So was I. We were dancing around it because, hell, this really isn't the kind of conversation people have.

I mean, I do, but only at home, when I'm around my aunts and my grandmother and my cousin. They're like me. They're exactly like me. Families tend to keep secrets like this. I've always kept it to myself. Usually the only people who find out about our family secret do so on their last and worst day.

On the other hand, I think I can say for certain that the people at Limbus—whoever or whatever the fuck they are—know. Why else would I be here? Cricket knew that I'd recognize the bite and claw patterns in those photos.

He was right.

"This has to go two ways," I said. "If I show you mine, you got to show me yours."

"You comfortable with the way that came out?" he asked.

"You know what I mean."

"Yeah. And…yes, this is a two-way street. Kind of has to be, don't you think?"

So, after another mile I began talking. Trees whipped past. The sky above us was blotted out by the canopy of fall foliage.

"It's a family thing," I said. "Going back like…forever. My bunch is more or less Irish-English mutts. Been here since five minutes after the Mayflower. But we have roots in Italy going back to Etruscan times. Like six, seven hundred years B.C., you dig?"

He nodded.

"We weren't always what you'd call saints, but I guess in our own way we've always been on the side of the angels. Not literally, 'cause that would be a little New Agey even for me. But in spirit. White hats, no matter how battered and stained those hats were."

"Nice to know," he said, then threw me a curveball. "Any relation to Theiss?"

I took a moment on that, then figured in for a penny, in for a pound. "Direct descent," I said.

"Wow."

"Wow," I agreed. "Not sure which version of the story you heard. The one that makes the history books is that back in 1692, in Jurgenburg, Livonia, a Benandanti named Theiss was arrested and put on trial for being...well, for being what he was."

"Say the word," said Crow. He cut me a glance out of the corner of his eye. "Really...say it."

I sighed. "Okay. Theiss was arrested for being a werewolf."

He took a deep breath, held it, let it out, then he picked up the story I'd started. "Theiss's defense was that at night he and the members of his order—"

"Family," I corrected.

"Family. Okay. He and the members of his family transformed into werewolves in order to fight demons and other kinds of evil. Witches, pernicious spirits. Like that. He was whipped for superstition and idolatry and let go."

"To paraphrase you," I said, "that's the story they sold to the press."

"And the real story?"

"He was tortured for a long damn time. They wanted him to confess to being an apostate of Hell and an enemy of God. But...Theiss was a tough old motherfucker. They tried it all on him. Thumbscrews, the rack, dunking. The church is nothing if not enthusiastic."

"They couldn't break him, though?" prompted Crow.

"No. In the end they let him go because they figured that he couldn't possibly endure all of the torture if he didn't have God's grace. Yada, yada, yada. So they let him go. They even gave him a nickname. You seem to know the story. What'd they call him?"

Crow smiled thinly. "The Hound of God."

"Right. The thing is, a lot of the history books get it wrong. They don't always connect the Benandanti with werewolves. Mostly 'cause there are a lot of New Age lamebrains who use that name like the Celts use 'wicca.' There are plenty of Benandanti in Europe today who come in to bless a new baby or sage a new house. Like that."

"Don't mock," said Crow. "They might be doing something useful."

"Maybe they are, but that doesn't make them true Benandanti."

"Ah," he said, "pride goeth before a fall."

"Yeah, well fuck you, too."

"Point taken."

We both smiled at that. Not sure what it meant, though.

"So," I said, "are you going to ask me the obvious question?"

"Do I need to?"

"I don't know. You tell me?"

"Sam," he said, "I knew what you were when you walked into my office."

"Why? Because Cricket told you?"

"Nope."

"Then how? I didn't wear my *'I'm A Werewolf, Ask Me How'* button today."

He didn't answer. We rounded a bend and on the other side was a parked police cruiser, lots of crime scene tape strung between tree trunks, and a big kid in a deputy's uniform leaning against the fender of the car. Maybe twenty-two. He was massive. Six-six, with more muscles than is necessary on any human being. He had his arms folded over his chest, a kitchen match between his teeth, and a scowl as dour as a country parson at a peep show.

I took one look at him and I knew why Crow knew what I was when he met me. This was his deputy.

And damn if he wasn't playing for the same team as me.

Shit.

Big Bad

The killer climbed another tree and hunkered down in the crotch, his body completely concealed by camouflage, his face painted green and brown. He had a pair of binoculars whose lenses were covered with a filter that would not reflect light. His clothes were daubed with a paste made from ground bird feathers, squirrel urine, owl feces, and insect larvae. Not even a bloodhound could smell him through that.

Not even one of his brothers could smell him.

Not unless they were very close, and the killer was six hundred feet away and fifty feet up a towering oak.

He watched the three figures below.

The smallest of the three men was strange. The killer knew him, had seen him many times in the town. Had read about him on the Internet. Chief of Police. Alcoholic. Husband to a farmer.

And, very likely, a killer, too. A man who was more dangerous than his size and age suggested.

The biggest of the three men was even harder to categorize. He was a monster, even by the killer's standards. Man, wolf and something else. There was a darkness in him that ran all the way to the soul. The killer feared him for reasons he could not name.

The third man looked weak, but wasn't. Middle-sized, middle-aged, thin and haggard. He looked like a salesman, and not a successful one. He looked tired and frail.

But the killer could smell the wolf in him.

It was a strong wolf.

A true hunter.

The killer wanted to fight him. To see which of them was stronger.

To see which of them deserved to live.

He would have to arrange that.

He knew, in fact, that he would have to face all of these men. And maybe the big man he'd seen earlier. He would have to kill them all.

He...and his family.

The slaughter would be so delicious.

Chap. 23

We sniffed each other.

I'm not proud of it.

And, don't get the wrong idea. We didn't sniff each other's asses. We're strange but we're not weird. We stood a few feet apart and took the air. His expression never flickered. Him I definitely wouldn't play poker with. If he was like me, he was cataloging everything he could from my smell. I sure as hell was.

He was bigger and stronger than me, but the wolf in him was younger. A lot younger. It was more savage than mine. Less controlled. I could feel it wanting to come out. The kid had some iron goddamn control, though.

"Okay, okay," said Crow, "you two are weirding me out. So cut the shit."

"He's the consultant?"

"Yes. Officer Mike Sweeney meet Sam Hunter, and vice versa. Shake hands and mind your manners. Both of you."

He didn't budge, so I took the cue and offered my hand. Sweeney looked at it for a moment, then without haste took it. And held it.

"Crow," he said, "this guy had blood on him. Been in a fight. Couple of different guys. No...three different guys."

My mouth went dry. No one's ever read me that way. The way I usually read people.

Crow came and stood beside Mike. "I won't ask if Mike's telling the truth," he said, "'cause Mike doesn't make those kinds of mistakes."

"Private matter," I said.

"Which you're going to tell us about," said Crow.

I shook my head. "I plead the fifth."

"No," said Crow.

"No," said Mike.

"Then we have a problem," I said. "I didn't come here to be blindsided by Sherriff Andy and Barney Fife."

"Who?" asked Mike.

Crow said, "Sam, I think it's fair to say that a lot of what's going on here isn't going to make it into any official report. If you're going to work with us, then it has to be by being straight up."

"You could arrest me."

"Pretend for a moment that I won't."

We stood there inside that moment, none of us budging.

"He killed someone," said Mike. "He changed and he killed someone."

Crow nodded. "Is that true?"

I shrugged.

"Did they need killing?" asked Mike.

I tilted my head to one side. "You hear about that case last year? Guy doping little girls and making rape porn?"

"I heard about it."

I shrugged again.

"There's not going to be a trial," said Crow, "is there?"

"Doesn't look like it."

Mike Sweeney took a step closer and sniffed again. Then he nodded and stepped back. "More than one guy."

"Even total assholes have friends."

"Had," he corrected.

"Had," I agreed.

He smiled then. A very small, thin smile. It was the kind of smile nobody—and I mean nobody—would ever want to see. There was no trace of humanity in it. No fragment of mercy.

"Fuck 'em," he said. "You're here as a consultant?"

"Yeah."

"Then consult."

With that, he turned his back on me and walked toward the crime scene.

Crow sighed.

"What was that all about?" I asked.

"Mike had a complicated childhood."

"I can imagine."

He shook his head. "No, I really don't think you could."

He turned to follow Mike, and I, feeling more awkward than I had since my first middle school dance, trudged along in his wake.

Chap. 24

I ducked under the yellow crime scene tape and moved into a space dense with shadows. A motorcycle was wrapped around a tree. Front wheel torn open, gas tank ruptured, seat dislodged, headlight glass twinkling in a thousand pieces. There was dried blood everywhere, though for once I had to rely more on sight than smell because of the presence of the spilled gasoline.

Mike took an iPad from a briefcase he'd laid on the edge of a plastic tarp near the crash site, called up an image folder and handed it to me.

"The body was transported last night. These are the photos."

I looked at them one at a time. High-res digital photography is very stark, very detailed. Artless and cruel. The body of a man lay partly atop the bike, partly on the grass. And partly fifteen feet away. He was literally torn to pieces. It was a very brutal kind of thing, and a very familiar kind of thing.

I tried my Richard Dreyfus line again.

"This was no boating accident."

Crow chuckled. Mike didn't.

"Sam used to be a cop," Crow said to Mike. To me he said, "Walk the scene. Tell me what you see."

I did. There were tire tracks that curved off the road and right into the tree. There was dead grass around the spilled gas. There was blood spatter. There was the ruined machine.

"This is bullshit," I said.

Crow and Mike exchanged a quick look.

"Walk us through it," said Crow.

We went back to the road and I reconstructed it for them. "Here's what is supposed to have happened," I said. "It rained last night, right?"

"Until ten."

"Ten. Okay. And when was the crash?"

"Passing motorist called it in at ten-twenty-one."

"Uh-huh. So, the story is this. Guy's tooling down this black as fuck road in the middle of a rainstorm at night. Loses control, goes into a skid, wraps his bike around the tree at high speed and goes splat."

Crow put a stick of gum into his mouth and began folding the little foil wrapper with great care. "Uh-huh," he said.

"Bike had to be going at high speed and for some reason the driver didn't throttle down when he lost control."

"Uh-huh."

"To do that much damage, he had to be going at a hundred or better."

"Uh-huh."

I looked at him. "All of which amounts to a yard-high pile of total bullshit."

"Why?"

"Let's start with the road. Why would anyone be on this road at night? Does it even go anywhere?"

"It's a fire access road and it's used by the forestry service," said Mike. "Kids come up here to make out."

"Not in the rain," I said. "And not on a bike. It's not a dirt bike, either."

"No."

"In the photos, the guy's wearing jeans and a sweatshirt. In the rain?"

Crow spread his hands.

"Where's his helmet?"

"He wasn't wearing one," said Mike.

"Again I say, in the rain?"

No one bothered to answer that. I squatted by the tire tracks. "No way these were made during the storm. Look at the ridges in the mud. Even if it was drizzling, they'd be smeared more than this."

They nodded.

"And over here," I said, moving from the road onto the dirt, to a point halfway to the impact point. "See how deep it is here? The bike accelerated right here. Right when the bike was lined up with the tree."

They nodded.

I went over to the bike now and bent over it, touching various points on the fractured frame. "This is all wrong. It looked like the bike was starting to tilt away from the line of impact, like the driver was trying to avoid collision by ditching sideways. That would be the natural thing, even if you lose control in the dark. But look at the underside of the frame, right here. That's crumpled the wrong way. It should be pushed up but it's pushed in. That means the bike, while slewing sideways was starting to stand back up."

"And what does that tell you?" asked Crow.

"It tells me that whoever was riding this bike jumped off right before it hit. Jumped off with a hell of a lot of force, enough to nearly stand the bike up while it was falling over. If that was the case, then the body should have landed over here. He wouldn't have been *on* the bike when it hit. At most, he'd have gotten a leg trapped under it, but he wouldn't have hit the tree hard enough to be splattered."

Crow said, "That's pretty good. What else?"

I bent over the bike again and spent some time with it. I've seen a lot of car and motorcycle accidents, accidental and criminal. I've also seen some faked accidents before. I've been in court plenty of times to hear expert testimony on the physics of high-speed vehicular impacts. What I was seeing here didn't square with my understanding of cause and effect. I said as much to them.

"This isn't something you probably want to put in your official report," I began, "but I think someone *bent* this bike around the tree."

"Bent," said Crow.

"Bent."

"That would take a lot of muscle."

"It would."

"Could *you* do it?"

I thought about it for a moment. "No. Under certain, um, circumstances, I could mangle it pretty good, but some of these bends...no. I couldn't."

"Which brings us to our problem, Mr. Consultant."

"Yeah."

"Mike and I walked this site together and we came up with the same read on it that you gave us. Nice work, by the way."

"Thanks."

"Once the forensics guys were gone, I asked Mike to see if he could duplicate those bends."

I stared at him. And at Mike, who continued to make his matchstick bob slowly up and down. "Well," I said, "that must have been interesting."

"It was instructive," admitted Crow. "Mike was able to bend it a little. But that was with the frame already fatigued and cracked. And, trust me when I say this, Mike is a very, very strong young man."

"Knock it off, Crow," said Mike.

"I'm making a point here."

Mike looked at the trees and sighed slowly.

"So," continued Crow, "what I'm wondering is whether you and Mike working together—under, as you say, certain circumstances—could do that kind of damage."

It was an interesting question.

We all stood there and thought about it.

I shook my head first. Then Mike.

"No," I said, "not even together."

Crow nodded. "What I thought. But someone did. And either it was one very, very, *very* strong son of a bitch—someone way outside of the normal range. Or...whatever passes for normal with you guys."

I said nothing.

"Or we're dealing with something even worse. Something that's stronger than two werewolves."

I said, "Well, shit."

Mike Sweeney grinned. "Yeah, and isn't that interesting as all shit?"

Chap. 25

The killer moved away from the kill site.

He was confused by the presence of two others like him. That was wrong. That made no sense. There should only be one wolf in these woods. The big, red-haired one. The one who seemed to belong here.

But now this other one was here.

The killer did not like it.

He wasn't afraid, though. Fear was not a factor in the killer's life. Not now anyway. He was beyond that now.

He faded into the woods and vanished.

Chap. 26

"The victim," I said. "The wounds in those photos...what's the coroner going to say about it?"

"Exactly what I want him to say," said Crow.

"He, um...knows?"

"He's the coroner for Pine Deep, Pennsylvania. He's come to accept certain realities."

"Shit."

"Tell me about it."

"But we all know those aren't injuries sustained in a crash."

"My guess," said Crow, "is that the body was torn up pretty good by whoever our Big Bad is, and then dropped off a roof. There are visible impact injuries."

"Unless they're stupid they'd have to know that an autopsy would—"

"We can assume they didn't choose Pine Deep by accident."

"Meaning you can keep secrets?"

"Meaning we've had to keep secrets."

Mike snorted but didn't say anything.

I walked past the scene into the woods and stood there for a while, letting the smells and sounds tell me whatever they wanted to share. After a few moments, Crow and Mike joined me.

"Shame it rained so hard last night," Crow said. "No scent to follow."

I glanced at Mike. "You tried?"

He shrugged. "Sure. Lots of scents, but they're all mingled. Rain, you know?"

I nodded. "Makes me wonder if the rain was part of an agenda. Not just to fake the slip and slide crash, but to wash away any useful spoor."

Mike grunted and nodded.

"What were the other crash sites like?" I asked.

"Similar," said Crow. "In each case there was some kind of accident—car wreck, farm accident, house fire—but the details don't completely square. Especially the pathology. Someone's killing people and doing a slightly better than half-assed job covering it up."

"Yeah, but how would a regular police department be reacting to this?"

Crow nodded his approval. "I did some checking to see if there are any similarly troubled cases."

"And?"

"There were four suspicious fatal accidents in upstate New York last August, in the Finger Lakes district. All ultimately ruled accidental, but with notations about anomalies in the case files. Another two in Cape May, New Jersey, in December. Same conclusions. And three out near Pittsburgh this past May. The pattern is the same. A couple of the investigating detectives have been sharing case information in hopes of getting somewhere, but there's so little conventional evidence that they keep hitting a wall."

"Because they don't have certain specialized knowledge," I suggested.

"Yup."

"This is interstate," I said. "That makes it Federal. A serial killer?"

"Maybe."

"Shame there isn't really something like the *X-Files*. Fox Mulder would go nuts for something like this."

"Can't call him, can't call the Ghostbusters," he said. "If wishes were horses."

We stood there and looked at the huge forest. Oaks and sycamores and pines, with underbrush so dense it seemed impenetrable.

"What do you know about the vics?" I asked.

Crow fielded that. "No obvious connections. Not between the victims here in Pine Deep or between ours and those in other towns. I have someone doing background checks—a computer geek friend of mine—but so far we got bupkiss."

"Balls," I said.

"Balls," he agreed.

Chap. 27

The killer ran through the darkening woods, exulting in the power that rippled through his muscles. The solidity of his bones. The song of hunger that shouted in his blood.

He would find something to kill.

Anything.

Animal.

Human.

Even a bear.

Anything that would scream.

Thinking red thoughts, he ran.

Chap. 28

We spent the rest of the afternoon going over the crime scene, which yielded a lot of information, none of which seemed particularly useful. Then we went back to the station and Crow walked me through the rest of the case file. Again, lots of forensic information—photos, hair and fiber samples, casts of tire tracks, coroner's reports, the works.

Bottom line?

Well, shit. We knew there was one or more werewolf killing people.

They were doing it in bunches and, apparently, moving on.

Motive? Unknown.

Identity? Unknown.

Anything of actual use?

Impossible to say.

"Have you reached out to the FBI about this?" I asked.

"I filed a report."

"And—?"

"You familiar with the word 'obfuscation?'"

"Ah."

"What about your own investigation? Do you have any leads?"

"Beyond guesswork on the nature of the killers?"

"Beyond that, yes."

"Nope."

"Oh."

"But," he said, "I've been hearing about strangers in town."

"What kind of strangers?"

"Unknown. I have my people running that down right now. All I know is that there have been a few out-of-towners around. One of them was over at the Scarecrow Inn asking questions about the accident. And either the same guy or a different guy asking questions at some of the farms."

"You have a description on him?"

"Big, blond guy. The one local I talked to said he looked 'mean.'"

"That's it?"

"Getting information from stubborn farm-country folk is like pulling your own teeth. You'll get it, but there's a lot of unpleasant effort involved."

"Ah. This guy flash a badge of any kind?"

"Not so far."

"You think he's a Fed?"

"Maybe. Who else would be asking questions?"

I thought about it. "Could be another P.I., maybe hired by the family of one of the victims."

"Our vics were locals."

"A vic from another town."

Crow pursed his lips, nodded. "Maybe. I'll bet a shiny nickel it's a Fed."

"There's another possibility."

"What's that?"

"Could be someone related to the killings asking around to see what the locals know."

"Or suspect," he suggested.

"Or suspect," I agreed.

We poked at it for another couple of minutes and got nowhere. Then I suggested we retire to the local bar and drown our sorrows in some beers. Crow smiled and shook his head.

"Gave up drinking. I go to meetings now."

"Balls."

"Mike doesn't drink, either."

"He in the same Twelve Step?"

"No. He's a purity freak. Organic foods, no drugs, no alcohol. Won't even take an aspirin."

"How come?"

Crow sucked his teeth for a moment. "He has some health concerns. He wants to make sure he stays ahead of them."

"Like...?"

"Like it's his business and there's no second half to this discussion." He said it pleasantly enough, but there was a finality to it.

"Well, shit," I said. "*I* need a beer. Maybe six or eight of them."

I left him at his office and walked up the street until I found a place called the Scarecrow Inn. It wasn't exactly a dive bar. Dive is an active word. This was more like "dove." Past tense. Dark as pockets. Bunch of little tables with old wooden chairs that didn't match. Visible ass-wear on the stools. Sawdust on the floor, like they do down south. Half the people were ignoring the No Smoking sign, including a table full of fat guys with cigars. A wooden bar that was probably two hundred years old, and a bartender who looked to have been here since the place was built. Tall, cadaverous, comprehensively wrinkled. Big jar of hard-boiled eggs by the beer taps. Country music on the jukebox. Travis Tritt, I think, but I'm not a country fan so what do I know.

I found an empty stool, ordered chili and a schooner of Yuengling to go with it. Dug into a bowl of peanuts while I was waiting.

Crow let me take the case file, so I made my way through the chili and two beers while reading every single word. I had a few pages of notes, mostly outside-chance connections I'd run down when I was in front of a computer again. I'd brought my iPad, but—big surprise— there was no Wi-Fi in the Scarecrow Inn. Too modern for them. They're probably still grousing about those newfangled electric lights.

As I read I became very slowly and subtly aware that I was being watched. At first I passed it off as the usual stranger-in-town thing, but then my spider sense really began tingling. So I used taking a sip of beer to check the room out in the mirror behind the bar. Everyone was a stranger, so that wasn't very helpful. There were about two dozen people in the place, either dressed for work on a farm or in casual clothes.

Then I spotted the two people who didn't belong.

They were seated alone at tables on opposite sides of the place, and they were so totally different from one another that it looked like they were here to make a statement. White guy, black guy. White guy was big in a jock ballplayer way. Not big like Mike Sweeney or the goons I danced with yesterday. Muscular, midthirties, blond. All-American looks. Kind of like the guy who plays Captain America in the movies. Mean-looking son of a bitch, though. Could be a cop, could be a soldier. Could be a freelance shooter. Something very dangerous about him. I could tell that right off. Sat there with half a smile on his face, nursing a beer, using the same mirror I was using to watch the other guy and, every once in a while, me.

The other guy was a black twenty-something. Short, skinny, bookish, with thick glasses and a fringe of beard. Not the only black guy I'd seen in Pine Deep, but one of maybe three or four. Gave off a pop-culture geek vibe.

The Geek was looking at me; the Jock was looking at him. And me.

I adjusted the way I was sitting so my gun was a little easier to reach.

The Geek caught me looking at him and looked away.

Then he looked back.

He did that a couple of times, and I kept looking at him until he caught and finally held my stare. I nodded. After a long five-count, he nodded back.

So, I figured fuck it. I picked up my beer and walked over to his table. For a moment, I thought he was going to bolt. He sat straight as a rake handle and looked up at me. I'm not that big, and I'm not what you'd call physically imposing. I've been told, however, that I give off a certain vibe. At times.

Like now.

He cut a look to the front door and then back at me. At close range I figured him closer to early twenties.

But here's the thing.

At close range, I could tell something about him I couldn't tell from across a smoky bar.

The kid had a certain scent.

A familiar scent. The kind I spent a lot of time every morning, with shampoo, skin creams and cologne trying to mask.

A smell most people can't smell.

Except guys like Mike Sweeney.

He looked up at me, and before I could even ask, he said, "I think we need to talk."

"Yeah," I said. "I think we'd better."

"Not here."

I nodded to the door. "Let's go."

Chap. 29

The killer smelled the hitchhiker before he saw her.

She smelled young.

She smelled afraid.

He knew that she would taste wonderful.

He knew that she would scream.

The young ones always screamed. They have so much to lose.

He raced down a hill and up the other side, then down again to the road. This was a lonely stretch. A stupid place for anyone to hitchhike. She couldn't have known that or she wouldn't have come this way.

Chap. 30

I stood aside to let him go first. If this was some kind of elaborate setup, I didn't want to be the first guy through the door.

It wasn't.

The kid stopped in the middle of the pavement, hands in his pockets. He wore a long black coat over jeans and a T-shirt with the words OBSCURE POP-CULTURE REFERENCE stenciled on it. He looked nervous. Maybe scared.

"There's a park up the street," he said, and we began walking that way.

"Let's start with the basics," I said. "Name?"

He hesitated.

I said, "Would you rather I held you down and stole your wallet?"

"Antonio," he said. "Antonio Jones."

"Real name?"

"Sure. Why?"

"Sounds like a stage name."

He shrugged. "Antonio Jones."

"Fair enough. I'm Sam Hunter."

"You're a cop?"

"Not anymore. Private investigator," I said as we crossed the street. There were only two traffic lights in town and they both blinked yellow continually. Either they were trying for a Twin Peaks thing, or all small towns are creepy like that. Yellow means "caution," so I figured a subtext was implied. Besides, it was that kind of a day.

Antonio said, "Working for the cops, though?"

"Why do you want to know?"

"I saw you with Chief Crow and Iron Mike."

"'Iron Mike?'"

"That's what people used to call him. In school, I mean. When he was little. Before the, um…"

"Before the Trouble?"

"Before that, yeah."

"Why? Was he always a body builder?"

"Huh? Oh…no. Mike used to be in his head all the time. Always dreaming up stuff. One day he'd be a Jedi, the next he'd be Sheriff Rick. Or Conan. Whatever. He spent a lot of time like that. Playing by himself. Daydreaming in school. Not sure if he started calling himself Iron Mike or the other kids did."

"You went to school with him?"

He shook his head. "Two years behind."

We crossed a side street and entered the park. Like most of the town of Pine Deep, the park was seedy, untended, and dark. Broken slats in the benches. Overflowing trash can. Beer bottles lying among the weeds. Indifferent lighting.

"Nice place for a mugging," I said to my new friend.

He stopped and looked at me. "I know," he said.

Which is when I felt the icy mouth of a gun barrel press into the base of my skull.

"Don't try anything funny," said a male voice. "And I'm pretty sure we both know what I mean by 'funny.'"

Chap. 31

The killer stalked her because stalking was fun.

One game was to see how close to the edge of the woods he could get without the hitchhiker seeing him. Then to make small, odd sounds so that she became aware of something. But unaware of what was in those shadowy woods.

That game was fun.

Then he changed his own rules. He ran ahead and stepped out of the woods. Very briefly. Just long enough for the girl to see him. A quick glance, then he was gone.

The way her lithe young body stiffened was very appealing. She had long legs and long hair and tiny little breasts. She was maybe sixteen, but young for it. Bruises on her face. Running away from a heavy-handed father, perhaps.

The girl stood there, uncertain, without a plan and without a direction, staring in the direction of the big, dark thing that had watched her from the road ahead.

She turned around, considering the road she'd walked. It was empty and it lead back in a direction she could not go. Not if something had been bad enough to put her out alone on a road like this.

The girl waited for almost five full minutes, looking at the road, looking under the trees, seeing nothing because the killer allowed her nothing to see. Not even when she was looking directly toward where he crouched. She had human eyes and they were so weak.

He waited until she began walking again. Hesitantly at first, and then at a rapid clip. The girl wanted to be past this stretch of road.

The killer circled around and came out of the woods behind her. He crept onto the asphalt and moved up behind her. Taking his time, waiting for that exquisite moment when the girl would inevitably turn to check behind her.

That was a new game.

He loved the way this one would end.

Chap. 32

I stood absolutely still.

No matter how fast I can do the change, it's not fast enough to dodge a bullet. Besides, little known fact about werewolves. Head shots? Pretty much does it. Head shots will pretty much flip the switch on everything. Vampires, zombies, me.

So, no, I didn't try anything funny.

I stood there.

"You carrying?" the voice asked.

"Shoulder holster," I told him.

"Take it out with two fingers. Hand it to Antonio."

I did. Antonio took it like it was radioactive. He looked scared and nervous and embarrassed. If this was a mugging, it wasn't following the right pattern.

"What else?" asked the guy with the gun.

"Blackjack. Rear pocket."

"Okay. Remove it the same way. Ditto for your wallet. Hand them to the kid."

"Got thirty bucks in my wallet," I said, just to see how he'd react.

"Cute. See that bench? Put your hands in your pants pockets and go sit down. Do it real slow and we'll stay friends."

I did what he asked and as I turned to sit, I got my first look at him. He was an All-American jock type. Six-two or so. Blond hair, blue eyes, white smile. Looked healthy but there was something in his eyes. Like maybe there was something freaky going on behind them. Something crazy, something dangerous. Something very, very dangerous. I discreetly sniffed but his scent was one hundred percent human.

Not a wolf, but definitely an alpha.

"What's the play?" I asked.

He ignored me and spoke to Antonio. "You sure this guy's playing for the same team as you?"

Antonio paused, sniffed the air in my direction, paused again. "Pretty sure."

"Check his I.D."

The kid did that. "Sam Hunter," he said, reading my driver's license. "Oh, hey. He has a private investigator's license."

"Read me the numbers."

He did.

The guy with the gun held his Beretta 92F in a rock-steady hand. He looked at me, taking stock. "Okay, Mr. Hunter," he said, "we're going to have us a nice chat."

"Uh-uh," I said. "I showed you mine, now you show me yours. Who the hell are you?"

"What, you don't think this is a mugging?"

I snorted.

"What would you say if I told you I was a cop?"

I shrugged. "You look the type. I used to be a cop."

"Where?"

"Minneapolis."

"What happened?"

"Got kicked out."

"Why?"

"I don't play well with others."

"Other cops?"

I shrugged again. "It's possible a couple of perps got dented while resisting."

"What kind of perps? This a racial thing?" he asked.

"No," I said. "I don't like bullies. Not too crazy about guys who hurt women and kids."

I watched his eyes while I said that. You can tell a lot from the way a guy reacts. Dickheads tend to grin. Closet-abusers get self-righteous about due process. By-the-book cops are merely disapproving. Guys who've walked some dark streets tend to connect with you on a purely nonverbal level—but the connection is there. Even guys who are good poker players always have a tell in moments like that.

This guy did.

There was the tiniest thinning of his lips. Not a smile. Nothing like that. More like a predatory smile. There are different kinds of predators. There are the kinds who target the weak. And there are those with more of a Dexter vibe who don't lose sleep if a child abuser has a hard time on the way to the station.

"Any of this going to come up if I run a background check on you?"

"My dismissal letter makes for quality reading," I told him.

"Okay," he said, though he didn't lower the gun. "New subject. What are you doing in Pine Deep?"

"What does it matter to you?"

"Not a two-way conversation, Sparky. Answer the question."

"I'm here on a case."

"What case?"

"A police case. I'm working with local law on a series of unexplained deaths."

"Who's your contact here?"

"The chief of police. Malcolm Crow."

Keeping his gun pointed at my forehead, he tapped his ear. "Bug, you get all this?"

I didn't hear anything, but the guy did. "Copy that."

"'Bug'?" I asked. "You wearing a wire?"

He ignored me and stood in an attitude of listening. I couldn't see his earbud or mike. Had to be high-tech stuff if it was that well-concealed. Which changed my estimation of him from cop to some kind of federal agent. FBI or higher. Which made some sense if someone in the Justice Department was taking these deaths seriously. If there was any evidence to link the kills, then it made this a federal case.

Didn't explain why he was holding a gun to my head.

"Okay," he said, "thanks, Bug. Hit me with anything else you dig up."

The jock looked me up and down for a few moments longer, then he lowered his gun. Lowered it, not put it away.

"You had a colorful career in the Cities," he said. "Samuel Taylor Coleridge Hunter. How the fuck did you get hung with a name like that?"

"My parents read a lot," I said. "And they're a little weird."

"Uh-huh."

"You got my background that fast?"

"I have good people."

"How long have you been tailing me?"

"Since you left the Scarecrow."

"Why'd you pick me?"

He nodded to Antonio. "My friend tagged you."

"He wearing a wire, too?"

"Does it matter?"

I changed tack. "You want to tell me who you are and why you pulled a gun on me?"

He glanced around at the darkened trees, then shrugged and holstered his piece.

"Joe Ledger," he said.

"FBI?"

"Same league, different team."

"Care to tell me which team?"

"Not really." He grinned at me. Son of a bitch had great teeth. I wanted to punch them down his throat.

"Can I have my gun and wallet back?"

"Antonio," said Ledger, "give the man his wallet."

The kid handed it to me and I slipped it into my pocket. I held my hand out for the gun.

"Let's pretend you don't need it right now," said Ledger.

I lowered my hand.

"Okay, Mr. Mysterious. How about you tell me what in the fuck is going on."

"You first," he said, "why don't you tell me why you're here in Pine Deep."

"I already told you."

He gestured to the bench. "You gave me a headline, now give me the story."

We sat, the two of us. Antonio stood a dozen feet apart, my gun in his pocket. He fidgeted and looked like he wanted to be anywhere else but here.

I looked at Ledger. "The chief said there was someone asking questions around town. That's you?"

He shrugged.

"If you're already looking into these deaths, then you must know what's going on. You know about me. Not about my background, but, you know…"

"You get weird and fuzzy," he said, "yeah, I know. Still borderline freaked out about it, but I know."

"Which means the government knows?"

"Some parts of it do. Most don't."

"Am I about to get myself onto some kind of watch list? You guys have an *X-Files* thing for real?"

"*X-Files* is fiction, and it's FBI," he said. "I personally don't give a rat's hairy nuts about the things that go bump in the night unless those bumpy things have a political agenda."

"I don't."

He touched his ear. "So I'm told. You're a lapsed Independent. You haven't voted since you left Minneapolis. Never been arrested at a rally. You're not a person of interest in any way that matters to guys like me."

"So why this setup? You had Knick-Knack here lure me to where you could blindside me. Very slick, and I fell for it. But as your mysterious Bug must have told you, I'm not a player in anything political. I don't even watch the debates. I think everyone in Washington needs a good foot up their ass, but I don't have any aspirations to be the one doing the kicking. Is there any chance you're going to stop being Mr. Cryptic and get to the fucking point?"

Ledger laughed. "Fair enough. This clandestine shit always makes me feel like a jackass."

"See it from my side."

He nodded. "But this isn't a discussion, Sam. This is me interrogating you. This is you cooperating without reservation. This is me—much as I hate to do it—waving the Patriot Act in your face and not having to play quid pro quo. Sorry, but life's a bitch like that."

"Why don't you just go ask the fucking chief of police?"

"I will. But he's lower priority. And, he's kind of a dick," said Ledger.

"You know him?"

"We've met. Besides, he's an ordinary guy. You're not. You're definitely not, if Antonio is certain."

"Absolutely," said Antonio. "He's like me."

"I'm neither short nor black," I said.

We all laughed.

Ledger said, "So, I want you to tell me why a werewolf private investigator—and I'm having a hard time saying those actual words—is in Pine Deep, Pennsylvania. I want to know what you know about the person or persons who committed these murders. I want to know if you have any connection to them, because I'm pretty damn sure you're all members of the Hair Club for Weirdos. So, talk."

"I think this conversation would make more sense if we included Chief Crow," I said.

"I don't."

A voice behind him said, "I do."

And there was the unmistakable sound of a pump shotgun being jacked.

Chap. 33

The girl turned around.

She saw the killer.

Of course she did. It was what she was meant to do.

He was fifty feet behind her, moving on all fours, grinning with all his teeth.

She screamed.

She screamed so loudly.

A shrill, piercing note that the killer was positive would live within his personal treasure trove of superb screams. It was a girl scream. A girl-woman scream. Filled with all of the dark imaginings of the child. And all of the understanding of the adult. It was as perfect as she was, this girl on the edge of womanhood. She, in all of her desperate, bruised beauty. Her defiled innocence. Her ripeness.

She ran.

Of course she ran.

He would have been disappointed, crushed, if she had not.

She dropped her backpack and her cheap little purse, and ran.

He let her run.

Another fifty feet. A hundred.
Two hundred.
And then he ran after.

Chap. 34

Joe Ledger turned. Slowly, without real concern.

Malcolm Crow stood twenty feet behind him, a Remington pump snugged into his shoulder.

Ledger smiled, got up, walked over, bent and picked up an unfired shell from where it had landed on the grass.

"Much as I appreciate the dramatics of pumping the shotgun—it's a real nut-twister—it's done purely for effect. You wouldn't have come out here without a shell being already in the breech. Which means you had to eject one to make your entrance."

He reached past the barrel and tucked the shell into the chief's pocket.

Crow sighed and lowered the gun.

"It scares the piss out of most people," he said.

"Hey," said Ledger, "I'm not saying it didn't work on me. I'll probably have a pee stain on my Joe Boxers. Just making an observation. You see that on TV?"

"Yeah."

"They always do it on TV. Saw one episode of *The Walking Dead* where a guy racked his gun twice."

"Nice."

They smiled at each other.

"Howdy, Chief Crow," said Ledger.

"Howdy, Duke."

I said, "Duke?"

Crow nodded. "First time we met he introduced himself as Marion Morrison. John Wayne's real name."

"Oh."

"Flashed an FBI badge."

Ledger shrugged. "It was convenient."

Crow pushed past him and walked over to Antonio. He held out a hand and waited as the kid looked for and received a nod from Ledger. He handed my gun to Crow, who exhaled through his nose and handed it to me.

I considered how much fun it would be to pistol-whip Ledger, but frankly didn't like my chances. Not without changing. He looked like a happy-go-lucky dumb jock, but there was something behind that façade that troubled me. I had the feeling he could turn mean as a snake if he wanted to. I didn't want him to.

Crow turned back to the agent. "We are going to have a frank conversation, Agent Whateveryournameis."

"Joe Ledger."

"Agent Ledger. Fine. We're going to have a pow-wow and if I get even a whiff of obstruction—"

"Or obfuscation," I amended.

"—I will kick your ass out of Pine Deep. And before you ask, yes I think it can be done and no I don't give a cold shit what kind of federal juice you have or which agency you belong to. Am I making myself clear?"

"Crystal," said Ledger, though it was also clear he was amused.

"Good. Let's all go over to the Scarecrow."

"Not your office?"

"No. The coffee sucks moose dick. Artie at the Scarecrow makes the best coffee in town."

I said, "You don't mind that it's a bar?"

"Son," he said, giving me a weary, pitying smile, "everyone I've ever met in this town drinks like a fish. Seeing it isn't going to knock me off the wagon. This is Pine Deep. Besides, you two ass-clowns could use a few beers. Maybe it'll help wash off the testosterone."

"I'm in," I said.

We all looked at Ledger.

"First round's on me."

Crow nodded to Antonio. "You want to do me a favor?"

"Um…sure."

"You know Mike Sweeney?"

He swallowed and nodded.

"Go find him. Tell him where we are."

Then Crow laid the barrel of his shotgun over his shoulder and nodded toward the lights of town. "Gentlemen, shall we—"

Chap. 35

The killer ran at half speed most of the way.
He didn't want to catch her.
Yet.
Where would the fun be in that?

He loped along, watching her legs pump, watching her hair bob. Watching her.

Aching for her.

Hungering.

In other times, in older times, he would have taken her a different way. Like he'd done in harbor towns throughout Southeast Asia. Like he'd done when crossing this country. Like he'd done more times than he could remember. Back then, when it was his old flesh that he wore and his weaker senses that he used, he still loved the chase, the catch, the tearing of clothes, the tearing of skin, the tearing of screams from young throats. Screams of fear. Screams of desperation. Screams of despair when they reached that critical moment when all fight and all flight were clearly failing. Screams of use. Screams of invasion. And screams filled with pleading as they tried to hold on to the bottom rung of life.

That had been different. Good for what it was, but not what it was now.

Now the killer wanted something different. Sex was fine, but it no longer thrilled him. It was too easy to get and too shallow a thing. No, what he wanted was the blood. The meat. The crack of bones between his teeth. The taste of all of the several parts that made up a human life. Oils of different pungencies. The flavor of skin on the hand and how different it was than the flavors of thigh and breast and hip and throat.

She ran so hard. She tried so much to be part of her own future.

But she could not run that fast.

Because he could run so much faster.

Chap. 36

So, three guys walk into a bar.

Pint-sized badass of a town cop. Scary jock government agent. And me. Werewolf ex-cop P.I.

Life has gotten very strange.

Even by my standards.

Chap. 37

We took a table in a corner that was so dark I needed my cell phone light to read the menu. I ordered a Philly cheesesteak, fries, and a beer. Ledger liked that and asked for the same thing. Crow had a Diet Coke.

"Okay," said Ledger, "cards on the table time."

"That'd make a refreshing change," observed Crow. "Let's start with your real name and official status."

There was no one seated within earshot, but even so, Ledger lowered his voice. "Captain Joseph Edwin Ledger," he said. "I work for a specialized group operating under executive order."

"Name?"

"If I told you I'd have to kill you." Ledger smiled as he said it.

"Not joking here," said Crow. "I'm a half step away from arresting you. I don't care if you could squeeze enough federal juice to beat an obstruction of justice charge. I'm the chief of police and you have to identify yourself."

Ledger nodded. "I used to be a cop," he said. "In Baltimore. Worked homicide and then I was attached to Homeland. Mostly sitting on my ass working wiretaps. Then I caught the tail of something, and when we yanked on it, there was a dragon at the other end. I was in on the bust, which went south and everyone thought it would be fun to be stupid with guns. After that I was scouted by a group called the Department of Military Sciences."

"Never heard of it," said Crow.

"You wouldn't. We fly pretty much below the radar."

"Part of Homeland?"

"Parallel. A lot smaller, less red tape and bullshit. We target groups with cutting-edge bioweapons and other tech. Designer pathogens, man-portable nukes, that sort of thing."

"Mad scientists?" said Crow, amused.

"The maddest."

"So," I said, "you're James Bond."

Ledger shook his head. "No laser-beam cufflinks. No ejector seats. And I prefer lagers to martinis."

Crow sipped his diet pisswater. "Which doesn't explain why you're here. Again. Last time you were here you pretended to be FBI and you brought two thugs with you who claimed to be Federal Marshals. Which they weren't."

"Not as such, no."

"You brought a lot of bad people to my town. You turned a farmhouse into the Battle of Bull Run."

"I didn't deal that play. We had a guy in witness protection who did something very stupid. Tried to reach out to some very bad people in hopes of uncovering some terrorists on American soil. Brought a lot of cockroaches out of the woodpile. Things got creative and the good guys rode their horses into the sunset." Ledger paused. "I never did thank you for stepping in on that."

Crow ran his finger around the rim of his glass. "I had no official involvement in that case. There was, I believe, no evidence of my ever having been there. Perhaps you're mistaken."

"Uh-huh," said Ledger. "Your nose grew two full inches when you said that."

They sat there and looked at each other, and I had the impression there was a lot I didn't know about them. Not sure I actually wanted to know. I was already creeped out and probably way out of my depth here.

"Guys...going on the assumption that I have no idea what the fuck you two jokers are talking about, how about we circle around to the matter at hand?"

Crow leaned back in his chair, effectively breaking the connection. "All cards on the table," he said.

"All cards on the table," echoed Ledger. "Tell me about your investigation and then I'll tell you why I'm here. I think we'll find we're working two ends of the same case."

Crow nodded and went through it all. The murders in other towns, the deaths here. The lack of any visible federal investigation. Ledger said nothing. He ate his cheesesteak and listened. I noticed Crow glossed over the part about who and what Mike Sweeney was. When he got to the part about Limbus, Ledger began asking questions. He wanted to know everything either of us knew about that organization. Unfortunately, we didn't know much.

When it was my turn, I told them about my previous case with the mysterious organization. Naturally, I omitted a few details—namely the nature of the real enemy in that case. I was still having nightmares about that.

I had my Limbus card with me and he used his phone to photograph it and send the picture to his office. His contact there— presumably the "Bug" he'd been talking to earlier—got back to him and Ledger relayed the information to us. We didn't like it.

"The number is fake. My guys traced it and it dead-ends. Understand something," Ledger said, "we have some pretty nifty toys and we can trace darn near anything. We can't trace that number. And it's not rerouting tech. Our pingbacks tell us that there is nothing at the end of that line. Database searches on Limbus came up empty, too. There are some obscure references to various groups using that name going back more than a hundred years, but so far we can't tie any of it together."

"You got all of this that fast?" asked Crow.

"Like I said, we have nifty toys. My people will continue to work on it. Maybe we'll come up with something. We have to assume, though, that your office is bugged, Crow. And maybe this Limbus group has some informants in town."

It was the logical answer, but Crow shook his head. "I don't think so."

"Has to be," insisted Ledger.

Crow shrugged. "Not sure it does."

Ledger let it go for now. The fact that he did made me wonder if he'd run up against other stuff that was equally weird. I sure as hell have. Ever since I went into business as a P.I., I've found that this world is a lot bigger, darker, and stranger than I ever thought. Werewolves are far from the only thing going bump in the night. And in my day, I've met things I don't understand and things that terrify me.

Crow had that look, too.

So did Ledger.

The three of us lapsed into a brief silence. We ate, we drank, we avoided each other's eyes.

Finally, Ledger said, "Super soldiers."

Crow paused, his glass halfway to his lips. "What now?"

"Super soldiers. That's what we think this is about."

"Super soldiers," repeated Crow.

"Super soldiers?" I asked.

"Super soldiers," said Ledger.

And when he said it, I could see it.

"Jesus Christ," I said.

Chap. 38

The killer dragged the girl into the woods and ate her.
Not all of her.
Just the good parts.
He nearly wept for the beauty of it.

Chap. 39

"We inherited this case," Ledger said. "The first attacks happened in a small town near Saskatoon, Saskatchewan. Local law was called in when a couple of joggers running back roads to prepare for a marathon smelled something nasty. Mounties checked out an abandoned warehouse and—"

"Seriously?" I asked. "An abandoned warehouse?"

"I know. It's cliché, but you have to respect the classics. Anyway, they found two bodies pretty much torn to beef jerky. Been there about a week. Back door was open, so the locals had to conclude that the corpses had been bitten post-mortem by animals."

"Let me guess which *kind* of animal," said Crow dryly.

"Wolves aren't entirely unknown in Canada," said Crow. "Even if they're not exactly common in Saskatoon. The coroner's report, though, cited blunt force trauma as the cause of death. Murder weapon unknown, but presumably heavy and soft."

He looked at me. So did Crow.

"What?"

"If you wanted to arrange a crime scene in a way that would muddy the investigation, how would you do it? Specifically, you."

I felt my face getting hot. I don't like to be put on the spot and I have never once in my adult life had anyone call me out for being what I was. Ledger was doing exactly that. It was so fucking weird. What was weirder still was that neither of these guys looked particularly freaked by this line of questioning. They weren't spooked by it. I was.

So fucked up.

I cleared my throat. "Um…well, I guess I'd, you know, *change*, and you know, maybe, um, hit the guys and, well…"

Crow and Ledger burst out laughing. They howled. Ledger slapped his thighs. Crow put his face in his hands and his whole body shook. My face was actually burning now.

In a creaking, wheezing voice, Crow said, "He's embarrassed by being a were…were…."

The rest of it dissolved into laughter.

Joe Ledger began singing "Werewolves of London," and Crow joined him for the "Wahoooo" chorus.

"I am going to kill both of you," I said.

That made them laugh harder.

"Seriously. Headshots. Bury you out in the country."

There were tears on Crow's cheeks.

I glared at them.

"Yeah, well…fuck you."

Then I was laughing, too.

Chap. 40

The killer heard something and he raised his head. He'd been cradling the girl's head, sniffing her hair, but now there was a sound in the woods.

The killer tossed the head into the bushes and rose to smell the breeze. He was covered in blood, and the smell of the girl's life was like strong perfume, blotting out most of what was exhaled on the forest's breath.

He moved away from the kill, going deeper into the woods, following the sound. Smelling the air. He changed halfway so he had arms but still had claws, and he climbed a tree.

There.

Way over there, a mile away or more, was the big red-haired policeman.

The local wolf, he thought.

Coming this way.

The killer shimmied down the tree, turned away from the half-eaten girl, and ran.

Was this local wolf blunted to the subtleties of the hunt? He wondered that as he ran.

He dared the wolf to pick up his scent. He dared him to follow.

He dared this pup to find him.

Chap. 41

Eventually Ledger got back to his story. More beer was involved. The other patrons at the Scarecrow moved even farther away from the three loud, obnoxious crazy people in the corner.

"Anyway, anyway," said Ledger, bringing it all down to earth, "there was a second set of murders in Manitoba. A third on Prince Edward Island. In each case there were two or more corpses. All mutilated. Each one in situations where there was another *convenient* possible cause of death. Industrial accidents, car crashes. You get the picture."

"Who put it all together?" asked Crow.

Ledger smiled. "A computer. We have a great pattern-recognition software package. It trolls interagency databases. Mostly used to scout for terrorist activity, but every once in a while, it coughs out something that's simply weird."

"Even so," I said, "what was the connecting factor? There are a lot of strange, violent deaths."

Ledger nodded his approval. "Location, location, location. In each case, the deaths occurred within twenty miles, give or take, of a known—or suspected—lab."

"What kind of lab?" I asked.

"Bioweapons research."

Crow shook his head. "Then your computer is wonky, 'cause there's nothing like that in Pine Deep. Nothing even remotely like it."

Ledger gave him a long, hard look. "How much of your pension would you like to bet on that?"

"Wait," said Crow, "what?"

"Yup, there is a bioweapons R&D facility in your own little slice of rural heaven."

"Run by whom?"

"That's a different question. It's sure as hell not run by the U.S. government. I know that for a fact."

"Are you talking about a private lab?" I asked. "Something attached to a pharmaceutical company?"

"No. We don't have those here, either," said Crow, who was getting very angry now.

"Then what?" I asked. "Private sector working on something they want to sell to Uncle Sam?"

Ledger shook his head. "I wish. No, gentlemen, I think what we have here is a clandestine and highly illegal lab. Probably funded by a terrorist group. And one that's highly mobile. I think it's been moving around North America doing research on the fly."

We digested that, and it was a hard pill to swallow.

"How sure are you?" I asked.

"Pretty sure."

"Based on what evidence?" demanded Crow.

"Based on a shitload of supposition and some negative reasoning," said Ledger. He drank the last of his beer and signaled for another. "Let's look at the facts, shall we? We have a series of murders in rural areas. Each murder has been orchestrated to look like an accident. Because of the nature of the injuries, they haven't been able to totally sell it, but enough so that no one in authority has been enthusiastic enough to start an international or even interstate investigation. Right now, there's too much room for doubt."

Crow and I reluctantly agreed.

"Whoever these folks are, they have access to, or have somehow created, lycanthropes."

"Look at you using technical words," said Crow.

"I went to college," said Ledger. "We can suppose that they have more than one because of the nature of the crime scenes. There's signs of evidence tampering that could not have been done in the absence of hypernormal physical strength."

"How did you make the jump from that to, um, *lycanthropes*?" I asked.

Ledger smiled. "Rumors in the pipeline." When it was clear that Crow and I wanted more than that, he explained. "There's been talk about this for a while now. Ever since Dr. Broussard found the lycanthropic gene and—"

"Whoa!" I said immediately. "Doctor who found what?"

"Ah," he said, "I would have thought that someone of your kind would have known about that. No? Okay, well Broussard is a French molecular biologist working with a team in Switzerland. They've been indexing the genes that are known in the tabloids as 'junk DNA.' Turns out, they're not junk. You guys up on your genetics? No? I'll try to flatten it out for you. In genomics they've found that about 98% of our DNA is what they called 'noncoding.' Some of this noncoding DNA is transcribed into functional noncoding RNA molecules, while others are not transcribed or give rise to RNA transcripts of unknown function. Follow me?"

"I have no idea what the fuck you just said," I admitted.

"Lost me on the first curve," said Crow.

Ledger grinned. "Yeah, a couple of years ago I didn't understand any of this shit. It's become a kind of job requirement."

"Weird job," I suggested.

"You have no idea. Anyway, the amount of this noncoding DNA varies species to species. Like I said, 98% of the human genome is noncoding while only about 2% of, say, a typical bacterial genome is noncoding."

"I think I almost understood that," said Crow.

"At first, most of the noncoding DNA had no *known* biological function—emphasis on *known*—and someone hung the nickname 'junk DNA' on it. But there are teams all over the world working to unlock the secrets of those genes. Dr. Broussard's team has been working on chimeric genes and—"

"On what?"

"Chimeric. Genes that change their nature, or that change what they code for. They're a brand-new branch of evolutionary science. Broussard's pretty much ready to prove that a lot of theriomorphic phenomena in world folklore—and that means things that change shape—"

"I know." Crow and I said it at the same time.

"—are not part of some weirdo supernatural shit," continued Ledger, "but are evidence that genetics is a much, much bigger field than we thought. It's Broussard's belief that werewolves are a genetic offshoot of good ol' *Homo sapiens*."

We said nothing.

"And, before you ask, there are other examples of chimeric genes. I had a tussle a couple of years ago with *Upierczy*."

"That's a kind of Russian vampire," said Crow quietly.

"*Homo vampiri*," said Ledger. "Now fully documented, though we haven't released that to the press yet. The *Upierczy* are some nasty fucks. They call themselves the Red Knights and even though they're not supernatural, they are still every damn bit as scary."

"You don't believe in the supernatural?" asked Crow.

"Not really," said Ledger, but his tone was mildly evasive. It was clear he didn't want to travel down that side road.

"How does that connect to an illegal bioweapons lab in my backyard?" asked Crow.

Ledger shrugged. "Most of the labs doing illegal bioweapons research tend to be either offshore or hidden."

"Hollowed-out volcanoes?" I suggested.

"Close enough. A few are on ships in international waters. Or hidden in oil refineries. Places where they can hide science teams, where people come and go, and where large shipments of supplies are routine. We busted one in a container yard in Baltimore last year and another on a freight train operating out of the Pacific Northwest. We've found minilabs in RVs, in mobile homes, and in your generic abandoned or short-leased warehouses. Computer and lab equipment is getting more compact every day and it's easier to have a grab-it-and-go lab than before. And there are what amounts to virtual labs, where everyone is networked through Wi-Fi so they don't all have to be in the same physical location. I think that's what we're hunting for here. Someone is messing around with lycanthrope DNA. Your basic *Homo sapiens canis lupis*. Broussard's term, not mine."

"Even so, how'd you get to werewolves?" asked Crow.

"Hair and fiber recovered from victims. We, um, *hijacked* some of the lab reports and sent it to Broussard's people for sequencing. Rang all the right bells. And the genes show clear sign of after-market manipulation. Transgenics, gene therapy, all sorts of stuff." He leaned forward and rested his elbows on the table. "Our theory is that someone is trying to build a better werewolf. I don't know about you gents, but that pretty much scares the shit out of me."

Chap. 42

The killer ran and the local wolf ran after.

They chased each other through the woods for long minutes, and then the killer broke and ran through a stream and shed his pursuer like a snake sheds a skin.

After ten full minutes of running, the killer stopped and went to high ground. He searched in all directions for the local wolf. For the pup.

And found nothing.

He sneered in contempt.

A wolf that could not follow a living scent was no wolf at all. He deserved to be gutted and left to rot.

The killer made a mental promise to see that done.

Chap. 43

"Why the fuck would someone want to do that?" I demanded.

"Two words," said Ledger. "Super soldier."

"Like Captain America with fur?" suggested Crow.

"More like Captain Russia or Captain North Korea, or something like that," said Ledger. "But in broad terms, sure. Why not? If you can make the science work, and if that science isn't all that expensive—and if you're starting with actual werewolves it wouldn't be—why not give it a shot? Of course, it's more cost effective and logistically sound to do something like this, to draw from the local populace of your enemy. If you can find lycanthropes within a target country and recruit them, then it reduces the likelihood of political fallout. It's always easier to disown a traitor than explain away a spy. Plus, given that there actually *are* werewolves, then imagine the psychological and religious implications. That kind of thing would do real harm. Actual monsters."

Crow and I sat there and chewed on that. Kind of choked on it going down.

It also made me review some of my own encounters with what I've always thought were supernatural elements. Was Ledger right? Were these things really part of a much bigger version of "natural science?" Like the way physics has had to expand to embrace both Einstein's relativity and Max Planck's quantum physics, and was being stretched further to take in chaos theory, string theory, and other crazy shit that I can't even begin to understand.

Vampires? Sure, the ones I met didn't turn into bats or command storms. None of that nonsense. And me? The phases of the moon didn't mean dick to me. Maybe it was all evidence that Mother Nature was a freaky bitch.

Demons and ghosts? Jury would have to deliberate a little longer on that. And that wasn't a topic I wanted to float with Ledger. Or Crow, though I was beginning to suspect that he knew more about this than all of us.

"What about that kid, Antonio?" I asked. "Is he part of this mad science bullshit?"

Ledger shook his head. "No. He's a friend of a friend."

Crow made a twirling motion with his index finger, indicating that he wanted more of an answer than that.

"One of the guys that works with me, a computer super-geek, travels in some of the same circles as Antonio. When the Broussard thing came up, this friend of mine did some covert net searches. Very much on the D.L., and based on message board posts, Facebook searches and other data, he made a list of people who might actually be lycanthropes hiding within regular society."

"More NSA spy shit?" asked Crow, but Ledger ignored that.

"How many names?" I asked.

"A few," said Ledger, but he wouldn't go any deeper into that. All he said was "Antonio Jones popped up on the list, and it happened to be that my friend knew him from some sci-fi and horror conventions. The kid's Facebook photo was of him in full makeup as a werewolf, except—"

"Except it was real?"

"Yup."

"That's nuts," I said, but I found it funny, too. "Hiding in plain sight."

Crow grunted. "Kind of makes you wonder."

"Yes it does," Ledger agreed.

"So where does all this leave us?" I asked. "I mean, I can kind of buy this werewolf super soldier thing, and I've seen firsthand the kind of damage these assholes are willing to do, but...what now? We have a theory and no facts. Do you *Mission Impossible* cats have any leads?"

Ledger sighed. "Not yet. I was kind of hoping you fellas could help with that."

"Why us?" asked Crow.

"'Cause, you got a werewolf working for you."

"Meaning me?" I asked.

"Meaning your deputy," said Ledger. "Meaning Officer Michael Sweeney. Meaning your adopted son."

Crow said nothing. His expression was completely blank. He hadn't mentioned Mike Sweeney.

So I asked. "What makes you think that?"

"Antonio," said Ledger.

"Balls," said Crow.

"Funny old world," said Ledger.

Which is when Crow's cell phone rang. He looked at it and made a face.

"It's him."

He held up a finger for silence as he took the call. Mostly, he listened.

Then he said, "Stay right there. Don't do anything. You hear me, Mike? You stay right where you are and wait. I'm bringing plenty of backup. No, I don't mean Otis and Farley. Don't worry, we'll be there in a hot minute."

He closed the phone and got to his feet.

"What is it?" Ledger and I both asked.

"Mike thinks he found them."

Chap. 44

Ledger's car was right outside. A Ford Explorer that had gotten some kind of upgrade. The engine was quiet as a whisper, but the fucking thing could move. Crow rode shotgun, I was in the back.

"Buckle up, kids," said Ledger. He wasn't joking. He drove it like a getaway car.

"I only have two spare magazines," said Crow.

Ledger laughed at that. "I got enough shit in the back to invade Iran. Now tell me about Sweeney. What exactly did he find?"

Crow said Mike was hunting the woods, trying to pick up the trail of the werewolves who'd wrecked the bike. He picked up a fresher scent, and for a while thought he was going to run another wolf to ground. Didn't happen that way, though, and he followed that to a blockhouse in the woods that was sometimes used by the EPA when they sent their teams in. Some universities leased it for use, too. There's some oddball flora and fauna in the woods near Pine Deep.

"Mike said that the trail led to a shed attached to the blockhouse, and he thought that the rear wall might be phony. That's when he backed out and called me."

"You know this blockhouse?" asked Ledger.

"Sure." Crow gave him precise directions out of town, then began calling turns onto small side roads. Pretty soon we were driving roads so narrow and overgrown that weeds and branches brushed both sides of the car.

"I bet the last guy to use this road wore feathers," complained Ledger.

We went deep into the state forest and way off the grid.

As we drove, Ledger caught my eye in the rearview. "This lycanthrope thing is pretty much new to me, and I'll be the first to admit that it's freaking me out."

"Doesn't show," I said.

"Feels it on the inside. My nuts crawled up inside my chest cavity and they don't seem to want to come down."

"You afraid of me?" I asked.

"Of course I am, you freak. You're a fucking werewolf. I have a fucking werewolf in my car. I am driving to meet *another* werewolf who is waiting to lead me to a nest of super-soldier werewolves. So, yeah, I'm afraid. I'd worry about anyone who said they weren't scared."

I grinned at him.

"Don't do that," he said. "You look like Hannibal fucking Lecter."

"Sorry."

"Tell me something," Ledger continued. "When you do that, um, change...how much of you is you and how much is the wolf?"

"One and the same."

"That's not enough of an answer, man. I need to know if I have to keep an eye on you. I mean, do I need to worry about you looking at me and thinking I'm on the menu?"

For some reason I couldn't adequately explain, I found that to be moderately offensive.

"No," I said.

"You're sure?"

"I'm sure."

He gave me another look. A hard one. "*Be* sure."

We drove the rest of the way in silence.

Chap. 45

Crow had Ledger pull off onto a side road that ran fifty feet and dead-ended in the woods.

"It's a mile from here," he said. "Best if we go in on foot."

We all agreed to that.

Ledger popped the back of the Explorer and opened a big, flat, metal box. Inside there were handguns, rifles, shotguns, boxes of rounds, and even some grenades.

"Party favors," said Ledger.

"Sweet Mother of Pearl," said Crow as he selected a bandolier fitted to hold a dozen loaded magazines. His sidearm was a Glock .40 and there were plenty of magazines for him. Ledger put one on as well, with mags for his Beretta. He also took an A-12 combat shotgun with a big drum filled with buckshot and Frag-12 fragmentation grenades.

"For when you want to send the very best," said Ledger. I saw him check the spring of his rapid-release folding knife, too. Then he glanced at me. "What about you?"

I had my gun and two magazines, but that was all I needed. "Less I carry, the less I have to go back later and find. But...any chance you have an extra pair of sweat pants or something?"

"I have BDU pants. My size, but you can roll up the cuffs. Why?"

"Because I tend to ruin my clothes when I change, unless I strip out first. And if we walk away from this, I doubt you want me going commando on your back seat."

He grinned, took the rolled-up extra pants, and tucked them into the back of his belt.

We moved off into the woods. Crow texted Mike to let him know we were coming. Ledger was good in the woods. Fast and silent, like me. Crow knew how to move through nature, too, but he had a limp. We had to slow down to let him keep pace with us. Even so, a mile was nothing and it fell away in a few quick minutes.

I smelled Mike before I saw him.

But he was closer than I would have liked. He was smart enough to come at us downwind. I turned a split second before he deliberately stepped on some dry grass. A moment later Crow and Ledger turned, too.

Mike waved us down behind some dense bushes. Beyond it, built into a downslope of a long hill, was a box made from cinderblock. Boring, utilitarian, and stained by forest rains and insect slime. The structure was sixty-by-ninety with a small shed built onto the east corner. Mike pointed to a clump of pines and in the shadows we could see three cars. An SUV and two sedans. Then he dug into a pocket and produced a handful of important-looking wires. Those cars weren't going anywhere.

The young officer nodded to the building. "I picked up a scent in the woods and followed it. Lost it a couple of times because I think he knew he was being followed. He went into the stream for a while, but I found him again. Stayed downwind and tracked him here. Saw him go inside the shed, but when I checked, he wasn't there. It's rigged to look like a tool shed, but the back wall's a dummy. Couldn't find the lock or handle, though."

Ledger nodded. "That's good police work, kid."

Sweeney gave him a stony go-fuck-yourself look. Crow patted him on the shoulder.

We watched the building for a few minutes.

"Don't see any security cameras," I said.

"Could be hidden," mused Ledger. "But I don't think so. I think this is a temporary setup. The fact that it's half a mile from No-fucking-Where is their security system. It'll be different inside. Guys like this always have lots and lots of guns."

"So do we," said Crow.

"They also have super soldiers."

"So do we."

Ledger nodded. He cut a look at Sweeney and at me. "And people wonder why I drink."

"Okay, coach," I said to Ledger. "This seems to be your ballgame. What's the play?"

Before he could answer, there was a sound behind us. Very small. Very furtive.

We spun around, guns coming up. The wolf that lives inside of me nearly jumped out. Must have been the same with Sweeney.

A small figure staggered out of the brush behind us.

Antonio Jones.

And he was covered in blood.

He reached out a hand toward us. His mouth worked as he fought to speak. Then his eyes rolled up and he pitched forward.

Chap. 46

Ledger and Sweeney moved at the same time. They closed on Antonio so fast it was like they blurred. With Mike I could understand the speed. The wolf was right there beneath his skin, it glared out through his eyes all the time. Ledger was just a man, but moved with a speed and economy of motion that called to mind an expression I once read in an article about Jesse Owens. Oiled grace.

He reached Antonio first and caught the kid as he fell and lowered him to the ground. We all huddled around him.

"Jesus," I breathed.

The kid was a mess.

Someone had beat the shit out of him. They'd cut him up. There were long, ragged gashes in his face and chest and stomach. His hands were bloody, his knuckles visibly broken. Whatever had happened, he'd put up one hell of a fight.

Ledger wiped blood from the kid's eyes and mouth. Crow took his pulse. Mike pulled off his own uniform shirt and began ripping it into strips that I pressed against the worst of the cuts. Antonio's eyelids fluttered and opened.

"What happened, kid?" asked Ledger, bending close.

"I...I...." The young man's voice faltered. "I...tried to...stop..."

He coughed and blood bubbled at the corners of his mouth.

It took a while, but the kid mastered himself through an admirable effort of will. Sometimes you find strength in the strangest of places. This kid had some grit.

He told us that he saw the three of us leave the Scarecrow and was hurrying down the street to catch up, but we drove off. Then he saw two men hurry out of the bar, get into a car and follow. Antonio didn't like the look of them. Or the smell. He got his scooter and tailed them. The car was well behind Ledger's Explorer, and once out in the country, it turned off and went up a logger's road. Antonio might have let it go, but he was positive that at least one of those men was a werewolf. So he followed. When he described the road, Crow and Mike nodded. The logger's road changed to a Forest Service road three miles outside of town and then crossed into the state forest. Antonio, thinking that these men might be heading for the hidden lab Ledger had told him about, kept following.

He lost the car twice, and when he found it a third time, not more than a mile east of where we all knelt, the men were in the process of hiding the car with boughs they cut from the trees. They heard the scooter, and before Antonio could turn it around and get the hell out of there, the two men changed into wolfshape and ran him down.

There was one hell of a fight.

Antonio was sure he injured one of them pretty badly, but he took too much damage to keep fighting. The other one—a big son of a bitch

Antonio described as "maybe Indian or Asian," was the one who took the kid apart. He slashed and bit him and beat him nearly to death. To get away, Antonio threw himself down a steep hill, fell into a river, and damn near drowned. The men gave up the chase, probably figuring him for dead. Antonio managed to get to the bank. When he climbed up the hill on the other side to try and find a road, he saw Ledger's car drive past with us in it.

He followed and found us here.

We exchanged looks. This was one impressive young man. Tougher than he looked with big, clanking balls.

Antonio, spent from telling his tale and nearly ruined by the fight with the other werewolves, passed out and lay silent.

Ledger leaned close to me. "You know this lycanthrope stuff, Sam. Aren't you guys supposed to be able to heal fast? Some kind of hyperactive wound repair system? Or is this kid going to die on us here?"

I hesitated. We Benandanti have a lot of specialized knowledge. Things about who we are and what we are. My mother, grandmother, and aunts were all very specific about keeping that information confidential. About sharing it with no one outside of the family. Not even with other werewolves.

So, naturally I had to give that a little thought before I answered. I glanced at Mike.

He shook his head. "I never had anyone to teach me how this all works," he admitted. "I've been hurt a few times. I know how fast *I* heal, but I'm not the same as Antonio. Or you."

His eyes were a strange and artificial blue. He reached up and pinched his eye, removing a contact lens. Then another. The eyes that were revealed were no human eyes at all. Nor were they werewolf eyes. They were as red as blood and ringed with gold.

Joe Ledger said, "What the fuck?"

I didn't say shit. Not sure I could have. Whatever he was, Mike Sweeney was a lot more than a werewolf. I was damn sure he wasn't even remotely human.

Ledger edged back, shaken and pale. "What in the wide blue fuck are you?"

Sweeney smiled. A rare thing for him. It was not the kind of smile you ever want to see. On anyone. Not even in a horror movie.

"What am I?" he asked, and for a moment, even the timbre of his voice was all wrong. Too deep. Too strange. "I have no idea."

Crow touched Mike's shoulder but looked at us. "Mike's family tree is moderately complicated. Maybe one of these days we can talk about it."

"Or maybe not," said Mike.

"Or maybe not," agreed Crow. "Right now, though, we got to help this kid. You have anything, Sam? Benandanti are supposed to be the secret keepers of the werewolves. Or something like that, am I right?"

"Something like that," I mumbled.

They all looked at me. I looked down at the kid.

Poor little bastard really put his ass on the line. Tried to make a difference.

"Sorry, Grandma," I said.

"What?" asked Ledger.

"Nothing." I held my hand out to him. "Give me your knife."

He didn't hesitate, but instead reached for the rapid-release knife, snapped his wrist to lock the blade in place, and offered it to me, handle-first.

I took it and looked at my reflection in the polished steel. "Understand something," I said, "I'm going on what I've been told. I've never actually done this before."

"Kid's going to die," said Ledger.

"This is a gamble," I said. "This might kill him faster."

Crow shook his head. "A small chance is better than none at all."

Ledger and Sweeney nodded.

"Do it," said Ledger.

I put the edge of the knife against the heel of my left palm, took a deep breath to steady my nerves, and let the wickedly sharp blade do its work. Bright red blood welled from the small cut.

"Open his mouth," I said, and Mike put two fingers between the kid's teeth and then splayed them to push open Antonio's mouth. I clenched my fist to increase the blood pressure and when the blood began rolling over my hand and down my wrist, I extended my arm and let the first fat drops fall. They splashed his lips, his teeth and then vanished into the darkness of his open mouth.

The old ritual says to use seven drops.

Seven, the number of heaven.

I gave him seven and one to grow on and then put my cut hand into my own mouth and sucked off the last drops of blood. When I removed my hand, the cut was already closed. Kind of freaky. Grandma hadn't told me about that part.

Ledger, who had gone pale earlier, went milk-white now.

"That," he said thickly, "is some weird-ass voodoo bullshit."

I grinned at him. I probably still had blood on my own teeth. "Welcome to my world."

Crow smiled, too. "Welcome to Pine Deep."

Mike Sweeney said nothing, but his red eyes burned into mine.

On the ground Antonio Jones groaned once, twitched.

And died.

Chap. 47

We tried everything.

CPR.

Mouth to mouth.

Everything.

But the kid's body settled into a terminal stillness. No pulse. No nothing.

I turned away and felt tears in my eyes. I balled my fist and drove it into the top of my thigh. Over and over again.

Son of a bitch.

Son of a motherfucking bitch.

This wasn't right.

It wasn't fair.

When I turned back, no one would meet my eyes.

Crow looked old and tired. Sweeney got up and walked back to the line of shrubs that separated us from the blockhouse. Ledger, he sat there looking down at the kid, shaking his head slowly.

He was the only one who said anything, though. "You tried, man. At least you tried."

Before I even knew I was going to do it, I grabbed a fistful of his shirt and pulled him halfway to his feet. "Fuck you, asshole. You should never have brought a kid into this. This shit is on you."

Ledger looked at me. If he was afraid of me, it no longer showed. He placed his hand on mine and pressed two fingers into nerve clusters. He did it without effort and my hand popped open. Just like that. Ledger gently pushed me back.

"Don't ever do that again, Sam." His voice was very calm. It wasn't a request and it was somehow more than a threat. He walked forward very slowly, which made me walk backward. Ledger got so close that his forehead and mine were touching. It might have looked like an intimate moment. Two close friends, two brothers, two mourners at a funeral.

But this wasn't that. This was alpha and wolf. His voice was very soft.

"You're letting emotions get in the way of your better sense. Don't. That's what happens to people when they get caught up in this kind of thing. They need to assign blame and because the bad guys are usually out of reach, they lash out at whoever's close. The thing about that is—it's what those assholes want. They count on it. Terrorism isn't about overwhelming force. It's about fear. It's about grief. It's about confusion."

"This isn't terrorism—" I began, but he cut me off.

"The fuck it isn't. That's the *only* thing this is about. These sons of bitches killed that kid. They fucked us all up in doing it."

"It's not right!" I growled.

"Shhh. Quiet now," he said. "No, it's not right. None of this is about right or wrong. None of it. It's about evil. It's about darkness. That's what this is about. These fuckers want to shut out all the lights. Everyone's lights. They want to be the boogeymen in the dark. That's what they do so they can feel powerful."

I said nothing. Ledger moved his head back a few inches so I could see his eyes. They were cold and they were hard, but I saw a bottomless pain there. Endless hurt. I could feel Crow and Sweeney watching us.

"Sam, the guys who did this are the same ones who killed the guy on the motorcycle and all of those other civilians. That's what they do. They don't have the balls to go to war with warriors, so they try to cripple us by targeting the innocent. The civilians. The ones who can't protect themselves. If you lose your shit, that guarantees a win for them. Is that what you want?"

"No," I said hoarsely.

"No," he agreed.

"This...this isn't my sort of thing," I said.

"What *is* your sort of thing?"

"When I take on a client, it's like they become part of my...." The word stuck in my throat. I wanted him to understand. I didn't want to sound like an idiot. But I said it anyway. "When I take on a client it's like they become part of my pack."

He studied me, and nodded slowly. "And you'll do anything for your pack."

It wasn't a statement.

I nodded.

He took his wallet out, removed a dollar bill and stuffed it into my shirt pocket. "Consider that a retainer from Antonio Jones. He's your client. When this is over, if we're both standing on our feet, you can bill me for the rest."

"I've already been paid."

"By who?"

"Limbus."

"Fuck Limbus. They're not here. That kid is. You're working for him. And if there was ever a client who deserved to be in your *pack*, then he's it."

I shook my head, but even I didn't know if that was a denial of his words or a refusal to accept all of this bullshit.

"So what's the alternative?" asked Ledger. "We could fall back and wait for reinforcements and hope that these bastards don't slip away while we're waiting."

"No."

"Or we can cowboy up and go in there and *prove* to these motherfuckers that they don't have a right to do these things. That they aren't allowed to do this. That there is punishment for it."

I cleared my throat. "We could be walking right into a trap. We don't know what's waiting for us in there."

Ledger smiled. His smile was every bit as alien and as awful as Mike Sweeney's had been. "Maybe," he conceded. "But they don't know what's waiting for them out here."

It took me a few seconds, but then I felt a smile growing on my own face. I couldn't see it, but I was sure it wasn't one I'd want to look at in the bathroom mirror.

Chap. 48

Ledger put a call into his people and told them to come running. But best estimate was forty minutes. We couldn't risk that kind of time.

We decided to hit the place ourselves.

Ledger mapped out a plan. It was ugly, dangerous as hell, probably insane, and definitely suicidal.

We all agreed to it.

It had somehow become that kind of day.

Chap. 49

We crowded into the shed.

Ledger took some goodies from his pockets and explained them as he set to work. The first thing was a pocket sensor that identified which wall of the shed had a door hidden behind it. That was easy. Finding the lock and door handle took a little longer, but Ledger found it. There was a knot in the wood of the back wall. It was phony and hid a pressure switch. Ledger produced a second gizmo that would let us know if the door was wired with bombs. It wasn't, which provided less of a relief than I would have thought. Then he took what looked like a Fruit Roll-Up from a metal tube, flatted it out, peeled off a plastic cover and pressed it in place over the switch. He pushed a small electronic detonator into the putty-like material.

"Blaster plaster," he explained. "Very high-tech pressure-reactive chemical explosive." He held up a small trigger device. "Let's get out of dodge."

We went outside and over the edge of the hill.

"Once I trigger it, we're committed. We go in hard and fast and it's fuck you to anyone inside. Anything past that door is no longer American soil and whoever's in there is to be considered an enemy combatant."

"Is that legal?" asked Crow.

"Do you care?" Ledger said.

"On the whole, not much."

Ledger nodded. "It'll get loud and smoky. Everyone keeps their shit wired tight. You check your targets. I do not want a bullet up my ass."

"What do we do if they want to surrender?" I asked.

"We let them," said Ledger. "We're not murderers, Sam. For right now, we're soldiers. Rules of engagement apply. You good with that?"

We all were.

We were all scared, too.

Even Mike, though it didn't show. I could smell it. Faint, but there.

Ledger was the coolest, but he had a fine sheen of sweat on his forehead. No doubt. After all, this wasn't a cell of al-Qaeda. These were monsters. Scary monsters. Scarier than me, and I have my moments. Super-soldier werewolves. If there's a worse-case scenario that trumps that, please do not fucking tell me.

Ledger held up the trigger. "Good guys win, bad guys lose."

We nodded.

As the Bible says, we girded our loins.

He pressed the trigger.

The blast was impressive.

The shed stopped being a shed and became a rapidly expanding cloud of splinters and dust that blew over and past us. The door disintegrated and a big chunk of the interior wall blew inward.

Ledger was up and moving before the first echo of the blast could bounce back at us from the surrounding trees. He had his pistol up, laser sight stabbing through the smoke. He bellowed through the thunder.

"Federal Agents! Put your weapons down. Put your hands in the air. Do it now! Do it now!"

It was rhetoric. It was like saying hello.

None of us expected them to comply.

And, fuck it, they didn't.

Chap. 50

We crowded behind him.

Crow and Mike Sweeney.

Me.

All of us with guns.

We ran into dense smoke and burst through into the blockhouse, none of us really knowing what to expect. I had a kind of Doctor Frankenstein thing in my head. Arcane science, secret experiments.

It wasn't like that.

There were two folding tables on which were laptops. And a third table crowded with some scientific junk. Open metal cases, high-pressure injection guns, alcohol swabs, IV bags. That was it. The whole shebang could have fit into the trunk of a midsized sedan. No exotic machinery, no bubbling vats or towering electrodes. This was Twenty-First Century microscience. Transgenics on the go.

But the equipment wasn't important to us. Not at the moment.

The occupants of the room were.

We were expecting two, maybe three of them. A handful at the outside. Some science geeks and a couple of their pet monsters.

Yeah, that's what we were hoping for.

Fuck.

There were fifteen people in the room.

Two of them were Korean. Both in lab coats. Both pencil-neck geeks. North Korean, as we later found out.

The others were homegrown. Twelve men, one woman. Americans and Canadians.

And every single one of them was a werewolf.

Every.

Single.

One.

Ledger put the red dot of his laser sight on the chest of the nearest man. A guy who looked like a baseball player. Fit, long-legged, rangy. The man was ten feet from Ledger.

"Hands on your head right now!" bellowed Ledger.

For just a split second it all held together. A tableau. Them and us, with ghosts of smoke drifting around us.

Then the man grabbed the shoulder of one of the Korean scientists and hurled him at Ledger.

Not shoved him.

Hurled.

The scientist went flying into the air, well off the ground, arms pinwheeling, legs kicking, right at Ledger. The agent was able to twist out of the way and the screaming Korean hit Crow. They went down hard.

Then all hell broke loose.

The crowd rushed at us, and even as I swung my gun toward the nearest, he stopped being a man and became a wolf. It was the fastest change I'd ever seen, and I've seen my grandmother do the shift. She could do it in the space of a finger-snap.

This guy was faster.

In a heartbeat he stopped being a man and became a thing.

When I change, I usually go the whole way into pure wolfshape. Most werewolves do. We're faster as wolves. We have four feet and keener senses.

He did not.

None of them did.

They shifted into wolfmen. A horror movie halfway point between man and wolf. He leapt at me and swatted the pistol from my hand. Claws like daggers dug into my chest, and if I hadn't begun the change as soon as he leapt, I'd have died as a man, right there and then. The man has more vulnerabilities.

He smashed me back and down, and immediately we were tearing into each other. Teeth and claws. Spit and blood.

I heard gunfire and didn't know who was shooting. Ledger, maybe.

Crow, too, if he could.

I doubted Mike Sweeney was still human.

There was a scream of fury higher and stranger than any wolf cry, and I knew at once it had to be him. It was almost the shriek of a jungle cat. What *was* he?

The wolfman who bore me to the ground was strong. Goddamn strong. He gripped my forelegs and tried to tear them apart. His grip alone was crushing. Pain exploded through my legs and shoulders. There was no way I was going to wrestle free. He was easily twice as strong as me.

Super soldiers.

What was it Ledger said? *Someone's trying to build a better werewolf.*

Yeah.

Shit.

So, fuck it, I stopped fighting a fight I couldn't win, and instead darted my head forward and bit his throat. I was in full wolfshape, and if my muscles weren't as powerful as his amped up physique, my jaws were. Wolf jaws were always stronger than wolfman jaws. My family's genetics don't go back to *Canis lupis*. Most werewolves do, we don't. We Benandanti are in a direct genetic line from *Canis dirus*. The massive, prehistoric Dire Wolves. No canine predator in history had a stronger bite. And as werewolves, we get something extra added to the package.

He tried to tough it out, to muscle through my bite.

Fuck him.

He didn't.

His throat tore away between my teeth.

Blood exploded from him with fire hose pressure, smashing into my face, hitting the wall. The evil bastard died right there. His strength evaporated and his powerful and scientifically enhanced physique became so much cooling meat. I threw him off of me and rose to four feet with bloody meat and fur hanging from my jaws.

The rest of the room was a madhouse.

Crow had his back to the wall and had Mike Sweeney's combat shotgun in his hands. He fired, pumped, fired, pumped, over and over again. I've been hit with shotgun shells before. Buckshot hurts. Bear shot will put me on my knees, but it won't kill a werewolf. Not unless you scored a headshot and blew apart the motor cortex or the brain stem.

The rounds in that shotgun were explosive.

He blew arms and legs off. He blew holes through chests.

Hard as balls to shake off a ten-inch hole through your sternum, supernatural or not.

Ledger didn't have his gun. It was somewhere on the floor.

Instead he had his rapid-release fighting knife in his hand and he was tackling two of the wolfmen at once.

He should have died. Right away. On the spot, end of story.

He was cut and bleeding, but damn it if that son of a bitch wasn't holding his own. He fought on the attack and with counterattacks. Nothing defensive. They came at him and he went for them. He didn't stab. Stabbing is for suckers who want to die. Ledger used lightning-fast slashes, jabs, and picks to open up dozens of wounds in arms, legs, bellies, groins, and faces. The wolfmen were the ones on the defensive. Maybe it was their arrogance, maybe they'd never fought a warrior before, but they were losing what should have been a nothing battle.

It couldn't last, though. Ledger was human. He'd tire.

They wouldn't.

And even as I watched, I could see some of their wounds beginning to close.

This could only end one way.

I began making my way toward him. On the other side of the room, Mike Sweeney—or what had been Mike Sweeney—was fighting with the largest of the wolfmen. Two giants colliding. Both standing on two legs and slashing with clawed hands. Sweeney and the giant were well-matched and there was no way to tell who was going to win that fight.

Before I could help him or Ledger, the only female werewolf in the room rushed at me. She was tall for a woman, and dishearteningly fast.

She laughed as she slashed at me.

If you haven't heard the cruel laughter of a werewolf, I hope you never do. It's so wrong in so many ways. There's no humanity in it. Just malicious glee and a red anticipation of what's to come.

She raked me from shoulder to hip as I tried to evade, the slashes burning like acid. I hissed and snapped at her, but she danced away, lithe as a dancer. Her riposte was a slash across my forehead that filled one eye with my own blood.

Bitch.

I darted in and she danced back, she slashed and I jumped sideways. And that started our gavotte. She caught me more times than I evaded. I nipped her twice and did no damage at all. Unlike the first wolfman I'd fought, she used cunning and speed rather than relying on her strength.

She was faster than me. By a mile.

I needed to get close enough to use my bite strength.

She did not let me.

So I changed the game; I played hers.

As she lunged for a long slash, I shifted from wolf to wolfman. I pivoted and whipped out my hand and caught her wrist. Then I clamped my teeth around it as I shifted back to werewolf.

Bite strength, baby. Nothing beats it.

Bones collapsed, meat burst, and then I had her hand. She screamed so loud I thought it would blow out my eardrums. I reeled, but it was all noise. She clutched her maimed arm to her body, trying to staunch the flow of blood that jetted from the stump. She backed away, the fight taken out of her.

I had other plans.

As she turned to flee, I hurled myself onto her back and slammed her down onto the floor. As we landed I buried my fangs in the back of her neck. I could feel the vertebrae break apart. I could taste the cerebral spinal fluid as it filled my mouth. I could feel the life as it fled from her like steam from a ruptured pipe.

I almost howled. Like a wolf does after a kill. Almost.

But there was too much going on.

Ledger was being pushed back now. Bloody cuts crisscrossed his body. But amazingly, one of the wolfmen lay dead at his feet, the rapid-release knife buried to the hilt in the top of the creature's skull. Ledger had no weapon. All he had was speed and training and whatever angels protected him.

He was going to die, though. I could see that without question.

He was also fifty feet away and I was never going to be able to get to him in time.

Crow was down on one knee, his whole side glistening red. The shotgun lay in pieces around him, but there were three dead werewolves, too. As I watched, Crow fumbled his pistol out of his holster and raised it. His hands trembled with pain and fatigue. And fear. I could see in his eyes that he thought he was going to die, too.

Maybe we all were.

I'd taken a hell of a lot of damage.

I started in his direction, but then my entire back exploded with searing, unbearable, blinding pain. I could feel nails rake across my spine and ribs. The force of the impact knocked me down and sent me sliding across the floor, riding a red carpet of my own blood. As my body spun, I saw a figure that I hadn't seen before.

A fourteenth werewolf.

Tall. Powerful.

He shifted back to his human aspect, standing there naked and indomitable.

With a face like an American Indian. High cheekbones, black eyes, straight black hair.

This was the werewolf who'd killed Antonio.

I was certain of it.

And, just as certainly, this was the alpha of this pack.

He exuded power.

Across the room, Mike Sweeney vanished beneath a pile of wolfmen. Blood geysered up around them and screams filled the air.

My pistol was on the floor near his feet. He bent and picked it up, dropped the magazine to inspect it, slapped it back in, racked it. The round that had already been in the chamber went arcing over his shoulder. The man looked around the room. His mouth turned down in a frown. Not of unhappiness at how many of his people were dead. It was a sneer of contempt. Everything he saw—us, his own pack, all of it—was nothing to him. He was a monster among monsters. I could *feel* that. I knew it to be true. We werewolves have certain instincts. I knew that this man was as close to death personified as ever walked the earth. Maybe he was the pinnacle of the twisted research being done in this place. Maybe he was the superior soldier they were looking for. An unstoppable force.

The pain in my back was excruciating, but I had to move. I had to try to fight. This wasn't just a bad guy, not some child abuser I was hunting or a bail skip I was paid to nab. This wasn't the kind of scum I chased for small bucks as a P.I. This was the kind of evil I became a cop to oppose. Actual evil.

Was this what the people at Limbus wanted stopped? They'd put me in the path of a monster before, and I'd nearly died fighting it. This time I was pretty sure that I *was* going to die. Limbus seemed so prescient, but as I struggled to get to my feet, I knew that their faith in me was badly misplaced.

The big man raised the pistol and pointed it. Not at me. He pointed it at Ledger. His mouth curled into a very small, very cruel little smile.

"No!" I snarled in a mouth that was not constructed for human speech. I flung myself at him. I tried to gut him with my claws. Tried to bite him with my teeth. But all I managed to do was bump against him and spoil his first shot. The round vanished into the smoke above Ledger's head.

The alpha grunted and clubbed me with the butt of the pistol. Once. Twice.

Again and again.

Beating me down. Breaking me.

Killing me.

And he wasn't even in wolfshape.

I collapsed onto the ground.

The man gave a single little nod and raised the pistol again.

This time there was nothing I could do to prevent that shot.

Nothing.

Chap. 51

I didn't have to.

There was a flash of movement. A blur, as fast as when Ledger and Mike had moved. Faster.

The hand holding the gun leaped into the air, trailed by rubies. The gun fired, but the barrel was pointing nowhere. The bullet struck the body of the dead werewolf woman, adding neither insult nor injury. Her flesh quivered but a little.

The alpha howled in agony. He spun around, and in doing so, changed from bleeding man to maimed wolfman. The thing that had attacked him, the creature that had taken his hand, landed ten feet beyond me. It whirled and bared its bloody teeth at the towering killer.

It was another werewolf.

Smaller than me. Darker fur. Eyes as hot as hell's furnaces.

It stood on four legs, claws flexing with such fury they scored the concrete floor. Hair rose along its spine, its ears were back. It was the picture of savage rage, of a total commitment to hate.

The killer looked into those eyes.

So did I.

I think we both recognized them.

I spoke the name.

"Antonio."

I didn't ask how. The blood. The old ritual I'd performed had done its work. Its magic. It had brought this young man back from the dark place. It had restored him, healed the terrible wounds that had been torn into his flesh. It had brought him to the peak of his feral power. Maybe to a greater peak than ever before.

Even maimed and bleeding, the alpha was still twice his size. He'd beaten this young man before. Easily.

He bared his teeth, and in that leer there was a promise of even greater harm and humiliation. The alpha suddenly rushed at him and though Antonio tried to dodge away, the killer was insanely fast. He struck Antonio with his stump, and it was like being smashed with a club. The younger werewolf yelped in pain and slammed into me so hard we rolled over and over. Blood welled from his mouth and nose and splashed my face.

Then he scrambled to get off of me, slashing me by accident as he sought to evade the next blow. The alpha caught him on the hip and sent him slewing sideways.

I snapped at the alpha and caught his ankle. With all of my rage, I tried to bite hard enough to cripple him, but he squatted, twisted and struck me on the side of the head hard enough to knock the world off its hinges.

Everything went dark.

I felt like I was falling from a great height. Falling through smoke for an endless time. I spun sideways and lay on the floor. Through shadows and blood, I saw the fight between Antonio and the alpha.

It was heroic, what that kid tried to do.

He gave as good as got for as long as he could. Tearing and slashing. Leaping and biting. Fighting with fury. Fighting like a Benandanti. Had my blood given him that edge?

If so, it was not enough.

Not enough.

Which is a damn shame because that was one hell of a comeback. One hell of an entrance. Heroism of that kind should be rewarded. Not pissed on.

I wished I could help.

I wished I had something left.

All I could do was lay there and feel myself die. I could feel Antonio's blood seep into my mouth. I could feel my own blood leak out. I could feel the coldness creep in.

Except...

Except that wasn't what was happening.

The taste of blood in my mouth was strange. It was his blood, but it tasted familiar. Like my own. It burned. It burned its way through the flesh of my mouth and into my blood. It burned through my blood.

It burned so goddamn bad.

And it burned so goddamn good.

The fire tore through me. It felt like there was acid in my veins. Lava. I screamed so loud blood flew from my lips.

I was wolf.

I was a human.

I was both.

I screamed as I changed and changed and changed.

The alpha swatted Antonio aside and turned to see what was happening. He frowned again. This time in doubt. I changed and changed and changed and changed.

And all the time I burned.

I had no idea what was happening to me. It was ripping me apart. Burning me at the cellular level. Destroying me.

Except…

The burning stopped.

Like that.

Like a switch being thrown.

I collapsed onto the bloody floor, gasping, human, naked, covered in blood and sweat.

The alpha watched me with narrowed eyes.

Antonio, gasping on the floor, watched me.

In the reflecting surface of the pool of blood beneath me, I watched myself. I saw my human face. I looked for the cuts. The slashes. The exposed bone.

And I saw none of it.

What I saw was whole skin. Painted with blood, but no longer gaping, no longer bleeding.

On the floor, Antonio shifted back to human form. His eyes were bugged in amazement. But he was also smiling.

The alpha was not.

This was not the science he knew. This was not the work of some super-soldier formula. This must have looked like sorcery to him.

Magic.

Pretty much was like that for me.

Except that I understood it. As I lay there, whole once again, I understood it. Antonio's blood in my mouth. Somehow in performing the ritual on him, I'd changed his nature. From *Canis lupis* to *Canis dirus*. He was a Dire Wolf now. Not sure if that made him a Benandanti, but definitely a cousin. Enough so that his blood did for me what mine had done for him.

I rolled onto my hands and knees, and in doing so raised my head to look up at the alpha.

"Surprise, surprise," I said. My voice was filled with ugly promise. Fine.

"You were dead," he said.

"Yeah, well, fuck it," I said.

And I launched myself at him.

It was the man who started that lunge, it was the wolf who buried his teeth in the alpha's throat.

He tried to change.

He tried to make a fight of it.

As the saying goes, that ship had sailed.

Beside me I saw Antonio struggle to his feet. He shifted back into wolfshape and raced across the room to help Joe Ledger.

I killed the alpha.

God, did I kill that son of a bitch.

I tore him to pieces.

Pieces.

Never in my life had I ever felt that powerful.

Across the room I heard a howl of agony. I looked up from the steaming corpse and saw a badly wounded Mike Sweeney struggling with two of the wolfmen. I saw Crow crawling toward a pistol that lay out of reach. Still alive, both of them.

There were more of the wolfmen in the room. The odds were still not in our favor.

And right then, at that moment, it didn't matter.

The wolf in me had never been this strong before. Maybe it never would be again. I threw back my head and howled. The howl of an alpha triumphant. It shook the walls. It knocked plaster from the ceiling. It shocked everyone and everything in that room into silence and stillness.

I howled again, louder still.

The alpha.

The master of this pack.

I screamed at them.

And one by one, the remaining wolfmen stopped their attacks.

One by one, they lay down on the bloody ground.

And goddamn it if they didn't roll to me.

In a pack, when the other wolves do that, the alpha bites them gently on the throat or belly, establishing dominance. Adopting them into the pack.

I came to them and bit them. One by one.

You couldn't, by any definition, call those bites *gentle*.

No, you couldn't.

When it was over, there were only five members of the pack.

Two of them were human.

Mike Sweeney and Antonio Jones looked at me. I lifted my head and howled.

And they howled with me.

Chap. 52

Joe Ledger and Malcolm Crow were in bad shape.

We left Mike at the scene, but Antonio and I had to get them to the hospital, so we broke a lot of traffic laws doing it. We almost didn't make it in time.

While they were still in the E.R., a black helicopter landed in the parking lot and three men came into the hospital. Two were clearly military, in unmarked black BDUs and wires behind their ears. One was a tall, blond-haired guy with lots of muscles. One was a black man in his early forties who looked like he ate crocodiles, uncooked. The third guy, though, was in his sixties, wearing a very expensive suit. Tall, blocky, with dark hair shot through with gray. Even at night he wore tinted glasses. He exuded a kind of personal power I have never before encountered. I would not have wanted to match my alpha status against his. No, sir, I would not.

He introduced himself as Mr. Church. No badge, no I.D.

He told me to wait for him, and he left the other two guys with me in the waiting room. Mike Sweeney was still at the crime scene. Antonio was in the waiting room with me.

The two military guys didn't say a fucking word. They stood waiting. They exchanged a few looks. They studied me. One chewed gum, the other didn't.

After twenty minutes, their boss came out of the E.R. and motioned for his men and Antonio to leave. When the door was closed, Mr. Church sat down opposite me.

"Captain Ledger will survive," he said.

I let out a breath I hadn't realized I was holding. "How is he?"

"He's had worse," said Church. No trace of sympathy in his voice. No trace of anything.

"He's a good guy," I said. "But this wasn't his kind of fight."

Church eyed me. "And was it your kind of fight?"

I said nothing.

Church nodded.

"What about Chief Crow?"

"He'll have some challenging rehab, but they expect him to make a full recovery."

"Guess we got lucky."

"Apparently so."

I chewed my lip for a moment. "Did you talk to Ledger?"

"Briefly. He's been sedated."

"Did he tell you what we found?"

"He did."

"Tell me something, Mr. Church," I said. "I know this isn't my business and you can pull rank and tell me to go piss up a rope. I'm Joe Nobody to you."

"Ask your question."

"That science...the, um, super soldier stuff?"

"What about it?"

"What happens to it? I mean, from what Ledger said, this is some kind of foreign terrorist thing."

"Multinational," agreed Church. "Funded covertly by North Korea."

"Okay. But it was terrorist science. What happens to it? I mean, does our government take it and start making its own monsters? Is that how it works?"

He leaned back in his chair, fished a small packet of vanilla wafers from his coat pocket, tore it open, and offered me one. I passed. Never been a vanilla wafer fan. He took one and bit off a piece, chewed, and studied the remaining cookie for a long few seconds.

"What do you think we should do with it, Mr. Hunter? This is science that could put superior soldiers into battle against an enemy that is both relentless and determined to see America burn. That science could give us an edge. What do you think we should do with it?"

"Are you really asking or jerking me off here?"

"Asking."

I crossed my legs and stretched my arms across the backs of the seats to either side of me. "I think you should burn it. I think you should destroy whatever's in there. Burn it down and scatter the ashes. There are enough monsters in the world already."

"Not all monsters are the enemy, Mr. Hunter."

"Maybe not, but should we be in the business of making more?"

Church finished his cookie. He brushed a stray crumb from his tie, rewrapped the package and put it into his coat pocket. Then he stood up.

"Wait," I said, "is that it? You never answered my question."

Church reached for the door handle, then paused. "Fifteen minutes ago, a Black Hawk helicopter fired four hellfire missiles at a blockhouse in the state forest. The news reports will all say that this was done to destroy a rogue laboratory making weaponized anthrax."

"That's bullshit."

"It's a useful story. And it will explain why that building and all of its contents have been reduced to hot ash." He opened the door, but paused one more time. "The world has enough monsters already, Mr. Hunter."

"Wait," I said, rising to my feet. "What about this Limbus thing. They must have known about that lab and what was in it. You need to find them and find out how they know what they know. You need to find out who they *are*."

His eyes glittered behind the tinted lenses.

He smiled faintly. "Thank you for your assistance in this matter."

And he went out.

An hour later Joe Ledger was medevac'd out of there. I knew that if I tried to find him or Mr. Church, I'd find nothing but shadows.

Antonio was in the hall, and we walked together to the doors to the E.R., then followed the gurney with Crow to his new room. We sat there all night. Crow's wife came in, glared at us, and went in to be with her husband. Hours passed.

We didn't say a word.

Not one fucking word.

The night seemed to last a million years.

In the morning, when Crow was awake, I said my goodbyes and left Pine Deep. All the way home I blasted music because I didn't want to listen to my own thoughts. As I neared the bridge out of town, I saw a police cruiser parked by the side of the road. Mike Sweeney leaned against it, big arms folded. He had bandages on his arms, his throat, his face. They did not make him look weak or injured.

He stared at me with eyes that burned like fire.

He nodded to me.

I nodded to him.

And I drove out of Pine Deep under a morning sky that was dark with clouds and offered nothing but the promise of coming rains.

Epilogue

The story finished, but this time, the words did not fade away into a maelstrom of code. Instead, another story, one that Conrad somehow knew was to be his own, began to fill the screen. It read...

The fire had died away to embers as he sat alone in the darkened tavern 'neath the ageless mountains of that ancient city. But the noose was tightening around his neck. A man can't run forever. Not from his past. Not from the dogs on his heels. Unless he escapes.

Unless he gets lucky.

The cursor on the screen blinked before him. He read the words. He saw the offer. He knew what he must do. There was a sound behind him, the creaking of footsteps on wooden floorboards. And yet he did not turn. Not yet. For to turn was to accept the contract that the man who left the card, the man who had written his name beneath the Limbus logo, the man named Hawthorne, would make.

But Conrad needed that chance. He needed that escape. He didn't know what the job was or how in the world he would pull it off, but he knew that he was the perfect man for it, and he knew that he was just desperate enough to take it.

Conrad turned. The man stood before him, wrapped in a dark great-cloak, his eyes burning in the night.

"Hello, Mr. McKay," Recruiter Hawthorne said. "I am sure that you have many, many questions. But I suppose there is only one that matters, only one that needs answering. Tell me Conrad—

"How lucky do you feel?"

About the Authors

Jonathan Maberry is a *NY Times* bestselling author, multiple Bram Stoker Award winner, and freelancer for Marvel Comics. His novels include *Code Zero, Rot & Ruin, Ghost Road Blues, Patient Zero, The Wolfman,* and many others. Nonfiction books include *Ultimate Jujutsu, The Cryptopedia, Zombie CSU,* and others. Several of Jonathan's novels are in development for movies or TV including *V-Wars, Extinction Machine, Rot & Ruin,* and *Dead of the Night.* He's the editor/co-author of *V-Wars,* a vampire-themed anthology, and was a featured expert on The History Channel special *Zombies: A Living History.* Since 1978 he's sold more than 1200 magazine feature articles, 3000 columns, two plays, greeting cards, song lyrics, and poetry. His comics include *Captain America: Hail Hydra, Bad Blood, Marvel Zombies Return,* and *Marvel Universe vs. the Avengers.* He lives in Del Mar, California with his wife, Sara Jo and their dog, Rosie. www.jonathanmaberry.com

Joe R. Lansdale is the author of over thirty novels and numerous short stories. His work has appeared in national anthologies, magazines, and collections, as well as numerous foreign publications. He has written

for comics, television, film, newspapers, and Internet sites. His work has been collected in eighteen short-story collections, and he has edited or co-edited over a dozen anthologies. He has received the Edgar Award, eight Bram Stoker Awards, the Horror Writers Association Lifetime Achievement Award, the British Fantasy Award, the Grinzani Cavour Prize for Literature, the Herodotus Historical Fiction Award, the Inkpot Award for Contributions to Science Fiction and Fantasy, and many others. His novella "Bubba Hotep" was adapted to film by Don Coscarelli, starring Bruce Campbell and Ossie Davis. His story

"Incident On and Off a Mountain Road" was adapted to film for Showtime's *Masters of Horror*. He is currently co-producing several films, among them *The Bottoms*, based on his Edgar Award-winning novel, with Bill Paxton and Brad Wyman, and *The Drive-In*, with Greg Nicotero. He is Writer In Residence at Stephen F. Austin State University, and is the founder of the martial arts system Shen Chuan: Martial Science and its affiliate, Shen Chuan Family System. He is a member of both the United States and International Martial Arts Halls of Fame. He lives in Nacogdoches, Texas with his wife, dog, and two cats.

Gary A. Braunbeck is the author of the acclaimed Cedar Hill Cycle of novels and stories, which includes *In Silent Graves, Keepers, Coffin County,* and the forthcoming *A Cracked and Broken Path.* He has published over 20 books, evenly split between novels and short-story collections, and his work has earned six Bram Stoker Awards, an International Horror Guild Award, three Shocker Awards, a Black Quill Award, and a World Fantasy Award nomination. He doesn't get out much, which everyone agrees is probably for the best. Find out more about his work on-line at garybraunbeck.com.

Joe McKinney has been a patrol officer for the San Antonio Police Department, a homicide detective, a disaster mitigation specialist, a patrol commander, and a successful novelist. His books include the four-part Dead World series, *Quarantined, Inheritance, Lost Girl of the Lake, Crooked House* and *Dodging Bullets.* His short fiction has been collected in *The Red Empire and Other Stories* and *Dating in Dead World and Other Stories.* In 2011, McKinney received the Horror Writers Association's Bram Stoker Award for Best Novel. For more information go to http://joemckinney.wordpress.com.

Harry Shannon has been an actor, Emmy-nominated songwriter, recording artist, a VP at Carolco Pictures and a Music Supervisor for motion pictures. His novels include *CLAN, Daemon, Dead and Gone,* The Hungry trilogy (co-written with Steven W. Booth), the thriller *The Pressure of Darkness"* as well as the Mick Callahan suspense series. He has won the Tombstone for Best Novel and the Dark Scribble from *Dark Scribe* magazine. His story "Night Nurse" and collection *A Host of Shadows* were each nominated for a Stoker Award by the Horror Writer's Association. Otto Penzler selected "Fifty Minutes" (co-written with Joe Donnelly of *Slake* magazine) as one of the Best American Mystery Stories of 2011. He has recently published his novella "Biters" for JournalStone's DoubleDown series. Readers may contact him via www.harryshannon.com

A native of the South, **Brett J. Talley** received a philosophy and history degree from the University of Alabama before moving to witch-haunted Massachusetts. When people ask, Brett tells them he writes for fortune and glory. But the truth is the stories in his head simply refuse to stay put. Brett loves every kind of fiction—from horror to literary to historical to sci-fi—as long as there are fantastic characters with a compelling purpose. Since his first novel, *That Which Should Not Be,* was a Bram Stoker Award finalist, he has contributed to the first *Limbus, Inc.* installment, published the sci-fi thriller *The Void,* numerous short stories, and recently released his post-apocalyptic novel *The Reborn* as part of JournalStone's DoubleDown series. There's still magic to be found in fiction, the mysterious and the unknown still beckon there, and the light can always triumph over the darkness, no matter how black the night may be. Brett writes when he can, though he spends most of his time working as a lawyer so that he can put food on the table. That is, until the air grows cool and crisp and fall descends. For then it is football time in the South, and Brett lives and dies with the Alabama Crimson Tide. Roll Tide. Brett can be found on-line at www.brettjtalley.com.

JONATHAN MABERRY, JOSEPH NASSISE,
BENJAMIN KANE ETHRIDGE,
BRETT J. TALLEY, and ANNE C. PETTY

LIMBUS
INC.

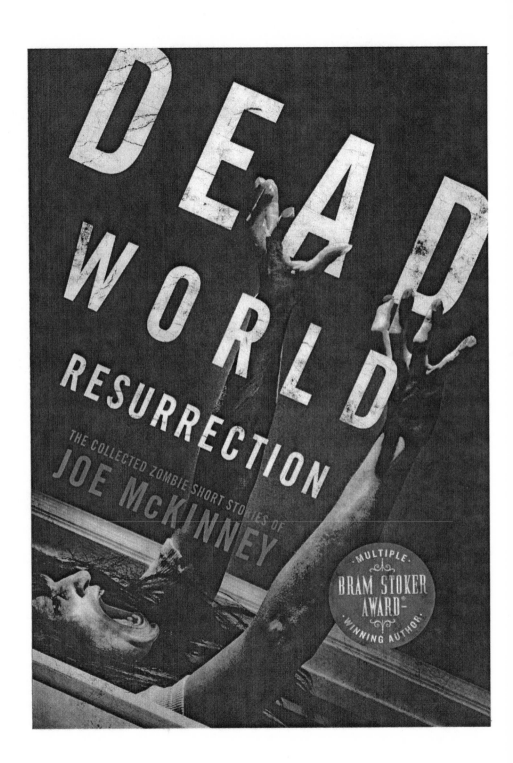

OUT OF TUNE

Christopher Golden

David Liss

Del Howison

Gary Braunbeck

Gregory Frost

Jack Ketchum

Jeff Strand

Nancy Keim-Comley

Keith R. A. DeCandido

Kelley Armstrong

Nancy Holder

Seanan McGuire

Simon R. Green

Lisa Morton

Jeffrey Mariotte

Marsheila Rockwell

EDITED BY

JONATHAN MABERRY

NEW YORK TIMES BESTSELLER

CPSIA information can be obtained at www.ICGtesting.com
Printed in the USA
LVOW08*1213061214

417479LV00002B/18/P

9 781940 161358